The F...
Companion

The
Household
Companion

Eliza Smith

WORDSWORTH CLASSICS

Readers who are interested in other titles from
Wordsworth Editions are invited to visit our website at
www.wordsworth-editions.com

For our latest list and a full mail-order service contact
Bibliophile Books, 5 Thomas Road, London E14 7BN
TEL: +44 (0)20 7515 9222 FAX: +44 (0)20 7538 4115
e-mail: orders@bibliophilebooks.com

Originally published in 1758 as *The Compleat Housewife or
Accomplished Gentlewoman's Companion*
This edition first published in 2006 by
Wordsworth Editions Limited
8B East Street, Ware, Hertfordshire SG12 9HJ

ISBN 1 84022 489 4

© Wordsworth Editions Limited 2006

Wordsworth® is a registered trademark of
Wordsworth Editions Limited

Typeset in Great Britain by Antony Gray
Printed and bound by Clays Ltd, St Ives plc

This edition of
Eliza Smith's *Companion*
is dedicated to
ANTHONY RANSON
and his grandmother
ROSE HOLLIS

Contents

Publisher's Preface to the New Edition

For many years this ancient and worthy book has been published in facsimile, preserving all the eighteenth-century typographic conventions. Some of these, in particular the use of the old-fashioned long s, which today looks like an f, have reduced the modern reader's pleasure in perusing the work. We hope that in resetting the book, using more current typography and spelling and making some slight revisions to the order of the contents, we will help our readers to a greater enjoyment of the extraordinary receipts which Eliza Smith describes in her preface as being 'what are approved and practicable'. Although Eliza claims to have 'omitted odd and fantastical messes' (the likes of which we can only speculate on), we may still find many of her recipies bizarre and extravagant.

This book is published for reading at your fireside or in bed; it can no longer be thought of as a kitchen manual. Though some of the many receipts may be easy to follow and yield delicious results, the publisher most fervently implores you not to attempt any of the more recherché concoctions, remedies or methods described; we cannot be held responsible for the consequences that may result if you choose to disregard this warning.

There have been added several illustrations in keeping with the spirit of a book whose contents we hope will transport the reader into the marketplaces, kitchens and dining-rooms of the long lost Georgian world where he or she will spend many happy hours – *Bon appétit!*

Author's Original Preface

It being grown as unfashionable for a book now to appear to people without a preface as for a lady to appear at a ball without a hoop-petticoat, I shall conform to custom for fashion' sake and not through any necessity. The subject being both common and universal needs no arguments to introduce it, and being so necessary for the gratification of the appetite stands in need of no encomiums to allure persons to the practice of it, since there are but few nowadays who love not good eating and drinking; therefore I entirely quit those two topics; but having three or four pages to be filled up previous to the subject itself, I shall employ them on a subject I think new and not yet handled by any of the pretenders to the art of cookery: and that is, the antiquity of it; which, if it either instruct or divert, I shall be satisfied if you are so.

Cookery, confectionary, etc., like all other arts, had their infancy, and did not arrive at a state of maturity but by slow degrees, various experiments and a long track of time; for in the infant age of the world, when the new inhabitants contented themselves with the simple provision of nature – viz. the vegetable diet, the fruits and productions of the earth as they succeeded one another in their several peculiar seasons – the art of cookery was unknown: apples, nuts and herbs were both meat and sauce, and mankind stood in no need of additional sauces, ragouts, etc., to procure a good appetite; for a healthful and vigorous constitution, a clear, wholesome, odoriferous air, moderate exercise and an exemption from anxious cares always supplied them with it.

We read of no palled appetites, but such as proceeded from the decays of nature by reason of an advanced old-age; but on the contrary, a craving stomach even upon a deathbed, as in Isaac, nor no sickness, but those that were both the first and the last, which proceeded from the struggles of nature, which abhorred the separation of soul and body; no physicians to prescribe for the sick nor apothecaries to compound medicines for two thousand years and upwards; food and physic were one and the same thing.

But when man began to pass from a vegetable to an animal diet, and feed on flesh, fowls and fish, then seasonings grew necessary, both to render it more palatable and savoury, and also to preserve that part which was not immediately spent from stinking and corruption; and probably salt was the first seasoning discovered; for of salt we read in Genesis 14.

And this seemed to be necessary, especially for those who were advanced in age, whose palates, with their bodies, had lost their vigour as to taste, whose digestive faculty grew weak and impotent; and thence proceeded the use of soups and savoury messes, so that cookery then began to be in use, though luxury had not brought it to the height of an art. Thus we read that Jacob made such palatable pottage that Esau purchased a mess of it at the extravagant price of his birthright. And Isaac, before he bequeathed by his last will and testament his blessing to his son Esau, required him to make some savoury meat such as his soul loved – i.e. such as was relishable to his blunted appetite.

So that seasonings of some sort were then in use, though whether they were salt, savoury herbs or roots only, or spices, the fruits of trees (such as pepper, cloves, nutmegs), bark (as cinnamon) and roots (as ginger), etc., I shall not determine.

As for the methods of the cookery of those times, boiling or stewing seems to have been the principal; broiling or roasting the next; besides which, l presume scarce any other were used for two thousand years and more, for I remember no other in the history of Genesis.

That Esau was the first cook, I shall not presume to assert; for Abraham gave orders to dress a fatted calf; but Esau is the first person mentioned that made any advances beyond plain dressing, as boiling, roasting, etc. For though we find, indeed, that Rebecca, his mother, was accomplished with the skill of making savoury meat as well as he, yet whether he learned it from her, or she from him, is a question too knotty for me to determine.

But cookery did not long remain a bare piece of housewifery or family economy; but in process of time, when luxury entered the world, it grew to an art, nay a trade: for in 1 Samuel 8:13, when the Israelites grew fashionists, and would have a king, that they might be like the rest of their neighbours, we read of cooks, confectioners, etc.

This art, being of universal use and in constant practice, has been ever since upon the improvement; and we may, I think, with good reason believe it is arrived at its greatest height and perfection, if it is not got beyond it, even to its declension; for whatsoever new, upstart out-of-the-way messes some humourists have invented, such as stuffing a roasted leg of mutton with pickled herring, and the like, are only the sallies of a capricious appetite, and debauching rather than improving the art itself.

The art of cookery, etc., is indeed diversified according to the diversity of nations or countries, and to treat of it in that latitude would fill an unportable volume, and rather confound than improve those who would accomplish themselves with it. I shall therefore confine what I have to communicate both within the limits of practicalness and usefulness and within the compass of a manual that shall neither burthen the hands to hold, the eyes in reading, nor the mind in conceiving.

What you will find in the following sheets are directions generally for dressing, after the best, most natural and wholesome manner, such provisions as are the product of our own country, and in such a manner as is most agreeable to English palates; saving that I have so far temporised as (since we have, to our disgrace, so fondly admired the French tongue, French modes, and also French messes) to present you now and then with such receipts of the French cookery as I think may not be disagreeable to English palates.

There are indeed already in the world various books that treat on this subject, some of which bear great names, such as those of cooks to kings, princes and noblemen; of these one might justly expect something more than many, if not most, of those I have read perform; but I have found myself deceived in my expectations; for many of them to us are impracticable, others whimsical, others unpalatable, unless to depraved palates; some unwholesome; many things copied from old authors, and recommended without (as I am persuaded) the copiers ever having had any experience of the palatableness or any regard for the wholesomeness of them; which two things ought to be standing rules that no pretenders to cookery ought to deviate from. And I cannot but believe that these celebrated performers, notwithstanding all their professions of having ingeniously communicated their art, industriously concealed their best receipts from the public.

But what I here present the world with is the product of my own experience, and that for the space of thirty years and upwards; during which time I have been constantly employed in fashionable and noble families, in which the provisions ordered according to the following directions have had the general approbation of such as have been at many noble entertainments,

These receipts are all suitable to English constitutions and English palates, wholesome, toothsome, all practicable and easy to be performed; here are those proper for a frugal and also for a sumptuous table, and if rightly observed, will prevent the spoiling of many a good dish of meat, the waste of many good materials, the vexation that frequently attends such mismanagement, and the curses not infrequently bestowed on cooks, with the usual reflection that whereas God sends good meat, the devil sends cooks. As to those parts that treat of confectionary, pickles, cordials, English wines, etc., what I have said in relation to cookery, is equally applicable to them also.

It is true, I have not been so numerous in receipts as some who have gone before me, but I think I have made amends in giving none but what are approved and practicable and fit either for a genteel or a noble table; and although I have omitted odd and fantastical messes, yet I have set down a considerable number of receipts.

The treatise is divided into ten parts: cookery contains above an hundred receipts; pickles, fifty; puddings above fifty; pastry, above forty; cakes, forty; creams and jellies, above forty; preserving, a hundred; made wines, forty; cordial waters and powders, above seventy; medicines and salves, above three hundred; in all, near eight hundred.

I have likewise presented you with schemes, engraven on copper-plates, for the regular disposition or placing of the dishes of provision on the table, according to the best manner, both for summer and winter, first and second courses, etc.

As for the receipts for medicines, salves and ointments, good in several diseases, wounds, hurts, bruises, aches, pains, etc., which amount to above three hundred, they are generally family receipts that have never been made public, excellent in their kind, and approved remedies, which have not been obtained by me without much difficulty, and of such efficacy in distempers, etc., to which they are appropriated that they have cured when all other means have failed; and a few of them, which I have communicated to a friend, have procured a very handsome livelihood.

They are very proper for those generous, charitable and Christian gentlewomen who have a disposition to be serviceable to their poor country neighbours, labouring under any of the afflicting circumstances mentioned; who by making the medicines, and generously contributing as occasions offer, may help the poor in their afflictions, gain their goodwill and wishes, entitle themselves to their blessings and prayers, and also have the pleasure of feeling the good they do in this world and have good reason to hope for a reward (though not by way of merit} in the world to come.

As the whole of this collection has cost me much pains, and thirty years' diligent application, and as I have had experience of their use and efficacy, I hope they will be as kindly accepted as by me they are generously offered to the public; and if they prove to the advantage of many, the end will be answered that is proposed by her that is ready to serve the public in what she may.

It may be necessary to observe that the proprietors, being desirous of rendering this edition as complete and useful as possible, have (besides many new receipts) added directions for marketing, or the best method of choosing butcher's meat, fish, fowl, etc., also directions for boiling, roasting, broiling, etc., which were wanting in the former impressions. And, as these additions have rendered the work more beneficial and useful, it is to be hoped that this edition will meet with as favourable a reception from the public as any of the former.

Opposite is a facsimile of the title page from the sixteenth edition

THE
Compleat Houſewife:
OR,
Accompliſhed Gentlewoman's
COMPANION.
BEING
A COLLECTION of upwards of Six Hundred
of the moſt approved RECEIPTS in

COOKERY,	CAKES,
PASTRY,	CREAMS,
CONFECTIONARY,	JELLIES,
PRESERVING,	MADE WINES,
PICKLES,	CORDIALS.

With COPPER PLATES, curiouſly engraven, for
the regular Diſpoſition or Placing of the various
DISHES and COURSES.

AND ALSO
BILLS of FARE for every Month in the Year.

To which is added,

A COLLECTION of above Three Hundred Family RECEIPTS of
MEDICINES; *viz. Drinks, Syrups, Salves, Ointments,* and
various other Things of ſovereign and approved Efficacy in
moſt Diſtempers, Pains, Aches, Wounds, Sores, &c. particularly Mrs. *Stephens's* Medicine for the Cure of the Stone
and Gravel, and Dr. *Mead's* famous Receipt for the Cure of a
Bite of a mad Dog; with ſeveral other excellent Receipts for
the ſame, which have cured when the Perſons were diſordered,
and the ſalt Water fail'd; never before made publick; fit
either for private Families, or ſuch publick-ſpirited Gentlewomen as would be beneficent to their poor Neighbours.

WITH
DIRECTIONS for MARKETING
By *E. SMITH.*

The SIXTEENTH EDITION, with ADDITIONS.

LONDON:
Printed for C. HITCH and L. HAWES, JOHN RIVINGTON,
JAMES RIVINGTON and J. FLETCHER, J. WARD, W.
JOHNSTON, S. CROWDER, P. DAVEY and B. LAW, T.
LONGMAN, C. WARE, and M. COOPER. MDCCLVIII.

Price FIVE SHILLINGS.

Directions for Marketing

MEAT

To choose Beef

If it be true ox-beef it will have an open grain, and the fat, if young, of a crumbling or oily smoothness, except it be the brisket and neck pieces, with such others as are very fibrous. The colour of the lean should be of a pleasant carnation red, the fat rather inclining to white than yellow, and the suet of a curious white colour.

Cow-beef is of a closer grain, the fat whiter, the bones less, and the lean of a paler colour. If it be young and tender the dent you make with your finger by pressing it will, in a little time, rise again.

Bull-beef is of a more dusky red, a closer grain, and firmer than either of the former; harder to be indented with your finger, and rising again sooner. The fat is very gross and fibrous, and of a strong rank scent. If it be old it will be so very tough that if you pinch it you will scarce make any impression in it. If it be fresh it will be of a lively fresh colour, but if stale of a dark dusky colour, and very clammy. If it be bruised, the part affected will look of a more dusky or blackish colour than the rest.

To choose Pork

Pinch the lean between your fingers: if it break, and feel soft and oily, or if you can easily nip the skin with your nails, or if the fat be soft and oily, it is young; but if the lean be rough, the fat very spongy, and the skin stubborn, it is old. If it be a boar, or a hog gelded at full growth, the flesh will feel harder and rougher than usual, the skin thicker, the fat hard and fibrous, the lean of a dusky red, and of a rank scent. To know if it be fresh or stale, try the legs and hands at the bone, which comes out in the middle of the fleshy part, but putting in your finger, for as it first taints in those places, you may easily discover it by smelling to your finger; also the skin will be clammy and sweaty when stale, but smooth and cool when fresh.

To Choose Brawn

The best method of knowing whether brawn be young or old, is by the extraordinary or moderate thickness of the rind, and the hardness and softness of it; for the thick and hard is old, the moderate and soft is young. If the rind and fat be remarkably tender it is not boar brawn, but barrow or sow.

To Choose dried Hams and Bacon

Take a sharp-pointed knife, run it into the middle of the ham on the inside under the bone, draw it out quickly and smell to it; if its flavour be fine and relishing, and the knife little daubed, the ham is sweet and good; but if, on the contrary, the knife be greatly daubed, has a rank smell, and a hogoo issues from the vent, it is tainted. Or you may cut off a piece at one end to look on the meat: if it appear white and be well scented, it is good; but if yellowish, or of a rusty colour, and not well scented, it is either tainted or rusty, or at least, will soon be so. A gammon of bacon may be tried in the same manner, and be sure to observe that the flesh stick close to the bones, and the fat and lean to each other; for if it does not, the hog was not sound. Take care also that the extreme part of the fat near the rind be white, for if that be of a darkish or dirty colour, and the lean pale and soft, it is rusty.

To Choose Venison

Try the haunches, shoulders, and fleshy parts of the sides with your knife, in the same manner as before directed for ham, and in proportion to the sweet or rank smell it is new or stale. With relation to the other parts, observe the colour of the meat; for if it be stale or tainted it will be of a black colour intermixed with yellowish or greenish specks. If it be old the flesh will be tough and hard, the fat contracted, the hoofs large and broad, and the heel horny and much worn.

To Choose Mutton

Take some of the flesh between your fingers and pinch it: if it feels tender, and soon returns to its former place, it is young; but if it wrinkles, and remains so, it is old. The fat will, also, easily separate from the lean if it be young; but if old it will adhere more firmly, and be very clammy and fibrous. If it be ram mutton the fat will be spongy, the grain close, the lean rough and of a deep red, and when dented by your finger will not rise again. If the sheep had the rot, the flesh will be palish, the fat a faint white, inclining to yellow; the meat will be loose at the bone, and if you squeeze it hard some drops of water resembling a dew or sweat will appear on the surface. If it be a fore quarter, observe the vein in the neck, for if it look ruddy, or of an azure colour it is fresh; but if yellowish, it is near tainting, and if green, it is already so. As for the hindquarter, smell under the kidney, and feel whether the knuckle be stiff or limber; for if you find a faint or ill scent in the former, or an unusual limberness in the latter, it is stale.

To Choose Veal

Observe the vein in the shoulder, for if it be of a bright red it is newly killed; but if greenish, yellowish, or blackish, or be more clammy, soft, and limber than usual, it is stale. Also if it has any green spots about it, it is either tainting or already tainted. If it be wrapped in wet cloths it is apt to be musty; therefore always observe to smell to it. The loin taints first under the kidney, and the flesh, when stale, will be soft and slimy. The neck and breast are first tainted at the upper end, and when so will have a dusky, yellowish, or greenish appearance, and the sweetbread on the breast will be clammy. The leg, if newly killed, will be stiff in the joint; but if stale, limber and the flesh clammy, intermixed with green or yellowish specks. The flesh of a bull-calf is firmer grained and redder than that of a cow-calf, and the fat more curdled.

To Choose a Hare

If the claws of a hare are blunt and ragged, her ears dry and tough, and the cleft in her lip spread much, she is old; but the opposite if young. If new and fresh killed, the flesh will be white and stiff; if stale, limber and blackish in many places.

To Choose a Leveret

The newness or staleness may be known by the same signs as the hare; but in order to discover if it be a real leveret, feel near the foot on its fore leg: if you find there a knob or small bone, it is a true leveret; but if not a hare.

To Choose a Rabbit or Coney

If a rabbit or coney be old, the claws will be very long and rough, and grey hairs intermixed with the wool; but if young, the claws and wool smooth; if stale, it will be limber, and the flesh will look blueish, having a kind of slime upon it; but if fresh it will be stiff, and the flesh white and dry.

DAIRY PRODUCTS

To choose Butter and Eggs

When you buy butter taste it yourself at a venture, and do not trust to the taste they give you, lest you be deceived by a well tasted and scented piece artfully placed in the lump. Salt butter is better scented than tasted, by putting a knife into it, and putting it immediately to your nose; but if it be a cask it may be purposely packed, therefore trust not to the top alone, but unhoop it to the middle, thrusting your knife between the staves of the cask, and then you cannot be deceived.

When you buy eggs put the great end to your tongue: if it feels warm, it is new; but if cold it is stale; and according to the heat or coldness of it, the egg is newer or staler. Or take the egg and hold it up against the sun or a candle: if the white appears clear and fair, and the yolk round, it is good; but if muddy or cloudy, and the yolk broken, it is nought. Or take the egg and put it into a pan of cold water: the fresher it is the sooner it will sink to the bottom; but if it be rotten, or addled, it will swim on the surface of the water. The best way to keep them is in bran or meal; though some place their small ends downwards in fine wood-ashes.

To choose Cheese

When you buy cheese observe the coat; for if the cheese be old, and its coat be rough, rugged, or dry at top, it indicates mites, or little worms. If it be spongy, moist, or full of holes, it is subject to maggots. If you perceive on the outside any perished place, be sure to examine its deepness.

POULTRY

To know if a Capon be a true one or not, or whether it be young, or old, new or stale

If a capon be young his spurs will be short and blunt, and his legs smooth. If a true capon, he will have a fat vein on the side of the breast, a thick belly and rump, and his comb will be short and pale. If he be new he will have a close hard vent; but if stale an open loose vent.

To choose a Cock or Hen Turkey, Turkey Poults, &c.

If the spurs of a turkey cock are short, and his legs black and smooth, he is young; but if his spurs be long, and his legs pale and rough, he is old. If long killed, his eyes will be funk into his head, and his feet feel very dry; but if fresh his feet will be limber, and his eyes lively. For the hen, observe the same signs. If she be with egg she will have an open vent; but if not, a close hard vent. The same signs will serve to discover the newness or staleness of turkey poults; and, with respect to their age, you cannot be deceived.

To choose a Cock, Hen, &c.

If a cock be young his spurs will be short and dubbed (but be sure to observe that they are not pared or scraped to deceive you); but if sharp and standing out he is old. If his vent be hard and close, it is a sign of his being newly killed; but if he be stale his vent will be open. The same signs will discover whether a hen be new or stale; and if old her legs and comb will be rough; but if young, smooth.

To know if Chickens are new or stale

If they are pulled dry, they will be stiff when new; but when stale they will be limber and their vents green. If they are scalded, or pulled wet, rub the breast with your thumb or finger, and if they are rough and stiff they are new; but if smooth and slippery, stale.

To choose a Goose, wild Goose, and bran Goose

If the bill and foot be red, and the body full of hairs, she is old; but if the bill be yellowish, and the body has but few hairs, she is young. If new, her feet will be limber, but if stale, dry. Understand the same of a wild goose, and bran goose.

To choose wild and tame Ducks

These fowls are hard and thick on the belly when fat, but thin and lean when poor; limber footed when new, but dry footed when stale. A wild duck may be distinguished from a tame one by its foot being smaller and reddish.

To choose the Bustard

Observe the same rules in choosing this curious fowl, as those already given for the turkey.

To choose the Shuffler, Godwitz, Marrel Knots, Gulls, Dotters, and Wheat-Ears

These birds, when new, are limber footed; when stale, dry footed. When fat, they have a fat rump; when lean, a close and hard one. When young their legs are smooth; when old, rough.

To choose the Pheasant Cock and Hen

The spurs of the pheasant cock, when young, are short and dubbed, but long and sharp when old; when new he has a firm vent, when stale an open and flabby one. The pheasant hen, when young, has smooth legs, and her flesh is of a fine and curious grain; but when old her legs are rough, and her flesh hairy when pulled. If she be with egg her vent will be open, if not closed. The same signs, as to newness or staleness, are to be observed as were before given for the cock.

To choose Heath and Pheasant Poults

The feet of these, when new, are limber, and their vents white and stiff; but when stale, are dry footed, their vents green, and if you touch it hard, will peel.

To Choose the Heath-Cock and Hen

The newness or staleness of these are known by the same signs as the foregoing; but when young their legs and bills are smooth; when old both are rough.

To Choose the Woodcock and Snipe

These fowls are limber-footed when new, but stale if dry-footed. If fat, thick and hard; but if their noses are snotty, and their throats moorish and muddy, they are bad.

To Choose the Partridge Cock or Hen

These fowls, when young, have black bills and yellowish legs; when old, white bills and bluish legs; when new, a fast vent; when stale a green and open one, which will peel with a touch: If they have fed lately on green wheat, and their crops be full, smell to their mouths, lest their crops be tainted.

To Choose Doves or Pigeons, Plovers, &c.

The turtledove is distinguished by a bluish ring round its neck, the other parts being almost white. The stock-dove exceeds both the wood-pigeon and ring-dove in bigness. The dove-house pigeons are red-legged when old. If new and fat they are limber-footed and feel full in the vent; but when stale, their vents are green and flabby.

After the same manner you may choose the grey and green plover, thrush, mavis, lark, blackbird, &c.

To Choose Teal and Widgeon

These, when new, are limber-footed; when stale, dry footed. Thick and hard on the belly if fat, but thin and soft if lean.

FISH

To choose Salmon, Trout, Carp, Tench, Pike, Graylings, Barbel, Chub, Whiting, Smelt, Ruff, Eel, Shad, &c.

The newness or staleness of these fish are known by the colour of their gills, their being hard or easy to be opened, the standing out or sinking of their eyes, their fins being stiff or limber, and by smelling to their gills.

To choose the Turbot

If this fish be plump and thick, and its belly of a cream colour, it is good; but if thin, and of a blueish white on the belly, not so.

To choose Soles

If these are thick and stiff, and of a cream colour on the belly, they will spend well; but if thin, limber, and their bellies of a blueish white, they will eat very loose.

To choose Plaice and Flounders

When these fish are new they are stiff, and the eyes look lively, and stand out; but when stale, the contrary. The best plaice are blueish on the belly; but flounders are of a cream colour.

To choose Cod and Codling

Choose those which are thick towards the head, and their flesh, when cut very white.

To choose fresh Herrings and Mackerel

If these are new, their gills will be of a lively shining redness, their eyes sharp and full, and the fish stiff; but if stale, their gills will look dusky and faded, their eyes dull and sunk down, and their tails limber.

To choose pickled Salmon

The scales of this fish, when new and good, are stiff and shining, the flesh oily to the touch, and parts in flakes without crumbling; but the opposite when bad.

To choose pickled and Red Herrings

Take the former and open the back to the bone: if it be white, or of bright red, and the flesh white, oily, and flaky, they are good. If the latter smell well, be of a good gloss, and part well from the bone, they are also good.

To choose dried Ling

The best sort of dried ling is that which is thickest in the pole, and the flesh of the brightest yellow.

To choose pickled Sturgeon

The veins and gristle of the fish, when good, are of a blue colour, the flesh white, the skin limber, the fat underneath of a pleasant scent, and you may cut it without its crumbling.

To choose Lobsters

If a lobster be new, it has a pleasant scent at that part of the tail which joins to the body, and the tail will, when opened, fall smart like a spring; but when stale it has a rank scent, and the tail limber and flagging. If it be spent, a white scurf will issue from the mouth and roots of the small legs. If it be full, the tail about the middle will be full of hard reddish skin'd meat, which you may discover by thrusting a knife between the joints, on the bend of the tail. The heaviest are best if there be no water in them. The cock is generally smaller than the hen, of a deeper red when boiled, has no spawn or seed under its tail, and the uppermost fins within its tail are stiff and hard.

To choose Crab-fish, great and small

When they are stale their shells will be of a dusky red colour, the joints of their claws limber; they are loose and may be turned any way with the finger, and from under their throat will issue an ill smell; but if otherwise they are good.

To choose Prawns and Shrimps

If they are hard and stiff, of a pleasant scent, and their tails turn strongly inward, they are new; but if they are limber, their colour faded, of a faint smell, and feel slimy, they are stale.

Cookery, &c.

The Preparation of Meat, Poultry, Fish, &c.

General directions for Boiling

Let your pot be very clean; and as a scum will arise from everything, be sure to shake a small handful of flour into it, which will take all the scum up, and prevent any from falling down to make the meat black. All salt meat must be put in when the water is cold; but fresh meat, not till it boils; and as many pounds as your piece weighs, so many quarters of an hour it will require in boiling.

To boil a Tongue

If it be a dry tongue it must be laid in warm water for six hours, then change your water, and let it lay three hours more; the second water must be cold. Then take it out and boil it three hours, which will be sufficient. If your tongue be just out of pickle it must lay three hours in cold water, and boil it till it will peel.

To boil a Ham

Lay your ham in cold water for two hours, wash it clean, and tie it up in clean hay; put it into fresh water, boil it very slow for one hour, and then very briskly an hour and an half more. Take it up in the hay and let it lie in it till cold, then rub the rind with a clean piece of flannel.

To boil House-Lamb, or Fowls

These are the best boiled in milk and water, being tied up in a clean cloth well floured. An hour will boil it if large, and so in proportion if smaller.

To boil pickled Pork

Wash your pork, and scrape it clean; then put it in when the water is cold, and boil it till the rind be tender.

To dress Greens, Roots, &c.

When you have nicely picked and washed your greens, lay them in a colander to drain, for if any cold water hang to them they will be tough; then boil them alone in a copper saucepan, with a large quantity of water, for if any meat be boiled with them it will discolour them. Be sure not to put them in till the water boils.

To dress Spinach

Wash it in several waters, put it into a saucepan with no more water than what hangs to it; when it boils up pour the liquor from it, and put in a piece of butter and some salt; then boil it till the spinach falls to the bottom; take it up, press it very dry, and serve it up with melted butter.

To dress Carrots

Scrape them very clean, and when the water boils, put them into your pot or saucepan; if they are young spring carrots, they will be boiled in half an hour, but if large they will require an hour. Then take them out, slice them into a plate, and pour over them some melted butter.

To dress Parsnips

Boil them in a large quantity of water, after they are cleanly scraped, and when they are enough, which may be known by their being soft, take them up, and separate from them all the sticky parts; then put them in a saucepan with some milk, a proper quantity of butter, and some salt; set them over the fire, stir them till they are thick, taking great care that they do not burn, and when the butter is melted send them to table.

To dress Potatoes

Put your potatoes into the saucepan with a proper quantity of water; and when they are enough, which may be known by their skins beginning to crack, drain all the water from them, and let them stand close covered up for two or three minutes; then peel them, place them in a plate, and pour over them a proper quantity of melted butter. Or after you have peeled them, lay them on a gridiron, and, when they are of a fine brown, send them to table. Or you may cut them into slices, fry them in butter, and season them with pepper and salt.

To dress Turnips

They are best boiled in the pot; when they are enough put them into a pan with some butter and salt, and after you have mashed them send them to table. Or, after your turnips are pared, you may cut them into small pieces, and boil them in a saucepan with as much water as will just cover them; when they are enough, put them into a sieve to drain; then put them into a saucepan with a proper quantity of butter, and, after stirring them five or six minutes over the fire, send them to table.

To dress Broccoli

After you have separated the small branches from the large ones, and taken off the hard outside skin, throw them into water; then place your stew-pan, containing a sufficient quantity of water mixed with some salt, on the fire, and when the water boils put in your broccoli; when they are enough, which may be known by the stalks being tender, send them to table with melted butter in a cup.

To dress Asparagus

Let all the stalks be carefully scraped till they look white, cut them of an equal length, and throw them into water; set your stew-pan with a proper quantity of water, having some salt in it, on the fire, and when the water boils put in your asparagus, after being tied up in small bundles. When they are enough, which may be known by their being somewhat tender, take them up, for if they boil too long, they will lose both their colour and taste. Then cut a round off a small loaf, and having toasted it brown on both sides, dip it in the liquor of the asparagus, laying it in your dish. Melt some butter, and pour it on the toast, laying the asparagus on it round the dish, with the bottom part of the stalks outward. Put the remaining part of the butter in a basin, because pouring it over the asparagus makes them greasy, and send them to table.

To dress French Beans

Take your beans, string them, cut them in two and then across, or else into four and then across, and put them into water with some salt; set your saucepan full of water over the fire, cover it close, and when it boils put in your beans, with a little salt. They will be soon done, which you may know by their being tender; then take them up before they lose their fine green, and having put them in a plate, send them to table with butter in a cup.

To dress Artichokes

After you have twisted the heads from the stalks, put them into the saucepan with the water cold, placing their tops downwards, by which means all the dust and sand contained between the leaves will boil out. When they have boiled about an hour and a half they will be enough; then take them up, and send them to table with melted butter in a basin.

To dress Cauliflowers

Cut off all the green part from your flowers, and divide them into four parts, laying them in water for an hour. Put some milk and water into your saucepan, and set it over the fire; when it boils put in your cauliflowers, observing to skim your saucepan well. When they are enough, which you may know by the stalks being tender, take them up into a colander to drain. Take a quarter of a pound of butter, a spoonful of water, a little flour, and a little pepper and salt; put them into a stew-pan, place it on the fire, shaking it often till the butter is melted; then take half of the cauliflower, divide it into small pieces, and put them into the stew-pan, shaking it often for ten minutes; place the boiled round the sides of the plate, and the stewed in the middle; pour the butter you stewed it in over it, and send it to table.

Rules to be observed in roasting

Let your fire be made in proportion to the piece you are to dress; that is, if it be a little or thin piece, make a little brisk fire that it may be done quick and nice; but if a large joint observe to lay a good fire to cake, and let it be always clear at the bottom.

When your meat is about half done, move it and the dripping-pan a little distance from the fire, which stir up and make it burn brisk; for the quicker your fire is, the sooner and better will your meat be done.

To roast Beef

If the rib, sprinkle it with salt for half an hour, dry and flour it; then butter a piece of paper very thick, fasten it on the beef, with the buttered side next it. If a rump or sirloin, do not salt it, but lay it a good distance from the fire; baste it once or twice with salt and water, then with butter, flour it, and keep it basting with what drops from it. Take three spoonfuls of vinegar, a pint of water, a shallot, a small piece of horseradish, two spoonfuls of ketchup, and one glass of claret, baste it with this once or twice, then strain it and put it under your beef; garnish with horseradish and red cabbage.

To roast Pork

All pork must be flour'd thick, and laid at first a good distance from the fire; and when the flour begins to dry, wipe it clean. Then with a sharp knife cut the skin across. Heighten the fire, and put your meat near it, baste, and roast it as quick as you can. If a leg, you must cut it very deep. When almost done, fill the cuts with grated bread, sage, parsley, a small piece of lemon-peel cut small, a piece of butter, two eggs, a little pepper, salt and nutmeg, mixed together: when it is enough send it to table with gravy and apple-sauce. If you roast a spare-rib, baste it with a little butter, flour, and sage shred small. When it is ready send it to table with apple-sauce.

To roast a Pig

Lay your pig in warm milk for a quarter of an hour, and wipe it very dry. Take of butter and crumbs of bread, of each a quarter of a pound, a little sage, thyme, parsley, sweet-marjoram, pepper, salt, and nutmeg, the yolks of two eggs, mix these together, and sew it up in the belly. Flour it very thick; then spit it, and lay it to the fire, taking care that your fire burns well at both ends, or till it does, hang a flat iron in the middle of the grate. When you find the crackling grows hard, wipe it clean with a cloth wet in salt and water, and baste it with butter. As soon as the gravy begins to run, put basins in the dripping-pan to receive it. When the pig is enough, take about a quarter of a pound of butter, put it into a coarse cloth, and, having made a brisk fire, rub the pig all over with it, till the crackling is quite crisp, and then take it from the fire. Cut off the head, and cut the pig in two, before you take it from the spit. Then having cut the ears off and placed one at each end, and, also, the under-jaw in two, and placed one part on each side, take some good butter, melt it, mix it with the gravy, the brains bruised, and some sage shred small, and send it to table.

To roast Mutton and Lamb

Before you lay the mutton down, take care to have a clear quick fire; baste it often, and when it is almost done, dredge it with a little flour. If it be a breast, skin it before you lay it down.

To roast Veal

If a shoulder baste it with milk till half done, then flour it and baste it with butter. A fillet must be stuffed with thyme, marjoram, parsley, a small onion, a sprig of savoury, a bit of lemon-peel cut very small, nutmeg, pepper, mace, salt, crumbs of bread, four eggs, and a quarter of a pound of butter or marrow, mixed with a little flour to make it stiff. Half of the above must be put into the udder, and the other into holes made in the fleshy part.

If it be a loin, paper the fat, that as little of it may be lost as possible. If it be the breast you must cover it with the caul, and fasten the sweetbread on the backside of it with a skewer. When it is almost done, take off the caul, baste and dredge it with a little flour. Send it up with melted butter, and garnish'd with lemon.

To roast a Hare

Take crumbs of bread, and suet cut small, of each half a pound; some parsley and thyme shred small; some salt, pepper, cloves, mace, and nutmegs pounded; three dried mushrooms cut small, two eggs, a glass of claret, two spoonfuls of ketchup; mix all these together, and sew it up in the belly of the hare; lay it down to a very slow fire and baste it with milk till it becomes very thick; then make a brisk fire, roast it for half an hour, baste it with butter, and dredge it with a little flour.

To roast Venison

Wash your venison in vinegar and water, dry it with a cloth, and cover it with the caul, or, instead of that, a buttered paper. Make a brisk fire, lay it down, and baste it with butter till it is almost done. Then take a pint of claret, boil it in a saucepan with some whole pepper, nutmeg, cloves and mace. Pour this liquor twice over your venison. Have your dish on a chafing-dish of coals to keep it hot. Then take it up, strain the liquor you poured over the venison, and serve it in the same dish with the venison, with good gravy in one basin and sweet sauce in another.

To roast Rabbits

When you have lain your rabbits down to the fire, baste them with good butter, and then dredge them with flour. If they are small, and your fire quick and clear, half an hour will do them, but if large they will require three quarters of an hour. Melt some good butter, and having boiled the livers with a bunch of parsley, and chop'd them small, put half into the butter, and pour it into the dish, garnishing it with the other half.

To roast a Tongue, or Udder

Take your tongue or udder and parboil it; then stick into it ten or twelve cloves, and while it is roasting baste it with butter. When it is ready take it up, and send it to table with some gravy and sweet sauce.

To roast Mutton like Venison

Take a fat hind quarter of mutton, and cut the leg like a haunch of venison, rub it well with salt petre, hang it in a moist place for two days, wiping it two or three times a day with a clean cloth. Then put it into a pan, and having boiled a quarter of an ounce of allspice in a quart of red wine, pour it boiling hot over your mutton, cover it close for two hours; take it out, spit it, lay it down to the fire and constantly baste it with the same liquor and butter. If you have a good quick fire, and your mutton not prodigious large, it will be ready in an hour and a half. Then take it up and send it to table with some good gravy in one cup, and sweet sauce in another.

To roast Woodcocks and Snipes

Put them on the spit without taking anything out of them; baste them with butter, and when the tail begins to drop, put into the dish to receive it a round of a threepenny loaf toasted brown. When they are done put the toast into the dish, with about a quarter of a pint of good gravy, put the woodcocks on it, and set it over a lamp or chafing-dish of coals for about three minutes, and send them to table.

To roast the hind quarter of a Pig Lamb fashion

Take the hind quarter of a large pig, skin it, and when it is roasted, which will be in three quarters of an hour, send it to table with mint sauce, a salad, or a Seville orange.

To roast Pigeons

Take a little pepper and salt, a small piece of butter, and some parsley cut small; mix these together, put them into the bellies of your pigeons, tying the neck ends tight; take another string, fasten one end of it to their legs and rumps, and the other to the mantle-piece. Keep them constantly turning round, and baste them with butter. When they are done, take them up, lay them in a dish, and they will swim with gravy.

To roast a Goose

Take a little sage, and a small onion chopped small, some pepper and salt, and a bit of butter; mix these together, and put it into the belly of the goose. Then spit it, singe it with a bit of white paper, dredge it with a little flour, and baste it with butter. When it is done, which may be known by the leg being tender, take it up, and pour thro' it two glasses of red wine, and serve it up in the same dish, and apple sauce in a basin.

To roast a Turkey

Take a quarter of a pound of lean veal, a little thyme, parsley, sweet-marjoram, a sprig of winter savoury, a bit of lemon-peel, one onion, a nutmeg grated, a dram of mace, a little salt, and half a pound of butter; cut your herbs very small, pound your meat as small as possible, and mix all together with three eggs, and as much flour or bread as will make it of a proper consistence. Then fill the crop of your turkey with it, paper the breast and lay it down at a good distance from the fire. An hour and a quarter will roast it if not very large.

General directions for broiling

First, take care that your fire be very clear before you lay your meat on the gridiron.

Second, turn your meat, when it is down, quick, having at the same time a dish placed on a chafing-dish of hot coals to put your meat in as fast as it is ready, and carry it to the table covered hot.

Third, observe never to baste anything on the gridiron, for that causes it to be both smoked and burnt.

To broil Steaks

When you have made a clear brisk fire, make your gridiron very clean, put some hot coals from the fire into a chafing-dish, and place a dish over them, in order to receive your steaks when ready; take rump-steaks, which should be about half an inch thick; after you have thrown over them a little pepper and salt, place them on the gridiron, and do not turn them till that side be done; when you have turned them you will soon perceive a fine gravy lying on the upper part of the steak, which you must carefully preserve by taking the steaks when ready warily from your gridiron, and placing them in your dish. Then covering your dish, send them hot to table with the cover on. Some, before they take the steak from the gridiron, cut into the dish a shallot or two, or a fine onion, and a little vinegar.

To broil a Pigeon

You may either split and broil them with a little pepper and salt; or you may take a small piece of butter, a little pepper and salt, and having put it into their bellies, tie both ends close. Then lay them on your gridiron, taking care to place it high that they may not burn, and when they are ready send them to table with a little melted butter in a cup.

To bake a Pig

Take your pig, flour it well, and having butter'd your dish, lay your pig into it, and put it into the oven. When it is ready and you have drawn it out of the oven, rub it all over with a buttery cloth; then put it again into the oven, and when it is dry take it out, lay it in your dish, and cut it up. Take the gravy which remains in the dish you baked it in, after you have skimmed off the fat; mix it with some good gravy, a sufficient quantity of butter rolled in flour, and a glass of white-wine; set it on the fire, and as soon as it boils, pour it into the dish with the brains and the sage which was roasted in its belly.

To bake a Leg of Beef

Take a leg of beef, cut it and break the bones; put it into an earthen pan with a spoonful of whole pepper, a few cloves and blades of mace, two onions, and a bundle of sweet herbs; cover it with water, and, having tied the pot down close with brown paper, put it into the oven to bake. When it is enough strain it through a sieve, and pick out all the fat and sinews, putting them into a saucepan with a little gravy, and a piece of butter rolled in flour. Set the saucepan on the fire, shaking it often, and when it is thoroughly hot pour it into the dish, and send it to table.

To bake an Ox's Cheek

Observe the same directions as those given for baking a leg of beef.

Sauce for boiled Ducks or Rabbits

Take a sufficient quantity of onions, peel them, and boil them in a large quantity of water: When they are about half boiled, throw that water away and fill your saucepan with half milk and half water, in which let them boil till they are enough; then take them up into a colander, and when they are drained, chop them with a knife; put them into a saucepan with a piece of butter rolled in flour; set the saucepan over the fire, shaking it often till the butter is melted, then pour it over your boiled ducks or rabbits, and send them to table.

Sauce for a boiled Turkey

Take a piece of white bread, put it into a quart of water, with a blade of mace, a little pepper and salt, and a bit of onion. Boil it to a pint; strain it, and add to it the yolk of an egg beat, a piece of butter rolled in flour, and a glass of white wine. Garnish with forc'd-meat balls and oysters.

Sauce for a boiled Goose

You may either make onion sauce as directed for boiled ducks, &c. or you may boil some cabbage, and then stew it a small time in butter.

Sauce for roast Venison

Take a pound of lean beef, and a quarter of a pound of lean bacon, cut into small pieces; put it into a stew-pan with three pints of water, a bunch of sweet herbs, and an onion; boil it till half is consumed. Strain it, and add to it two spoonfuls of ketchup, as much oyster-liquor, and thicken it with brown-butter.

Or take half the crumb of a halfpenny loaf, a large stick of cinnamon, some mace and nutmeg and a race of ginger, put these into a saucepan with a pint of water; boil it; beat it very fine, and strain it through a sieve, adding to it half a pint of red wine, and sweeten it to your taste.

Different sauces for a Hare

Take some good gravy, and a proper quantity of butter rolled in flour; when it is melted pour it into your dish. Or take half a pound of butter, put it into a saucepan, set it over the fire, keeping it continually stirred till the butter is melted, and the sauce thick; then take it from the fire and pour it into the dish. Or take a pint of red wine and half a pound of sugar, and after it has simmer'd about a quarter of an hour over the fire, pour it into the dish.

Different sauces for a Pig

Take a good piece of crumb of bread, a little whole pepper, and a blade of mace, boil these about six minutes in a pint of water; then pour off the water, take out the spice, and beat up the bread with a proper quantity of butter. Some add a few currants, a glass of wine, and a little sugar. Or take the gravy which dropped from the pig, half a pint of good gravy, three spoonfuls of ketchup, and a piece of butter rolled in flour; boil these together, and mix it with the brains of the pig. If you have not gravy enough from the pig you may supply its place by stewing the petty-toes.

Sauce for Larks

Take for every dozen of larks a quarter of a pound of butter, the crumb of a halfpenny loaf rubbed small; when the butter is melted put in your bread, keeping it constantly stirring till it becomes brown; then drain it through a sieve, and place it round your larks.

To make a Soup

Take a leg of beef, and boil it down with some salt, a bundle of sweet herbs, an onion, a few cloves, a bit of nutmeg; boil three gallons of water to one; then take two or three pounds of lean beef cut in thin slices; then put in your stew-pan a piece of butter as big as an egg, and flour it, and let the pan be hot, and shake it till the butter be brown; then lay your beef in your pan over a pretty quick fire, cover it close, give it a turn now and then, and strain in your strong broth, with an anchovy or two, a handful of spinach and endive boiled green, and drained and shred gross; then have pallets ready boiled and cut in pieces, and toasts fry'd and cut like dice, and forc'd-meat balls fry'd: take out the fry'd beef, and put all the rest together with a little pepper, and let it boil a quarter of an hour, and serve it up with a knuckle of veal, or a fowl boiled in the middle.

Another Gravy Soup

Take a leg of beef, and a piece of the neck, boil it till you have all the goodness out of it; then strain it from the meat; take half a pound of fresh butter, and put it in a stew-pan, and brown it; adding an onion stuck with cloves, some endive, celery and spinach, and your strong broth, seasoning it to your palate with salt, pepper, and spices; let it boil together, and put in chips of French bread dry'd by the fire, and serve it with a French roll toasted in the middle.

To make Crawfish or Lobster-Soup

Take whitings, flounders, and grigs, put them in a gallon of water, with pepper, salt, cloves, mace, a bunch of sweet herbs, a little onion, and boil them to pieces, and strain them out of the liquor; then take a large carp, and cut off the fish of one side of it, and put some eel to it; and make forc'd-meat of it, and lay it on the carp as before; dredge grated bread over it, butter a dish well, put it in an oven, and bake it; take an hundred of crawfish, break all the shells of the claws and tails, and take out the meat as whole as you can; then break all the shells small, and the spawn of a lobster, putting them to the soup, and if you please, some gravy; and give them a boil together, and strain the liquor out into another saucepan, with the tops of French rolls dried, beat, and sifted, and give it a boil up to thicken; then brown some butter, and put in the tails and claws of your crawfish, and some of your forc'd-meat made into balls, putting your baked carp into the middle of the dish, and pour your soup on boiling hot, and your crawfish or lobster in it; garnish the dish with lemon and scalded greens.

A Fasting-Day Soup

Take spinach, sorrel, chervil, and lettuce, and chop them a little; then brown some butter, and put in your herbs, keep them stirring that they don't burn; then, having boiling water over the fire, put to it a very little pepper, and some salt, a whole onion stuck with cloves, a French roll cut in slices and dried very hard, some Pistachio kernels, blanched and shred fine, and let all boil together; then beat up the yolks of eight eggs with a little white wine and the juice of a lemon; mix it with your broth, toast a whole French roll, and put it in the middle of your dish, pouring your soup over it; garnish your dish with ten or twelve poach'd eggs and scalded spinach.

Savoury Balls

Take part of a leg of lamb or veal, and scrape it fine, with the same quantity of minc'd beef-suet, a little lean bacon, sweet herbs, a shallot, and anchovies; beat it in a mortar till it is as smooth as wax, season it with savoury spice, and make it into little balls.

Another way

Take the flesh of fowl, beef-suet, and marrow, the same quantity; six or eight oysters, lean bacon, sweet herbs and savoury spices; pound it, and make it into little balls.

A Ragout for made Dishes

Take claret, gravy, sweet herbs, and savoury spice, toss up in it lamb-stones, cockcombs, boiled, blanched, and sliced, with sliced sweetmeats, oysters, mushrooms, truffles, and murrels; thicken these with brown butter; use it when called for.

To make Plum Porridge

Take a leg and shin of beef to ten gallons of water, boil it very tender, and when the broth is strong, strain it out; wipe the pot, and put in the broth again; slice six penny loaves thin, cutting off the top and bottom: put some of the liquor to it, cover it up, and let it stand a quarter of an hour, and then put it in your pot; let it boil a quarter of an hour, then put in five pounds of currants; let them boil a little, and put in five pounds of raisins, and two pounds of prunes, and let them boil till they swell, then put in three quarters of an ounce of mace, half an ounce of cloves, two nutmegs, all of them beat fine, and mix it with a little liquor cold, and put them in a very little while; then take off the pot, and put in three pounds of sugar, a little salt, a quart of sack, a quart of claret, and the juice of two or three lemons; you may thicken with sago instead of bread, if you please; pour them into earthen pans, and keep them for use.

A Soup or Pottage

Take several knuckles of mutton, a knuckle of veal, a shin of beef, and put to these twelve quarts of water, cover the pot close, and set it on the fire; let it not boil too fast; skim it well, and let it stand on the fire twenty-four hours; then strain it through a colander, and when it is cold take off the fat, and set it on the fire again, and season it with salt, a few cloves, pepper, a blade of mace, a nutmeg quarter'd, a bunch of sweet herbs, and a pint of gravy; let all these boil up for half an hour, and then strain it; put in spinach, sorrel, green peas, asparagus, or artichoke-bottoms, according to the time of the year; then thicken it up with the yolks of three or four eggs; have in readiness some sheep's tongues, cockscombs and sweetbreads, sliced thin and fry'd, and put them in; also some mushrooms, and French bread dry'd and cut in little bits, some forc'd-meat balls, and some very thin slices of bacon; make all these very hot, and garnish the dish with coleworts and spinach scalded green.

To make Peas Pottage

Take a quart of white peas, a piece of neck-beef, and four quarts of fair-water; boil them till they are all to pieces, and strain them thro' a colander; then take a handful or two of spinach, a top or two of young coleworts, and a very small leek; shred the herbs a little, and put them into a frying-pan, or stew-pan, with three quarters of a pound of fresh butter, but the butter must be very hot before you put in your herbs; let them fry a little while, then put in your liquor, and two or three anchovies, some salt and pepper to your taste, a sprig of mint rubb'd in small, and let it all boil together till you think it is thick enough; then have in readiness some forc'd-meat, and make three or four score balls, about the bigness of large peas, fry them brown, and put them in the dish you serve it in, and fry some thin slices of bacon, put some in the dish, and some on the rim of the dish, with scalded spinach: fry some toasts after the balls are brown and hard, and break them into the dish; then pour your pottage over all, and serve to the table.

To burn Butter

Shake some flour upon two or three ounces of butter, put it into a hot frying-pan that it may hiss; let it boil, and do not stir it; when it turns brown, put in the liquor you intend to thicken, and keep it quick stirring; boil it well, or it will taste raw.

To make Strong Broth to keep for use

Take part of a leg of beef, the scrag end of a neck of mutton, break the bones in pieces, put to it as much water as will cover it, and a little salt; when it boils skim it clean, and put into it a whole onion stuck with cloves, a bunch of sweet herbs, some pepper, and a nutmeg quartered; let these boil till the meat is boiled in pieces, and the strength boiled out of it; then put to it two or three anchovies; when they are dissolved, strain it out, and keep it for any sort of hash or fricassee.

To make Forc'd-Meat

Take part of a leg of mutton, veal, or beef, and pick off the skins and fat, and to every pound of meat put two pounds of beef-suet; shred them together very fine, then season it with pepper, salt, cloves, mace, nutmeg, and sage; put all into a stone mortar, and to every two pounds of meat put half a pint of oysters, and six eggs well beaten, then mix them all together, beat it very well, and keep it in an earthen pot for your use; put a little flour on the top, and when you roll them up flour your hands.

Another

Take a piece of a leg of veal, the lean part, and some lean bacon; mince them very fine, and add a double quantity of suet: put it all in a marble mortar, beat it well, sprinkle it with a little water in the beating; season it with pepper, salt, and a little cloves and mace, to your taste; shred spinach very fine if you would have it look green, or else without; make it up as you use it, with an egg or two, and roll it in long or round balls.

To Stew a Rump of Beef

Stuff the under part of the beef with forc'd-meat made of grated bread, beef-suet, sweet herbs, spice, anchovy, a little salt, fresh oysters or mushrooms, and two or three eggs beaten fine to mix up with the stuffing; then put it into a pot to stew, with as much water as will near cover it, some whole pepper, three or four cloves, and a little shred-nutmeg, or a few blades of mace; take up the beef, and separate all the fat, putting in a pint of stale beer, with a good quantity of strong gravy, and let it stew in a small quantity of liquor; it must be turned once or twice: fry some crumbs of bread brown, strain the liquor, and put in these crumbs to thicken it; then put in your gravy and not before; let it just simmer a little; you may put in some oysters, mushrooms, and ox's palate: this requires six or seven hours' stewing. Make some sauce of the liquor.

To roast a Rump of Beef

Let your beef lie two days in salt, then wash it, and lay it one hour in a quart of red wine and a pint of elder vinegar, with which baste the beef very well while it is roasting; then take two palates well boiled, and sliced thin; make your sauce with burnt butter, gravy, mushrooms and oysters; to which add the palates, and serve it up.

To roast a Loin of Mutton

Flay off the skin, and when it drips, dredge it with grated bread and molehill-thyme powder'd; do so till it is enough: you may run a long case-knife into the flesh on the inside, and stuff the whole full of forc'd-meat, with bread, herbs, lemon-peel, and an egg beat up; make savoury sauce.

To roast a Breast of Mutton

A breast of mutton dress'd thus is very good; the forc'd-meat must be put under the skin at the end, and then the skin pinn'd down with thorns; before you dredge it, wash it over with a bunch of feathers dipped in eggs.

To roast a Shoulder of Mutton in blood

Cut the shoulder as you do venison, take off the skin, let it lie in the blood all night; then take as much powder of sweet herbs as will lie on a sixpence, a little grated bread, some pepper, nutmeg and ginger, a little lemon-peel, the yolks of two eggs boil'd hard, and about twenty oysters and salt; temper all together with some of the blood, and stuff the meat thick with it, and lay some of it about the mutton; then wrap the caul of the sheep round the shoulder; roast it, and baste it with blood till it is near roasted; then take off the caul, dredge it, and baste it with butter and serve it to the table with venison-sauce in a basin. If you do not cut it venison-fashion, yet take off the skin, because it eats tough; let the caul be spread while it is warm, or it will not do well; and next day when you are to use it, wrap it up in a cloth that has been dipped into hot water; for sauce, take some of the bones of the breast, chop them, and put to them a whole onion. a bay-leaf, a piece of lemon-peel, two or three anchovies, with spices that please; stew these, then add some red wine, oysters and mushrooms.

To Stew a Head, Chine, and Neck of Venison

First take off all the fat, then cut it in pieces to your liking, and season it with your compound seasoning, an onion or two quartered, and two or three bay-leaves; put them in a stew-pan, with water near enough to cover them; let it stew till it is almost enough, and then put in a bottle of stale beer, or half red wine and half beer; it may stew two hours before this is in, and one after; burn a quarter of a pound of butter pretty thick with the liquor of the venison, and mix it with it when you serve it: the fat taken off must be put in some time before the venison has done stewing. If you put in beer instead of red wine, boil it and skim it before you put it in.

To collar Eels

Take your eel, and cut it open; take out the bones, cut off the head and tail, and lay the eel flat on a dresser; shred sage as fine as possible, and mix it with black pepper beat, nutmeg grated, and salt, and lay it all over the eel, and roll it up hard in little cloths, and tie it up tight at each end: then set over some water with pepper and salt, five or six cloves, three or four blades of mace, a bay-leaf or two; boil it and the bones and head and tail together; then take out the head and tail, and put it away, and put in your eels, and let them boil till they are tender; then take them out of the liquor and boil the liquor longer; then take it off, and when it is cold put it to your eels, but do not take off the little cloths till you use them.

To pot Lobsters

Take a dozen of large lobsters; take out all the meat of their tails and claws after they are boiled; then season them with beaten pepper, salt, cloves, mace, and nutmeg, all finely beaten and mixed together; then take a pot, put therein a layer of fresh butter, upon which put a layer of lobsters, and then strew over some seasoning, and repeat the same till your pot is full, and your lobster all in; bake it about an hour and a half, then set it by two or three days, and it will be fit to eat. It will keep a month or more, if you pour from it the liquor when it comes out of the oven, and fill it up with clarified butter. Eat it with vinegar.

Hung Beef

Make a strong brine with bay-salt, peter-salt, and pump water, and steep therein a rib of beef for nine days; then hang it up a chimney where wood or sawdust is burnt; when it is a little dry, wash the outside with blood two or three times to make it look black, and when it is dryed enough, boil it for use.

To roast a Cod's Head

Take the head, wash and scour it very clean, then scotch it with a knife, strew a little salt on it, and lay it on a stew-pan before the fire, with something behind it; throw away the water that runs from it the first half hour, then strew on it some nutmeg, cloves, mace, and salt, and baste it often with butter, turning it till it is enough. If it be a large head it will take four or five hours roasting; then take all the gravy of the fish, as much white-wine, and more meat gravy, some horseradish, one or two eschalots, a little slic'd ginger, some whole pepper, cloves, mace, and nutmeg, a bay-leaf or two; beat this liquor up with butter and the liver of the fish boiled, broke, and strained into it with the yolks of two or three eggs, some oysters and shrimps, balls made of fish and fried fish round it. Garnish with lemon and horseradish.

To make a Ragout of Pigs' Ears

Take a quantity of pigs' ears, and boil them in one half wine and the other water; cut them in small pieces, then brown a little butter, and put them in, and a pretty deal of gravy, two anchovies, an eschalot or two, a little mustard, and some slices of lemon, some salt and nutmeg: stew all these together, and shake it up thick. Garnish the dish with barberries.

Beef to collar

Take beef and season it with salt, pepper, and spice, and put in a pound of butter with a pint of claret, then roll it up with tape, and bake it in this liquor with brown bread.

To make collar'd Beef

Take a flank of beef, salt it with white salt, and let it lie forty-eight hours; then wash it, and hang it in the wind to dry twenty-four hours; then take pepper, salt, cloves, mace, nutmegs, and saltpetre, all beaten fine; mix them together, and rub it all over the inside; roll it up hard, and tie it fast with tape; put it in a pan with a few bay-leaves, and four pounds of butter, covering the pot with rye-paste; bake it with household bread.

Oyster Loaves

Take a quart of middling oysters, and wash them in their own liquor; then strain them thro' a flannel, and put them on the fire to warm; then take three quarters of a pint of gravy and put to the oysters, with a blade of mace, a little white pepper, a little horseradish, a piece of lean bacon, and half a lemon; then stew them leisurely. Take three penny loaves, and pick out the crumb clean; then take a pound of butter, and set it on the fire in a saucepan that will hold the loaves, and when it is melted, take it off the fire, and let it settle; then pour off the clear liquid, and set it on the fire again with the loaves in it, turning them about till you find them crisp; then put a pound of butter in a frying-pan, and with a dredging-box dust in flour till you find it of a reasonable thickness, then mix that and the oysters together; when they are stewed enough take out the bacon, and put the oysters into the loaves; then put them into a dish, and garnish the loaves with the oysters you cannot get in, and with slices of lemon; and when you have thickened the liquor, squeeze in lemon to your taste; or you may fry the oysters with batter to garnish the loaves.

To Stew Oysters in French Rolls

Take a quart of large oysters; wash them in their own liquor, strain it, and put them in it with a little salt, some pepper, mace, and sliced nutmeg; let the oysters stew a little with all these things, and thicken them up with a great deal of butter; then take six French rolls, cut a piece off the top, and take out the crumbs; take your oysters boiling hot, and fill the rolls full, set them near the fire on a chafing-dish of coals, and let them be hot through; as the liquor soaks in, fill them up with more, if you have it, or some hot gravy: So serve them up instead of a pudding.

A Marrow Pudding

Boil a quart of cream or milk, with a stick of cinnamon, a quarter'd nutmeg and a large blade of mace; then mix it with eight eggs well beat, a little salt, sugar, sack, and orange-flower-water; strain it; then put to it three grated biscuits, an handful of currants, as many raisins of the sun, and the marrow of two bones, all in four large pieces; put it into a dish, having the brim thereof garnished with puff-paste, and raised in the oven; then lay on the four pieces of marrow, knots and pastes, sliced citron and lemon-peel.

A Calves'-Foot Pudding

Take calves' feet, shred them very fine, and mix them with a penny-loaf grated and scalded with a pint of cream; put to it half a pound of shred beef-suet, eight eggs, and a handful of plump'd currants;

season it with sweet spice and sugar, a little sack, orange-flower-water, and the marrow of two bones; then put it in a veal caul, being washed over with batter of eggs; then wet a cloth and put it therein; tie it close up; when the pot boils, put it in; boil it about two hours, and turn it in a dish, sticking in it sliced almonds and citron; let the sauce be sack and orange-flower-water, with lemon-juice, sugar and drawn butter.

To Stuff a Shoulder or Leg of Mutton with Oysters

Take a little grated bread, some beef-suet, yolks of hard eggs, three anchovies, a bit of an onion, salt, pepper, thyme, winter-savoury, twelve oysters, and some nutmeg grated. Mix all these together, shred them very fine, and work them up with raw eggs, like a paste; stuff your mutton under the skin in the thickest place, or where you please, and roast it; for sauce take some of the oyster liquor, some claret, two or three anchovies, a little nutmeg, a bit of onion, and the rest of the oysters: stew all these together, then take out the onion, and put it under the mutton.

Sauce for boil'd Mutton

Take a piece of liver as big as a pigeon's egg, and boil it tender, with half a handful of parsley and a few sprigs of pot thyme, with the yolks of three or four eggs boiled hard; bray them with a spoon till they are dissolved; then add one anchovy washed and stripped from the bone, thyme, beaten pepper and grated nutmeg, with a little salt; put all these together in a saucepan, with a glass of white wine, and the gravy that has drained from your leg of mutton after it is taken out of the pot, or a quarter of a pint of the liquor the mutton is boiled in; mix it all together, and give it a boil, then beat it up with three ounces of butter; you may add a teaspoonful of vinegar, which takes off a sweetness it's apt to have: it's best to make the sauce thick, or it will be too thin when the mutton is cut.

To boil a Pike

Cut open the pike, gut it, and scour the outside and inside very well with salt, then wash it clean, and have in readiness the following pickle to boil it in: water, vinegar, mace, whole pepper, a bunch of sweet herbs, and a small onion; there must be liquor enough to cover it; when the liquor boils put in the pike, and make it boil soon (half an hour will boil a very large pike); make your sauce with white wine, a little of the liquor, two anchovies, some shrimps, lobster, or crab; beat and mix with it grated nutmeg, and butter floured to thicken it; pour your sauce over the fish, garnish with horseradish and sliced lemon.

Soles to Stew

When your soles are wash'd, and the fins cut off, put them into a stew-pan, with no liquor but a quarter of a pint of white wine, some mace, whole pepper, and salt; when they are half stew'd, put in some thick cream, and a little piece of butter dipp'd in flour; when that is melted, put in some oysters with their liquor; keep them often shaking, till the fish and oysters are enough, or that the oysters will break; squeeze in a little piece of lemon, give them a scald, and pour it into the dish.

To roast a Pike

Take a large pike, gut it, clean it, and lard it with eel and bacon, as you lard a fowl; then take thyme, savoury, salt, mace, nutmeg, some crumbs of bread, beef-suet, and parsley; shred all very fine, and mix it up with raw eggs; make it in a long pudding, and put it in the belly of your pike; sew up the belly, and dissolve the anchovies in butter, basting it with it; put two splints on each side the pike, and tie it to the spit; melt butter thick for the sauce, or if you please, oyster-sauce, and bruise the pudding in it. Garnish with lemon.

To roast a Pike in Embers

When your fish is scal'd, and well dry'd in a cloth, make a pudding with sweet herbs, grated bread and onion wrapped up in butter; put it into the belly, and sew it up, turn the tail into the mouth, and roll it up in white paper, and then in brown, wet them both, and tie them round with packthread; then rake it up in the embers, and let it lie two or three hours; then take it up, and take the pudding out of the belly; mix it with sauce, such as is usually made for fish, and serve it up.

A Ragout of Sweetbreads

Take your sweetbreads and skin them; put some butter in the frying-pan, brown it with flour, and put the sweetbreads in; stir them a little, and turn them; then put in some strong broth and mushrooms, some pepper, salt, cloves and mace; let them stew half an hour; then put in some forc'd-meat balls, some artichoke bottoms cut small and thin; make it thick, and serve it up with slic'd lemon.

A Ragout of Oysters

Put into your stew-pan a quarter of a pound of butter, and let it boil; then take a quart of oysters, strain them from their liquor, and put them to the butter; let them stew with a bit of eschalot shred very fine, some grated nutmeg, and a little salt; then beat the yolks of three or four eggs with the oyster liquor and half a pound of butter; shake all very well together till 'tis thick, and serve it up with sippets, and garnish with sliced lemon.

To mumble Rabbits and Chickens

Put into the bellies of your rabbits, or chickens, some parsley, an onion, and the liver; set it over the fire in the stew-pan with as much water mixed with a little salt as will cover them; when they are half boiled take them out, and shred the parsley, liver, and onion; tear the flesh from the bones of the rabbit in small flakes, and put it into the stew-pan again with a very little of the liquor it was boiled in, a pint of white-wine, some gravy, half a pound or more of butter, and some grated nutmeg; when 'tis enough, shake in a little flour, and thicken it up with butter. Serve it on sippets.

To Stew Mushrooms

Take some strong broth, season it with a bunch of sweet herbs, some spice and anchovies, setting it over the fire till 'tis hot; then put in the mushrooms, and just let them boil up; then take the yolks of eggs, with a little minced thyme, parsley, and some grated nutmeg; and stir it over the fire till 'tis thick. Serve it up with sliced lemon.

To collar a Calf's Head

Take a calf's head with the skin and hair upon it; scald it to fetch off the hair; parboil it, but not too much; then get it clean from the bones while it is hot; you must slit it in the forepart; season it with pepper, salt, cloves, mace, nutmeg, and sweet herbs, shred small, and mix'd together with the yolks of three or four eggs; spread it over the head, and roll it up hard. Boil it gently for three hours, in just as much water as will cover it; when it is tender it is boiled enough. If you do the tongue, first boil it and peel it, and slice it in thin slices, and likewise the palate, putting them and the eyes in the inside of the head before you roll it up. When the head is taken out, season the pickle with salt, pepper, and spice, and give it a boil, adding to it a pint of white wine, and as much vinegar. When it is cold, put in the collar; and when you use it, cut it in slices.

To collar Cow-Heels

Take five or six cow-heels or feet, and bone them while they are hot; lay them one upon another, strewing some salt between; then roll them up in a coarse cloth, and squeeze in both ends, and tie them up very hard; boil it an hour and a half; then take it out, and when it is cold put it in common souce-drink for brawn. Cut off a little at each end, it looks better. Serve it in slices, or in the collar, as you please.

A Tansy

Boil a quart of cream or milk with a stick of cinnamon, quarter'd nutmeg, and a large blade of mace; when half cold, mix it with twenty yolks of eggs, and ten whites; strain it, then put to it four grated biscuits, half a pound of butter, a pint of spinach-juice, a little tansy, sack, orange-flower-water, sugar, and a little salt; then gather it to a body over the fire, and pour it into your dish, being well butter'd. When it is baked turn it on a pie plate; squeeze on it an orange, grate on sugar, and garnish it with slic'd orange and a little tansy. Made in a dish; cut as you please.

Scotch Collops

Cut your collops off a fillet of veal; cut them thin, hack them and fry them in fresh butter; then take them out and brown your pan with butter and flour, as you do for a soup. Do not make it too thick; put in your collops and some bacon cut thin and fry'd, and some forc'd-meat balls fry'd, some mushrooms, oysters, artichoke bottoms, sliced lemon, and sweetbreads, or lamb-stones; some strong broth, gravy, and thick butter; toss up all together. Garnish the dish with sliced lemon.

Another

Cut thin slices out of a leg of veal, as many as you think will serve for a dish, hack them, and lard some with bacon, and fry them in butter; then take them out of the pan, and keep them warm; clean the pan, and put into it half a pint of oysters, with their liquor, some strong broth, one or two eschalots, a glass of white wine, two or three anchovies minced, some grated nutmeg; let these have a boil up, and thicken it with four or five eggs and a piece of butter; then put in your collops, and shake them together till it is thick; put dried sippets on the bottom of the dish, and put your collops in, and so many as you please of the things in your hash.

Another

Take the skin from a fillet of veal, and cut it in thin collops, hack and scotch them with the back of a knife, lard half of them with bacon, and fry them with a little brown butter; then take them out and put them into another tossing-pan; then set the pan they were fry'd in over the fire again, and wash it out with a little strong broth, rubbing it with your ladle, then pour it to the collops; do this every panful till all are fried; then stew and toss them up with a pint of oysters, two anchovies, two shiver'd palates, cockscombs, lamb-stones, and sweetbreads, blanch'd and sliced, savoury balls, onions, a faggot of sweet herbs; thicken it with brown butter, and garnish it with lemons.

Another

Cut thin slices of a fillet of veal, and hack them; then take the yolks of four eggs; beat a little melted butter, a little salt, and some nutmeg, or lemon-peel grated in it; then dip in each collop, lay them in a pewter dish, flour them and let them lie till you want them. Put a bit of butter in the frying-pan, and your collops, and fry them quick, shaking them all the while to keep the butter from oiling; then pour it into a stew-pan cover'd close, and keep it warm; then put to them some good gravy, some mushrooms, or what else you like, a bit of butter, toss it up thick, and squeeze an orange over it.

To Stew a Rump of Beef

Season your rump of beef with two nutmegs, some pepper and salt, and lay the fat side downward in your stew-pan; put to it a quarter of a pint of vinegar, a pint of claret, three pints of water, three whole onions stuck with a few cloves, and a bunch of sweet herbs; cover it close, and let it stew over a gentle fire four or five hours; scum off the fat from the liquor. Lay your meat on sippets, and pour your liquor over it. Garnish your dish with scalded greens.

To roast an Eel

Take a large eel, and scour him well with salt; skin him almost to the tail; then gut, and wash, and dry him; take a quarter of a pound of suet, shred as fine as possible; put to it sweet herbs, an eschalot likewise, shred very fine, and mix it together with some salt, pepper, and grated nutmeg; scotch your eel on both sides, the breadth of a finger's distance, and wash it with yolks of eggs, and strew some seasoning over it, and stuff the belly with it; then draw the skin over it, put a long skewer thro' it, and tie it to the spit, baste it with butter, and make the sauce of anchovy and butter melted.

To make a pale Fricassee

Take lamb, chicken, or rabbits, cut in pieces, wash it well from the blood, then put it in a broad pan or stew-pan; put in as much fair-water as will cover it; add salt, a bunch of sweet herbs, some pepper, an onion, two anchovies, and stew it till it is enough; then mix in a porringer six yolks of eggs, a glass of white wine, a nutmeg grated, a little chop'd parsley, a piece of fresh butter, and three or four spoon-fuls of cream; beat these together, and put it in a stew-pan, shaking it together till thick. Dish it on sippets, and garnish with sliced lemon.

To hash a Calf's Head

Boil your calf's head almost enough, and when it is cold, cut the meat in thin slices clean from the bones; put it into a stew-pan, with some strong broth, a glass of white wine, some oysters and their liquor, a bunch of sweet herbs, two or three eschalots, a nutmeg quarter'd, and let these stew over a slow fire till they are enough; then put in two or three anchovies, the yolks of four eggs well beaten and a piece of butter, and thicken it up; then have ready fry'd some thin slips of bacon, some forc'd-meat balls, some large oysters dipp'd in butter, the brains first boiled and then fried, some sweet herbs cut in slices and some lamb-stones cut in rounds; then put your hash in your dish, and the other things, some round and some on it. Garnish the dish with sliced lemon.

A Fricassee of Veal

Cut a fillet of veal in thin slices, a little broader than a crown-piece, beat them with a rolling-pin to make them tender; then steep them in milk three hours, take a blade or two of mace, a few corns of pepper, a small sprig of thyme, a little piece of lemon-peel, a bone of mutton and the veal-bones; stew them gently all together for sauce; if you have no mutton, a little piece of beef, if no beef, a spoonful of gravy at least; then drain the milk from the veal, and put fresh milk into a stew-pan, and stew the veal in it without salt, for that curdles the milk; stew it till it is enough, or you may half stew it, and fry it as pale as possible; then drain it, and strain the sauce, which beat up with some salt, flour, and butter, a pretty deal of cream, and some white wine; just at the last you may shred a little parsley, and scalding it, strew it upon the veal, and squeeze a little lemon, which will thicken the sauce. You may make the same sauce for this as you do for the boiled turkey, if you like it better.

Pulled Chickens

Boil six chickens near enough; flay them and pull the white flesh all off from the bones; put it in a stew-pan with half a pint of cream, made scalding hot, the gravy that runs from the chickens, a few spoonfuls of that liquor they were boil'd in; to this add some raw parsley shred fine, give them a toss or two over the fire, and dust a little flour upon some butter, and shake up with them. Chicks done this way must be killed the night before, and a little more than half boiled, and pulled in pieces as broad as your finger, and half as long; you may add a spoonful of white wine.

A Fricassee of Chickens

After you have drawn and washed your chickens, half boil them; then take them up, cut them in pieces, put them into a frying-pan, and fry them in butter; then take them out of the pan, clean it, and put in some strong broth, some white wine, some grated nutmeg, a little pepper, salt, a bunch of sweet herbs, and an eschalot or two; let these, with two or three anchovies, stew on a slow fire and boil up; then beat it up with butter and eggs till it is thick; put your chickens in, and toss them well together; lay sippets in the dish, and serve it up with sliced lemon and fried parsley.

A fine Side-Dish

Take veal, chicken, or rabbit, with as much marrow, or beef-suet, as meat; a little thyme, lemon-peel, marjoram, two anchovies, washed and boned; a little pepper, salt, mace, and cloves; bruise the yolks of hard eggs, some oysters, or mushrooms; mix all these together, chop them, and beat them in a mortar very fine; then spread the caul of a breast of veal on a table, and lay a layer of this, and a layer of middling bacon, cut in thin small pieces, rolling it up hard in the caul; roast or bake it, as you like; cut it into thin slices, and lay it in your dish, with a rich gravy sauce.

Gravy to keep for use

Take a piece of coarse beef, cover it with water; when it has boiled some time, take out the meat; beat it very well, and cut it in pieces to let out the gravy; then put it in again, with a bunch of sweet herbs, an onion stuck with cloves, a little salt, and some whole pepper; let it stew, but not boil; when it is of a brown colour it is enough; take it up; put it in an earthen pot, and let it stand to cool; when it is cold skim off the fat. It will keep a week unless the weather be very hot. If for a brown fricassee, put some butter in your frying pan, and shake in it a little flour as it boils, and put in some gravy, with a glass of claret, and shake up the fricassee in it. If for a white fricassee, then melt your butter in the gravy, with a little white wine, a spoonful or two of cream, and the yolks of eggs.

An Amulet of Eggs the savoury way

Take a dozen of eggs, beat them very well, season them with salt, and a little pepper, then have your frying-pan ready with a good deal of fresh butter in it, and let it be thoroughly hot; then put in your eggs, with four spoonfuls of strong gravy, and have ready parsley, and a few chives cut, and throw them over it, and when it is enough turn it; and when done, dish it, and squeeze orange or lemon over it.

A Fricassee of Rabbits

Cut and wash your rabbits very well; put them in a frying-pan, with a pound of butter, an onion stuck with cloves, a bunch of sweet herbs, and some salt; let it stew till it is enough; then beat up the yolks of six eggs, with a glass of white wine, a little parsley shred, a nutmeg grated, and mix it by degrees with the liquor in your pan; shake it till it is thick, and serve it up on sippets. Garnish the dish with sliced lemon.

A Fricassee of Tripe

Take lean tripes, cut and scrape them from all the loose stuff; cut them in pieces two inches square, and then cut them across from corner to corner, or in what shape you please; put them into a stew-pan, with half as much white wine as will cover them, sliced ginger, whole pepper, a blade of mace, a little sprig of rosemary, a bay-leaf, an onion, or a small clove of garlic; when it begins to stew, a quarter of an hour will do it; then take out the herbs and onion, and put in a little shred parsley, the juice of a lemon, and a little piece of anchovy shred small, a few spoonfuls of cream, the yolk of an egg, or a piece of butter: salt it to your taste; when it is in the dish, you may lay on a little boiled spinach and sliced lemon.

A Fricassee of double Tripe

Cut your tripe in slices two inches long, and put it into a stew-pan; put to it a quarter of a pound of capers, as much samphire shred, half a pint of strong broth, as much white wine, a bunch of sweet herbs, a lemon shred small; stew all these together till it is tender; then take it off the fire, and thicken up the liquor with the yolks of three or four eggs, a little parsley boiled green and chopped, some grated nutmeg and salt; shake it well together; serve it on sippets; garnish with lemon.

A Fricassee of Ox-Palates

Make the gravy thus: Take two pounds of beef, cut it in little bits, and put it in a saucepan, with a quart of water, some salt, some whole pepper, an onion, an eschalot or two, or three anchovies, a bit of horseradish; let all these stew till it is strong gravy; then strain it out, and set it by; then have ten or twelve ox-palates, boil them till they are tender, peel them, and cut them in square pieces; then flay and draw two or three chickens, cut them between every joint, season them with a little nutmeg, salt, and shred thyme, put them in a pan, and fry them with butter; when they are half fry'd, put in half your gravy, and all your palates, and let them stew together; put the rest of your gravy into a saucepan, and when it boils, thicken it up with the yolks of three or four eggs, beaten with a glass of white wine, a piece of butter, and three or four spoonfuls of thick cream; then pour all into your pan, shake it well together, and dish it up; garnish with pickled grapes.

A Fricassee of great Plaice or Flounders

Run your knife all along upon the bone on the backside of your plaice, then raise the flesh on both sides from the head to the tail, and take out the bone clear; then cut your plaice in six collops, dry it very well from the water, sprinkle it with salt, flour it well, and fry it in a very hot pan of beef-dripping, so that it may be crisp; take it out of the pan, and keep it warm before the fire; then make clean the pan, and put into it oysters and their liquor, some white wine, the meat of the shell of a crab or two; mince half the oysters, some grated nutmeg, three anchovies; let all these stew up together; then put in half a pound of butter, and put in your plaice; toss them well together, dish them on sippets, and pour the sauce over them; garnish the dish with yolks of hard eggs minced, and sliced lemon. After this manner do salmon, or any firm fish.

To fricassee Fish

Melt butter according to the quantity of fish you have, melt it thick, cut your fish in pieces in length and breadth three fingers, then put them and your butter into a frying or stew-pan; it must not boil too fast, for fear of breaking the fish, and turning the butter into oil; turn them often till they are enough; put in a bunch of sweet herbs at first, an onion, two or three anchovies cut small, a little pepper, nutmeg, mace, lemon-peel, two or three cloves; when all these are in, put in some claret, and let them stew all together; beat up six yolks of eggs and put them in, with such pickles as you please, as oysters, mushrooms, and capers; shake them well together that they do not curdle; if you put the spice in whole, take it out when it is done; the seasoning ought to be stewed first in a little water, and then the butter melted in that and wine before you put the fish in. Jacks do best this way.

A Crawfish Soup

Cleanse your crawfish, and boil them in water, salt and spice, pull off their feet and tails, and fry them; break the rest of them in a stone mortar, season them with savoury spice and an onion, hard eggs, grated bread, and sweet herbs boiled in strong broth; strain it; put to it scalded chopped parsley and French rolls, then put them therein with a few dry'd mushroom; garnish the dish with sliced lemon, and the feet and tails of the crawfish. A lobster-soup is done the same way.

To boil Mullet, or any sort of Fish

Scale your fish, and wash them, saving their liver, or tripes, roes or spawn; boil them in water seasoned with salt, white-wine vinegar, white wine, a bunch of sweet herbs, a sliced lemon, one or two onions, some horseradish; and when it boils up put in your fish; and for sauce, a pint of oysters with their liquor, a lobster bruised or minced, or shrimps, some white wine, two or three anchovies, some large mace, a quartered nutmeg, a whole onion; let these have a boil up, and thicken it with butter and the yolks of two or three eggs; serve it on sippets, and garnish with lemon.

To butter Shrimps

Stew a quart of shrimps in half a pint of white wine, a nutmeg grated, and a good piece of butter; when the butter is melted, and they are hot through, beat the yolks of four eggs, with a little white wine, and pour it in; shake it well, till it is of the thickness you like; then dish it on sippets, and garnish with sliced lemon.

To butter Crabs or Lobsters

Your crabs and lobsters being boiled and cold, take all the meat out of the shells and body, break the claws, and take out all their meat, mince it small, and put it altogether, adding to it two or three spoonfuls of claret, a very little vinegar, a nutmeg grated; let it boil up till it is thorough hot; then put in some butter melted, with some anchovies and gravy, and thicken up with the yolks of an egg or two; when it is very hot put it in the large shell, and stick it with toasts.

Another

Take the meat out of the shells, and mix it well together with some white wine, grated nutmeg, salt, and the juice of a lemon, or a little vinegar, put it into a saucepan and stir it over a slow fire, with a piece of butter. If they are crabs, warm the shells and put the meat in again; if lobsters, in a china dish; some beaten pepper does well.

To roast Lobsters

Tie your lobsters to the spit alive, baste them with water and salt till they look very red, and are enough; then baste them with butter and salt, take them up, and set little dishes round with the sauce, some plain melted butter, some oyster-sauce.

To Stew Carp

Take a live carp, cut him in the neck and tail, and save the blood; then open him in the belly; take care you do not break the gall; put a little vinegar in the belly, to wash out the blood; stir all the blood with your hand; then put your carp into a stew-pan; if you have two carps, you may cut off one of their heads an inch below the gills, and slit the body in two, and put it into your stew-pan after you have rubbed them with salt; but before you put them in, your liquor must boil – a quart of claret, or as much as will cover them, the blood you saved, an onion stuck with cloves, a bunch of sweet herbs, some gravy, three anchovies. When this liquor boils up, put in your fish, cover it close, and let it stew up for about a quarter of an hour; then turn it, and let it stew a little longer; then put your carp into a dish, and beat up the sauce with butter melted in oyster-liquor, and pour your sauce over it. Your milt, spawn, and rivets must be laid on the top: garnish the dish with fry'd smelts, oysters, or pitchcock-eel, lemon and fry'd parsley.

Another way to Stew Carp

Take two carps, scale and rub them well with salt; cut them in the nape of the neck and round the tail, to make them bleed; cut up the belly, take out the liver and guts, and if you please to cut each carp in three pieces they will eat the firmer; then put them in a stew-pan, with their blood, a quart of claret, a bunch of sweet herbs, an onion, one or two eschalots, a nutmeg, a few cloves, mace, whole pepper; cover them close and let them stew till they are half enough, then turn them, and put half a pound of fresh butter, four anchovies, the liver and guts taking out the gall, and let them stew till they are enough; then beat the yolks of five or six eggs with a little verjuice, and by degrees mix it with the liquor the carp was stewed in: just give it a scald to thicken it; then put your carp in a dish, and pour this over it; garnish the dish with a sliced lemon.

To collar Salmon

Take a side of salmon, and cut off about a handful of the tail; wash your large piece very well, and dry it with a cloth; wash it over with the yolks of eggs; then make some forc'd-meat with that you cut off the tail; but take off the skin, and put to it a handful of parboil'd oysters, a tail or two of lobster, the yolks of three or four eggs boil'd hard, six anchovies, a good handful of sweet herbs chopped small, a little salt, cloves, mace, nutmeg, pepper, and grated bread; work all these together into a body with the yolks of eggs, and lay it all over the fleshy part, and a little more pepper and salt over the salmon; so roll it up in a collar, and bind it with broad tape; then boil it in water and salt and vinegar; but let the liquor boil first; then put in your collars, and a bunch of sweet herbs, sliced ginger and nutmeg; let it boil, but not too fast; it will require near two hours' boiling; when it is near enough, take it up; put it in your sousing-pan, and when the pickle is cold, put it to your salmon, and let it stand in it till used; otherwise you may pot it after it is boiled, and fill it up with clarified butter, as you pot fowls; that way will keep longest and best.

Eels to collar

Split them down the belly, and take the bones out clean, make a seasoning with spice powder'd, and herbs chopped fine; strew it in, and roll them up, and sew a cloth over each eel, so boil them in a pickle made as for tench, and when they are boiled enough, lay them out and keep them in it; the cloths must be taken off when the eels are cold.

To collar Venison

Take a side of venison, bone it, and take away all the sinews, and cut it into square collars, of what bigness you please; it will make two or three collars; lard it with fat clear bacon, cut your lards as big as the top of your finger, and as long as your little finger, then season your venison with pepper, salt, cloves, mace, and nutmeg; roll up your collars, and tie them close with coarse tape; them put them into deep pots; put seasoning at the bottom of the pot, with fresh butter, and three or four bay-leaves; then put in your venison, some seasoning, and butter on the top, and over that some beef-suet finely shred and beaten; then cover up your pot with coarse paste; they will take four or five hours baking; then take them out of the oven, and let it stand a little; then take out your venison, and let it drain well from the gravy: take off all the fat from the gravy, and add more butter to that fat, and set it over a gentle fire to clarify; then take it off, and let it stand a little, and skim it well; then make your pots clean, or have pots fit for each collar: put a little seasoning at the bottom, and some of your clarified butter; then put in your venison, and fill up your pots with clarified butter; and be sure your butter be an inch above the meat; and when it is thorough cold, tie it down with double paper, and lay a tile on the top; they will keep six or eight months: you may, if you please, when you use a pot, put it in boiling water a minute, and it will come whole out: Let it stand till it is cold, and stick it round with bay-leaves, and one sprig on the top.

To pot Neats' Tongues

Take neats' tongues, and rub them very well with salt and water (bay-salt is best); then take pump-water, with a good deal of saltpetre, some white salt, and some cloves and mace; boil it well and skim it; when it is cold put your tongues in, and let them lie in it six days; then wash them out of the liquor, put them in a pot, and bake them with bread till they are very tender; when they are taken out of the oven, pull off their skins, put them in the pot you intend to keep them in, and cover them over with clarified butter: they will keep four or five months.

To collar a Breast of Veal

Take a breast of veal, bone it, wash it, and dry it in a clean cloth; then shred thyme, winter-savoury, and parsley, very small, and mix it with salt, pepper, cloves, mace, and nutmeg; then strew it on the inside of your meat, and roll it up hard, beginning at the neck end; tie it up with tape, and put it in a pot fit to boil it in, standing upright: you must boil it in water and salt, and a bunch of sweet herbs; when it is boiled enough take it off the fire, put it in an earthen pot, and when the liquor is cold pour it over, or else boil salt and water strong enough to bear an egg; and when that is cold, pour it on your veal: when you serve it to the table, cut it in round slices. Garnish with laurel and fennel.

To collar a Pig

Cut off the head of your pig, and the body asunder; bone it, and cut two collars off each side; lay it in water to take out the blood; then take sage and parsley, shred them very small, mix them with pepper, salt, and nutmeg, strewing some on every side, or collar, and roll it up, and tie it with coarse tape; boil them in fair-water and salt, till they are very tender; put two or three blades of mace in the kettle, and when they are enough, take them up and lay them in something to cool; strain out some of the liquor, and add to it some vinegar and salt, a little white wine, and three or four bay-leaves; give it a boil up, and when it is cold put it to the collars, and keep them for use.

To pot Beef

Take a good buttock of beef, cut out the bone, lay it flat, and slash it in several places; salt it well, and let it lie in the salt three days; then take it out, and let it lie in running water with a handful of salt three days longer; then take it out, dry it with a cloth, and season it with pepper, salt, nutmeg, cloves, mace, and two ounces of saltpetre finely beaten; then shred two or three pounds of beef-suet, and one pound in lumps, and three pounds of butter, put some in the bottom of the pot you bake it in; then put in your beef and the rest of the butter and suet on the top; cover your pot over with coarse paste, and set it in all night with household-bread; in the morning draw it, and pour off all the fat into a pot, and drain out all the gravy; pull the meat all to pieces, fat and lean, and work it into your pots that you keep it in while it is hot, or it will not close so well; then cover it with the clear fat you poured off; paper it when it is cold; it will keep good a month or six weeks.

To make artificial Venison

Bone a rump of beef, or a large shoulder of mutton; then beat it with a rolling-pin; season it with pepper and nutmeg; lay it twenty-four hours in sheep's-blood; then dry it with a cloth, and season it again with pepper, salt, and spice. Put your meat in the form of a paste, and bake it as a venison-pasty, and make a gravy with the bones, to put in when it is drawn out of the oven.

Chickens forced with Oysters

Lard and truss them; make a forcing with oysters, sweetbreads, parsley, truffles, mushrooms, and onions; chop these together, and season it; mix it with a piece of butter and the yolk of an egg; then tie them at both ends and roast them; then make for them a ragout, and garnish them with sliced lemon.

A Calf's Head hashed

Your calf's head being slit and cleansed, half boiled and cold, cut one side into thin pieces and fry it in butter; then having a tossing-pan on the stove with a ragout for made-dishes, toss it up and stew it together, and scotch the other side cross and cross, flour, baste, and boil it. The hash being thickened with brown butter, put it in the dish; lay over and about it fried balls, and the tongue sliced and larded with bacon, lemon-peel, and beetroot; then fry the batter of eggs, sliced sweetbreads, carv'd sippets and oysters; lay in the head, and place these on and about the head; garnish with sliced orange and lemon.

A Ragout of a Breast of Veal

Bone a breast of veal, cut a handsome square piece, and the other part into small pieces; brown it in butter; then stew and toss it up in your ragout for made-dishes; thicken it with brown butter; put then the ragout in the dish, lay on the square piece dic'd, with lemon, sweetbreads, sippets, and bacon fry'd in the batter of eggs, and garnish it with sliced orange.

To recover Venison when it Stinks

Take as much cold water in a tub as will cover it a handful over, and put in a good store of salt, and let it lie three or four hours; then take your venison out, and let it lie in as much hot water and salt; and let it lie as long as before; then have your crust in readiness, and take it out, and dry it very well, and season it with pepper and salt pretty high, and put it in your pasty. Do not use the bones of your venison for gravy, but get fresh beef or other bones.

How to force a Fowl

Take a good fowl, kill, pull and draw it; slit the skin down the back, take off the flesh from the bones; mince it very small, and mix it with one pound of beef-suet shred, and a pint of large oysters chop'd, two anchovies, an eschalot, a little grated bread, some sweet herbs; shred all these very well, mix them, and make it up with yolks of eggs, put all these ingredients on the bones again, and draw the skin over again; sew up the back, and put the fowl in a bladder; boil it an hour and a quarter; then stew some more oysters in gravy, bruise in a little of your forc'd-meat, and beat it up with fresh butter; put the fowl in the middle; pour on the sauce and garnish with sliced lemon.

To boil Fowls and Cabbage

Take a well-shap'd cabbage, peel off some of the outside leaves, and cut a piece out of the top; then scoop out the inside, and fill the hole with savoury forc'd-meat beat up with two eggs; let it be tied up as a pudding in a cloth, but first put back the top of the cabbage. When the outside is tender, lay it between two bon'd fowls, and on them all some melted butter and slices of fried bacon.

To marinade a Leg of Lamb

Take a leg of lamb, cut it in pieces the bigness of a half crown; hack them with the back of a knife; then take an eschalot, three or four anchovies, some cloves, mace, nutmeg, all beaten; put your meat in a dish, strew the seasoning over it, put it in a stew-pan, with as much white wine, as will cover it, and let it lie two hours; then put it all together in a frying-pan, and let it be half enough; then take it out, drain it through a colander, saving the liquor, and put to it a little pepper and salt, and half a pint of gravy; dip your meat in yolks of eggs, and fry it brown in butter; thicken up your sauce with yolks of eggs and butter, and pour it in the dish with your meat; lay sweetbreads and forc'd-meat balls over your meat; dip them in eggs, and fry them. Garnish with lemon.

To force a Leg of Veal, Mutton, or Lamb

Take out all the meat, and leave the skin whole; then take the lean of it and make it into forc'd-meat thus: to two pounds of your lean meat, three pounds of beef-suet; take away all skins from the meat and suet; then shred both very fine, and beat it with a rolling-pin, till you know not the meat from the suet; then mix with it four spoonfuls of grated bread, half an ounce of cloves and mace beaten, as much pepper, some salt, a few sweet herbs shred small; mix all these together with six raw eggs, and put into the skin again, and sew it up. If you roast it, serve it with anchovy-sauce; if you boil it, lay cauliflower or French beans under it. Garnish with pickles, or stew oysters and put under it, with forc'd-meat balls, or sausages fry'd in butter.

To ragout a Breast of Veal

Lard your breast of veal with bacon; then half boil it in water and salt, whole pepper, and a bunch of sweet herbs; take it out, and dust it with some grated bread, sweet herbs shred small, and grated nutmeg and salt, all mixed together; then broil it on both sides, and make a sauce of anchovies and gravy thicken'd up with butter. Garnish with pickles.

To fry Oysters

Beat eggs with a little salt, grated nutmeg, and thicken it like thick batter, with grated white bread and fine flour; then dip the oysters in it, and fry them brown with beef-dripping.

Beef-à-la-mode

Take a good buttock of beef interlarded with great lard, roll'd up in savoury spice and sweet herbs; put it in a great saucepan, and cover it close, and set it in the oven all night. This is fit to eat cold.

A Goose, Turkey, or Leg of Mutton, à-la-daube

Lard it with bacon, and half roast it; take it off the spit, and put it in as small a pot as will boil it, put to it a quart of white wine, strong broth, a pint of vinegar, whole spice, bay-leaves, sweet-marjoram, winter-savoury, and green onions. When it is ready, lay it in the dish, make sauce with some of the liquor, mushrooms, dic'd lemon, two or three anchovies, thicken it with brown butter, and garnish it with sliced lemon.

A Leg of Mutton à-la-royal

Lard your mutton and slices of veal with bacon roll'd in spice and sweet herbs; bring them to a brown with melted lard; boil the leg of mutton in strong broth, with all sorts of sweet herbs, and an onion stuck with cloves; when it is ready lay it on the dish, lay round the collops, then pour on it a ragout; garnish with lemon and orange.

A brown Fricassee of Chickens or Rabbits

Cut them in pieces, and fry them in butter; then having ready hot a pint of gravy, a little claret, white wine, strong broth, two anchovies, two shiver'd palates, a faggot of sweet herbs, savoury balls and spice, thicken it with brown butter, and squeeze on it a lemon.

A white Fricassee of the same

Cut them in pieces, wash them from the blood, and fry them on a slow fire; then put them in a tossing pan, with a little strong broth; season them, and toss them up with mushrooms, and oysters; when almost enough, put to them a pint of cream, thicken it with a bit of butter rolled up in flour.

A Fricassee of Lamb

Cut an hind quarter of lamb into thin slices, season it with savoury spice, sweet herbs, and a shallot; then fry them, and toss them up in strong broth, white wine, oysters, balls and palates, a little brown butter to thicken it, or a bit of butter roll'd up in flour.

Sauce for a Woodcock

Take a very little claret, some good gravy, a blade of mace, some whole pepper, an eschalot; let these stew a little, then thicken it up with butter; roast the guts in the woodcock, and let them run on sippets, or a toast of white bread, and lay it under your woodcock, and pour the sauce into the dish.

White Cucumber Sauce

Take six or eight cucumbers for six chickens, according as they are in bigness; pare and slice them with a piece of onion, some pepper, and salt, and as much water as will stew them till they are tender; then toss them up in some butter roll'd in flour; it must be as thick as you can well make it, without burning it, which it is subject to; you may strain it through a thin colander into another saucepan, to take out the seeds, then heat it, and you may pour it upon the chickens, rabbits, or neck of veal.

Brown Cucumber Sauce

Pare and slice them with a piece of onion, then put a piece of butter in the frying-pan, and when it is hot put in your cucumbers with flour on them, and stew them till they are brown; then take them out of the pan with a slice, and put them into a saucepan, with a little sauce made of broth or gravy, that is savoury; when you have so done, burn a piece of butter in a pan, and when it is sufficiently burnt, put your cucumber sauce in by degrees, and season it with salt to your taste.

To fry Cucumbers for Mutton Sauce

You must brown some butter in a pan, and cut the cucumbers in thin slices; drain them from the water, then fling them into the pan, and when they are fry'd brown, put in a little pepper and salt, a bit of onion and gravy, and let them stew together, and squeeze in some juice of lemon; shake them well, and put them under your mutton.

To hash roasted Mutton

Take your mutton half roasted, and cut it in pieces as big as a half-crown; then put into your saucepan half a pint of claret, as much strong broth or gravy (or water, if you have not the other), one anchovy, an eschalot, a little whole pepper, some nutmeg sliced, salt to your taste, some oyster-liquor, a pint of oysters; let these stew a little, then put in the meat, and a few capers and samphire shred; when it is hot through, thicken it up with a piece of fresh butter roll'd in flour; toast sippets, and lay in your dish, and pour your meat on them. Garnish with lemon.

To hash a Lamb's Pumice

Boil the head and neck at most a quarter of an hour, the heart five minutes, and the lights half an hour; the liver boil'd or fry'd in slices (but not hash'd), slice all the rest very thin, put in the gravy that runs from it, and a quarter of a pint of the liquor they are boiled in, a few spoonfuls of walnut liquor, or a little elder vinegar, a little ketchup, pepper, salt, and nutmeg, the brains a little boil'd and chopped, with half a spoonful of flour and a piece of butter as big as a walnut mixed up with them; but before you put in the butter, put in four middling cucumbers slic'd thin and stew'd a little time, or you may fry them in butter before you put them into the hash, and shake them up together; but they are excellent good if only stew'd; at the time of the year, green gooseberries scalded, and in grape time, green grapes, to stew on the top.

To make a savoury dish of Veal

Cut large collops out of a leg of veal, spread them abroad on a dresser, hack them with the back of a knife, dip them in the yolks of eggs, and season them with cloves, mace, nutmeg, salt, pepper; then make forc'd-meat with some of your veal, beef-suet, oysters chopped, sweet herbs shred fine, and the aforefaid spice, and strew all these over your collops; roll and tie them up, put them on skewers, tie them to a spit, and roast them; to the rest of your forc'd-meat add the yolk of an egg or two, make it up in balls, and fry them; put them in the dish with your meat when roasted, and make the sauce with strong broth, or anchovy, an eschalot, and a little white wine and spice; let it stew, and thicken it up with butter.

Mutton Cutlets

Cut a neck of mutton bone by bone, and beat it flat with your cleaver; have ready seasoning, with grated bread, a little thyme rubb'd to powder, shred parsley, with grated nutmeg, and some lemon-peels minced; then beat up two eggs, flour your cutlets on both sides; dip them in the eggs beat up with a little salt, and roll them in the grated bread and seasoning; put some butter in your frying-pan, and when it is hot lay in your cutlets, and fry them brown on both sides; for sauce, take gravy or strong broth, an onion, some spice, a bit of bacon and a bay-leaf, and boil them well together; then beat it up with an anchovy, or some oysters, and a quarter of a pint of red wine; strew upon your cutlets pickled walnuts in quarters, barberries, samphire or cucumbers and a little sliced lemon.

To Stew a Knuckle of Veal

Cut your veal in proper pieces, season it with salt, whole pepper, and large mace, and put the bone chopped amongst the meat; fill it a little more than half full with water; stew it slowly near an hour; then take up the meat, and cover it up warm, strain out the spice and bones, bray the mace with a little of the liquor, and put in a quarter of a pint of thick cream and the yolk of an egg; if you have no cream, some butter dipped in flour; scald it in well over the fire with the rest of the liquor, then pour upon the veal, and serve it.

To dress a Neck of Mutton

Take the best end of a neck of mutton, cut it into steaks, and beat them with a rolling-pin; then strew some salt on them, and lay them in a frying-pan; hold the pan over a slow fire that may not burn them; turn them as they heat, and there will be gravy enough to fry them in till they are half enough; then put to them broth made thus: take the scrag end of the mutton, break it in pieces, and put it in a pipkin with three pints of water, an onion, and some salt; when it first boils skim it very well, cover it, and let it boil an hour; then put to it half a pint of white wine, a spoonful of vinegar, a nutmeg quarter'd, a little pepper, a bunch of sweet herbs; cover it again, and let it boil till it comes to a pint; then strain it thro' a hair sieve, and put this liquor in the frying-pan, and let it fry together till it is enough; then put in a good piece of butter, shake it together, and serve it up. Garnish with pickles.

Collar'd Mutton to eat hot

Take two loins of mutton, or a neck and breast, bone them, and take off all the skin; then take some of the fat off from the loins, and make savoury forc'd-meat to spread on them, and clap the two insides together, and where the flesh is thick, cut it, and put in some of the forc'd-meat (first beating it with a rolling-pin), and season it well with pepper and salt, besides the spice that is in the forc'd-meat; roll this up as close as you can, and then bind a cloth over it, and sew it up close; boil it in broth, or salt and water, and when it is more than half boiled, straiten the cloth; when enough, cut the collar into three pieces and lay upon them heaps of boiled spinach, sliced lemon, and pickled barberries. Before you divide your collar, cut a little slice off from each end, that they may stand well in the dish; make sauce with the bones of the mutton boiled in some of the broth, an onion, some whole spice, a piece of bacon, a bay-leaf, an anchovy, a little piece of lemon-peel, and some red wine; beat it up with butter, and some oysters, if you have them; this will require near four hours boiling. Your collar may be made overnight; you may boil a little brown toast in your sauce with walnut pickle; you ought to make forc'd-meat enough for balls, to fry and put into the sauce.

To collar a Breast of Mutton

Take a large breast of mutton, cut off the red skin, the bones and gristles, then grate white bread, a little cloves, mace, salt, and pepper, the yolks of three hard eggs bruised small, and a little lemon-peel shred fine; make your meat even and flat, and strew your seasoning over it, with four or five anchovies wash'd and bon'd; then roll your meat like a collar, and bind it with coarse tape, and bake, boil, or roast it; cut it into three or four pieces, and dish it with strong gravy sauce thickened with butter; you may fry oysters and forc'd-meat balls on it if you please; it is very good cold: cut it in slices like collar'd beef.

To collar Beef

Take a flank and cut the skin off, lay it in pump-water, with three handfuls of bay-salt and an ounce of saltpetre; let it lie in the brine three days; then take some pepper, two nutmegs, and a good handful of green sweet-marjoram, half a handful of sage, some rosemary and thyme, all green, with a good handful of parsley; chop the herbs small, then lay the beef on the table; cut the lean piece, and put in the thick fat part, strew it all over with the herbs and spice; roll it up as close as you can, tie it very well with tape bound about it; then put it into a long pot, and fill it up with the brine it was laid in, tie a wet paper over it, put it in an oven when your bread is drawn, let it stand all night; next day heat your oven hot, and let your beef stand four hours, then draw it out, and let it stand in the liquor till it is half cold, then take it out, and strain your tape and bind it up closer; you must put two middling handfuls of salt into the herbs when you roll it up, besides the brine; the rosemary ought to be chopped fine by itself; and then with the rest of the herbs.

Another

Lay your flank of beef in ham-brine eight or ten days, then dry it in a cloth, and take out all the leather and the skin; scotch it cross and cross, season it with savoury spice, two or three anchovies, an handful or two of thyme, sweet-marjoram, winter-savoury, and onions; strew it on the meat, and roll it in a hard collar in a cloth; sew it close, and tie it at both ends; put it in a long pan, with a pint of claret, and cochineal, and two quarts of pump-water, and bake it all night; then take it out hot, and tie it close at both ends; then set it upon one end, put a weight upon it, and let it stand till it is cold; then take it out of the cloth, and keep it dry.

To keep collared Beef

You may keep a collar of beef two months in a liquor made of one quart of cyder and two of stale small beer, boil'd with a handful of salt; if it mothers, take it off, and boil it again, and when cold put in your beef; first keep it as long as you can dry, which is to be done by rolling it up in a cloth when it is first baked, tying it up at both ends, hanging it up to dry till cold, then taking off the cloth; wrap it up in white paper and keep it in a dry place, but not near the fire; when you have kept it dry as long as you can, put it into the pickle as before.

To collar Pig

Slit the pig down the back, take out all the bones, wash it from the blood in three or four waters, wipe it dry, and season it with savoury spice, thyme, parsley, and salt, and roll it in a hard collar; tie it close in a dry cloth, and boil it with the bones in three pints of water, a handful of salt, a quart of vinegar, a faggot of sweet herbs, whole spice; when it is boiled tender take it off, and when cold take it out of the cloth, and keep it in the pickle.

To pot Ducks or any Fowls, or small Birds

Break all the bones of your ducks with a rolling-pin, take out the thighbones, and as many others as you can, keeping the ducks whole; season them with pepper, salt, nutmeg, and cloves; lay them close in a pot with their breast down, put in a little red wine, a good deal of butter, and lay a small weight upon them; when they are bak'd, let them stand in the pot till they are near cold, to suck up the seasoning the better; then put them in another pot, and pour clarified butter on them; if they are to keep long, put away the gravy; if to spend soon, put it in. Take care to season them well.

To pot a Swan

Bone and skin your swan, and beat the flesh in a mortar, taking out the strings as you beat it; then take some clear fat bacon and beat with the swan, and when it is of a light flesh-colour there is bacon enough in it; when it is beaten till it is like dough, it is enough; then season it with pepper, salt, cloves, mace, and nutmeg, all beaten fine; mix it well with your flesh, and give it a beat or two all together; then put it in an earthen pot, with a little claret and fair-water, and at the top two pounds of fresh butter spread over it; cover it with coarse paste, and bake it with bread; then turn it out into a dish; squeeze it gently to get out the moisture; then put it in a pot fit for it; and when it is cold cover it with clarified butter, and next day paper it up; in this manner you may do goose, duck, or beef, or hare's flesh.

To dress a Hare

Flay your hare, and lard it with bacon; take the liver, give it one boil; then bruise it small, and mix it with some marrow, or a quarter of a pound of beef-suet shred very fine, two anchovies chopped small, some sweet herbs shred very small, some grated bread, a nutmeg grated, some salt, a little bit of eschalot cut fine; mix these together with the yolks of two or three eggs; then work it up in a good piece of butter; flour it, and when your hare is spitted, put this pudding in the belly, and sew it up, and lay it to the fire; put a dish under to receive what comes from the hare; baste it well with butter, and when it is enough, put in the dish with it a sauce made with strong broth, the gravy of your hare, the fat being taken off, and some claret; boil these up, and thicken it up with butter; when the hare is cut up, mix some of the pudding with your sauce. Garnish the dish with sliced lemon.

Some, instead of the pudding in the belly, roast a piece of bacon, with some thyme; and for sauce, have melted butter and thyme mixed with what comes from the hare.

To make Westphalia Bacon

Make a pickle as follows: take a gallon of pump-water, a quarter of a peck of bay-salt, as much of white salt, a pound of petre-salt and a quarter of a pound of saltpetre, a pound of coarse sugar, and an ounce of socho tied up in a rag; boil all these together very well, and let it stand till it is cold; then put in the pork, and let it lie in this pickle a fortnight; then take it out, and dry it over sawdust: this pickle will do tongues, but you must first let the tongues lie six or eight hours in pump-water, to take out the sliminess; and when you have laid them in the pickle, dry them as your pork.

To salt and dry a Ham of Bacon

Take bay-salt and put it in a vessel of water suitable to the quantity of hams you do; make your pickle strong enough to bear an egg with your bay-salt; then boil and scum it very well; then let the pickle be thoroughly cold, and put into it so much red saunders as will make it of the colour of claret; then let your pickle stand three days before you put your hams into it; the hams must lie in the pickle three weeks; then carefully dry them where wood is burnt.

To dry Tongues

Take to every two ounces of saltpetre, a pint of petre-salt, and rub it well; after it is finely beaten, strew it over your tongue, and then beat a pint of bay-salt, and rub that on over it, and every three days turn it; when it has lain nine or ten days, hang it in wood-smoke to dry. Do a hog's-head this way. For a ham of pork or mutton, have a quart of bay-salt, half a pound of petre-salt, a quarter of a pound of saltpetre, a quarter of a pound of brown sugar, all beaten very fine, mix'd together, and rubb'd well over it; let it lie a fortnight; turn it often, and then hang it up a day to drain, and dry it in wood-smoke.

To salt Hams, or Tongues, &c.

Take of bay-salt a peck, of saltpetre four ounces; three pounds of very brown sugar: put to all these water till it will but just bear an egg; after it is well stirred lay in the hams so that they are covered with the pickle; let them lie three weeks, if middling hams, if large a month; when you take them out, dry them well in a cloth and rub them with bay-salt, then hang them up to dry, and smoke them with sawdust every day for a fortnight together; the chimney you hang them in must be of a moderate heat, the pickle must be raw, and not boil'd. This quantity is enough to salt six hams at a time. When you take them out, you may boil the pickle, and skim it clean, putting in some fresh salt. If you keep your hams till they are dry and old, lay them in hot grains, and let them lie till cold, then wrap them up in hay, and boil them tender; set them on in cold water when they are dry, the houghs being before stop'd with salt, and tied up close in brown paper, to keep out the flies.

Neats' hearts, tongues, or Hogs' cheeks, do well in the same pickle; the best way is to rub hams with bay-salt and sugar three or four days before you put them in this pickle.

Another

Take three or four gallons of water, put to it four pounds of bay-salt, four pounds of white-salt, a pound of petre-salt, a quarter of a pound of saltpetre, two ounces of prunella-salt, a pound of brown sugar; let it boil a quarter of an hour; scum it well, and when it is cold sever it from the bottom into the vessel you keep it in. Let hams lie in this pickle four or five weeks. A clod of Dutch beef as long. Tongues a fortnight. Collared beef eight or ten days. Dry them in a stove, or with wood in a chimney.

To make Dutch Beef

Take the lean part of a buttock of beef raw; rub it well with brown sugar all over, and let it lie in a pan or tray two or three hours, turning it three or four times; then salt it well with common salt and saltpetre, and let it lie a fortnight, turning it every day; then roll it very strait in a coarse cloth, and put it in a cheese-press a day and a night, and hang it to dry in a chimney. When you boil it, you must put it in a cloth; when it is cold, it will cut out into shivers as Dutch beef.

To dry Mutton to cut out into shivers as Dutch Beef

Take a middling leg of mutton, then take half a pound of brown sugar, rub it hard all over your mutton, and let it lie twenty-four hours; then take an ounce and half of saltpetre, and mix it with a pound of common salt, and rub that all over the mutton every other day, till it is all on, and let it lie nine days longer; keep the place free from brine, and hang it up to dry three days; then smoke it in a chimney where wood is burnt; the fire must not be too hot; a fortnight will dry it; boil it like other hams, and when it is cold cut it out in shivers like Dutch beef.

To dry a Leg of Mutton like Pork

Take a large leg of mutton, and beat it down flattish with a cleaver, to make it like Westphalia ham; then take two ounces of saltpetre, beat it fine, rub it all over your mutton, and let it lie all night; then make a pickle with bay-salt and pump-water, strong enough to bear an egg, put your mutton into it, and let it lie ten days; then take it out and hang it in a chimney where wood is burnt, till it is thorough dry, which will be about three weeks. Boil it with hay, till it is very tender; do it in cool weather, or it will not keep well.

To salt Bacon

Cut your flitches of bacon very smooth, make no holes in it; to about three score pounds of bacon, ten pounds of salt; dry your salt very well, and make it hot, then rub it hard over the outside, or skinny part, but on the inside lay it all over, without rubbing, only lightly on, about half an inch thick. Let it lie on a flat board, that the brine may run from it nine days; then mix with a quart of hot salt, two ounces of saltpetre, and strew it all over your bacon; then heat the rest of your salt, put over it, and let it lie nine days longer; then hang it up a day, and put it in a chimney, where wood is burnt, and there let it hang three weeks or more, as you see occasion.

To pot Salmon

Scale and chine your salmon down the back, and dry it well; cut it as near the shape of your pot as you can; take two nutmegs, near an ounce of cloves and mace, half an ounce of white pepper, about an ounce of salt; take out all the bones, and cut off the joll below the fins; cut off the tail; season the scaly side first, and lay that at the bottom of the pot; then rub the seasoning on the other side; cover it with a dish, and let it stand all night. It must be put double, and the scaly side top and bottom. Put butter on the bottom and top; cover the pot with some stiff coarse paste; three hours if it is a large fish, if not, two hours will bake it. When it comes out of the oven, let it stand half an hour; then uncover it, and raise it up at one end that the gravy may run out; then put a trencher and a weight on it, to press out the gravy, melt the butter that came from it, but let no gravy be in it, let the butter boil up, and add more butter to it, if there be occasion. Scum it, and fill the pot with the clear butter; when 'tis cold, paper it up.

Salmon or Mackerel to pot

After you have washed and cleans'd them, dry them in a cloth, cut off the heads, tails and fins, cut them down the bellies, take out the roes, and wipe the black that lies under the roes; take out the bones as clean as you can; season twelve or thirteen with four ounces of salt, half an ounce of nutmeg, as much pepper, a quarter of an ounce of cloves, as much ginger beat very fine; mix with the salt and season them; lay them into a long pot with a few bay-leaves and lemon-peel on the top, a good quantity of fresh butter, and bake them with household bread at least three hours: lay on a double brown paper wetted and tied close. When they are baked, take them out of the pot while hot, and pull them in small pieces with your fingers; place them close in your potting-pots, and pour clarified butter on the top.

To pot Beef

Take six pounds of the buttock of beef, cut it in pieces as big as your fist, season it with a large spoonful of mace, a spoonful of pepper, with twenty-five or thirty cloves, and a good race of ginger; beat them all very fine, mix them with salt, and put them to the beef; lay it in a pot, and upon it two pounds of butter; bake it three or four hours, well cover'd up with paste; before it is cold take out the beef, beat it fine, putting in the warm butter as you do it, and put it down close in pots; if you keep it long, keep back the gravy, and if it wants seasoning, add some in the beating; pour on clarified butter.

To Stew Pigeons

Season your pigeons with pepper, salt, cloves and mace, with some sweet herbs; wrap a seasoning up in a bit of butter, and put it in their bellies, then tie up the neck and vent, and half roast them; then put them in a stew-pan, with a quart of good gravy, a little white wine, some pickled mushrooms, a few peppercorns, three or four blades of mace, a bit of lemon-peel, a bunch of sweet herbs, a bit of onion, some oyster-pickle: let them stew till they are enough; then thicken it up with butter and yolks of eggs. Garnish with lemon. Do ducks the same way. You may put forc'd-meat in their bellies, or shred thyme wrap'd up in butter. Put forc'd-meat balls in both.

To fricassee a Pig

Half roast your pig, then take it up, and take off the coat, pull the meat in flakes from the bones, and put it in a stew-pan, with some strong broth, some white wine, a little vinegar, an onion stuck with cloves, some mace, a bunch of sweet herbs, and some salt, and lemon-peel; when it is almost done, take out the onions, herbs, and lemon-peel, and put in some mushrooms, and thicken it with cream and eggs. The head must be roasted whole, and set in the middle, and the fricassee round it. Garnish with lemon.

To Stew Cod

Cut your cod in thin slices, and lay them one by one in the bottom of a dish; put in a pint of white wine, half a pound of butter, some oysters and their liquor, two or three blades of mace, a few crumbs of bread, some pepper and salt, and let it stew till it is enough. Garnish the dish with lemon.

To make Skuets

Take fine, long and slender skewers; then cut veal sweetbreads into pieces like dice, and some fine bacon in thin square bits; season them with forc'd-meat, and then spit them on the skewers, a bit of sweetbread, a bit of bacon, till all is on; roast them, and lay them round a fricassee of sheep's tongues.

To pot a Hare

Take three pounds of the pure flesh of hare, and a pound and half of the clear fat of pork or bacon, and beat them in a mortar, till you cannot distinguish each from the other; then season it with pepper, salt, a large nutmeg, a large handful of sweet herbs, sweet-marjoram, thyme, and a double quantity of parsley; shred all very fine, mix it with the seasoning, and beat it all together, till all is very well mingled; then put it into a pot, laying it lower in the middle than the sides, and paste it up; two hours will bake it. When it comes out of the oven, have clarified butter ready; fill the pot an inch above the meat while it is hot; when it is cold, paper it up, and keep it; which you may do three or four months before it is cut: the fat of pork is much better than the fat of bacon.

To make a Bisk of Pigeons

Take twelve pigeons, fill the bellies with forc'd-meat, and half roast them, or half boil them in strong broth; then have slices of French bread, toasted hard and stew'd in strong broth, and have in readiness some lamb-stones, and sweetbreads, and palates, they being first boiled tender; then stew them with your pigeons in your strong broth; add balls of forc'd-meat first stewed or fry'd; lay your pigeons in a dish; lay on them thin slices of broiled bacon, and your other ingredients, and pour in your strong broth, and garnish with lemon. You may leave out the sweetbreads, palates, and lamb-stones, and put in scalded herbs, as for soups, and turnips half boil'd, cut like dice, and fry'd brown, and so serve it like a soup, using but six pigeons.

To do Pigeons in Jelly

Take a knuckle of veal, and a good piece of isinglass, and make a strong jelly; season it with mace, white pepper, salt, bay-leaves, and lemon-peel; then truss your pigeons as for boiling, and boil them in the jelly; when they are cold, put them in the dish you serve them in; then add the juice of a lemon to your jelly, clarify it with the whites of eggs, run it through a jelly-bag into a pan, and keep it till 'tis cold: with a spoon lay it in heaps, on and between your pigeons. Garnish with sliced lemon and bay-leaves.

To make a Poloe

Take a pint of rice, boil it in as much water as will cover it; when your rice is half boiled put in your fowl, with a small onion, a blade or two of mace, some whole pepper, and some salt; when 'tis enough, put the fowl in the dish, and pour the rice over it.

To Stew Cucumbers

Pare twelve cucumbers, slice them as for eating, put them to drain, and lay them in a coarse cloth till they are dry; flour them, and fry them brown in butter; then put to them some gravy, a little claret, some pepper, cloves and mace, and let them stew a little; then roll a bit of butter in flour, and toss them up; put them under mutton or lamb roasted.

To pot Goose and Turkey

Take a fat goose, and a fat turkey; cut them down the rump, and take out all the bones; lay them flat open, and season them very well with white pepper, nutmeg and salt, allowing three nutmegs, with the like proportion of pepper, and as much salt as both the spices; when you have season'd them all over, let your turkey be within the goose, and keep them in season two nights and a day; then roll them up as collared beef, very tight, and as short as you can, and bind it very fast with strong tape. Bake it in a long pot, with good store of butter, till it is very tender, as you may feel by the end; let it lie in the hot liquor an hour, then take it out, and let it stand till next day; then unbind it, place it in your pot, and melt butter, and pour over it. Keep it for use, and slice it out thin.

To make a Fricassee of Eggs

Boil your eggs hard, and take out a good many of the yolks whole, then cut the rest in quarters, yolks and whites together. Set on some gravy, with a little shred thyme and parsley in it, give it a boil or two; then put in your eggs, with a little grated nutmeg; shake it up with a bit of butter, till it be as thick as another fricassee: then fry artichoke bottoms in thin slices, and serve it up. Garnish with eggs shred small.

Another Fricassee of Eggs

Boil six eggs hard, slice them in round slices, then stew some morels in white wine, with an eschalot, two anchovies, a little thyme, a few oysters or cockles, and salt to your taste; when they have stew'd well together, put in your eggs and a bit of butter; toss them up together till it is thick, and then serve it up.

To fricassee Artichoke-bottoms for a side-dish

Boil your artichokes tender, take off the leaves and choke; when cold split every bottom, dredging them with flour, and then dip them in beaten eggs, with some salt and grated nutmeg; then roll them up in grated bread, fry them in butter; make gravy sauce thicken'd with butter, and pour under them.

To keep Smelts in Jelly

Take smelts alive, if you can get them; choose out the firmest without spawn, set them a-boiling in a gallon of water, a pint of wine vinegar, two handfuls of salt, and a bunch of sweet herbs, and lemon-peel; let them boil three or four walms, and take them up before they break. The jelly make thus: take a quart of the liquor, a quart of vinegar, a quart of white wine, one ounce of isinglass, some cloves, mace, sliced ginger, whole pepper, and salt; boil these over a gentle fire till a third part be consumed, and the isinglass be melted; then set it by till almost cold: lay your smelts in a china plate one by one, then pour it on your smelts; set it in a cool place; it will jelly by next day.

To Stew a Turkey

Take a fine young turkey, kill'd, pull'd, and drawn, fill the skin on the breast with forc'd-meat, and lard it on the sides with bacon; put into the belly half an eschalot, two anchovies, and a little thyme shred small; brown it in a pan with a little butter; when it is very brown put it in a stew-pan, with strong gravy, some white wine, or claret, two or three anchovies, some mace, sweet herbs, and a little pepper; let it stew till it is thoroughly enough, then thicken the liquor with butter and eggs; fry some French loaves dipped in cream, after the top and the crumb is taken out; then fill them with stewed oysters, or shrimps, or cockles, and with them garnish the dish, or with slic'd lemon. A hen, goose, or duck, does well this way.

To bake a Rump of Beef

Bone a rump of beef, beat it very well with a rolling-pin, cut off the sinew, and lard it with large pieces of bacon; roll your lards in seasoning, which is pepper, salt, and cloves; lard athwart the meat, that it may cut handsomely; then season it all over the meat with pepper and salt pretty thick, tie it with packthread cross and cross, and put the top under the bottom, and tie it up tight; put it in an earthen pot, break all the bones, and put in the sides and over, to keep it fast that it cannot stir; then put in half a pound of butter, some bay-leaves, whole pepper, an eschalot or two, and some sweet herbs; cover the top of the pot with coarse paste; put it in the oven, and let it stand eight hours. Serve it up with its own liquor, and some dry'd sippets.

To make Veal Cutlets

Cut your veal steaks thin, hack them, and season them with pepper and salt, and sweet herbs; wash them over with eggs, and strew over them some forc'd-meat; put two steaks together, and lard them with bacon; wash them over with melted butter, and wrap them in white papers butter'd; roast them on a lark spit, or bake them; when they are enough, unpaper them, and serve them with good gravy and sliced lemon.

To dress a Calf's Head

Scald the hair off, and take out the bones, then have in readiness palates boiled tender, yolks of hard eggs, oysters scalded, and forc'd-meat; stuff all this into your head, and sew it up close in a cloth; boil it three hours; make a strong gravy for sauce, and garnish with fry'd bacon.

To make a Pulpatoon of Pigeons

Take mushrooms, palates, oysters, sweetbreads, and fry them in butter; then put all these into a strong gravy; give them a heat over the fire, and thicken up with an egg and a bit of butter; then half roast six or eight pigeons, and lay them in a crust of forc'd-meat, as follows: scrape a pound of veal and two pounds of marrow, and beat it together in a stone mortar, after it is shred very fine; then season it with salt, pepper, spice, and put in hard eggs, anchovies, and oysters; beat all together, and make the lid and sides of your pie of it; first, lay a thin crust in your pattipan, then put in your forc'd-meat, then lay an exceeding thin crust over it, then put in your pigeons and other ingredients, with a little butter on the top; bake it two hours.

To pot Mushrooms

Take of the best mushrooms, and rub them with a woollen cloth; those that will not rub, peel, and take out the gills, and throw them into water, as you do them; when they are all done, wipe them dry, and put them in a saucepan, with a handful of salt and a piece of butter; stew them till they are enough, shaking them often for fear of burning; then drain them from their liquor, and when they are cold wipe them dry, and lay them in a pot one by one as close as you can, till your pot be full; then clarify butter; let it stand till it is almost cold, and pour it into your mushrooms; when cold, cover them close in your pot; when you use them, wipe them clean from the butter, and stew them in gravy thicken'd, as when fresh.

To pot Herrings

Cut off their heads, and put them in an earthen pot, lay them close, and between every layer of herrings strew some salt, not too much; put in cloves, mace, whole pepper, and nutmeg cut in bits; fill up the pot with vinegar, water and a quarter of a pint of white wine; cover it with brown paper, tie it down, and bake it with brown bread. When cold it is fit to eat.

To bake Herrings

Take thirty herrings, scale them, cut off their heads, pull out their roes, wash them very clean, and lay them to drain four or five hours; roll them in a dry cloth, season them with pepper and salt, and lay them in a long venison pot at full length; when you have laid one row, shred a large onion very small, and mix it with a little cloves, mace and ginger cut small, and strew it all over the herrings; and then another row of herrings, and seasoning; and so do till all is in the pot; let it stand season'd an hour before it is put in the oven, then put in a quart of claret, and tie it over with paper, and bake it with household bread.

To make a Soup

Take twelve pounds of beef, a scrag of mutton, and knuckle of veal; it must be neck-beef, and the sticking piece; put your beef in a saucepan, and half fry it with a bit of butter; then put all in a pot, with nine quarts of water, a good handful of salt, and a piece of bacon; boil and skim it, then season it with three onions stuck with cloves, whole pepper, Jamaica pepper, and a bunch of sweet herbs; let it boil five or six hours close covered; then strain it out, and put it in your dish, with stew'd herbs and toasted bread.

To make Mushroom Liquor and Powder

Take a peck of mushrooms, wash and rub them clean with a piece of flannel, cutting out all the gills, but not peeling off the skins; put to them sixteen blades of mace, four cloves, six bay-leaves, twice as much beaten pepper as will lie on a half-crown, a handful of salt, a dozen onions, a piece of butter as big as an egg, and half a pint of vinegar; stew them up as fast as you can, keeping them stirring till the liquor is out of your mushrooms; drain them thro' a colander, save the liquor and spice, and when cold bottle it up for use; dry the mushrooms first on a broad pan in the oven, afterwards put them on sieves, till they are dry enough to pound to powder. This quantity usually makes about half a pound.

Peas Soup

Take the broth of a leg of beef, and boil in it a piece of bacon and a sheep's-head, to mash with a good quantity of peas; strain the broth from the husks, then take half a nutmeg, four cloves, and a race of ginger, some pepper, a pretty deal of mint, some sweet-marjoram and thyme; bruise the spice, powder the herbs, and put them into the soup; boil leeks in two or three waters till they are tender, and the rankness out of them; put in what other herbs you please, as spinach, lettuce, beets, &c. – forget not to boil an onion or two in the broth at first; some will burn butter in a stew-pan, and when it is boiling put in a large plate of sliced onions, let them boil till they are tender, keeping them stirring all the time, and boil them in a soup; others will scrape a little cheshire cheese, and strew in the butter and onions; it ought to be old cheshire-cheese; if you put in the onions mentioned last, they must be fry'd in butter, brown, before they are put into the soup; when you put them into the frying-pan flour them well, put in celery and turnips, if you like the taste, but strain the turnips out: to throw an old pigeon in with the meat at first, gives a high taste, or a piece of lean bacon dry'd.

Oyster Soup

Take a quart of small oysters, put them into a colander to drain; then strain the liquor through a muslin rag, and put to it half a pint of water, and a quarter of a pint of white wine; let them stew with a few sprigs of parsley, and a little thyme, a little eschalot or onion, a little lemon-peel, a few cloves, a blade of mace, and a little whole pepper; let them stew gently a pretty while; take a quarter of a pound of butter and put it into a pan, but flour it well first, then fry it till it has done hissing; dry the oysters in a cloth, and flour them; put them into the butter, and fry them till they are plump; then take one anchovy and dissolve in the liquor; add some fresh wine, and the yolks of two eggs, well beaten; put all into the pan together, and give it a scald, keeping it stirring all the time it is on the fire;

before you put the soup into the dish, lay the crust of a French loaf, or a toast, at the bottom, which must soak with some of the liquor over coals. Before you put in the whole, you may add strong broth or fried gravy, if not in Lent. This soup must be thick with butter'd crumbs: you may add burnt butter or sago, but that you must boil in several waters, the more, the whiter it looks. Vermicelli is good in this, but that must boil but little time. Crawfish and shrimps do well in this soup; if you have shrimps, the fewer oysters will do.

To make green Peas Soup

Take half a bushel of the youngest peas, divide the great from the small; boil the smallest in two quarts of water, and the biggest in one quart; when they are well boil'd, bruise the biggest, and when the thin is drain'd from it, boil the thick in as much cold water as will cover it; then rub away the skins, and take a little spinach, mint, sorrel, lettuce, parsley, and a good quantity of marigolds; wash, shred, and boil these in half a pound of butter, and drain the small peas; save the water, and mingle all together, with a spoonful of whole pepper; then melt a quarter of a pound of butter, shake a little flour into it, and let it boil; put the liquor to the butter, and mingle all well together, and let them boil up; so serve it with dry'd bread.

To keep green Peas till Christmas

Shell what quantity you please of young peas, put them in the pot when the water boils, let them have four or five walms; then first pour them into a colander, and then spread a cloth on a table, and put them on that, and dry them well in it; have bottles ready dried, and fill them to the necks, and pour over them melted mutton fat, and cork them down very close, that no air come to them; set them in your cellar, and when you use them, put them into boiling water, with a spoonful of fine sugar, and a good piece of butter; and when they are enough, drain and butter them.

To make Asparagus Soup

Take twelve pounds of lean beef, cut in thin slices; then put a quarter of a pound of butter in a stew-pan over the fire, and put your beef in; let it boil up thick till it begins to brown; then put in a pint of brown ale, and a gallon of water; cover it close, and let it stew gently for an hour and half; put in what spice you like in the stewing, and strain out the liquor, and skim off all the fat; then put in some vermicelli, some celery wash'd and cut small, half a hundred of asparagus cut small, and palates boiled tender and cut; put all these in, and let them boil gently till tender; just as it is going up fry a handful of spinach in butter, and throw in a French roll.

Asparagus Soup, or green Peas

Take some strong broth of beef, mutton, or both, boil in it a large brown toast, a little flour sifted from oatmeal, and three or four handfuls of asparagus cut small, so far as they are green (or green peas) some spinach, white beets, and what herbs you like, a little celery, and a few sprigs of parsley; toast little white toasts, butter them, and pour your soup upon them; the brown bread ought to be strain'd off before your asparagus goes in; season it with salt to your taste.

White Soup

Take some liquor that has had a leg of mutton boil'd in it, in which you may stew a knuckle of veal, an onion, and a bay-leaf; strain it off and put it again into your stew-pan, with a handful of shred celery, and a good quantity of oysters; let them boil till they will break, then put in such a quantity of butter'd crumbs as will make it thick; you may boil in this some vermicelli; grate in half a nutmeg, salt it to your taste; some celery if you please.

A brown Fricassee

Take lamb or rabbit cut in small pieces; grate on it a little nutmeg, or lemon-peel; fry it quick and brown with butter, then have some strong broth, in which put your morels and mushrooms, a few cockscombs boil'd tender, and artichoke-bottoms; a little walnut-liquor, and a bay-leaf; then roll a bit of butter in flour, shake it well, and serve it up; you may squeeze an orange or lemon over it.

To make Hams of Pork like Westphalia

To two large hams, or three small ones, take three pounds of common salt, and two pounds and a half of brown coarse sugar; mix both together, rub it well into the hams, let them lie seven days, turning them every day, and rub the salt in them when you turn them; then take four ounces of saltpetre beat small, and mix with two handfuls of common salt, and rub that well in your hams, and let them lie a fortnight longer; then hang them up high in a chimney to smoke.

To make Sausages

Take three pounds of fat, and three pounds of lean pork; cut the lean into thin slices; and scrape every slice, and throw away the skin; have the fat cut as small as can be; mix fat and lean together, shred and mix them well; two ounces and a half of salt, half an ounce of pepper, thirty cloves, and three or four large blades of mace, six spoonfuls of sage, two spoonfuls of rosemary cut exceeding fine, with three nutmegs grated; beat six eggs, and work them well together with a pint of water that has been boil'd, and is perfectly cold. If you put in no herbs, slice a penny white loaf in cream, steep it all night, and work it in well with the sausagemeat, with as much cream as will infuse the bread. If you put in raw water, the sausages are said not to keep so well as when it is boiled.

Very fine Sausages

Take a leg of pork or veal; pick it clean from skin or fat, and to every pound of lean meat put two pounds of beef-suet pick'd from the skins; shred the meat and suet severally very fine; then mix them well together, and add a large handful of green sage shred very small, season it with grated nutmeg, salt and pepper; mix it well, and press it down hard in an earthen pot, and keep it for use. When you use them roll them up with as much egg as will make them roll smooth, but use no flour; in rolling them up, make them the length of your finger, and as thick as two fingers; fry them in clarified suet, which must be boiling hot before you put them in. Keep them rolling about in the pan, when they are fried through, they are enough.

To Stew Pigeons with Asparagus

Draw your pigeons, and wrap up a little shred parsley, with a very few blades of thyme, some salt and pepper in a piece of butter; put some in the belly, some in the neck, and tie up the vent and the neck, and half roast them; then have some strong broth and gravy, put them together in a stew-pan; stew the pigeons till they are full enough; then have tops of asparagus boil'd tender, and put them in, and let them have a warm or two in the gravy, and dish it up.

To Stew Pigeons

Season eight pigeons with pepper and salt only; take a middling cabbage cut across the middle, and lay the bottom with the thick pieces in the stew-pan; then lay on your pigeons, and cover 'em with the top of your cabbage; pour in a pint of red wine, and a pint of water; let it stew slowly an hour or more.

Another

Stuff your pigeons with sweet herbs chop'd small, some bacon minced small, grated bread, spice, butter, and yolk of egg; sew them up top and bottom, and stew them in strong broth, with half a pint of white wine to six pigeons, and as much broth as will cover them well, with nutmeg, whole pepper, mace, salt, a little bundle of sweet herbs, a bit of lemon-peel, and an onion; when they are almost done, put in some artichoke bottoms ready boiled, and fried in brown butter, or asparagus-tops ready boiled; thicken up the liquor with the stuffing out of the pigeons, and a bit of butter roll'd in flour; take out the lemon-peel, bunch of herbs, and onion. Garnish the dish with sliced lemon, and very thin bits of bacon toasted before the fire.

To pickle Hams or Ribs of Beef

Take six gallons of your bloody beef-brine, or from pork, and put to it two pounds of brown sugar, and a pound of saltpetre; boil 'em together, and skim it well; when 'tis cold put it into the thing you design to pickle in, and put in your hams; large ones must lie in the pickle three weeks; small ones but a fortnight, sometimes turning them; the pickle must be strong enough to bear an egg; this way is only for great families that kill or use a great deal of beef.

To stew Green Peas

Take five pints of young green peas, put them into a dish with a little spring-water, savoury, some sweet-marjoram, thyme, and onion, a few cloves, and a little whole pepper; melt half a pound of sweet butter, with a piece of dried fat bacon the bigness of an egg, in a stew-pan, and let it boil till it is brown; take the white part of three hard lettuces cut very small, and put them into the butter; set it again on the fire for half a minute, stirring the lettuces four or five times; then put in the peas, and after you have given them five or six tosses, put in as much strong broth as will stew them; then add half a pint of cream, and let them boil till the liquor is almost wasted; bruise them a little with a spoon, and put a quarter of a pint more of cream to them; toss them five or six times, and dish them. Any good gravy may be added.

To make Green Peas Soup

Make strong broth of a leg of beef, a knuckle or scrag end of veal, and scrag of mutton; clear it off; then chop some cabbage lettuce, spinach, and a little sorrel; then put half a pound of butter in a flat saucepan, dredge in some flour, put it over the fire until 'tis brown: then put in your herbs and toss them up a little over the fire; then put in a pint and half of green peas, half boiled before, adding your strong broth, and let it just simmer over the fire half an hour; then cut some French bread very thin, dry it well before the fire, put it in, and let it stew half an hour longer; season your broth with pepper, salt, and a few cloves and mace. Garnish the dish with spinach scalded green, and some very thin bits of bacon toasted before the fire.

Strong Broth

Take twelve quarts of water, two knuckles of veal, a leg or two shins of beef, two pair of calf's-feet, a chicken, a rabbit, two onions, cloves, mace, pepper, salt, a bunch of sweet herbs; cover it close, and let it boil till six quarts are consumed; strain it out, and keep it for use.

To make Crawfish Soup

Take a gallon of water, and set it a-boiling; put in it a bunch of sweet herbs, three or four blades of mace, an onion stuck with cloves, pepper, and salt; then have about two hundred of crawfish; save out about twenty; pick the rest from their shells; save the tails whole, the bodies and shells beat in a mortar, with a pint of peas, green or dry, that have been boiled tender; put your boiling water to it, and strain it boiling hot through a cloth, till you have got all the goodness out, and some good gravy; then slice French bread very thin, and set it to dry very hard; set your soup over a stew in a dish, and the French bread in it; cover it, and let it stew till it is served up; then brown a piece of butter in a broad saucepan, and put into it your tails, a ladleful of broth, and an onion; cover that, and set it over a stew, and when you are ready to use it, take out the onion, and put all together in the dish you serve it in, with a whole French roll toasted and put in the middle of the dish, and the twenty crawfish you saved out, fried, and laid round the dish to garnish it.

If you have a carp, scale and flay it, take the fish from the bones, and mince the fish small, with a very little bit of eschalot, an anchovy, some parsley and thyme, some spice, salt, a little grated bread, and the yolks of two eggs; make it up, and sew it in the skin of the carp; then boil it, but not long, and put it in the middle of your soup, instead of your French roll.

To Stew a Neck of Veal

Cut your neck of veal in steaks; beat them flat and season them with salt, grated nutmeg, thyme and lemon-peel, shred very fine; when you put it into your pan, put to it some thick cream, according to the quantity you do, and let it stew softly till enough; then put into your pan two or three anchovies, a little gravy, or strong broth, a bit of butter, and some flour dusted in, and toss it up till 'tis thick, then dish it. Garnish with lemon.

To Stew Carps

Scale and gut your carp, and wash the blood out of their bellies with vinegar; then flour them well, and fry them in butter till they are thorough hot, then put them into your stew-pan, with a pint of claret, two anchovies, an onion stuck with three or four cloves, two or three blades of mace, a bunch of sweet herbs, and a pound of fresh butter; put them over a soft fire, three quarters of an hour will do them; then take your fish up, and put them in the dish you serve them in; if your sauce is not thick enough, boil it a little longer; then strain it over your carp. This is a very good way to stew eels, only cut them in pieces, and do not fry them. Garnish with horseradish and lemon.

To pot Eels

Case your eels and gut them, wash them, and dry them, slit them down the back, and take out the bones; cut them in pieces to fit your pot; then rub every piece on both sides with pepper, salt, and grated nutmeg; then lay them close in the pot till 'tis full; cover the pot with close paste, and bake them. A pot that holds eight pound weight must have two hours baking; when they come out of the oven open the pot and pour out all the liquor, then cover them with clarified butter.

Mackerel to caveack

Cut your mackerel in pieces; season them as for potting, and rub it in well; fry them in oil or clarified butter, then lay them on straw by the fire to drain; when cold put them in vinegar, and cover them with oil, dry them before you season them. They will keep, and are extremely good.

To hash a Calf's Head

Boil the head almost enough, then cut it in half, the fairest half scotch and strew it over with grated bread, and a little shred parsley; set it before the fire to broil, and baste it with butter.

Cut the other half and the tongue in thin slices as big as a crown piece: have some strong gravy ready, and put it in a stew pan with your hash, an anchovy washed, boned, the head and tail off; a bit of onion, two or three cloves, and two blades of mace, just bruised and put into a rag; then strew in a little flour, and set it to stew; when it is enough have in readiness the yolks of four eggs well beaten, with two or three spoonfuls of white wine, and some grated nutmeg, and stir it in your hash till it is thick enough; then lay your broiled head in the middle, and your hash round. Garnish with lemon and little slices of bacon; always have forc'd-meat balls. You may add sweetbreads, lamb-stones, &c.

To jug a Hare

Cut a hare in pieces, but do not wash it; season it with half an onion shred very fine, a sprig of thyme, a little parsley all shred, beaten pepper and salt, as much as will lie on a shilling, half a nutmeg, and a little lemon-peel; strew all these over your hare, and cut half a pound of fat bacon into thin slices; then put your hare into a jug, a layer of hare, and the slices of bacon on it; so do till all is in the jug; stop the jug close that not any steam can go out; then put it in a pot of cold water, lay a tile on the top, and let it boil three hours; take the jug out of the kettle, put half a pound of butter in it, and shake it together till the butter is melted; then pour it in your dish. Garnish with lemon.

To jug Pigeons

Pull, crop, and draw your pigeons, but not wash them; save the livers, put them in scalding water, and set them on the fire for a minute or two; then take them out, and bruise them small with the back of a spoon; mix them with a little pepper, salt, grated nutmeg, lemon-peel shred very fine, chopped parsley, two yolks of eggs very hard, and bruised as you did the liver, suet shaved exceeding fine, and some grated bread; work these together with raw eggs, roll it in butter, putting a bit into the crop and belly of your pigeon, and sew up the neck and vent; then dip your pigeons in water, seasoning them with pepper and salt, as for a pie; then put them into your jug, with a piece of celery; stop them up close, set them in a kettle of cold water, with a tile on the top, and let it boil three hours; then take them out of the jug, and put them in your dish; take out the celery, and put in a piece of butter roll'd in flour; shake it till it is thick, and put it on your pigeons. Garnish with lemon.

To make Pockets

Cut three slices out of a leg of veal, the length of a finger, the breadth of three fingers, the thickness of a thumb, with a sharp penknife; give it a slit thro' the middle, leaving the bottom and each side whole, the thickness of a straw, then lard the top with small fine lards of bacon; then make a forc'd-meat of marrow, sweetbreads and lamb-stones just boiled; make it up after it is seasoned and beaten together with the yolks of two eggs, and put it into your pockets, as if you were filling a pincushion; then sew up the top with fine thread, flour them, put melted butter on them, and bake them; roast three sweetbreads to put between, and serve them with gravy sauce.

To make Rennet

Take a calf's bag, skewer it up, and let it lie a night in cold water, then turn out the curd into fresh water, wash and pick it very clean, and scour the bag inside and outside; then put a handful of salt to the curd, put it into a bag, skewer it up, and let it lie in a clean pot a year; then put half a pint of sack into the bag, and as much into the pot, and prick the bag, then bruise one nutmeg, four cloves, a little mace, and tie them up in a bit of thin cloth; put it into the pot, and now and then squeeze the spice cloth; in a few days you may use it; put a spoonful, or at most a spoonful and half, to twenty quarts of milk.

To make a Summer Cream Cheese

Take three pints of milk just from the cow, and five pints of good sweet cream, which you must boil free from smoke; then put it to your milk, cool it till it is but blood-warm, and then put in a spoonful of rennet; when it is well come, take a large strainer, lay it in a great cheese-fat, then put the curd in gently upon the strainer, and when all the curd is in, lay on the cheese-board, and a weight of two pound; let it so drain three hours, till the whey be well drained from it, then lay a cheese-cloth in your lesser cheese-fat, and put in the curd, laying the cloth smooth over it as before, the board on the top of that, and a four-pound weight on it; turn it every two hours into dry cloths before night, and be careful not to break it next morning; salt it, and keep it in the fat till next day; then put it into a wet cloth, which you must shift every day till it is ripe.

To make a Newmarket Cheese to cut at two years old

Any morning in September take twenty quarts of new milk warm from the cow, and colour it with marigolds; when this is done, and the milk not cold, get ready a quart of cream and a quart of fair-water, which must be kept stirring over the fire till it is scalding hot, then stir it well into the milk and rennet, as you do other cheese; when it is come, lay cheese-cloths over it, and fettle it with your hands; the more hands the better; as the whey rises, take it away, and when it is clean gone, put your curd into your fat, breaking it as little as you can; then put it in the press, and press it gently an hour; take it out again, and cut it in thin slices, and lay them singly on a cloth, and wipe them dry; then put it in a tub, and break it with your hands as small as you can, and mix it with a good handful of salt, and a quart of cold cream; put it in the fat, and lay a pound weight on it till next day; then press and order it as others.

To make a Rennet-Bag

Let the calf suck as much as he will just before he is kill'd, then take the bag out of the calf, and let it lie twelve hours, cover'd over in stinging nettles till it is very red; then take out your curd, wash your bag clean, salt it within-side and without, letting it lie sprinkled with salt twenty-four hours; then wash your curd in warm new milk, pick it, and put away all that is yellow and hollow, keep what is white and close; then wash it well, and sprinkle it with salt; when the bag has lain twenty-four hours, put it into the bag again, and put to it three spoonfuls of the stroakings of a cow, beat up with the yolk of an egg or two, twelve cloves, and two blades of mace; put a skewer thro' it, and hang it in a pot; then make the rennet-water thus:

Take half a pint of fair-water, a little salt, and six tops of the red buds of blackthorn, as many sprigs of burnet, and two of sweet-marjoram; boil these in the water, and strain it out; when it is cold put one half in the bag, and let the bag lie in the other half, taking it out as you use it; when you want, make more rennet, which you may do six or seven times; three spoonfuls of this rennet will make a large cheshire or cheddar cheese, and half as much to a common cheese.

To make a Cheddar Cheese

Take the new milk of twelve cows in the morning, and the evening cream of twelve cows, putting to it three spoonfuls of rennet; when it is come, break it, and whey it; that being done, break it again, work into the curd three pounds of fresh butter, put it in your press; turn it very often for an hour or more, and change the cloths, washing them every time you change them; you may put wet cloths at first to them, but towards the last put two or three fine dry cloths; let it lie thirty or forty hours in the press, according to the thickness of the cheese; then take it out, wash it in whey, and lay it in a dry cloth till it is dry; then lay it on your shelf, and turn it often.

French Butter

Take the yolks of four hard eggs, half a pound of loaf sugar beat and sifted, and half a pound of sweet butter; bray them in a marble mortar, or some other convenient thing, with a spoonful or two of orange flower water; when it is well mix'd force it thro' the corner of a coarse cloth, in little heaps on a china-plate, or through the top of a dredging-box.

To make Butter

As soon as you have milked, strain your milk into a pot, and stir it often for half an hour, then put it in your pans or trays; when it is cream'd, skim it exceeding clean from the milk, and put your cream into an earthen pot; if you do not churn immediately for butter, shift your cream once in twelve hours into another clean scalded pot, and if you find any milk at the bottom of the pot, put it away; when you have churned, wash your butter in three or four waters, and then salt it to your taste, and beat it well, but not wash it after it is salted; let it stand in a wedge, if it be to pot, till the next morning, and beat it again, and make your layers the thickness of three fingers, and then strew a little salt on it, and so do till your pot is full.

The Queen's Cheese

Take six quarts of the best stroakings, and let them stand till they are cold, then set two quarts of cream on the fire till it is ready to boil, take it off, and boil a quart of fair-water, and take the yolks of two eggs, one spoonful of sugar, and two spoonfuls of rennet; mingle all these together, and stir it till it is but blood warm; when the cheese is come, use it as other cheese; set it at night, and the third day lay the leaves of nettles under and over it; it must be turn'd and wip'd, and the nettles shifted every day, and in three weeks it will be fit to eat. This cheese is made between Michaelmas and All Hallowtide.

To make a thick Cream Cheese

Take the morning's milk from the cow, and the cream of the night's milk and rennet, pretty cool together, and when it is come, make it pretty much in the cheese-fat, and put in a little salt, and make the cheese thick in a deep mould, or a melon-mould, if you have one; keep it a year and half, or two years before you cut it; it must be well salted on the outside.

To make Slip-Coat Cheese

Take new milk and rennet, quite cold, and when it is come, break it as little as you can in putting it into the cheese-fat; let it stand and whey itself for some time; then cover it, and set about two pounds' weight on it; when it will hold together, turn it out of that cheese-fat, and keep it turning upon clean cheese-fats for two or three days, till it has done wetting, and then lay it on sharp pointed dock-leaves till it is ripe; shift the leaves often.

A Cream Cheese

Take six quarts of new milk warm from the cow, and put it to three quarts of good cream, and rennet it; when it comes, put a cloth in the cheese-mould, and with your slitting dish take it out in thin slices, and lay on your mould by degrees till it is all in; then let it stand with a cheese-board upon it till it is enough to turn, which will be at night: then salt it on both sides a little, and let it stand with a two-pound weight on it all night; then take it out, and put it into a dry cloth; and so do till it is dry; ripen it with laying it on nettles; shift the nettles every day.

Sauce for boiled Turkey or Chickens

Boil a spoonful of the best mace very tender, and the liver of the turkey, but not too much, for then it will be hard; bray the mace with a few drops of liquor to a very fine pulp, then bray the liver and put about half of it to the mace with a little pepper, and some salt; if you please you may put the yolk of an egg boil'd hard and

dissolved; to this add by degrees a little of the liquor that drains from the turkey, or some other gravy; put these liquors to the pulp, and boil them some time; then take half a pint of oysters and boil them no longer than till they will break; and last put in white wine and butter wrapped in flour; let it boil but a little, lest the wine make the oysters hard, and just at the last scald four or five spoonfuls of thick new cream, with a few drops of lemon or vinegar; mushrooms pickled do well, but then leave out the other acids; some like this sauce best thicken'd with yolks of eggs and no butter.

Sauce for Fish or Flesh

Take a quart of verjuice, and put it into a jug; then take Jamaica pepper whole, some sliced ginger, some mace, a few cloves, some lemon-peel, horseradish root sliced, some sweet herbs, six eschalots peeled, eight anchovies, and two or three spoonfuls of shred capers; put all these into a linen bag, and put the bag into your verjuice; stop the jug close, and keep it for use – a spoonful cold or mixed in sauce for fish or flesh.

Sauce for Fish in Lent, or at any time

Take a little thyme, horseradish, a bit of onion, lemon-peel, and whole pepper; boil them in a little fair-water; then put in two anchovies, and four spoonfuls of white wine; strain them out, and put the liquor into the same pan again, with a pound of fresh butter; when 'tis melted take it off the fire; and stir in the yolks of two eggs well beaten, with three spoonfuls of white wine; set it on the fire again, and keep it stirring till 'tis the thickness of cream, and pour it hot over your fish. Garnish them with lemon and horseradish.

All Sorts of Pickles

To pickle Mushrooms

Gather your mushrooms in the morning, as soon as possible after they are out of the ground, for one of them that are round and unopened is worth five that are open; if you gather any that are open, let them be such as are reddish in the gills, for those that have white gills are not good; having gathered them, peel them into water; when they are all done, take them out and put them into a saucepan; then put to them a good quantity of salt, whole pepper, cloves, mace, and nutmeg quartered; let them boil in their own liquor a quarter of an hour with a quick fire; then take them off the fire, and drain them thro' a colander, and let them stand till they are cold; then put all the spice that was used in the boiling them to one half white wine and the other half white-wine vinegar, some salt, and a few bay-leaves: then give them a boil or two; there must be liquor enough to cover them; when they are cold, put a spoonful or two of oil on the top to keep them; you must change the liquor once a month.

An excellent way to pickle Mushrooms

Put your mushrooms into water, and wash 'em clean with a sponge, throw them into water as you do them; then put in water and a little salt, and when it boils put in your mushrooms; when they boil up scum them clean, and put them into cold water, and a little salt: let them stand twenty-four hours, and put them into white-wine vinegar, and let them stand a week; then take your pickle from them, and boil it very well with pepper, cloves, mace, and a little all spice; when your pickle is cold, put it to your mushrooms in the glass or pot you keep them in; keep them close tied down with a bladder as the air will hurt them; if your pickle mothers, boil it again: you may make your pickle half white wine, and half white-wine vinegar.

Another

After your mushrooms are well cleansed with a woollen cloth in salt and water, boil milk and water and put them in; let them boil eight or ten minutes; drain them in a sieve; put them immediately into cold water that has been boiled and made cold; take them out of it, and put them into boil'd vinegar that is cold also; let them stand twenty-four hours, and in that time get ready a pickle with white-wine vinegar, a few large blades of mace, a good quantity of whole pepper and ginger sliced; boil this, and when cold put in your mushrooms from the other vinegar. Put them into wide-mouth glasses, and oil upon them; they will keep a great while, if you put them thus in two pickles.

To make Melon Mangoes

Take small melons not quite ripe, cut a slice out of the side, and take out the inside very clean; beat mustard seeds, and shred garlic, which mix with the seeds, and put in your mangoes; put the pieces you cut out into their places again, tie them up, and put them into your pot; then boil some vinegar (as much as you think will cover them) with whole pepper, some salt, and Jamaica pepper, which pour in scalding hot over your mangoes, and cover them close to keep in the steam; repeat this nine days, and when they are cold cover them with leather.

To pickle Walnuts

Take walnuts about midsummer, when a pin will pass through them, put them in a deep pot, and cover them over with ordinary vinegar; change them into fresh vinegar once in fourteen days for six weeks; then take two gallons of the best vinegar, and put into it coriander seeds, caraway seeds, and dill seeds, of each an ounce grossly bruised, ginger sliced three ounces, whole mace one ounce, nutmeg and pepper bruised, of each two ounces; give all a boil or two over the fire, and have your nuts ready in a pot, and pour the liquor boiling hot over them; repeat this nine times.

To pickle Cucumbers in slices

Slice your cucumbers pretty thick, and to a dozen of cucumbers cut in two or three good onions, strew on them a large handful of salt, and let them lie in their liquor twenty-four hours: then drain them, and put them between two coarse cloths; then boil the best white-wine vinegar, with some cloves, mace and Jamaica pepper in it, and pour it scalding hot over them, as much as will cover them all over; when they are cold, cover them up with leather, and keep them for use.

To pickle Sprats for Anchovies

Take an anchovy-barrel, or a deep glazed pot, put a few bay-leaves at the bottom, a layer of bay-salt, and some petre-salt mixed together; then a layer of sprats, crowded close, then bay-leaves, and the same salt and sprats and so till your barrel or pot be full; then put in the head of your barrel close, and once a week turn the other end upwards; in three months they will be fit to eat as anchovies raw, but they will not dissolve.

To pickle Sparrows, or Squab-Pigeons

Take your sparrows, pigeons, or larks, draw them, and cut off their legs; then make a pickle of water, a quarter of a pint of white wine, a bunch of sweet herbs, salt, pepper, cloves and mace; when it boils put in your sparrows, and when they are enough take them up, and when they are cold put them in the pot you keep them in; then make a strong pickle of rhenish wine and white-wine vinegar; put in an onion, a sprig of thyme and savoury, some lemon-peel, some cloves, mace, and whole pepper; season it pretty high with salt; boil all these together very well; then set it by till it is cold, and put it to your sparrows; once in a month new boil the pickle, and when the bones are dissolv'd they are fit to eat; put them in china saucers and mix with your pickles.

To pickle Nasturtium Buds

Gather your little knobs quickly after your blossoms are off; put them in cold water and salt for three days, shifting them once a day; then make a pickle (but do not boil it at all) of some white wine, some white-wine vinegar, eschalot, horseradish, pepper, salt, cloves and mace whole, and nutmeg quartered; then put in your seeds and stop them close; they are to be eaten as capers.

To keep Quinces in pickle

Cut five or six quinces all to pieces, and put them in an earthen pot or pan, with a gallon of water, and two pounds of honey; mix all these together well, and then put them in a kettle to boil leisurely half an hour, and then strain your liquor into an earthen pot; and when 'tis cold, wipe your quinces clean, and put them into it: They must be covered very close, and they will keep all the year.

To pickle Asparagus

Gather your asparagus, and lay them in an earthen pot; make a brine of water and salt strong enough to bear an egg, pour it hot on them, and keep it close covered: when you use them hot, lay them in cold water for two hours, then boil and butter them for the table; if you use them as a pickle, boil them and lay them in vinegar.

To pickle Ashen-Keys

Take ashen-keys as young as you can get them, and put them in a pot with salt and water; then take green whey, when 'tis hot, and pour over them; let them stand till they are cold before you cover them; when you use them, boil them in fair-water till they are tender; then take them out, and put them in salt and water.

To pickle Samphire

Pick your samphire from dead or withered branches; lay it in a bell metal or brass pot, then put in a pint of water and a pint of vinegar; so do till your pickle is an inch above your samphire; have a lid for the pot, and paste it close down, that no steam may go out; keep it boiling an hour, take it off, and cover the pot close with old sacks, &c.; when 'tis cold, put it up in tubs or pots; the best by itself; the great stalks lay uppermost in boiling; it will keep the cooler and better. The vinegar you use must be the best.

To mango Cucumbers

Cut a little slice out of the side of the cucumber, and take out the seeds, but as little of the meat as you can; then fill the inside with mustard seed bruised, a clove of garlic, some slices of ginger, and some bits of horseradish; tie the piece in again, and make a pickle of vinegar, salt, whole pepper, cloves and mace, boil it and pour it on the mangoes, and do so for nine days together; when cold, cover them with leather.

Another way to pickle Walnuts

Take walnuts about Midsummer, when a pin will pass through them, and put them in a deep pot, and cover them over with ordinary vinegar; change them into fresh vinegar once in fourteen days, and repeat this four times; then take six quarts of the best vinegar, and put into it an ounce of dill weeds grossly bruised, ginger sliced three ounces, mace whole one ounce, nutmegs quartered two ounces, whole pepper two ounces; give all a boil or two over the fire; then put your nuts into a crock, and pour your pickle boiling hot over them; cover them up close till 'tis cold, to keep in the steam; then have gallipots ready, and place your nuts in them till your pots are full; put in the middle of each pot a large clove of garlic stuck full of cloves; strew over the tops of the pots mustard seed finely beaten, a spoonful, more or less, according to the bigness of your pot; then put the spice on, lay vine-leaves, and pour on the liquor, laying a slate on the top to keep them under the liquor. Be careful not to touch them with your fingers, lest they turn black; but take them out with a wooden spoon; put a handful of salt in with the spice. When you first boil the pickle, you must likewise remember to keep them under the pickle they are first steeped in, or they will loose their colour. Tie down the pots with leather. A spoonful of this liquor will relish sauce for fish, fowl, or fricassee.

To pickle Lobsters

Boil your lobsters in salt and water, till they will easily slip out of the shell; take the tails out whole, just crack the claws, and take the meat out as whole as possible; then make the pickle half white wine and half water; put in whole cloves, whole pepper, whole mace, two or three bay-leaves; then put in the lobsters, and let them have a boil or two in the pickle; then take them out, and set them by to be cold, boil the pickle longer, and when both are cold put them together, and keep them for use. Tie the pot down close; eat them with oil, vinegar, and lemon.

Tench to pickle

When your tench are cleansed, have a pickle ready boil'd, half white wine and half vinegar, a few blades of mace, some slic'd ginger, whole pepper, and a bay-leaf, with a piece of lemon-peel and some salt; boil your tench in it, and when it is enough, lay them out to cool, and when the liquor is cold, put them in; it will keep but few days.

To pickle Oysters

Wash your oysters in their own liquor, squeezing them between your fingers, that there be no gravel in them; strain the liquor, and wash the oysters in it again; put as much water, as the liquor, set it on the fire, and as it boils skim it clean; then put a pretty deal of whole pepper, boil it a little, then put in some blades of mace, and your oysters, stirring them apace, and when they are firm in the middle-part, take them off, pour them quick into an earthen pot, and cover them very close; put in a few bay-leaves; be sure your oysters are all under the liquor; the next day put them up for use, cover them very close. When you dish them to eat, put a little white wine or vinegar on the plate with them.

Another

Take a quart of oysters, and wash them in their own liquor very well, till all the grittiness is out; put them in a saucepan or stew-pan, and strain the liquor over them, set them on the fire, and scum them; then put in three or four blades of mace, a spoonful of whole peppercorns; when you think they are boiled enough, throw in a glass of white-wine; let them have a thorough scald; then take them up, and when they are cold, put them in a pot, and pour the liquor over them, and keep them for use. Take them out with a spoon.

Another

Open your oysters, get the grit from them, and stew them in their own liquor in an earthen pipkin till they are tender; then take up the oysters, and cover them, that they may not be discoloured; then increase the liquor with as much more water, and let it boil till one third is consumed; then put your oysters into your pot or barrel, laying between the rows some whole pepper and spice, and a few bay-leaves; and when the pickle is cold, put it to your oysters, and keep them very close covered.

Another

Take a hundred and half of large oysters, wash them and scald them in their own liquor; then take them out, and lay them on a clean cloth to cool; strain their liquor, and boil and skim it clean, adding to it one pint of white wine, half a pint of white-wine vinegar, one nutmeg beat grossly, one onion slit, an ounce of white pepper, half whole the other half just bruised, six or eight blades of mace, a quarter of an ounce of cloves, and five or six bay-leaves; boil up this pickle till it is of a good taste, then cool it in broad dishes, and put your oysters in a deep pot or barrel, and when the pickle is cold put it to them; in five or six days they will be ready to eat, and will keep three weeks or a month, if you take them out with a spoon, and not touch them with your fingers.

To pickle Cucumbers

Wipe your cucumbers very clean with a cloth, then get so many quarts of vinegar as you have hundreds of cucumbers, and take dill and fennel, cut it small, put to it vinegar, set it over the fire in a copper kettle, and let it boil; then put in your cucumbers till they are warm through, but do not boil the liquor while they are in; when they are warm thro', pour all out into a deep earthen pot, and cover it up very close till the next day; then do the same again; but the third day season the liquor before you set it over the fire; put in salt till 'tis brackish, some sliced ginger, whole pepper, and whole mace; then set it over the fire again, and when it boils put in your cucumbers; when they are hot through, pour them into the pot, cover it close; when they are cold, put them in glasses, and strain the liquor over them; pick out the spice, and put it to them; cover them with leather.

To pickle French Beans

Pick the small slender beans from the stalks, and let them lie fourteen days in salt and water, then wash them clean from the brine, and put them in a kettle of water over a slow fire, covered over with vine-leaves; let them stew, but not boil, till they are almost as tender as for eating; then strain them off, laying them on a coarse cloth to dry; then put them in your pots. Boil alegar, skim it and pour it over them, covering them close; boil it so three or four days together, till they be green. Put spice, as to other pickles; and when cold cover with leather.

Another way to pickle French Beans

Take young slender French beans; cut off top and tail; then make a brine with cold water and salt, strong enough to bear an egg; put your beans into that brine, and let them lie fourteen days; then take them out, wash them in fair-water, set them over the fire in cold water, without salt, and let them boil till they are so tender as to eat; when they are cold, drain them from their water, and make a pickle for them. To a peck of French beans, you must have a gallon of white-wine vinegar; boil it with some cloves, mace, whole pepper, and sliced ginger; when 'tis cold put it and your beans into a glass, and keep them for use.

To pickle Pods of Radishes

Gather the youngest pods, and put them in water and salt twenty-four hours; then make a pickle for them of vinegar, cloves, mace, and whole pepper; boil this, drain the pods from the salt and water, and pour the liquor on them boiling hot; put to them a clove of garlic a little bruised.

French Beans to keep

Take a peck of French beans, break them every one in the middle; to them put two pounds of beaten salt; ram them well together, and when the brine arises put them in a narrow-mouth'd jar; press them down close, and lay somewhat that will keep them down with a weight, and tie them up close, that no air comes to them; the night before you use them, lay them in water.

To pickle Currants for present use

Take either red or white, being not thorough ripe; give them a warm in white-wine vinegar, with as much sugar as will indifferently sweeten them; keep them well covered with liquor.

To pickle Asparagus

Take of the largest asparagus, cut off the white at the ends, and scrape them lightly to the head, till they look green; wipe them with a cloth, and lay them in a broad gallipot very even; throw over them whole cloves, mace, and a little salt; put over them as much white-wine vinegar as will cover them very well. Let them lie in the cold pickle nine days, then pour the pickle out into a brass kettle, and let it boil; then put them in, stove them down close, and set them by a little; then set them over again, till they are very green; but take care they don't boil to be soft; then put them in a large gallipot, place them even, and pour the liquor over them; when cold tie them down with leather. 'Tis a good pickle, and looks well in a savoury made dish or pie.

To pickle Broom-Buds

Put your broom-buds into little linen-bags, tie them up; make a pickle of bay-salt and water boiled, and strong enough to bear an egg; put your bags in a pot, and when your pickle is cold, put it to them; keep them close, and let them lie till they burn black: then shift them two or three times, till they change to green; then take them out, and boil them as you have occasion for them: When they are boiled, put them out of the bag; in vinegar they will keep a month after they are boiled.

To pickle Purslane Stalks

Wash your stalks, and cut them in pieces six inches long; give them in water and salt a dozen walms; take them up, drain them, and when they cool make a pickle of stale beer, white-wine vinegar, and salt; put them in, and cover them close.

Another

Take the largest and greenest purslane stalks, gather them dry, and strip off all the leaves; lay the stalks close in an earthen pot; you may lay kidney-beans among them, for you may do them the same way; then lay a stick or two across to keep them under the pickle, which must be made thus: take whey, and set it on the fire, with as much salt as will make it almost as salt as brine; skim off all the curd, and let it boil a quarter of an hour longer, with Jamaica pepper in it; next day, when it is cold, pour the clear liquor thro' a clean cloth upon the pickles, and tie it down close, and set it in a cool cellar; in winter, take a few out as you use them; wash them till the water runs clean; then put your beans or stalks into cold water, and set them over the fire, very close cover'd, and let them scald two hours; and tho' they be as black as ink or stink before you put them in, they will be very green and good when done; then boil vinegar, salt, pepper, Jamaica pepper, ginger, for half a quarter of an hour; and when your stalks are well drain'd from the water thro' a colander, then put your pickle to them, and when these are used, green more, but do not do many at a time.

Cabbage Lettuce to keep

About the latter end of the season take very dry sand, and cover the bottom of a well seafon'd barrel; then set your lettuces in so as not to touch one another: you must not lay above two rows one upon another; cover them well with sand, and set them in a dry place, and be careful that the frost come not at them. The lettuce must not be cut, but be pull'd up by the roots.

To pickle Red Cabbage

Take your close-leav'd red cabbage, and cut it in quarters; when your liquor boils put in your cabbage, and give it a dozen walms; then make the pickle of white-wine vinegar and claret; you may put to it beetroot, boil them first, and turnips half boiled; it is very good for garnishing dishes, or to garnish a salad.

To pickle Barberries

Take of white-wine vinegar and fair-water an equal quantity, and to every pint of this liquor put a pound of sixpenny sugar; set it over the fire, and bruise some of the barberries and put in it a little salt; let it boil near half an hour, then take it off the fire, and strain it, and when it is pretty cold pour it into a glass over your barberries; boil a piece of flannel in the liquor and put over them, and cover the glass with leather.

Another way to pickle Barberries

Take water, and colour it red with some of the worst of your barberries, and put salt to it, and make it strong enough to bear an egg; then set it over the fire, and let it boil half an hour; skim it, and when it is cold strain it over your barberries; lay something on them to keep them in the liquor, and cover the pot or glass with leather.

To pickle Salmon

Take two quarts of good vinegar, half an ounce of black pepper, and as much Jamaica pepper, cloves and mace, of each a quarter of an ounce, near a pound of salt; bruise the spice grossly, and put all these to a small quantity of water, put just enough to cover your fish; cut the fish round, three or four pieces, according to the size of the salmon, and when the liquor boils put in your fish, boil it well; then take the fish out of the pickle, and let it cool; and when it is cold put your fish into the barrel or stein you keep it in, strewing some spice and bay-leaves between every piece of fish; let the pickle cool, and skim off the fat, and when the pickle is quite cold pour it on your fish, and cover it very close.

To pickle Mackerel

Slit your mackerel in halves, take out the roes, gut and clean them, strew salt over them, and lay one on another, the back of one to the inside of the other; let them lie two or three hours, then wipe every piece clean from the salt, and strew them over with pepper beaten, and grated nutmeg; let them lie two or three hours longer; then fry them well, take them out of the pan, and lay them on coarse cloths to drain; when cold put them in a pan, and cover them over with a pickle of vinegar boiled with spice, when it is cold.

The Lemon Salad

Take lemons and cut them into halves, and when you have taken out the meat, lay the rinds in water twelve hours; then take them out, and cut the rinds into spirals; boil them in water till they are tender; take them out and dry them; then take a pound of loaf sugar, putting to it a quarter of a pint of white wine, and twice as much white-wine vinegar, and boil it a little; then take it off, and when it is cold put it in the pot to your peels; they will be ready to eat in five or six days; it is a pretty salad.

To pickle Pigeons

Take your pigeons and bone them, beginning at the rump; take cloves, mace, nutmegs, pepper, salt, thyme, and lemon-peel; beat the spice, shred the herbs and lemon-peel very small, and season the inside of your pigeons; then sew them up, and place the legs and wings in order; then season the outside, and make a pickle for them: to a dozen of pigeons two quarts of water, one quart of white wine, a few blades of mace, some salt, some whole pepper; and when it boils put in your pigeons, and let them boil till they are tender; then take them out, and strain out the liquor, and put your pigeons in a pot, and when the liquor is cold pour it on them; when you serve them to table, dry them out of the pickle, and garnish the dish with fennel or flowers; eat them with vinegar and oil.

To make English Ketchup

Take a wide-mouth'd bottle, put therein a pint of the best white-wine vinegar, putting in ten or twelve cloves of eschalot peeled and just bruised; then take a quarter of a pint of the best langoon white wine, boil it a little, and put to it twelve or fourteen anchovies, washed and shred, and dissolve them in the wine, and when cold, put them in the bottle; then take a quarter of a pint more of white wine, and put in it mace, ginger sliced, a few cloves, a spoonful of whole pepper just bruised, and let them boil all a little; when near cold, slice in almost a whole nutmeg, and some lemon-peel, and likewise put in two or three spoonfuls of horseradish; then stop it close, and for a week shake it once or twice a day; then use it; it is good to put into fish sauce, or any savoury dish of meat; you may add to it the clear liquor that comes from mushrooms.

Another way to pickle Cucumbers in slices

Take your cucumbers at the full bigness, but not yellow, and slice them half an inch thick; cut an onion or two with them, and strew a pretty deal of salt on them, and let them stand to drain all night; then pour the liquor clear from them; dry them in a coarse cloth, and boil as much vinegar as will cover them, with whole pepper, mace, and a quarter'd nutmeg; pour it scalding hot on your cucumbers, keeping them very close stopt; in two or three days heat your liquor again, and pour over them; so do two or three times more; then tie them up with leather.

To pickle small Onions

Take young white unset onions, as big as the tip of your finger; lay them in water and salt two days; shift them once, then drain them in a cloth; boil the best vinegar with spice according to your taste, and when it is cold, keep them in it, covered with a wet bladder.

Another Way to pickle Walnuts

Take your nuts fit to preserve, prick them full of holes, and cut the slit in the crease half through; put them as you do them into brine; let them lie three weeks, changing the brine every four days; take them out with a cloth, and wipe them dry; put them in a pot, with a good deal of bruised mustard seed; then have your pickle ready, which must be wine vinegar, as much as will cover them; put in cloves, mace, ginger, pepper, salt, three or four cloves of garlic stuck with cloves, and pour the liquor boiling hot upon them, and keep them close tied for a fortnight; boil the pickle again, so do three times; put oil on the top.

To diſtil Vinegar for Mushrooms

To a gallon of vinegar put an ounce and half of ginger sliced, one ounce of nutmegs, bruised, half an ounce of mace, half an ounce of white pepper, as much Jamaica pepper, both bruised, a few cloves; distil this: take care it does not burn in the still.

Another way to pickle Mushrooms

Take only the buttons, wash them in milk and water with a flannel; put milk on the fire, and when it boils put in your mushrooms, and give them four or five boils; have in readiness a brine made with milk and salt, and take them out of the boiling brine, and put them into the milk-brine, covering them up all night; then have a brine with water and salt; boil it, and let it stand to be cold, and put in your buttons, and wash them in it. When you first boil your mushrooms, you must put with them an onion and spice; then have in readiness a pickle made with half white wine, and half white-wine vinegar; boil in it ginger, mace, nutmegs, and whole white pepper; when it is quite cold put your mushrooms into the bottle, and some bay-leaves on the sides; and strew between some of your boiled spice; then put in the liquor, and a little oil on the top; cork and rosin the top; set them cool and dry, and the bottom upwards.

To marinate Smelts

Take your smelts, gut them neatly, wash and dry them, and fry them in oil; lay them to drain and cool, and have in readiness a pickle made with vinegar, salt, pepper, cloves, mace, onion, horseradish; let it boil together half an hour; when it is cold put in your smelts.

To pickle Lemons

Take twelve lemons, scrape them with a piece of broken glass, then cut them cross into four parts downright, but not quite through, but that they will hang together; then put in as much salt as they will hold, rub them well, and strew them over with salt: let them lie in an earthen dish, and turn them every day for three days; then slice an ounce of ginger very thin, and salted for three days, twelve cloves of garlic parboil'd and salted three days, a small handful of mustard seed bruised, and forced thro' a hair sieve, some red Indian pepper, one to every lemon; take your lemons out of the salt, and squeeze them gently, and put them into a jar with the spice, and cover them with the best white-wine vinegar; stop them up very close, and in a month's time they will be fit to eat.

To keep Artichokes in pickle, to boil all winter

Throw your artichokes into salt and water half a day, then make a pot of water boil, and put in your artichokes, and let them boil till you can just draw off the leaves from the bottom; then cut off the bottom very smooth and clean, and put them into a pot with pepper, salt, cloves, mace, two bay-leaves, and as much vinegar as will cover them; then pour as much melted butter over them as will cover them inch thick; tie it down close, and keep them for use; when you use them put them into boiling water, with a piece of butter in the water to plump them; then use them for what you please.

Another way to pickle Mushrooms

Rub your mushrooms with a piece of flannel in a little water, and as you clean them, put them into the pot you design to use them in; then set them into a pot of hot water, as if you were going to infuse them; let them be covered close, and boil them till they be settled about half from what they were at first; take them out into a sieve to let the liquor run off; and immediately spread them on a clean coarse cloth, and smother them up close; when cold put them in the best white-wine vinegar and salt, and let them lie nine or ten days in it; then make your pickle with fresh white-wine vinegar, white pepper whole, and a little salt.

Another way to pickle Walnuts

In July gather the largest walnuts, and let them lie nine days in salt and water, shifting them every third day; let the salt and water be strong enough to bear an egg; then put two pots of water on the fire; when the water is hot put in your walnuts; shift them out of one pot into the other, for the more clean water they have the better; when some of them begin to rise in the water they are enough; then pour them into a colander, and with a woollen cloth wipe them clean, and put them in the jar you keep them in; then boil as much vinegar as will cover them, with beaten pepper, cloves, mace, and nutmeg, just bruised, and put some cloves of garlic into the pot to them, with whole spice, and Jamaica pepper; when they are cold put into every half hundred of nuts three spoonfuls of mustard seed; tie a bladder over them and leather.

Another way to pickle Mushrooms

Scrape the buttons carefully with a penknife, and throw them into cold water, as you scrape them; and put them into fresh water, and set them close cover'd over a quick clear fire; blow under it, to make it boil as fast as possible half a quarter of an hour; strain them off, and turn the hollow end down upon a wooden board as quick as you can, whilst they remain hot, and then sprinkle them over with a little salt; when they are cold put them into bottles or glasses, with a little mace, and sliced ginger, and cover them with cold white-wine vinegar; tie bladders or leather over them.

To make Gooseberry Vinegar

Take gooseberries full ripe, bruise them in a mortar, then measure them, and to every quart of gooseberries put three quarts of water, first boiled, and let it stand till cold; let it stand twenty-four hours; then strain it thro' a canvas, then a flannel; and to every gallon of this liquor put one pound of brown sugar; stir it well, and barrel it up; at three quarters of a year old it is fit for use; but if it stands longer it is the better; this vinegar is likewise good for pickles.

To make the Mushroom Powder

Take the large mushrooms, wash them clean from grit, cut off the stalks, but do not peel or grill them; so put them into a kettle over the fire, but no water; put a good quantity of spice of all sorts, two onions stuck with cloves, a handful of salt, some beaten pepper, and a quarter of a pound of butter; let all these stew, till the liquor is dried up in them; then take them out, and lay them on sieves to dry, till they will beat to powder; press the powder hard down in a pot, and keep it for use, what quantity you please at a time, in sauce.

Another way to pickle Mushrooms

Take your mushrooms fresh gathered, peel or rub them, and put them in milk, with water and salt; when they are all peeled, take them out of that, and put them into fresh milk, water, and salt to boil, adding an onion stuck with cloves; when they have boiled a little, take them off, and take them out of that, and smother them between two flannels; then take as much good alegar as you think will cover them, and boil it with ginger, mace, nutmeg, and whole pepper; when it is cold, let it be put on your mushrooms, and cover them close.

To pickle Mussels or Cockles

Take your fresh mussels or cockles, wash them very clean, and put them in a pot over the fire till they open; then take them out of their shells, pick them clean, and lay them to cool; then put their liquor to some vinegar, whole pepper, ginger sliced thin, and mace, setting it over the fire; when it is scalding hot, put in your mussels, and let them stew a little; then pour out the pickle from them, and when both are cold put them in an earthen jug, and cork it up close; in two or three days they will be fit to eat.

To pickle Ox Palates

Take your palates and wash them well with salt in the water, and put them in a pipkin, with water and some salt, and when they are ready to boil scum them very well, and put into them whole pepper, cloves and mace, as much as will give them a quick taste: when they are boiled tender (which will require four or five hours) peel them and cut them into small pieces, and let them cool; then make the pickle of white-wine vinegar, and as much white wine; boil the pickle, and put in the spicE as was boil'd in the palates, adding a little fresh spice; put in six or seven bay-leaves, and let both pickle and palates be cold before you put them together; then keep them for use.

To make a Pickle for Tongues

Make your pickle with bay-salt, some saltpetre, coarse sugar, and spring-water; make it strong, boil and skim it, and when 'tis cold put in your tongues; turn them often; let them be three weeks, then dry them.

A Pickle for either Tongues or Hams.

Take what quantity of water you please, and with bay-salt and common salt make it strong enough to bear an egg; then to every gallon of this pickle add half a pound of petre-salt, a pound of coarse sugar, and two or three ounces of saltpetre beat fine; boil it and skim it, and when it is thorough cold put in your hams or tongues; turn them often; the hams may lie in pickle about a month, the tongues three weeks; then hang them up to dry.

To make hung Beef

To a pound of beef, put a pound of bay-salt, two ounces of saltpetre, and a pound of sugar mix'd with the common salt; let it lie six weeks in this brine, turning it every day, then dry it and boil it

To do the fine hanged Beef

The piece that is fit to do is the navel-piece, and let it hang in your cellar as long as you dare for stinking and till it begins to be a little sappy; take it down, and wash it in sugar and water; wash it with a clean rag very well, one piece after another, for you may cut that piece in three; then take sixpennyworth of saltpetre, and two pounds of bay-salt; dry it, and pound it small, and mix with it two or three spoonfuls of brown sugar, and rub your beef in every place very well with it; then take of common salt, and strew all over it as much as you think will make it salt enough; let it lie close, till the salt be dissolved, which will be in six or seven days; then turn it every other day, the undermost uppermost, and so for a fortnight; then hang it where it may have a little warmth of the fire; not too hot to roast it. It may hang in the kitchen a fortnight; when you use it, boil it in hay and pump-water, very tender; it will keep boiled two or three months, rubbing it with a greasy cloth, or putting it two or three minutes into boiling water to take off the mouldiness.

To distil Verjuice for pickles

Take three quarts of the sharpest verjuice, and put in a cold still, and distil it off very softly; the sooner it is distill'd in the spring, the better for use.

Another way to pickle Mushrooms

Take your mushrooms as soon as they come in; cut the stalks off, and throw your mushrooms into water and salt as you do them; then rub them with a piece of flannel, and as you do them, throw them into another vessel of salt and water, and when all is done, put some salt and water on the fire, and when 'tis scalding hot, put in your mushrooms, and let them stay in as long as you think will boil an egg; throw them into cold water as soon as they come off the fire; but first put them in a sieve, and let them drain from the hot water, and be sure to take them out of the hot water immediately, or they will wrinkle and look yellow. Let them stand in the cold water till next morning; then take them out, and put them into fresh water and salt, and change them every day for three or four days together; then wipe them very dry, and put them into distill'd vinegar: the spice must be distilled in the vinegar.

All Sorts of Puddings

To make an Orange Pudding

Take two large Seville oranges, and grate off the rind, as far as they are yellow; then put your oranges in fair-water, and let them boil till they are tender, shift the water three or four times to take out the bitterness; when they are tender cut them open, take away the seeds and strings, and beat the other part in a mortar, with half a pound of sugar, till 'tis a paste; then put in the yolks of six eggs, three or four spoonfuls of thick cream, half a Naples biscuit grated; mix these together, and melt a pound of very good fresh butter, and stir it well in; when 'tis cold, put a bit of fine puff paste about the brim and bottom of your dish; put it in and bake it about three quarters of an hour.

Another sort of Orange Pudding

Take the outside rind off three Seville oranges, boil them in several waters till they are tender; then pound them in a mortar with three quarters of a pound of sugar; then blanch and beat half a pound of almonds very fine, with rose-water to keep them from oiling; then beat sixteen eggs, but six whites, and a pound of fresh butter; beat all these together very well till it is light and hollow; then put it in a dish with a sheet of puff-paste at the bottom, and bake it with tarts; grate sugar on it, and serve it up hot.

To make a Carrot Pudding

Take raw carrots, scrape them clean, and grate them with a grater without a back. To half a pound of carrots, take a pound of grated bread, a nutmeg, a little cinnamon, a very little salt, half a pound of sugar, half a pint of sack, eight eggs, a pound of butter melted, and as much cream as will mix it well together; stir it and beat it well up, and put it in a dish to bake; put puff-paste at the bottom of your dish.

To make an Almond Pudding

Take a pound of the best Jordan almonds blanched in cold water, and beat very fine with a little rose-water; then take a quart of cream, boiled with whole spice, and taken out again, and when it is cold, mix it with the almonds, and put to it three spoonfuls of grated bread, one spoonful of flour, nine eggs, but three whites, half a pound of sugar, and a nutmeg grated; mix and beat these well together, put some puff-paste at the bottom of a dish; put your stuff in, and here and there stick a piece of marrow in it. It must bake an hour, and when it is drawn, grate sugar on it, and serve it up.

To make a Marrow Pudding

Take out the marrow of three or four bones, and slice it in thin pieces; and take a penny loaf, cut off the crust, and slice it in as thin slices as you can, and stone half a pound of raisins of the sun; then lay a sheet of thin paste in the bottom of a dish; so lay a row of marrow, or bread, and of raisins, till the dish is full; then have in readiness a quart of cream boiled, and beat five eggs, and mix with it; put to it nutmeg grated, and half a pound of sugar. When 'tis just going into the oven, pour in your cream and eggs; bake it half an hour, grate sugar on it when it is drawn, and serve it up.

A Bread-and-Butter Pudding for fasting-days

Take a twopenny loaf, and a pound of fresh butter; spread it in very thin slices, as to eat; cut them off as you spread them, and stone half a pound of raisins, and wash a pound of currants; then put puff-paste at the bottom of a dish, and lay a row of your bread and butter, and strew a handful of currants, a few raisins, and some little bits of butter, and so do till your dish is full; then boil three pints of cream and thicken it when cold with the yolks of ten eggs, a grated nutmeg, a little salt, near half a pound of sugar, and some orange flower-water; pour this in just as the pudding is going into the oven.

Another baked Bread Pudding

Take a penny loaf, cut it in thin slices, then boil a quart of cream or new milk, and put in your bread, and break it very fine; put five eggs to it, a nutmeg grated, a quarter of a pound of sugar, and half a pound of butter; stir all these well together; butter your dish, and bake it an hour.

A Lemon Pudding

Take two clear lemons, grate off the outside rinds; then grate two Naples biscuits, and mix with your grated peel, adding to it three quarters of a pound of fine sugar, twelve yolks and six whites of eggs, well beat, three quarters of a pound of butter melted, and half a pint of thick cream; mix these well together, put in a sheet of paste at the bottom of the dish, and just as the oven is ready put your stuff in the dish; sift a little double-refined sugar over it before you put it in the oven; an hour will bake it.

To make a Calf's-Foot-Pudding

Take two calf's-feet finely shred; then take of biscuits grated, and stale macaroons broken small, the quantity of a penny loaf; then add a pound of beef-suet, very finely shred, half a pound of currants, a quarter of a pound of sugar; some cloves, mace, and nutmeg, beat fine; a very little salt, some sack and orange-flower water, some citron and candied orange-peel; work all these well together with yolks of eggs; if you boil it, put it in the caul of a breast of veal, and tie it over with a cloth, it must boil four hours. For sauce, melt butter, with a little sack and sugar; if you bake it, put some paste in the bottom of the dish, but none on the brim, then melt half a pound of butter, which mix with your stuff, and put it in your dish, sticking lumps of marrow in it: bake it three or four hours; grate sugar over it, and serve it hot.

A Rice Pudding

Set a pint of thick cream over the fire, and put into it three spoonfuls of the flour of rice, stir it, and when 'tis pretty thick, pour it into a pan, adding to it a pound of fresh butter; stir it till 'tis almost cold; then add to it a grated nutmeg, a little salt, some sugar, a little sack, the yolks of six eggs; stir it well together; put some puff paste in the bottom of the dish, pour it in; an hour or less will bake it.

An Apple Pudding

Peel and quarter eight golden rennets, or twelve golden pippins; put them into water, in which boil them as you do apple-sauce; sweeten them with loaf sugar, squeeze in two lemons, and grate in their peels; break eight eggs, and beat them all well together; pour it into a dish covered with puff-paste, and bake it an hour in a slow oven.

To make an Oatmeal Pudding

Take three pints of thick cream, and three quarters of a pound of beef-suet shred very fine; when the cream boils, put into it the suet, a pound of butter, half a pound of sugar, a nutmeg grated, and a little salt; then thicken all with a pint of fine oatmeal; stir all together; pour it into a pan, and cover it up close till 'tis almost cold; then put in the yolks of six eggs; mix it all well together, and put a very thin paste at the bottom of the dish, and stick lumps of marrow in it; bake it two hours.

To make a French Barley Pudding

Take a quart of cream, and put to it six eggs well beaten, but three of the whites; then season it with sugar, nutmeg, a little salt, orange-flower water, and a pound of melted butter; then put to it six handfuls of French barley that has been boiled tender in milk. Butter a dish, and put it in, and bake it. It must stand as long as a venison-pasty, and it will be good.

A colouring liquor for Puddings

Beat an ounce of cochineal very fine, put it in a pint of water in a skillet, and a quarter of an ounce of roach alum, boil it till the goodness is out; strain it into a phial, with two ounces of fine sugar; it will keep six months.

A good boiled Pudding

Take a pound and a quarter of beef-suet, after it is skin'd, and shred very fine; then stone three quarters of a pound of raisins, and mix with it, as also a grated nutmeg, a quarter of a pound of sugar, a little salt, a little sack, four eggs, four spoonfuls of cream, and about half a pound of fine flour; mix these well together pretty stiff, tie it in a cloth, and let it boil four hours; melt butter thick for sauce.

Another Orange Pudding

Take half a pound of loaf sugar, beat half a pound of fresh butter, the yolks of six eggs beaten, half a candied orange cut as small as you can; melt the butter, and put in the sugar and eggs, stir it over the fire a pretty while, then put in your orange; keep it stirring over the fire till it be pretty thick, then take it off the fire, and let it stand till cold, then put it into a dish with puff-paste under and over it; half an hour will bake it; then make them into little pats like cheesecakes; it is good cold.

To make a Quaking Pudding

Take a pint of cream, and boil it with nutmeg, cinnamon and mace; take out the spice, when it is boiled; then take the yolks of eight eggs, and four of the whites, beat them very well with some sack; then mix your eggs and cream, with a little salt and sugar, and a stale halfpenny white-loaf, one spoonful of flour, and a quarter of a pound of almonds blanch'd and beat fine, with some rose-water; beat all these well together; then wet a thick cloth, flour it, and put it in when the pot boils; it must boil an hour at least; melt butter, sack and sugar for the sauce; stick blanch'd almonds and candied orange-peel on the top.

To make a Cow-Heel Pudding

Take a large cow-heel, and cut off all the meat but the black toes; put them away, but mince the rest very small, and shred it over again, with three quarters of a pound of beef-suet; put to it a penny loaf grated, cloves, mace, nutmeg, sugar, a little salt, some sack, and rose-water; mix these well together with six raw eggs well beaten; butter a cloth, put it in, and boil it two hours; for sauce, melt butter, sack and sugar.

To make a Curd Pudding

Take the curd of a gallon of milk, whey it well, and rub it thro' a sieve; then take six eggs, a little thick cream, three spoonfuls of orange-flower water, one nutmeg grated, bread and flour, of each three spoonfuls, a pound of currants and stoned raisins; mix all these together; butter a thick cloth, and tie it up in it; boil it an hour; for sauce, melt butter with orange-flower water and sugar.

To make a Pith Pudding

Take a quantity of the pith of an ox, and let it lie all night in water to soak out the blood; the next morning strip it out of the skins, and beat it with the back of a spoon in orange-flower water till it is as fine as pap; then take three blades of mace, a nutmeg quartered, a stick of cinnamon; then take half a pound of the best Jordan almonds, blanch'd in cold water, beat them with a little of the cream, and as they dry put in more cream, and when they are all beaten, strain the cream from them to the pith; then take the yolks of ten eggs, the whites of but two, beat them very well, and put them to the ingredients; then take a spoonful of grated bread, or Naples biscuit; mingle all these together, with half a pound of fine sugar, the marrow of four large bones, and a little salt; fill them in small ox or hog's guts, or bake it with puff-crust.

A Rice Pudding

Take two large handfuls of rice well beaten and sieved; then take two quarts of milk or cream, set it over the fire with the rice, put in cinnamon and mace, let it boil a quarter of an hour; it must be as thick as hasty pudding; then stir in half a pound of butter while it is over the fire; then take it off to cool, and put in sugar, and a little salt; when it is almost cold put in ten or twelve eggs, take out four of the whites; butter the dish; an hour will bake it; sift sugar over it.

Butter'd Crumbs

Put a piece of butter into a saucepan, and let it run to oil; then skim it clean, and pour it off from the settlement; to this clear oil put grated crumbs of bread, and keep them stirring till they are crisp.

Orange-Custard or Pudding

Take Seville oranges, and rub the outside with a little salt very well, pare them, and take half a pound of the peel, and lay them in several waters till the bitterness is abated; beat them small in a stone or wooden mortar, then put in ten yolks of eggs and a quart of thick cream, mix them well, and sweeten them to your taste; melt half a pound of butter and stir it well in, if you design it for a pudding, and pour it into a dish covered with paste; if for custards, leave out the butter, and pour it into China cups, and bake it to eat cold.

A Pudding for little dishes

Take a pint of cream, boil it, and slice a halfpenny loaf, and pour your cream over it hot, and cover it close till it is cold; then put in half a nutmeg grated, a quarter of a pound of sugar, the yolks of four eggs, the whites of but two; butter your dish and put it in, and let it boil an hour; melt butter, sack and sugar for sauce.

A Hasty Pudding to butter itself

Set a quart of thick cream upon the fire, put into it the crumb of a penny white loaf grated, boil it pretty thick together, with often stirring it; a little before you take it up, put in the yolks of four eggs, with a spoonful of sack, or orange-flower water and some sugar; boil it very flow, keeping it stirring; some make it with grated Naples biscuit and put no eggs in; you may know when it is enough by an oil round the edge of the skillet, and soon all over it; then pour it out; it will require half an hour or more before it is enough; some put a few almonds blanched, and beat very fine, with a spoonful of wine, to keep them from oiling.

Another Hasty Pudding

Break an egg into fine flour, and with your hand work it up as much as you can into as stiff a paste as possible; then mince it as small as if it were to be sifted; then set a quart of milk a-boiling, and put in your paste, so cut as before mentioned; put in a little salt, some beaten cinnamon and sugar, a piece of butter as big as a walnut, and keep it stirring all one way, till it is as thick as you would have it; and then stir in such another piece of butter; and when it is in the dish stick it all over with little bits of butter.

To make Stew'd Pudding

Grate a twopenny loaf, and mix it with half a pound of beef-suet finely shred, and three quarters of a pound of currants, and a quarter of a pound of sugar, a little cloves, mace, and nutmeg; then beat five or six eggs, with three or four spoonfuls of rose-water, beat all together, and make them up in little round balls the bigness of an egg, some round and some long, in the fashion of an egg; then put a pound of butter in a pewter dish, when it is melted and thorough hot, put in your puddings, and let them stew till they are brown; turn them, and when they are enough, serve them up with sack, butter, and sugar for sauce.

To make a Cabbage Pudding

Take two pounds of the lean part of a leg of veal, of beef-suet the like quantity, chop them together, then beat them together in a stone mortar, adding to it half a little cabbage scalded, and beat that with your meat; then season it with mace and nutmeg, a little pepper and salt, some green gooseberries, grapes, or barberries in the time of the year; in the winter put in a little verjuice, then mix all well together, with the yolks of four or five eggs, well beaten; wrap it up in green cabbage leaves, tie a cloth over it, boil it an hour; melt butter for sauce.

A Venison Pasty

Bone your venison, take out the gristles, skin and films; to a side of doe venison three ounces of salt, and three quarters of an ounce of pepper: or to seven pounds of lean venison, without the bones, put in two ounces and a half of salt, and half an ounce of pepper.

Very fine Hog's Puddings

Shred four pounds of beef-suet very fine, mix with it two pounds of fine sugar powder'd, two grated nutmegs, some mace beat, a little salt, and three pounds of currants wash'd and pick'd; beat twenty-four yolks, twelve whites of eggs, with a little sack; mix all well together, and fill your guts, being clean and steep'd in orange-flower water; cut your guts quarter and half long, fill them half full; tie at each end, and at intervals along their length; boil them as others, and cut them in balls when sent to the table.

To make Almond Hog's Puddings

Take two pounds of beef-suet, or marrow shred very small, a pound and a half of almonds blanched and beaten very small with rose-water, one pound of grated bread, a pound and a quarter of fine sugar, a little salt, one ounce of mace, nutmeg and cinnamon, twelve yolks of eggs, four whites, a pint of sack, a pint and a half of thick cream, some rose- or orange-flower water; boil the cream; tie a little saffron in a rag, and dip it in the cream, to colour it; first beat your eggs very well, then stir in your almonds, then the spice, salt, and suet; then mix all your ingredients together; fill your guts but half full, put some bits of citron in the guts as you fill them; tie them up, and boil them about a quarter of an hour.

To make Hog's Puddings with Currants

Take three pounds of grated bread to four pounds of beef-suet finely shred, two pounds of currants, cloves, mace, and cinnamon, of each half an ounce beaten fine, a little salt, a pound and a half of sugar, a pint of sack, a quart of cream, a little rose-water, twenty eggs well beaten, but half the whites; mix all these well together, and fill the guts half full; boil them a little, and prick them as they boil, to keep them from breaking the guts; take them up on clean cloths.

Another Sort of Hog's Puddings

To half a pound of grated bread put half a pound of hog's liver, boil'd, cold and grated, a pound and a half of suet finely shred, a handful of salt, a handful of sweet herbs, chopped small, some spice; mix all these together, with six eggs well beaten, and a little thick cream; fill your guts and boil them; when cold, cut them in round slices an inch thick; fry them in butter, and garnish your dish of fowls, hash, or fricassee.

To make black Hog's Puddings

Boil all the hog's harslet in about four or five gallons of water till it is very tender, then take out all the meat, and in that liquor steep near a peck of groats; put in the groats as it boils, and let them boil a quarter of an hour; then take the pot off the fire, and cover it up very close, and let it stand five or six hours; chop two or three handfuls of thyme, a little savory, some parsley, and pennyroyal, some cloves and mace beaten, a handful of salt; mix all these with half the groats and two quarts of blood; put in most part of the leaf of the hog; cut it in square bits like dice, and some in long bits; fill your guts, and put in the fat as you like it; fill the guts three quarters full, put your puddings into a kettle of boiling water, let them boil an hour, and prick them with a pin, to keep them from breaking; lay them on clean straw when you take them up.

The other half of the groats you may make into white puddings for the family; chop all the meat very small, and shred two handfuls of sage very fine, an ounce of cloves and mace finely beaten, and some salt; work all together very well with a little flour, and put into the large guts; boil them about an hour, and keep them and the black near the fire till used.

To make Rice Pancakes

Take a quart of cream and three spoonfuls of the flour of rice, boil it till it is as thick as pap, and as it boils stir in half a pound of butter, a nutmeg grated; then pour it out into an earthen pan, and when it is cold put in three or four spoonfuls of flour, a little salt, some sugar, nine eggs well beaten; mix all well together, and fry them in a little pan, with a small piece of butter; serve them up four or five in a dish.

To make a Chestnut Pudding

Take a dozen and half of chestnuts, put them in a skillet of water, and set them on the fire till they will blanch; then blanch them, and when cold put them in cold water, then stamp them in a mortar, with orange-flower water and sack till they are very small; mix them in two quarts of cream, and eighteen yolks of eggs, the whites of three or four; beat the eggs with sack, rose-water, and sugar, put it in a dish with puff-paste; stick in some lumps of marrow or fresh butter, and bake it.

To make a brown Bread Pudding

Take half a pound of brown bread, and double the weight of it in beef-suet, a quarter of a pint of cream, the blood of a fowl, a whole nutmeg, some cinnamon, a spoonful of sugar, six yolks of eggs, three whites; mix it all well together, and boil it in a wooden dish two hours; serve it with sack and sugar, and butter melted.

To make a baked Sack Pudding

Take a pint of cream, and turn it to a curd with sack; bruise the curd very small with a spoon, and grate in two Naples biscuits, or the inside of a stale penny loaf, mix it well with the curd, and half a nutmeg grated, some fine sugar, and the yolks of four eggs, the whites of two, beaten with two spoonfuls of sack; then melt half a pound of fresh butter, and stir all together till the oven is hot; butter a dish, put it in, and sift some sugar over it just as it is going into the oven; half an hour will bake it.

To make a Marjoram Pudding

Take the curd of a quart of milk finely broken, a good handful or more of sweet-marjoram chopped as small as dust, and mingle with the curd five eggs, but three whites, beaten with rose-water, some nutmeg and sugar, and half a pint of cream; beat all these well together, and put in three quarters of a pound of melted butter; put a thin sheet of paste at the bottom of your dish, then pour in your pudding, and with a spur cut out little strips of paste the breadth of a little finger, and lay them over cross and cross in large diamonds; put some small bits of butter on the top, and bake it. This is old fashioned, and not good.

To make Pancakes

Take a pint of cream, and eight eggs, whites and all, a whole nutmeg grated, and a little salt; then melt a pound of rare dish butter, and a little sack; before you fry them, stir it in: it must be made as thick with three spoonfuls of flour as ordinary batter, and fried with butter in the pan, the first pancake, but no more: strew sugar, garnish with orange, turn it on the back side of a plate.

To make a Tansy to bake

Take twenty eggs, but eight whites, beat the eggs very well, and strain them into a quart of thick cream, one nutmeg, three Naples biscuits grated, and as much juice of spinach, with a sprig or two of tansy, as will make it as green as grass; sweeten it to your taste; then butter your dish very well, and set it into an oven, no hotter than for custards; watch it, and as soon as it is done, take it out of the oven, and turn it on a pie-plate; scrape sugar, and squeeze orange upon it. Garnish the dish with orange and lemon, and serve up.

To make a Gooseberry Tansy

Put some fresh butter in a frying-pan; when it is melted put into it a quart of gooseberries, fry them till they are tender, and break them all to mash; then beat seven eggs, but four whites, a pound of sugar, three spoonfuls of sack, as much cream, a penny loaf grated, and three spoonfuls of flour; mix all these together, then put the gooseberries out of the pan to them, and stir all well together, and put them into a saucepan to thicken; then put butter into the frying-pan, and fry them brown; strew sugar on the top.

To make Curd Fritters

Take a handful of curds, a handful of flour, ten eggs well beaten and strained, some sugar, some cloves, mace, nutmeg, and a little saffron; stir all well together, and fry them in very hot beef-dripping; drop them in the pan by spoonfuls; stir them about till they are of a fine yellow brown; drain them from the suet, and scrape sugar on them when you serve them up.

To make fried Toasts

Chip a manchet very well, and cut it round-ways into toasts; then take cream and eight eggs, season'd with sack, sugar, and nutmeg, and let these toasts steep in it about an hour; then fry them in sweet butter; serve them up with plain melted butter, or with butter, sack and sugar, as you please.

To make Parsnip Fritters

Boil your parsnips very tender, peel them and beat them in a mortar; rub them through a hair sieve, and mix a good handful of them with some fine flour, six eggs, some cream, and new milk, salt, sugar, a little nutmeg, a small quantity of sack and rose-water; mix all well together a little thicker than pancake batter; have a frying-pan ready with a good store of hog's lard very hot over the fire, and put in a spoonful in a place, till the pan be so full as you can fry them conveniently; fry them a light brown on both sides. For sauce, take sack and sugar, with a little rose-water or verjuice; strew sugar on them when in the dish.

To make Apple Fritters

Take the yolks of eight eggs, the whites of four, beat them well together, and strain them into a pan; then take a quart of cream, warm it as hot as you can endure your finger in it; then put to it a quarter of a pint of sack, three quarters of a pint of ale, and make a posset of it; when your posset is cool, put to it your eggs, beating them well together; then put in the nutmeg, ginger, salt, and flour to your liking; your batter should be pretty thick; then put in pippins sliced or grated; fry them in a good store of hot lard with a quick fire.

To make an Apple Tansy

Take three pippins, slice them round in thin slices, and fry them with butter; then beat four eggs, with six spoonfuls of cream, a little rose-water, nutmeg, and sugar; stir them together, and pour it over the apples; let it fry a little, and turn it with a pie-plate. Garnish with lemon and sugar strew'd over it.

To make a Lemon Tart

Take three clear lemons, and grate off the outside rinds; take the yolks of twelve eggs, and six whites; beat them very well, squeeze in the juice of a lemon; then put in three quarters of a pound of fine powdered sugar, and three quarters of a pound of fresh butter melted; stir all well together, put a sheet of paste at the bottom, and sift sugar on the top; put it in a brisk oven, three quarters of an hour will bake it; so serve it to the table.

A Rye-bread Pudding

Take half a pound of sour rye-bread grated, half a pound of beef-suet finely shred, half a pound of currants clean washed, half a pound of sugar, a whole nutmeg grated; mix all well together, with five or six eggs; butter a dish, boil it an hour and a quarter, and serve it up with melted butter.

A baked Pudding

Blanch half a pound of almonds, and beat them fine with sweet water, ambergris dissolv'd in orange-flower water, or in some cream; then warm a pint of thick cream; and melt in it half a pound of butter, then mix it with your beaten almonds, a little salt, a grated nutmeg, and sugar, and the yolks of six eggs; beat it up together, and put it in a dish with puff-paste, the oven not too hot; scrape sugar on it just before it goes into the oven.

To make a Custard Pudding

Take a pint of cream, and mix with it six eggs well beat, two spoonfuls of flour, half a nutmeg grated, a little salt, and sugar to your taste; butter a cloth, put it in when the pot boils; boil it just half an hour; melt butter for sauce.

Boil'd Custards

Take a pint of cream, and put into it two ounces of almonds, blanch'd and beaten very fine with rose- or orange-flower water, or a little cream; let them boil till the cream is a little thickened, then sweeten your eggs, and keep it stirring over the fire till it is as thick as you would have it; then put into it a little orange-flower water, stir it well together, and put it into China cups.

Note You may make them without almonds.

Rice Custards

Take a quart of cream, and boil it with a blade of mace, and a quarter'd nutmeg; put into it boiled rice, well beat with your cream; mix them together, and stir them all the while it boils on the fire; when 'tis enough take it off, and sweeten to your taste; put in a little orange-flower water and pour it in your dishes; when cold serve it.

To make Almond Tort

Blanch and beat half a pound of Jordan almonds very fine; use orange-flower water in the beating your almonds; pare the yellow rind of a lemon pretty thick; boil it in water till 'tis very tender, beat it with half a pound of sugar, and mix it with the almonds, and eight eggs, but four whites, half a pound of butter melted, almost cold, and a little thick cream; mix all together, and bake it, in a dish with paste at bottom. This may be made the day before 'tis used.

To make Hasty Puddings, to boil in custard dishes

Take a large pint of milk, put to it four spoonfuls of flour; mix it well together, set it over the fire, and boil it into a smooth hasty pudding; sweeten it to your taste, grate nutmeg in it, and when 'tis almost cold, beat five eggs very well, and stir into it; then butter your custard-cups, put in your stuff, and tie them over with a cloth, put them in the pot when the water boils, and let them boil something more than half an hour; pour on them melted butter.

To make a Sweetmeat Pudding

Put a thin puff paste at the bottom of your dish, then have of candied orange, lemon, and citron peel, of each an ounce; slice them thin, and put them in the bottom on your paste; then beat eight yolks of eggs, and two whites, near half a pound of sugar, and half a pound of butter melted; mix and beat all well together, and when the oven is ready, pour it on your sweetmeats in the dish. An hour or less will bake it.

To make Carrot or Parsnip Puffs

Scrape and boil your carrots and parsnips tender; then scrape or mash them very fine, add to it a pint of pulp, the crumb of a penny loaf grated, or some stale biscuit, if you have it, some eggs, but four whites, a nutmeg grated, some orange-flower water, sugar to your taste, a little sack, and mix it up with thick cream; they must be fried in rendered suet, the liquor very hot when you put them in: put in a good spoonful in a place.

To make New College Puddings

Grate a penny stale loaf, put to it a like quantity of beef-suet finely shred, a nutmeg grated, a little salt, and some currants; then beat some eggs in a little sack, and some sugar; mix all together, knead it as stiff as for manchet, and make it up in the form and size of a turkey egg, but a little flatter; then take a pound of butter, put it in a dish, set the dish over a clear fire in a chafing dish, and rub your butter about the dish till 'tis melted; put your puddings in, and cover the dish, but often turn your puddings, until they are all brown alike, and when they are enough, scrape sugar over them, and serve them up hot for a side-dish.

You must let the paste lie a quarter of an hour before you make up your puddings.

To make an Oatmeal Pudding

Take a pint of great oatmeal, beat it very small, then sift it fine; take a quart of cream, boil it and your oatmeal together, stirring it all the while until 'tis pretty thick; then put it in a dish, cover it close, and let it stand a little; then put into it a pound and half of fresh butter, and let it stand two hours before you stir it; put to it twelve eggs, a nutmeg grated, a little salt, sweeten it to your taste; a little sack, or orange-flower water; stir all very well together, put paste at the bottom of your dish, and put in your pudding-stuff, the oven not too hot; an hour will bake it.

To make fine Fritters

Take half a pint of thick sweet cream, put to it four eggs well beaten, a little brandy, some nutmeg and ginger; make this into a thick batter with flour; your apples must be golden pippins pared and cut in thin slices; dip them in batter, and fry them in lard. It will take up two pounds of lard to fry this quantity.

To make a Marrow Pudding

Take a quart of cream, and three Naples biscuits grated, a nutmeg grated, the yolks of ten eggs, the whites of five well beaten, and sugar to your taste; mix all well together, and put a little bit of butter in the bottom of your saucepan; then put in your stuff, and set it over the fire, and stir it till it is pretty thick; then put it into your pan, with a quarter of a pound of currants that have been plump'd in hot water; stir it together, and let it stand all night. The next day put some fine paste rolled very thin at the bottom of your dish, and when the oven is ready, pour in your stuff, and on the top lay large pieces of marrow. Half an hour will bake it.

Another Lemon Pudding

Grate the peels of three large lemons, only the yellow, then take two lemons more, and the three you have grated, and roll them under your hand on a table till they are very soft; but be careful not to break them; then cut and squeeze them, and strain the juice from the seeds to the grated peels; then grate the crumb of three halfpenny loaves (or ten ounces of the crumb of white loaves) into a basin, make a pint of white wine scalding hot, pour it to your bread, and stir it well together to soak, then put to it the grated peel and juice; beat the yolks of eight eggs and four whites together, and mingle with the rest three quarters of a pound of butter that is fresh and melted, and almost a pound of white sugar; beat it well together till it be thoroughly mixed, then lay a sheet of puff-paste at the bottom and brim, cutting it into what form you please; the paste that is left roll out, and with a jagging iron cut them out in little stripes, neither so broad or long as your little finger, and bake them on a floured paper; let the pudding bake almost an hour, when it comes out of the oven stick the pieces of paste on the top of it to serve it to table. It eats well either hot or cold.

The Ipswich Almond Pudding

Steep somewhat above three ounces of the crumb of white bread sliced in a pint and a half of cream, or grate the bread; then beat half a pound of blanched almonds very fine, till they do not glister, with a small quantity of perfumed water; beat up the yolks of eight eggs and the whites of four; mix all well together, put in a quarter of a pound of white sugar, then set it into the oven, but stir in a little melted butter before you set it in; let it bake but half an hour.

Oatmeal Pudding

A wine pint of oatmeal pick'd from the blacks, a pint and a quarter of milk warmed; let it steep one night; three quarters of a pound of beef-suet shred, one nutmeg, three spoonfuls of sugar, a small handful of flour, four eggs, and salt to your taste; make two puddings, and boil them three hours; if the oatmeal be too large, beat it, and if you make it into but one pudding, boil it four hours.

To make a fine Bread Pudding

Take three pints of milk and boil it; when it is boiled, sweeten it with half a pound of sugar, a small nutmeg grated, and put in half a pound of butter; when it is melted, pour it in a pan over eleven ounces of grated bread and cover it up; the next day put to it ten eggs well beaten, stir all together, and when the oven is hot, put it in your dish, three quarters of an hour will bake it; boil a bit of lemon-peel in the milk, take it out before you put your other things in.

To make a Spread-Eagle Pudding

Cut off the crust of three halfpenny rolls, and slice them into your pan; then set three pints of milk over the fire, make it scalding hot, but do not boil it, put it over your bread, cover it close, and let it stand an hour; then put in a good spoonful of sugar, a very little salt, a nutmeg grated, a pound of suet after it is shred, half a pound of currants wash'd and pick'd, four spoonfuls of cold milk, ten eggs, but five of the whites, and when all is in stir it, but not till all is in; then mix it well and butter a dish; less than an hour will bake it.

To make a very fine Plain Pudding

Take a quart of milk, and put six laurel leaves into it; when it has boil'd a little, take out your leaves, and with fine flour make that milk into hasty pudding, pretty thick; then stir in half a pound of butter, a quarter of a pound of sugar, a small nutmeg grated, twelve yolks, six whites of eggs well beaten; mix and stir all well together, butter a dish, and put in your stuff; a little more than half an hour will bake it.

A fine Rice Pudding

Take of the flour of rice six ounces, put it in a quart of milk and let it boil till it is pretty thick, stirring it all the while; then pour it into a pan, and stir in it half a pound of fresh butter, and a quarter of a pound of sugar, or sweeten it to your taste; when it is cold grate in a nutmeg, and beat six eggs, with a spoonful or two of sack, and beat and stir all well together; put a little fine paste at the bottom of your dish, and bake it.

To make a Ratafia Pudding

Take a quart of cream, boil it with four or five laurel leaves; then take them out, and break in half a pound of Naples biscuit, half a pound of butter, some sack, nutmeg, and salt; take it off the fire, cover it up; when it is almost cold put in two ounces of almonds blanched, and beaten fine, with the yolks of five eggs; mix all well together, and bake it in a moderate oven half an hour; scrape sugar on it as it goes into the oven.

Vermicelli Pudding

Boil five ounces of vermicelli in a quart of milk till it is tender, with a blade of mace, and a rind of lemon or Seville orange; sweeten it to your taste and add the yolks of six eggs, and four whites; have a dish ready cover'd with paste, and just before you set it into the oven, stir in half a pound of melted butter; a very little salt does well; if you have no peels, put in a little orange-flower water.

All Sorts of Pastry

To make a Tureiner

Take a china pot or bowl, and fill it as follows: at the bottom lay some fresh butter, then put in three or four beef-steaks larded with bacon; then cut some veal-steaks from the leg, hack them, and wash them over with the yolk of an egg; and afterwards lay it over with forc'd-meat, and roll it up, and lay it in with young chickens, pigeons and rabbits, some in quarters, some in halves; sweetbreads, lamb-stones, cockscombs; palates after they are boiled, peeled and cut in slices; tongues, either hog's or calf's, slic'd, and some larded with bacon; whole yolks of hard eggs, pistachio nuts peel'd, forc'd balls, some round, some like an olive, lemon sliced, some with the rind on, barberries and oysters; season all these with pepper, salt, nutmeg, and sweet herbs, mix'd together after they are cut very small, and strew it on everything as you put in your pot; then put in a quart of gravy, and some butter on the top; cover it close with a lid of puff-paste pretty thick; eight hours will bake it.

A Caudle for sweet Pies

Take sack and white wine alike in quantity, a little verjuice and sugar, boil it, and brew it with two or three eggs, as butter'd ale; when the pies are baked, pour it in with a funnel, and shake it together.

A Lear for savoury Pies

Take claret, gravy, oyster-liquor, two or three anchovies, a faggot of sweet herbs and an onion; boil it up and thicken it with brown butter, then pour it into your savoury pies when called for.

A Lamb Pie

Cut a hind quarter of lamb into thin slices, season it with sweet spices, and lay it in the pie, mix'd with half a pound of raisins of the sun, stoned, half a pound of currants, and two or three Spanish potatoes, boil'd, blanched, and sliced; or an artichoke bottom or two, with prunellas, damsons, and gooseberries; and close the pie; when 'tis baked make a caudle for it.

A Chicken Pie

Take six small chickens; roll up a piece of butter in sweet spice, and put it into them; then season them, and lay them in the pie, with the marrow of two bones, with fruit and preserves, and, as the lamb pie, with a caudle.

A Lumber Pie

Take a pound and a half of fillet of veal, and mince it with the same quantity of beef suet; season it with sweet spice, five pippins, an handful of spinach, and a hard lettuce, thyme and parsley; mix it with a penny white loaf grated, the yolks of eggs, sack and orange-flower water, a pound and a half of currants and preserves, and, as the lamb pie, with a caudle. An umble pie is made the same way.

A Lamb Pie

Cut a hind quarter of lamb into thin slices; season it with savoury spice, and lay them in the pie with a hard lettuce, artichoke bottoms and the tops of an hundred of asparagus: lay on butter, and close the pie. When it is baked, pour into it a lear.

A Mutton Pie

Season your mutton-steaks with savoury spice; fill the pie, lay on the butter, and close the pie: when it is baked, toss up a handful of chop'd capers, cucumbers and oysters, in gravy, anchovy, and drawn butter.

A Pigeon Pie

Truss and season your pigeons with savoury spice, lard them with bacon, stuff them with forc'd-meat, and lay them in the pie with the ingredients for savoury pies, with butter, and close the pie. When it is baked, pour into it a lear. A chicken or capon pie is made the same way.

A Battalia Pie

Take four small chickens, four squab pigeons, four sucking rabbits: cut them in pieces, season them with savoury spice, and lay them in the pie, with four sweetbreads sliced, and as many sheep's-tongues, two shiver'd palates, two pair of lamb-stones, twenty or thirty cockscombs, with savoury balls and oysters. Lay on butter, and close the pie. When it is baked, pour into it a lear.

A Neats'-Tongue Pie

Half boil the tongues, blanch and slice them; season them with savoury spice, with balls, sliced lemon and butter, and close the pie. When it is baked pour into it a ragout.

A Veal Pie

Raise an high pie, then cut a fillet of veal into three or four slices, season it with savoury spice, a little minced sage and sweet herbs; lay it in the pie, with slices of bacon at the bottom, and betwixt each piece lay on butter, and close the pie.

A Turkey Pie

Bone the turkey, season it with savoury spice and lay it in the pie with two capons, or two wild-ducks cut in pieces to fill up the corners; lay on butter, and close the pie.

A Florendine of a Kidney of Veal

Shred the kidney, fat and all, with a little spinach, parsley and lettuce, three pippins and orange-peel; season it with sweet-spice, sugar, a good handful of currants, two or three grated biscuits, sack, orange-flower-water, and two or three eggs; mix it into a body, and put it into a dish, being cover'd with puff-paste; lay on a cut-lid, and garnish the brim.

Another Battalia Pie or Bride Pie

Take young chickens as big as blackbirds, quails, young partridges, larks, and squab-pigeons, truss them, and put them in your pie; then have ox-palates boiled, blanched, and cut in pieces, lamb-stones, sweetbreads, cut in halves or quarters, cockscombs blanched, a quart of oysters dipped in eggs, and dredged over with grated bread and marrow; sheep's-tongues boiled, peeled, and cut in slices; season all with salt, pepper, cloves, mace, and nutmegs, beaten and mix'd together; put butter at the bottom of the pie, and place the rest in with the yolks of hard eggs, knots of eggs, forc'd-meat balls; cover all with butter, and close up the pie; put in five or six spoonfuls of water when it goes into the oven, and when it is drawn pour it out and put in gravy.

To make an Oyster Pie

Make good puff-paste, and lay a thin sheet in the bottom of your pattipan; then take two quarts of large oysters, wash them well in their own liquor, take them out of it, dry them, and season them with salt, spice, and a little pepper, all beaten fine; lay some butter in the bottom of your pattipan, then lay in your oysters and the yolks of twelve hard eggs whole, two or three sweetbreads cut in slices, or lamb-stones, or for want of these a dozen of larks, two marrowbones, the marrow taken out in lumps, dipped in the yolks of eggs, and seasoned as you did your oysters, with some grated bread dusted on it, and a few forc'd-meat balls; when all these are in put some butter on the top, and cover it over with a sheet of puff-paste, and bake it; when it is drawn out of the oven, take the liquor of the oysters, boil it, skim it, and beat it up thick with butter, and the yolks of two or three eggs; pour it hot into your pie, shake it well together, and serve it hot.

To make a Salmon Pie

Make a good puff-paste, and lay it in your pattipan, then take the middle piece of salmon, season it pretty high with pepper, salt, cloves and mace, cut it in three pieces, then lay a layer of butter and a layer of salmon, till all is in; make forc'd-meat balls of an eel, chop it fine with the yolks of hard eggs, two or three anchovies, marrow (or, if for a fasting-day, butter), sweet herbs, some grated bread, and a few oysters and grated nutmeg, some small pepper, and a little salt; make it up with raw eggs into balls, some long, some round, and lay them about your salmon; put butter over all, and lid your pie; an hour will bake it.

To make Egg Pies

Take the yolks of two dozen of eggs boiled hard, and chopped with double the quantity of beef-suet, and half a pound of pippins pared, cored, and sliced; then add to it one pound of currants wash'd and dried, half a pound of sugar, a little salt, some spice beaten fine, the juice of a lemon, and half a pint of sack, candied orange and citron cut in pieces, of each three ounces, some lumps of marrow on the top, fill them full; the oven must not be too hot; three quarters of an hour will bake them; put the marrow only on them that are to be eaten hot.

To make a Sweetbread Pasty to fry or bake

Parboil your sweetbreads, and shred them very fine, with an equal quantity of marrow; mix with them a little grated bread, some nutmeg, salt, the yolks of two hard eggs, bruised small, and sugar; then mix up with a little cream and the yolk of an egg: make paste with half a pound of the finest flour, an ounce of double-refined sugar, beat and sifted, the yolks of two eggs, and white of one, and fair-water; then roll in half a pound of butter, and roll it out in little pasties the breadth of your hand; put your meat in, close them up well, and fry or bake them; a very pretty side-dish.

To make a Lumber Pie

Take a pound and a half of veal, parboil it, and when it is cold chop it very small, with two pounds of beef-suet, and some candied orange-peel, some sweet herbs, as thyme and sweet-marjoram, and an handful of spinach; mince the herbs small before you put them to the other; chop all together, and a pippin or two, then add a handful or two of grated bread, a pound and half of currants wash'd and dried, some cloves, mace, nutmeg, a little salt, sugar and sack, adding to all these as many yolks of raw eggs, and whites of two, as will make it a moist forc'd-meat; work it with your hands into a body, and make it into balls as big as a turkey's egg, then having your coffin made, put in your balls; take the marrow out of three or four bones as whole as you can; let your marrow lie a little in water, to take out the blood and splinters; then dry it, and dip it in yolks of eggs; season it with a little salt, nutmeg grated, and grated bread; lay it on and between your forc'd-meat balls, and over that sliced citron, candied orange and lemon, eringo-roots, and preserved barberries; then lay on sliced lemon, and thin slices of butter over all; then lid your pie, and bake it; and when it is drawn, have in readiness a caudle made of white wine and sugar, and thickened with butter and eggs, and pour it hot into your pie.

To make little Pasties to fry

Take the kidney of a loin of veal or lamb, fat and all, shred it very small, season it with a little salt, cloves, mace, nutmeg, all beaten small, some sugar, and the yolks of two or three hard eggs minc'd very fine; mix all these together with a little sack or cream; put them in puff-paste and fry them; serve them hot.

To make Custards

Take two quarts of thick sweet cream, boil it with some bits of cinnamon, and a quartered nutmeg, keep it stirring all the while, and when it has boil'd a little time, pour it into a pan to cool, and stir it till it is cool, to keep it from creaming; then beat the yolks of sixteen eggs, the whites of but six, and mix your eggs with the cream when it is cool, and sweeten it with fine sugar to your taste, put in a very little salt, and some rose- or orange-flower water; then strain all thro' a hair sieve, and fill your cups or crust; it must be a pretty quick oven; when they boil up they are enough.

To make Cheesecakes

Take a pint of cream and warm it, and put to it five quarts of milk warm from the cow, then put rennet to it, and when it is come, put the curd in a linen bag or cloth, and let it drain well from the whey, but do not squeeze it much; then put it in a mortar, and break the curd as fine as butter; then put to your curd half a pound of almonds blanched, and beaten exceeding fine (or half a pound of dry macaroons beat very fine); if you have almonds, grate in a Naples biscuit, but if you use macaroons, you need not; then add to it the yolks of nine eggs beaten, a whole nutmeg grated, two perfumed plums dissolved in rose- or orange-flower water, half a pound of fine sugar; mix all well together; then melt a pound and a quarter of butter, and stir it well in, and half a pound of currants plump'd; let it stand to cool till you use it. Then make your puff-paste thus: take a pound of fine flour, and wet it with cold water, roll it out, and put into it by degrees a pound of fresh butter; use it just as it is made.

Another way to make Cheesecakes

Take a gallon of new milk, set it as for a cheese, and gently whey it; then break it in a mortar, sweeten it to your taste; put in a grated nutmeg, some rose-water and sack; mix these together, and set it over the fire with a quart of cream and make it into a hasty pudding; fill your pattipans just as they are going into the oven; your oven must be ready, that you may not stay for that; when they rise well up they are enough. Make your paste thus: take about a pound of flour, and strew into it three spoonfuls of loaf sugar beaten and sifted, and rub into it a pound of butter, one egg, and a spoonful of rose-water, the rest cold fair-water; make it into a paste, roll it very thin, and put it into your pans, and fill them almost full.

Paste for Pasties

Rub six pounds of butter into fourteen pounds of flour, put to it eight eggs, whip the whites to snow, and make it into a pretty stiff paste with cold water.

To make Cheesecakes without Rennet

Take a quart of thick cream, and set it over a clear fire, with some quarter'd nutmeg in it; just as it boils up, put in twelve eggs well beaten, and a quarter of a pound of fresh butter; stir it a little while on the fire, till it begins to curdle; then take it off, and gather the curd as for cheese; put it in a clean cloth, tie it together, and hang it up, that the whey may run from it; when it is pretty dry, put it in a stone mortar, with a pound of butter, a quarter of a pint of thick cream, some sack, orange-flower water, and half a pound of fine sugar; then beat and grind all these very well together for an hour or more, till it is very fine; then pass it thro' a hair sieve, and fill your pattipans but half full; you may put currants in half the quantity if you please; a little more than a quarter of an hour will bake them; take the nutmeg out of the cream when it is boiled.

To make Orange or Lemon Tarts

Take six large lemons, and rub them very well with salt, and put them in water for two days, with a handful of salt in it; then change them into fresh water without salt every other day for a fortnight; then boil them for two or three hours till they are tender; then cut them in half quarters, and then slice them as thin as you can; then take pippins pared, cored and quartered, and a pint of fair-water, let them boil till the pippins break; put the liquor to your orange or lemon, half the pippins well broken, and a pound of sugar; boil these together a quarter of an hour; then put it in a gallipot, and squeeze an orange in it if it be lemon, or a lemon if it is orange; two spoonfuls are enough for a tart; your pattipans must be small and shallow; put fine puff-paste, and very thin; a little while will bake it. Just as your tarts are going into the oven, with a feather or brush do them over with melted butter, and then sift double-refin'd sugar on them, and this is a pretty icing on them.

To make Puff-Paste for Tarts

Rub a quarter of a pound of butter into a pound of fine flour; then whip the whites of two eggs to snow, and with cold water and one yolk make it into a paste; then roll it abroad, and put in by degrees a pound of butter, flouring it over the butter every time; roll it up, and roll it out again, and put in more butter; so do for six or seven times, till it has taken up all the pound of butter. This paste is good for tarts, or any small things.

Apple Pasties to fry

Pare and quarter apples, and boil them in sugar and water, and a stick of cinnamon, and when tender, put in a little white wine, the juice of a lemon, a piece of fresh butter, and a little amber-grease or orange-flower water; stir all together, and when it is cold put it in puff-paste, and fry them.

To season and bake a Venison Pasty

Bone your haunch or side of venison, and take out all the sinews and skin; and then proportion it for your pasty, by taking away from one part, and adding to another, till 'tis of an equal thickness; then season it with pepper and salt, about an ounce of pepper; save a little of it whole, and beat the rest; and mix with it twice as much salt, and rub it all over your venison, letting it lie till your paste is ready. Make your paste thus: a peck of fine flour, six pounds of butter, a dozen of eggs; rub your butter in your flour, beat your eggs, and with them and cold water make up your paste pretty stiff: then drive it forth for your pasty; let it be the thickness of a man's thumb; put under it two or three sheets of cap-paper well floured: then have two pounds of beef-suet, shred exceeding fine; proportion it on the bottom to the breadth of your venison, and leave a verge round your venison three fingers broad, wash that verge over with a bunch of feathers or brush dipp'd in an egg beaten, and then lay a border of your paste on the place you wash'd, and lay your venison on the suet; put a little of your seasoning on the top, a few corns of whole pepper, and two pounds of very good fresh butter; then turn over your other sheet of paste, so close your pasty. Garnish it on the top as you think fit; vent it in the middle, and set it in the oven. It will ask five or six hours baking. Then break all the bones, wash them, and add to them more bones, or knuckles; season them with pepper and salt, and put them with a quart of water, and half a pound of butter, in a pan or earthen pot; cover it over with coarse paste, and set it in with your pasty; and when your pasty is drawn and dish'd, fill it up with the gravy that came from the bones.

Balls for Lent

Grate white bread, nutmeg, salt, shred parsley, a very little thyme, and a little orange- or lemon-peel cut small; make them up into balls with beaten eggs, or you may add a spoonful of cream; and roll them up in flour, and fry them.

To keep Venison in Summer

Beat pepper very fine, and rub all over it.

Sauce for Roast Venison

Jelly of currants melted and serv'd hot, with a lemon squeez'd into it.

A fine Potato Pie for Lent

First make your forc'd-meat, about two dozen of small oysters just scalded, and when cold chop'd small, a stale roll grated, and six yolks of eggs boil'd hard and bruised small with the back of a spoon; season with a little salt, pepper, and nutmeg, some thyme and parsley, both shred small; mix these together well, pound them a little, and make it up in a stiff paste, with half a pound of butter and an egg work'd in it; just flour it to keep it from sticking, and lay it by till your pie is fit, and put a very thin paste in your dish, bottom and sides; then put your forc'd-meat, of an equal thickness, about two fingers broad, about the sides of your dish, as you would do a pudding crust; dust a little flour on it, and put it down close; then fill your pie, a dozen of potatoes, about the bigness of a small egg, finely pared, just boiled a walm or two, a dozen yolks of eggs boiled hard, a quarter of a hundred of large oysters just scalded in their own liquor and cold, six morels, four or five blades of mace, some whole pepper, and a little salt butter on the bottom and top; then lid your pie, and bake it an hour; when 'tis drawn, pour in a caudle made with half a pint of your oyster liquor, three or four spoonfuls of white wine, and thickened up with butter and eggs, pour it in hot at the hole on the top, and shake it together, and serve it.

Artificial Potatoes for Lent: A side-dish; second course

Take a pound of butter, put it into a stone mortar, with half a pound of Naples biscuit grated, and half a pound of Jordan almonds beat small after they are blanched, eight yolks of eggs, four whites, a little sack and orange-flower water; sweeten to your taste; pound all together till you don't know what it is, and with a little fine flour make it into stiff paste, lay it on a table, and have ready about two pounds of fine lard in your pan, let it boil very fast, and cut your paste the bigness of chestnuts, and throw them into the boiling lard, and let them boil till they are of a yellow brown; when they are enough, take them up in a sieve to drain the fat from them; put them in a dish, pour sack and melted butter over them and strew double-refined sugar over the brim of the dish.

Potato or Lemon Cheesecake

Take six ounces of potatoes, four ounces of lemon-peel, four ounces of sugar, four ounces of butter; boil the lemon-peel till tender, pare and scrape the potatoes, boil them tender and bruise them; beat the lemon-peel with the sugar, then beat all together very well, and melt the butter in a little thick cream; mix all together very well, and let it lie till cold; put crust in your pattipans, and fill them little more than half full. Bake them in a quick oven half an hour, sift some double-refined sugar on them as they go into the oven; this quantity will make a dozen small pattipans.

To make a savoury Lamb Pie

Season your lamb with pepper, salt, cloves, mace, and nutmeg: so put it into your coffin with a few lamb-stones and sweetbreads seasoned as your lamb; also some large oysters, and savoury forc'd-meat balls, hard yolks of eggs, and the tops of asparagus two inches long, first boiled green; then put butter all over the pie, lid it, and set it in a quick oven an hour and a half; then make the liquor with oyster liquor, as much gravy, a little claret, with one anchovy in it, a grated nutmeg. Let these have a boil, thicken it with yolks of two or three eggs, and when the pie is drawn, pour it in hot.

To make a sweet Lamb Pie

Cut your lamb into small pieces, and season it with a little salt, cloves, mace, and nutmeg; your pie being made, put in your lamb or veal; strew on it some stoned raisins and currants, and some sugar; then lay on it some forc'd-meat balls made sweet, and in the summer some artichoke bottoms boil'd, and scalded grapes in the winter. Boil Spanish potatoes cut in pieces; candied citron, candied orange- and lemon-peel, and three or four large blades of mace; put butter on the top; close up your pie and bake it. Make the caudle of white wine, juice of lemon and sugar; thicken it with the yolks of two or three eggs, and a bit of butter; and when your pie is baked, pour in the caudle as hot as you can, and shake it well in the pie, and serve it up.

A sweet Chicken Pie

Take five or six small chickens, pick, draw, and truss them for baking; season them with cloves, mace, nutmeg, cinnamon, and a little salt; wrap up some of the seasoning in butter, and put it in their bellies, and your coffin being made, put them in; put over and between them pieces of marrow, Spanish potatoes and chestnuts, both boiled, peeled and cut, a handful of barberries stripped, a lemon sliced, some butter on the top; so close up the pie and bake it, and have in readiness a caudle made of white wine, sugar, nutmeg; beat it up with yolks of eggs and butter; have a care it does not curdle; pour the caudle in, shake it well together, and serve it up hot.

Another Chicken Pie

Season your chickens with pepper, salt, cloves, mace, nutmeg, a little shred parsley, and thyme, mix'd with the other seasoning; wrap up some in butter, put it in the bellies of the chickens, and lay them in your pie; strew over them lemon cut like dice; a handful of scalded grapes, artichoke-bottoms in quarters; put butter on it, and close it up; when 'tis baked, put in a lear of gravy, with a little white wine and a grated nutmeg, thickened up with butter, and two or three eggs; shake it well together, serve it up hot.

To make an Olio Pie

Make your pie ready, then take the thin collops of the butt end of a leg of veal, as many as you think will fill your pie; hack them with the back of a knife, and season them with pepper, salt, cloves, and mace; wash over your collops with a bunch of feathers dipped in eggs, and have in readiness a good handful of sweet herbs shred small; the herbs must be thyme, parsley, and spinach; the yolks of eight hard eggs minced, a few oysters parboiled and chop'd, and some beef-suet shred very fine. Mix these together, and strew them over your collops, and sprinkle a little orange-flower water on them; and roll the collops up very close, and lay them in your pie, strewing the seasoning that is left over them; put butter on the top, and close up your pie; when 'tis drawn, put in gravy, and one anchovy dissolved in it, and pour it in very hot; you may put in artichoke-bottoms and chestnuts, if you please, or sliced lemon, or grapes scalded, or what else is in season: but if you will make it a right savoury pie, leave them out.

Another

Take a fillet of veal, cut it in large thin slices, and beat it with a rolling-pin; have ready some forc'd-meat made with veal and suet, grated bread, grated lemon-peel, some nutmeg, the yolks of two or three hard eggs; spread the forc'd-meat all over your collops, and roll them up, and place them in your pie, with yolks of hard eggs, lumps of marrow, and some water; lid it and bake it; when it is done, put in a caudle of strong gravy, white wine and butter.

To make a Florendine of Veal

Take the kidney of a loin of veal, fat and all, and mince it very fine; then chop a few herbs, and put to it, and add a few currants; season it with cloves, mace, nutmeg, and a little salt; and put in some yolks of eggs, and a handful of grated bread, a pippin or two chop'd, some candied lemon-peel minced small, some sack, sugar, and orange-flower water. Put a sheet of puff-paste at the bottom of your dish; put this in, and cover it with another; close it up, and when 'tis baked, scrape sugar on it; and serve it hot.

Another made Dish

Take half a pound of almonds, blanch and beat them very fine; put to them a little rose- or orange-flower water in the beating; then take a quart of sweet thick cream, and boil it with whole cinnamon, and mace, and quartered dates; sweeten your cream with sugar to your taste, and mix it with your almonds, and stir it well together, and strain it out through a sieve. Let your cream cool, and thicken it with the yolks of six eggs; then garnish a deep dish, lay paste at the bottom, and then put in sliced artichoke-bottoms, being first boiled, and upon that a layer of marrow, sliced citron, and candied orange; so do till your dish is near full; then pour in your cream, and bake it without a lid; when 'tis baked, scrape sugar on it, and serve it up hot. Half an hour will bake it.

To make an Artichoke Pie

Boil the bottoms of eight or ten artichokes, scrape and make them clean from the core; cut each of them into six parts; season them with cinnamon, nutmeg, sugar, and a little salt; then lay your artichokes in your pie. Take the marrow of four or five bones, dip your marrow in yolks of eggs and grated bread, and season it as you did your artichokes, and lay it on the top and between your artichokes; then lay on sliced lemon, barberries and large mace; put butter on the top, and close up your pie; then make your lear of white wine, sack, and sugar; thicken it with yolks of eggs, and a bit of butter; when your pie is drawn, pour it in, shake it together, and serve it hot.

To make a Skirret Pie

Boil your biggest skirrets, blanch them, and season them with cinnamon, nutmeg, and a very little ginger and sugar. Your pie being ready, lay in your skirrets; season also the marrow of three or four bones with cinnamon, sugar, a little salt and grated bread. Lay the marrow in your pie, and the yolks of twelve hard eggs cut in halves, a handful of chestnuts boiled and blanched, with some candied orange-peel in slices. Lay butter on the top, and lid your pie. Let your caudle be white wine, verjuice, some sack and sugar; thicken it with the yolks of eggs, and when the pie is baked, pour it in, and serve it hot. Scrape sugar on it.

To make a Turbot Pie

Gut, wash, and boil your turbot; season it with a little pepper, salt, cloves, mace, nutmeg, and sweet herbs shred fine; then lay it in your pie, or pattipan, with the yolks of six eggs boiled hard; a whole onion, which must be taken out when it is baked. Put two pounds of fresh butter on the top; close it up; when it is drawn, serve it hot or cold: it is good either way.

To make a Chervil or Spinach Tart

Shred a gallon of spinach or chervil very small; put to it half a pound of melted butter, the meat of three lemons picked from the skins and seeds, the rind of two lemons grated, a pound of sugar; put this in a dish or pattipan with puff-paste on the bottom and top, and so bake it; when it is bak'd, cut off the lid, and put cream or custard over it, as you do codlin tarts; scrape sugar over it; serve it cold; this is good among other tarts in the winter for variety.

To make Lemon Cheesecakes

Take the peel of two large lemons, boil it very tender, then pound it well in a mortar, with a quarter of a pound or more of loaf sugar, the yolks of six eggs, and half a pound of fresh butter; pound and mix all well together, and fill the pattipans but half full. Orange cheesecakes are done the same way, only you must boil the peel in two or three waters, to take out the bitterness.

A Fish Pie

Take of soles, or thick flounders, gut and wash them, and just put them in scalding water to get off the black skin; then cut them in scollops, or indented, so that they will join and lie in the pie as if they were whole; have your pattipans in readiness, with puff-paste at the bottom, and a layer of butter on it; then season your fish with a little pepper and salt, cloves, mace, and nutmeg, and lay it in your pattipans, joining the pieces together as if the fish had not been cut; then put in forced balls made with fish, slices of lemon with the rind on, whole oysters, whole yolks of hard eggs, and pickled barberries; then lid your pie and bake it; when it is drawn, make a caudle of oyster liquor and white wine thicken'd up with yolks of eggs and a bit of butter; serve it hot.

To make Marrow Pasties

Make your little pasties the length of a finger, and as broad as two fingers, put in large pieces of marrow dipped in eggs, and seasoned with sugar, cloves, mace, and nutmeg; strew a few currants on the marrow; bake or fry them.

To make Mince Pies of Veal

From a leg of veal cut off four pounds of the fleshy part in thick pieces, put them in scalding water, and let it just boil; then cut the meat in small thin pieces, and skin it; must be four pounds after it is scalded and skinned; to this quantity put nine pounds of beef-

suet well skinned; shred them very fine with eight pippins pared
and cored, and four pounds of raisins of the sun stoned; when it is
shred very fine put it in a large pan, or on a table, to mix, and put
to it one ounce of nutmegs grated, half an ounce of cloves, as much
mace, a large spoonful of salt, above a pound of sugar, the peel of a
lemon shred exceeding fine; when you have seasoned it to your
palate, put in seven pounds of currants, and two pounds of raisins
stoned and shred; when you fill your pies, put into every one some
shred lemon with its juice, some candied lemon-peel and citron in
slices; and just as the pies go into the oven, put into every one a
spoonful of sack and a spoonful of claret; so bake them.

To make butter'd Loaves to eat hot

Take eleven yolks of eggs, beat well, five spoonfuls of cream, and a
good spoonful of ale-yeast, stir all these together with flour, till it
comes to a little paste, not too stiff; work it well, cover it with a
cloth; lay it before the fire to rise a quarter of an hour; when it is
well risen, make it into a roll, cut it in five pieces, and make them
into loaves, flatting them down a little, or they will rise too much;
put them into an oven as hot as for manchet, and when they are
taken out of the oven, have at least a pound of butter beaten with
rose-water and sugar to your taste; cut all the loaves open at the
top, and pour the butter into them, and serve them hot to table.

To make Cheesecakes

Take a pound of potatoes when they are boiled and peeled, beat
them fine; put to them twelve eggs, six whites; then melt a pound
of butter and stir it in; grate half a nutmeg; you must sweeten it to
your palate with double-refined sugar; then put a piece of puff-
paste round the edges of the dish; it must not be overbak'd; when
the crust is enough draw it.

Another

Take four quarts of new milk and rennet very cold, and when it is come to a curd and whey take half a pound of butter and rub it with the curd; then boil a pint of cream with a blade of mace and cinnamon, and as much grated Naples biscuit as will make it of the thickness of pancake batter, and when it is almost cold put it to your curd; then put in a spoonful or two of sack, and as many currants as you like, and put them into a puff-paste.

To make Cheesecakes without Curd

Beat two eggs very well, then put as much flour as will make them thick; then beat three eggs more very well, and put in a pan, with a pint of cream and half a pound of butter; set it over the fire, and when it boils put in your two eggs and flour, stir them well, and let them boil till they be pretty thick; then take it off the fire, and season it with sugar, a little salt and nutmeg; put in the currants, and bake them in pattipans, as you do others.

To make a Cabbage-Lettuce Pie

Take some of the largest and hardest cabbage-lettuces you can get, boil them in salt and water till they are tender, then lay them in a colander to drain; have your paste laid in your pattipan ready, and lay butter on the bottom; then lay in your lettuce, some artichoke-bottoms, some large pieces of marrow, the yolks of eight hard eggs, and some scalded sorrel; bake it, and when it comes out of the oven, cut open the lid, and pour in a caudle made with white wine and sugar, thickened with eggs; so serve it hot.

To make the light Wigs

Take a pound and a half of flour, and half a pint of milk made warm, mix these together, and cover it up, and let it lie by the fire half an hour; then take half a pound of sugar and half a pound of butter, then work these in the paste, and make it into wigs, with as little flour as possible; let the oven be pretty quick, and they will rise very much.

To make little Plum-Cakes

Take two pounds of flour dried in the oven, half a pound of sugar finely powder'd, four yolks of eggs, two whites, half a pound of butter washed with rose-water, six spoonfuls of cream warmed, a pound and a half of currants unwashed, but pick'd and rubb'd very clean in a cloth; mix all together, make them into cakes, and bake them up in an oven almost as hot as for manchet; let them stand half an hour till they be coloured on both sides; then take down the oven lid, and let them stand a little to soak.

To make Puff-Paste

To a peck of flour you must have three quarters the weight in butter; dry your flour well, and lay it on a table; make a hole, and put in it a dozen whites of eggs well beaten, but first break into it a third part of your butter; then with water make up your paste, then roll it out, and by degrees put in the rest of the butter.

To make a Hare Pie

Skin your hare, wash her, dry her, and bone her; season the flesh with pepper, salt, and spice, beaten fine in a stone mortar; do a young pig at the same time in the same manner; then make your pie, and lay a layer of pig and a layer of hare till it is full; put butter at the bottom and on the top; bake it three hours; it is good hot or cold.

Another

Bone your hare as whole as you can, then lard it with the fat of bacon, first dipped in vinegar and pepper, then season it with pepper, salt, a little mace, and a clove or two; put it into a dish with puff-paste, and have in readiness gravy or strong broth made with the bones, and put it in just before you set it in the oven; when it comes out, pour in some melted butter with strong broth and wine; but before you pour it in, taste how the pie is seasoned, and if it wants, you may season the liquor accordingly; if you please, you may lay slices of butter upon the hare before it goes into the oven, which I think best, instead of the melted butter; after, a glass of claret does well, just before you serve it. To seven pounds of lean venison, without bones, put two ounces and a half of salt, and half an ounce of pepper, to season this in proportion; some choose to put in the legs and wings with the bones; divide them at every joint, and take the bones of the body, only cracking the other bones in the limbs

To ice Tarts

Take a little yolk of egg and melted butter, beat it very well together, and with a feather wash over your tarts, and sift sugar on them just as you put them into the oven.

To make very good Wigs

Take a quarter of a peck of the finest flour, rub into it three quarters of a pound of fresh butter, till it is like grated bread, something more than half a pound of sugar, half a nutmeg, and half a race of grated ginger, three eggs, yolks and whites, beaten very well, and put to them half a pint of thick ale-yeast, and three or four spoonfuls of sack; make a hole in your flour, and pour in your yeast and eggs, and as much milk just warm as will make it into a light paste; let it stand before the fire to rise half an hour, then make it into a dozen and a half of wigs; wash them over with eggs just as they go into the oven; a quick oven and half an hour will bake them.

To make Almond Cheesecakes

Take a good handful or more of almonds, blanch them in warm water, and throw them in cold; pound them fine, and in the pounding put a little sack, or orange-flower water, to keep them from oiling; then put to your almonds the yolks of two hard eggs, and beat them together; beat the yolks of six eggs, the whites of three, and mix with your almonds, and half a pound of butter melted, and sugar to your taste; mix all well together, and use it as other cheesecake stuff.

To make a Lumber Pie

Parboil the umbles of a deer, clear all the fat from them, and put more than their weight in beef-suet, and shred it together very small; then put to it half a pound of sugar, and season with cloves, mace, nutmeg, and salt, to your taste; and put in a pint of sack, half as much claret, and two pounds of currants wash'd and pick'd; mix all well together, and bake it in puff or other paste.

To make Lemon Cheesecakes

Take two large lemons, grate off the peel of both, and squeeze out the juice of one; add to it half a pound of fine sugar, twelve yolks of eggs, eight whites well beaten; then melt half a pound of butter in four or five spoonfuls of cream; then stir it all together and set it over the fire, stirring it till it begins to be pretty thick; take it off, and when it is cold fill your pattipans little more than half full; put a fine paste very thin at the bottom of the pattipans; half an hour with a quick oven will bake them.

To make Cream Cheese with old Cheshire

Take a pound and a half of old cheshire-cheese, shave it all very thin, then put it in a mortar and add to it a quarter of an ounce of mace beaten fine and sifted, half a pound of fresh butter, and a glass of sack; mix and beat all these together till they are perfectly incorporated; then put it in a pot what thickness you please, and cut it out in slices for cream cheese, and serve it with the desert.

All Sorts of Cakes

To make a rich great Cake

Take a peck of flour well dried, an ounce of cloves and mace, half
an ounce of nutmegs, as much cinnamon; beat the spice well, and
mix them with your flour, and a pound and half of sugar, a little
salt, thirteen pounds of currants well wash'd, pick'd and dried, and
three pounds of raisins stoned and cut into small pieces; mix all
these well together, then make five pints of cream almost scalding
hot, and put into it four pounds of fresh butter; then beat the yolks
of twenty eggs, three pints of good ale-yeast, a pint of sack, a
quarter of a pint of orange-flower water, three grains of musk, and
six grains of ambergris; mix these together, and stir them into your
cream and butter; then mix all in the cake, and set it an hour
before the fire to rise, before you put it into your hoop; mix your
sweetmeats in it, two pounds of citron, and one pound of candied
orange- and lemon-peel, cut in small pieces; you must bake it in a
deep hoop; butter the sides; put two papers at the bottom, flour it,
and put in your cake; it must have a quick oven, four hours will
bake it; when it is drawn, ice it over the tops and sides. Take two
pounds of double-refined sugar, beat and sifted, and the whites of
six eggs beaten to a froth, with three or four spoonfuls of orange-
flower water, and three grains of musk and ambergris together; put
all these in a stone mortar, and beat them with a wooden pestle till

it is as white as snow, and with a brush or bunch of feathers spread it all over the cake, and put it in the oven to dry, but take care the oven does not discolour it; when it is cold paper it; will keep good five or six weeks.

A Plum Cake

Take six pounds of currants, five pounds of flour, an ounce of cloves and mace, a little cinnamon, half an ounce of nutmegs, half a pound of pounded and blanched almonds, half a pound of sugar, three quarters of a pound of sliced citron, lemon- and orange-peel, half a pint of sack, a little honey-water, a quart of ale-yeast, a quart of cream, a pound and a half of butter melted and poured into the middle thereof; then strew a little flour thereon, and let it lie to rise; then work it well together, and lay it before the fire to rise; work it up till it is very smooth; put it in a hoop, with a paper floured at the bottom.

A good Seed Cake

Take five pounds of fine flour well dried, and four pounds of single-refined sugar, beaten and sifted; mix the sugar and flour together, and sift them through a hair sieve; then wash four pounds of butter in rose- or orange-flower water; you must work the butter with your hand till it is like cream, beat twenty eggs, half the whites, and put to them six spoonfuls of sack, then put all in your flour, a little at a time, keeping it stirring with your hand all the time; you must not begin mixing it till the oven is almost hot; you must let it lie a little while before you put the cake into the hoop; when you are ready to put it into the oven, put into it eight ounces of candied orange-peel sliced, as much citron, and a pound and half of caraway comfits; mix all well together, and put it in the hoop, which must be papered at bottom, and butter'd; the oven must be quick; it will take two or three hours baking; you may ice it if you please.

Another Seed Cake

Take seven pounds of fine flour well dried, mix with it a pound of sugar beaten and sifted, and three nutmegs grated; rub three pounds of butter into the flour; then beat the yolks of eight eggs, the whites of but four, and mix with them a little rose-water, a quart of cream blood warm, a quart of ale-yeast, and a little salt; strain all into your flour, and put a pint of sack in with it, and make up your cake; put it into a butter'd cloth, and lay it half an hour before the fire to rise; the meanwhile fit your paper, and butter your hoop; then take a pound and three quarters of biscuit comfits, and a pound and half of citron cut in small pieces, mix these in your cake, and put it into your hoop; run a knife cross down to the bottom; a quick oven, and near three hours will bake it.

Another

Dry two pounds of flour, then put two pounds of butter into it; beat ten eggs, leave out half the whites; then put to them eight spoonfuls of cream, six of ale-yeast, run it through a sieve into the batter, and work them well together, and lay it a quarter of an hour before the fire; then work into it a pound of rough caraways; less than an hour bakes it.

Another Plum-Cake

Take five pounds of fine flour, and put to it half a pound of sugar, of nutmegs, cloves, and mace finely beaten, of each half an ounce, and a little salt, mix these well together; then take a quart of cream, let it boil, take it off, and cut into it three pounds of fresh butter, let it stand till 'tis melted, and when 'tis blood warm, mix with it a quart of ale-yeast, a pint of sack, and twenty eggs, ten whites well beaten; put six pounds of currants to your flour, and make a hole in the middle, and pour in the milk and other things, and make up your cake, mixing it well with your hands; cover it warm, and set it before the fire to rise for half an hour; then put it in the hoop; if the oven be hot, two hours will bake it the oven must be quick; you may perfume it with ambergris, or put sweetmeats in it if you please. Ice it when cold, and paper it.

An ordinary Cake to eat with Butter

Take two pounds of flour, and rub into it half a pound of butter; then put to it some spice, a little salt, a pound and a half of sugar, half a pound of raisins stoned, and half a pound of currants; make these into a cake, with half a pint of ale-yeast, four eggs and as much warm milk as you see convenient; mix it well together; an hour and a half will bake it. This cake is good to eat with butter for breakfast.

A French Cake to eat hot

Take a dozen of eggs, a quart of cream and as much flour as will make it into a thick batter; put to it a pound of melted butter, half a pint of sack, and one nutmeg grated; mix it well, and let it stand three or four hours; then bake it in a quick oven, and when you take it out, slit it in two, and pour a pound of butter on it melted with rose-water; cover it with the other half, and serve it up hot.

To make Portugal Cakes

Take a pound and a quarter of fine flour well dried, and break a pound of butter into the flour, and rub it in, adding a pound of loaf sugar beaten and sifted, a nutmeg grated, four perfumed plums, or some ambergris; mix these well together, and beat seven eggs, but four whites, with three spoonfuls of orange-flower water; mix all these together, and beat them up an hour; butter your little pans, and just as they are going into the oven, fill them half full, and searce some fine sugar over them; little more than a quarter of an hour will bake them. You may put a handful of currants into some of them; take them out of the pans as soon as they are drawn, and keep them dry; they will keep good three months.

To make Jumbals

Take the whites of three eggs, beat them well, and take off the froth; then take a little milk, and a little flour, near a pound, as much sugar sifted, and a few caraway seeds beaten very fine; work all these in a very stiff paste, and make them into what form you please: bake them on white paper.

To make Marchpane

Take a pound of Jordan almonds, blanch and beat them in a marble mortar very fine; then put to them three quarters of a pound of double-refined sugar, and beat them with a few drops of orange-flower water; beat all together till 'tis a very good paste, then roll it into what shape you please; dust a little fine sugar under it as you roll it, to keep it from sticking. To ice it, searce double-refined sugar as fine as flour, wet it with rose-water, and mix it well together, and with a brush or bunch of feathers spread it over your marchpane: bake them in an oven that it not too hot; put wafer paper at the bottom, and white paper under that, so keep them for use.

To make Almond Puffs

Take half a pound of Jordan almonds, blanch and beat them very fine with three or four spoonfuls of rose-water; then take half an ounce of the finest gum-dragant steeped in rose-water three or four days before you use it, then put it to the almonds, and beat it together; then take three quarters of a pound of double-refined sugar beaten and sifted, and a little fine flour, and put to it; roll it into what shape you please; lay them on white paper, and put them in an oven gently hot, and when they are baked enough, take them off the papers and put them on a sieve to dry in the oven when 'tis almost cold.

To make Biscuits

Take a pound of loaf sugar beaten and sifted, and half a pound of almonds blanch'd and beat in a mortar, with the whites of five or six eggs; put your sugar in a basin, with the yolks of five eggs; when they are both mingled, strew in your almonds; then put in a quarter of a pound of flour, and fill your pans fast; butter them and put them into the oven; strew sugar over them, bake them quick, and then turn them on a paper, and put them again into the oven to harden.

Another

Take the whites of four eggs, the yolks of ten, beat them a quarter of an hour with four spoonfuls of orange-flower water; add to it one pound of loaf sugar beaten and sifted; then beat them together an hour longer; then stir in half a pound of dry flour, and the peel of a lemon grated; mix it well together, then butter the pans and fill them; searce some sugar over them as you put them into the oven; when they are risen in the oven, take them out and lay them on a clean cloth; and when the oven is pretty cool, put them in again on sieves, and let them stand till they are dry, and will snap in breaking.

To make little hollow Biscuits

Beat six eggs very well with a spoonful of rose-water, then put in a pound and two ounces of loaf sugar beaten and sifted; stir it together till 'tis well mixed in the eggs, then put in as much flour as will make it thick enough to lay out in drops upon sheets of white paper; stir it well together till you are ready to drop it on your paper; then beat a little very fine sugar and put it into a lawn sieve, and sift some on them, the oven must not be too hot, and as soon as they are baked, whilst they are hot, pull off the papers from them, and put them in a sieve, and set them in an oven to dry; keep them in boxes with papers between.

To make Wigs

Take two pounds of flour, and a quarter of a pound of butter, as much sugar, a nutmeg grated, a little cloves and mace, and a quarter of an ounce of caraway seeds, cream and yeast as much as will make it up into a pretty light paste; make 'em up, and set them by the fire to rise till the oven be ready; they will quickly be baked.

To make Gingerbread

Take a pound and half of treacle, two eggs beaten, half a pound of brown sugar, one ounce of ginger beaten and sifted; of cloves, mace and nutmegs all together half an ounce, beaten very fine, coriander seeds and caraway seeds of each half an ounce, two pounds of butter melted; mix all these together, with as much flour as will knead it into a pretty stiff paste; then roll it out, and cut it into what form you please; bake it in a quick oven on tin-plates; a little time will bake it.

Another sort of Gingerbread

Take half a pound of almonds, blanch and beat them till they have done shining; beat them with a spoonful or two of orange-flower water, put in half an ounce of beaten ginger, and a quarter of an ounce of cinnamon powder'd; work it to a paste with double-refined sugar beaten and sifted; then roll it out, and lay it on papers to dry in an oven after pies are drawn.

Another

Take one pound of flour, three quarters of a pound of sugar, and an ounce of nutmegs, ginger and cinnamon together, beaten and sifted; a quarter of a pound of candied orange-peels or fresh peel cut in small stripes; two ounces of sweet butter rubb'd in the flour; take the yolks of two eggs, beat with eight spoonfuls of sack, and six of yeast, make it up in a stiff paste; roll it thin, and cut it with a glass; bake them and keep them dry.

To make Dutch Gingerbread

Take four pounds of flour, and mix with it two ounces and a half of beaten ginger, then rub in a quarter of a pound of butter, and add to it two ounces of caraway seeds, as much orange-peel dried and rubb'd to powder, a few coriander seeds bruised, and two eggs; mix all up into a stiff paste with two pounds and a quarter of treacle; beat it very well with a rolling pin, and make it up into thirty cakes; put in a candied citron; prick them with a fork; butter papers, three double, one white, and two brown; wash them over with the white of an egg; put 'em into an oven, not too hot, for three quarters of an hour.

To make Buns

Take two pounds of fine flour, a pint of ale-yeast, put a little sack in the yeast and three eggs beaten, knead all these together with a little warm milk, a little nutmeg, and a little salt; then lay it before the fire till it rise very light; then knead in a pound of fresh butter, and a pound of round caraway comfits, and bake them in a quick oven on floured papers in what shape you please.

To make French Bread

Take half a peck of fine flour, put to it six yolks of eggs, and four whites, a little salt, a pint of good ale-yeast, and as much new milk, made a little warm, as will make it a thin light paste; stir it about with your hand, but by no means knead it; then have ready six wooden quart dishes, and fill them with dough; let them stand a quarter of an hour to heave, and then turn them out into the oven; and when they are baked, rasp them; the oven must be quick.

To make Wigs

Take three pounds and a half of flour, and three quarters of a pound of butter, and rub it into the flour till none of it be seen; then take a pint or more of new milk, and make it very warm, and half a pint of new ale-yeast, then make it into a light paste; put in caraway seeds, and what spice you please; then make it up, and lay it before the fire to rise; then work in three quarters of a pound of sugar, and then roll them into what form you please, pretty thin, and put them on tin plates, and hold them before the oven to rise again, before you set them in; your oven must be pretty quick.

To make Gingerbread

Take three pounds of fine flour, and the rind of a lemon dried and beaten to powder, half a pound of sugar or more, as you like it, and an ounce and a half of beaten ginger; mix all these well together, and wet it pretty stiff with nothing but treacle; make it into long rolls or cakes, as you please; you may put candied orange-peel and citron in it; butter the paper you bake it on, and let it be bak'd hard.

To make Shrewsbury Cakes

Take to one pound of sugar three pounds of the finest flour, a nutmeg grated, some beaten cinnamon; the sugar and spice must be sifted into the flour, and wet it with three eggs, and as much melted butter as will make it of a good thickness to roll into a paste; mould it well and roll it; cut it into what shape you please; perfume them, and prick them before they go into the oven.

To make Almond Cakes

Take a pound of almonds, blanch and beat them exceeding fine with a little rose- or orange-flower water; then beat three eggs, but two whites, and put to them a pound of sugar sifted; then put in your almonds, and beat all together very well; put sheets of white paper, and lay the cakes in what form you please, and bake them; you may perfume them if you like it; bake them in a cool oven.

To make Drop Biscuits

Take eight eggs, and one pound of double-refined sugar beaten fine, and twelve ounces of fine flour well dried; beat your eggs very well, then put in your sugar and beat it, and then your flour by degrees, beating it all very well together for an hour without ceasing; your oven must be as hot as for halfpenny bread; then flour some sheets of tin, and drop your biscuits what bigness you please, and put them into the oven as fast as you can; and when you see them rise, watch them; and if they begin to colour, take them out again, and put in more; and if the first are not enough, put them in again; if they are right done, they will have a white ice on them; you may put in caraway seeds if you please; when they are all bak'd, put them all in the oven again till they are very dry, and keep them in your stove.

To make little Cracknels

Take three pounds of flour finely dried, three ounces of lemon- and orange-peel dried and beaten to a powder, an ounce of coriander seeds beaten and searced, and three pounds of double-refined sugar beaten fine and searced; mix these together with fifteen eggs, half of the whites taken out, a quarter of a pint of rose-water, as much orange-flower water; beat the eggs and water well together, then put in your orange-peel and coriander seeds, and beat it again very well with two spoons, one in each hand; then beat your sugar in by little and little, then your flour by a little at a time; so beat with both spoons an hour longer; then strew sugar on papers, and drop them the bigness of a walnut, and set them in the oven; the oven must be hotter than when pies are drawn; do not touch them with your finger before they are bak'd; let the oven be ready for them against they are done; be careful the oven does not colour them.

To make the thin Dutch Biscuit

Take five pounds of flour, two ounces of caraway seeds, half a pound of sugar, and something more than a pint of milk; warm the milk, and put into it three quarters of a pound of butter; then make a hole in the middle of your flour, and put in a full pint of good ale-yeast; then pour in the butter and milk, and make these into a paste, letting it stand a quarter of an hour by the fire to rise; then mould it, and roll it into cakes pretty thin; prick them all over pretty much, or they will blister; bake them a quarter of an hour.

To make an ordinary Seed Cake

Take six pounds of fine flour, rub into it a thimble-full of caraway seeds finely beaten, and two nutmegs grated, and mace beaten; then heat a quart of cream hot enough to melt a pound of butter in it, and when it is no more than blood-warm, mix your cream and butter with a pint of good ale-yeast, and then wet your flour with it; make it pretty thin; just before it goes into the oven, put in a pound of rough caraways, and some citron sliced thin; three quarters of an hour in a quick oven will bake it.

To make the Marlborough Cake

Take eight eggs, yolks and whites, beat and strain them, and put to them a pound of sugar beaten and sifted; beat it three quarters of an hour together, then put three quarters of a pound of flour well dried, and two ounces of caraway seeds; beat it all well together, and bake it in a quick oven in broad tin pans.

Another sort of little Cakes

Take a pound of flour and a pound of butter, rub the butter into the flour, two spoonfuls of yeast and two eggs, make it up into a paste; slick white paper; roll your paste out the thickness of a crown; cut them out with the top of a tin canister, sift fine sugar over them, and lay them on the slick'd paper; bake them after tarts an hour.

To make the White Cake

Take three quarts of the finest flour, a pound and a half of butter, a pint of thick cream, half a pint of ale-yeast, half a quarter of a pint of rose-water and sack together, a quarter of an ounce of mace, nine eggs, abating four whites, beaten well, and five ounces of double-refined sugar; mix the sugar and spice and a very little salt with your dry flour, and keep out half a pint of the flour to strew over the cake; when it is all mix'd, melt the butter in the cream; when 'tis a little cool, strain the eggs into it, yeast, &c. make a hole in the midst of the flour, and pour all the wetting in, stirring it round with your hand all one way till well mix'd; strew on the flour that was saved out, and set it before the fire to rise, cover'd over with a cloth; let it stand so a quarter of an hour; you must have in readiness three pounds and a half of currants, wash'd and pick'd, and well dried in a cloth; mingle them in the paste without kneading; put it in a tin hoop; set it in a quick oven, or it will not rise; it must stand an hour and a half in the oven.

To make another sort of Gingerbread

Take a pound and a half of treacle, two eggs beaten, a pound of butter melted, half a pound of brown sugar, an ounce of beaten ginger, and of cloves, mace, coriander seeds and caraway seeds, of each half an ounce; mix all these together with as much flour as will knead it into a paste; roll it out, and cut it into what form you please; bake it in a quick oven on tin plates; a little time will bake it.

To make Biscuits

To a quart of flour take a quarter of a pound of butter, and a quarter of a pound of sugar, one egg, and what caraway seeds you please; wet it with milk as stiff as you can, then roll them out very thin, cut them with a small glass, bake them on tin plates; your oven must be slack; prick them very well just as you set them in, and keep them dry when bak'd.

To make brown French Loaves

Take a peck of coarse flour, and as much of the raspings of bread beaten and sifted as will make it look brown, then wet it with a pint of good yeast, and as much milk and warm water as will wet it pretty stiff; mix it well, and set it before the fire to rise; make it into six loaves; make it up as light as you can, and bake it well in a quick oven.

To make the Hard Biscuit

Take half a pound of fine flour, one ounce of caraway seeds, the whites of two eggs, a quarter of a pint of ale-yeast, and as much warm water as will make it into a stiff paste; then make it into long rolls, bake it an hour; the next day pare it round, then slice it in thin slices, about half an inch thick; dry it in the oven; then draw it, turn it, and dry the other side; they will keep the whole year.

To make Whetstone Cakes

Take half a pound of fine flour, and half a pound of loaf sugar searced, a spoonful of caraway seeds dried, the yolk of one egg, the whites of three, a little rose-water, with ambergris dissolved in it; mix it together, and roll it out as thin as a wafer; cut them with a glass, lay them on floured paper, and bake them in a slow oven.

To make a good Plum Cake

Take four pounds of flour, put to it half a pound of loaf sugar beaten and sifted, of mace and nutmegs half an ounce beaten fine, a little salt; beat the yolks of thirty eggs, the whites of fifteen, a pint and a half of ale-yeast, three quarters of a pint of sack, with two grains of ambergris and two of musk steep'd in it five or six hours; then take a large pint of thick cream, set it on the fire, and put in two pounds of butter to melt, but not boil; then put your flour in a bowl, make a hole in the midst, and pour in your yeast, sack, cream, and eggs; mix it well with your hands, make it up, not too stiff, set it to the fire a quarter of an hour to rise; then put in seven pounds of currants, pick'd and wash'd in warm water, then dried in a coarse cloth and kept warm till you put them into your cake, which mix in as fast as you can, and put candied lemon, orange and citron in it; put it in your hoop, which must be ready butter'd and fixed; set it in a quick oven, bake it two hours or more; when it is near cold, ice it.

Another Plum Cake

Take four pounds of flour, four pounds of currants, and twelve eggs, half the whites taken out, near a pint of yeast, a pound and a half of butter, a good half pint of cream, three quarters of a pound of loaf sugar, beaten mace, nutmegs and cinnamon, half an ounce, beaten fine; mingle the spices and sugar with the flour; beat the eggs well and put to them a quarter of a pint of rose-water that had a little musk and ambergris dissolved in it; put the butter and cream into a jug, and put it in a pot of boiling water to melt; when you have mixed the cake, strew a little flour over it; cover it with a very hot napkin, and set it before the fire to rise; butter and flour your hoop, and just as your oven is ready, put your currants into boiling water to plump; dry them in a hot cloth, and mix them in your cake; you may put in half a pound of candied orange, lemon, and citron; let not your oven be too hot, two hours will bake it, three if it is double the quantity; mix it with a broad pudding-stick, not with your hands; when your cake is just drawn, pour all over it a gill of brandy or sack; then ice it.

Another Plum Cake with Almonds

Take four pounds of fine flour dried well, five pounds of currants well pick'd and rubb'd, but not wash'd, five pounds of butter wash'd and beaten in orange-flower water and sack, two pounds of almonds beaten very fine, four pounds of eggs weighed, half the whites taken out, three pounds of double-refined sugar, three nutmegs grated, a little ginger, a quarter of an ounce of mace, as much cloves finely beaten; a quarter of a pint of the best brandy; the butter must be beaten to cream, then put in your flour and all the rest of the things, beating it till you put it in the oven; four hours will bake it, the oven must be very quick; put in orange- and lemon-peel candied, and citron, as you like.

A rich Seed Cake, call'd the Nun's Cake

Take four pounds of your finest flour, and three pounds of double-refined sugar beaten and sifted, mix them together, and dry them by the fire till you prepare your other materials. Take four pounds of butter, beat it in your hands till it is very soft like cream, then beat thirty-five eggs, leave out sixteen whites, and strain out the treddles of the rest, and beat them and the butter together till all appears like butter; put in four or five spoonfuls of rose- or orange-flower water, and beat it again; then take your flour and sugar, with six ounces of caraway seeds, and strew it in by degrees, beating it up all the time for two hours together; you may put in as much tincture of cinnamon or ambergris as you please; butter your hoop, and let it stand three hours in a moderate oven.

To ice a great Cake

Take two pounds of double-refined sugar, beat and sift it very fine, and likewise beat and sift a little starch and mix with it; then beat six whites of eggs to a froth, and put to it some gum-water; the gum must be steeped in orange-flower water; then mix and beat all these together two hours, and put it on your cake; when it is baked, set it in the oven a quarter of an hour.

Another Seed Cake

Take a pound of flour, dry it by the fire, add to it a pound of fine sugar beaten and sifted; then take a pound and a quarter of butter, and work it in your hand till it is like cream; beat the yolks of ten eggs, the whites of six; mix all these together with an ounce and half of caraway seeds, and a quarter of a pint of brandy; it must not stand to rise.

Creams and Jellies

Lemon Cream

Take five large lemons, and squeeze out the juice, and the whites of six eggs well beaten, ten ounces of double-refined sugar beaten very fine, and twenty spoonfuls of spring-water; mix all together and strain it through a jelly-bag; set it over a gentle fire, skim it very well; when it is as hot as you can bear your finger in it, take it off, and pour it into glasses; put shreds of lemon-peel into some of the glasses.

Another Lemon Cream

Take the juice of four large lemons, half a pint of water, a pound of double-refined sugar, beaten fine, the whites of seven eggs, and the yolk of one beaten very well; mix all together, strain it, set it on a gentle fire, stirring it all the while, and skim it clean; put into it the peel of one lemon when it is very hot, but not boil; take out the lemon-peel, and pour it into China dishes.

To make Orange Cream

Take a pint of the juice of Seville oranges, put to it the yolks of six eggs, the whites of four; beat the eggs very well, and strain them and the juice together; add to it a pound of double-refined sugar beaten and sifted; set all these together on a soft fire, and put the peel of half an orange into it, keep it stirring all the while, and when it is almost ready to boil, take out the orange-peel, and pour out the cream into glasses or China dishes.

To make Gooseberry Cream

Take two quarts of gooseberries, put to them as much water as will cover them; let them boil all to mash, and run them through a sieve with a spoon; to a quart of the pulp, you must have six eggs, well beaten, and when the pulp is hot, put in an ounce of fresh butter, sweeten it to your taste, put in your eggs, and stir them over a gentle fire till they grow thick; then set it by, and when it is almost cold, put into it two spoonfuls of juice of spinach, and a spoonful of orange-flower water or sack, stir it well together, and put it in your basins; when it is cold serve it to the table.

Some love the gooseberries only mashed, not pulped through a sieve, and put the butter, and eggs, and sugar as the other, but no juice of spinach.

To make Barley Cream

Take a small quantity of pearl barley, and boil it in milk and water till it is tender; then strain the liquor from it, and put your barley into a quart of cream, and let it boil a little; then take the whites of five eggs, and the yolk of one beaten with a spoonful of fine flour, and two spoonfuls of orange-flower water, then take the cream off the fire, and mix the eggs in by degrees, and set it over the fire again to thicken; sweeten it to your taste; pour it into basins, and when it is cold serve it up.

To make Steeple Cream

Take five ounces of hartshorn, and two ounces of ivory; put them into a stone-bottle, fill it up with fair-water to the neck, and put in a small quantity of gum-arabic and gum-dragant; then tie up the bottle very close, and set it into a pot of water with hay at the bottom, let it boil six hours; then take it out, and let it stand an hour before you open it, lest it fly in your face; then strain it in, and it will be a strong jelly; then take a pound of blanched almonds, beat them very fine, and mix it with a pint of thick cream, letting it stand a little; then strain it out and mix it with a pound of jelly; set it over the fire till it is scalding hot, sweeten it to your taste with double-refined sugar; then take it off, and put in a little amber, and pour it out into small high gallipots like a sugar loaf at top; when it is cold turn it out, and lay whipped cream about them in heaps.

To make Blanch'd Cream

Take a quart of the thickest sweet cream you can get, season with fine sugar and orange-flower water; then boil it; then beat the whites of twenty eggs with a little cold cream, take out the treddles, and when the cream is on the fire and boils, pour in your eggs, stirring it very well till it comes to a thick curd; then take it up and pass it through a hair sieve; then beat it very well with a spoon till it is cold, and put it in dishes for use.

To make Quince Cream

Take quinces, scald them till they are soft; pare them, mash the clear part of them, and pulp it through a sieve; take an equal weight of quince, and double-refined sugar beaten and sifted, and the whites of eggs, and beat it till it is as white as snow, then put it in dishes.

To make Almond Cream

Take a quart of cream, boil it with nutmeg, mace, and a bit of lemon-peel, and sweeten it to your taste; then blanch some almonds, and beat them very fine; then take nine whites of eggs well beaten, and strain them to your almonds, and rub them very well through a thin strainer; so thicken your cream; just give it one boil; and pour it into China dishes; and when it is cold serve it up.

To make Ratafia Cream

Take six large laurel leaves, and boil them in a quart of thick cream; when it is boiled, throw away the leaves, and beat the yolks of five eggs with a little cold cream, and sugar to your taste; then thicken your cream with your eggs, and set it over the fire again, but let it not boil; keeping it stirring all the while, and pour it into China dishes; when it is cold it is fit for use.

To make Sack Cream

Take the yolks of two eggs, three spoonfuls of fine sugar, and a quarter of a pint of sack; mix them together, and stir them into a pint of cream; then set them over the fire till it is scalding hot, but let it not boil. You may toast some thin slices of white bread, and dip them in sack or orange-flower water, and pour your cream over them.

To make Rice Cream

Take three spoonfuls of the flour of rice, as much sugar, the yolks of two eggs, two spoonfuls of sack, or rose- or orange-flower water; mix all these, and put them to a pint of cream, stir it over the fire till it is thick, then pour it into China dishes.

To make Hartshorn Jelly

Take a large gallipot, and fill it with hartshorn, and then fill it full with spring-water, and tie a double paper over the gallipot, and set it in a baker's oven with household bread; in the morning take it out, run it through a jelly-bag, season with juice of lemons, double-refin'd sugar, and the whites of eight eggs well beaten; let it have a boil, and run it through the jelly bag again into your jelly glasses; put a bit of lemon-peel in the bag.

To make Calf's-foot Jelly

To four calves' feet take a gallon of fair-water, cut them in pieces, put them in a pipkin close covered, and boil them softly till almost half be consumed; and run it through a sieve, and let it stand till it is cold; then with a knife take off the fat; and top and bottom, and the fine part of the jelly melt in a preserving pan or skillet, and put in a pint of rhenish wine, the juice of four or five lemons, double-refin'd sugar to your taste, the whites of eight eggs beaten to a froth; stir and boil all these together near half an hour; then strain it through a sieve into a jelly bag; put into your jelly bag a sprig of rosemary, and a piece of lemon-peel; pass it through the bag till 'tis as clear as water. You may cut some lemon-peel like threads, and put in half the glasses.

To make Whipped Cream

Take a quart of thick cream, and the whites of eight eggs beaten with half a pint of sack; mix it together, and sweeten it to your taste with double-refined sugar; you may perfume it if you please with some musk or ambergris tied in a rag, and steeped a little in the cream; whip it up with a whisk, and a bit of lemon-peel tied in the middle of the whisk; take the froth with a spoon, and lay it in your glasses or basins.

To make Whipped Syllabubs

Take a quart of cream, not too thick, a pint of sack, and the juice of two lemons; sweeten it to your palate, put it into a broad earthen pan, and with a whisk whip it; as the froth rises, take it off with a spoon, and lay it in your syllabub-glasses; but first you must sweeten some claret, sack, or white wine, and strain it, and put seven or eight spoonfuls of the wine into your glasses, and then gently lay in your froth. Set them by. Do not make them long before you use them.

To make a fresh Cheese

Take a quart of cream, and set it over the fire till it is ready to boil, then beat nine eggs, yolks and whites, very well; when you are beating them, put to them as much salt as will lie on a small knife's point; put them to the cream, with some nutmeg quartered, and tied up in a rag; let them boil till the whey is clear; then take it off the fire, put it in a pan, and gather it as you do cheese; then put it in a cloth, and drain it between two; then put it in a stone mortar, grind it, and season it with a little sack, orange-flower water and sugar; then put it in a little earthen colander, and let it stand two hours to drain out the whey, then put it in the middle of a China dish and pour thick cream about it. So serve it to the table.

To make Almond Butter

Take a pound of the best Jordan almonds, blanched in cold water, and as you blanch them throw them into fair-water; then beat them in a marble mortar very fine, with some rose- or orange-flower water, to keep them from oiling; then take a pound of butter out of the churn before 'tis salted, but it must be very well washed, and mix it with your almonds, with near a pound of double-refin'd sugar beaten and sifted; when 'tis very well mix'd, set it up to cool; when you are going to use it, put it into a colander, and pass it through with the back of a spoon into the dish you serve it in. Hold your hand high and let it be heaped up.

To make Ribbon Jelly

Take out the great bones of four calf's-feet, and put the feet into a pot with ten quarts of water, three ounces of hartshorn, three ounces of isinglass, a nutmeg quarter'd, four blades of mace; then boil this till it comes to two quarts, and strain it through a fine flannel bag; let it stand twenty-four hours; then scrape off all the fat from the top very clean; then heat it, and put it to the whites of six eggs beaten to a froth; boil it a little, and strain it again through a flannel bag; then run the jelly into little high glasses; run every colour as thick as your finger; one colour must be thorough cold before you put another on, and that you run on must not be blood-warm for fear it mixes together; you must colour red with cochineal, green with spinach, yellow with saffron, blue with syrup of violets, white with thick cream, and sometimes the jelly by itself.

To make Orange Cream

Take the juice of six oranges, set it on the fire, let it be scalding hot, but not boil; beat three yolks of eggs with as much sugar as will make it sweet enough to your taste; beat them up together, and let them have one boil up; keep it stirring, scum it, and put it into glasses, and serve it up cold.

To make Cream of any preserv'd Fruit

Take half a pound of the pulp of any preserv'd fruit, put it in a large pan, put to it the whites of two or three eggs; beat them together exceeding well for an hour; then with a spoon take it off, and lay it heaped up high on the dish or salver with other creams, or put it in the middle basin; raspberries will not do this way.

To make a Snow Posset

Take a quart of new milk, and boil it with a stick of cinnamon and quarter'd nutmeg; when the milk is boiled, take out the spice, and beat the yolks of sixteen eggs very well, and by degrees mix them in the milk till it is thick; then beat the whites of the sixteen eggs with a little sack and sugar into a snow; then take the basin you design to serve it up in, and put in it a pint of sack; sweeten it to your taste; set it over the fire, and let one take the milk, and another the whites of eggs, and so pour them together into the sack in the basin; keep it stirring all the while it is over the fire; when it is thorough warm take it off, cover it up, and let it stand a little before you use it.

To make a Jelly Posset

Take twenty eggs, leave out half the whites, and beat them very well; put them into the basin you serve it in, with near a pint of sack, and a little strong ale; sweeten it to your taste, and set it over a charcoal fire, stirring all the while; then have in readiness a quart of milk or cream boiled with a little nutmeg and cinnamon, and when your sack and eggs are hot enough to scald your lips, put the milk to it boiling hot; then take it off the fire, and cover it up half an hour; strew sugar on the brim of the dish, and serve it to the table.

To make Flummery Caudle

Take a pint of oatmeal, and put it to two quarts of fair-water; let it stand all night; in the morning stir it, and strain it into a skillet, with three or four blades of mace, and a nutmeg quartered; set it on the fire, and keep it stirring, and let it boil a quarter of an hour; if it is too thick, put in more water, and let it boil longer; then add a pint of rhenish white wine, three spoonfuls of orange-flower water, the juice of two lemons, and one orange, a bit of butter, and as much fine sugar as will sweeten it; let all these have a walm, and thicken it with the yolks of two or three eggs. Drink it hot for breakfast.

To make Tea Caudle

Make a quart of strong green tea, pour it out into a skillet, and set it over the fire; then beat the yolks of four eggs, and mix them with a pint of white wine, a grated nutmeg, sugar to your taste, and put all together; stir it over the fire till it is very hot, then drink it in China dishes as caudle.

A fine Caudle

Take a pint of milk, and turn it with sack; then strain it, and when it is cold, put it in a skillet with mace, nutmeg, and some white bread sliced; let all these boil, and then beat the yolks of four or five eggs, the whites of two, and thicken your caudle, stirring it all one way, for fear it curdles; let it warm together, then take it off and sweeten it to your taste.

To make Hartshorn or Calf's-foot Jelly without Lemons

Take a pair of calves' feet, boil them with six quarts of fair-water to mash; it will make three quarts of jelly; then strain it off, and let it stand still till 'tis cold, take off the top, and save the middle, and melt it again and scum it; then take six whites of eggs beaten to a froth, half a pint of rhenish wine, and one lemon juiced, and half a pound of fine powdered sugar; stir all together, and let it boil, then take it off, and put to it as much spirit of vitriol as will sharpen it to your palate, about one pennyworth will do; let it not boil after the vitriol is in; let your jelly-bag be made of thick flannel, then run it through till it is very clear; you may put the whites of the eggs that swim at the top into the bag first, and that will thicken the bag.

To make Oatmeal Caudle

Take two quarts of ale, one of stale beer, and two quarts of water; mix them all together, and add to it two spoonfuls of pot-oatmeal, twelve cloves, five or six blades of mace, and a nutmeg quartered or bruised; set it over the fire, and let it boil half an hour, stirring it all the while; then strain it out thro' a sieve, and put in near a pound of fine sugar, and a bit of lemon-peel; pour it into a pan, and cover it close, that it may not scum; warm it as you use it.

To make Salop

Take a quart of water, and let it boil a quarter of an hour, then put in a quarter of an ounce of salop finely powdered, and let it boil half an hour longer, stirring it all the while; then season it with white wine and juice of lemons, and sweeten it to your taste; drink it in China cups, as chocolate; it is a great sweetener of the blood.

Boil sago till it is tender and jellies, a spoonful and half to a quart of water, then season it as you do salop, and drink it in chocolate dishes; or if you please leave out the wine and lemon, and put in a pint of thick cream and a stick of cinnamon, and thicken it up with two or three eggs.

To make Lemon Syllabubs

Take a quart of cream, half a pound of sugar, a pint of white wine, the juice of two or three lemons, the peel of one grated; mix all these, and put them in an earthen pot, and milk it up as fast as you can till it is thick; then pour it into your glasses, and let them stand five or six hours; you may make them overnight.

To make white Leach

Take half a pound of almonds, blanch and beat them with rose-water, and a little milk; then strain it out, and put to it a piece of isinglass, and let it boil on a chafing-dish of coals half an hour; then strain it into a basin, sweeten it, and put a grain of musk into it; let it boil a little longer, and put to it two or three drops of oil of mace or cinnamon, and keep it till it is cold; eat it with wine or cream.

To make White-Wine Cream

Take a quart of cream, set it on the fire, and stir it till it is blood-warm; then boil a pint of white wine with sugar till it is syrup, and then mingle the wine and cream together; put it in a China basin, and when it is cold serve it up.

To make Strawberry or Raspberry Fool

Take a pint of raspberries, squeeze and strain the juice with orange-flower water; put to the juice five ounces of fine sugar; then set a pint of cream over the fire, and let it boil up; then put in the juice; give it one stir round, and then put it into your basin; stir it a little in the basin, and when it is cold use it.

To make Sack Cream

Take a quart of thick cream and set it over the fire, and when it boils take it off; put a piece of lemon-peel in it, and sweeten it very well; then take the China basin you serve it in, and put into the basin the juice of half a lemon, and nine spoonfuls of sack; then stir in the cream into the basin by a spoonful at a time, till all the cream is in; when it is little more than blood-warm, set it by till next day; serve it with wafers round it.

To make Ratafia Biscuit

Take four ounces of bitter almonds, blanch and beat them as fine as you can; in beating them put in the whites of four eggs, one at a time; then mix it up with sifted sugar to a light paste; roll them and lay them on wafer paper, and on tin plates; make the paste so light that you may take it up with a spoon; bake them in a quick oven.

To make Pistachio Cream

Peel your pistachios, beat them very fine, and boil them in cream; if it is not green enough, add a little juice of spinach; thicken it with eggs, and sweeten to your taste; pour it in basins, and set it by till it is cold.

To make Hartshorn Flummery

Take three ounces of hartshorn, and boil it with two quarts of spring-water; let it simmer over the fire six or seven hours, till half the water is consumed; or else put it in a jug, and set it in the oven with household bread; then strain it through a sieve, and beat half a pound of almonds very fine, with some orange-flower water in the beating; when they are beat mix a little of your jelly with it, and some fine sugar; strain it out and mix it with your other jelly; stir it together till it is little more than blood warm, then pour it into half-pint basins, fill them about half full; when you use them, turn them out of the dish as you do flummery; if it does not come out clean, hold the basin a minute or two in warm water; eat it with wine and sugar.

Put six ounces of hartshorn in a glaz'd jug with a long neck, and put in three pints of soft water; cover the top of the jug close, and put a weight on it to keep it steady; set it in a pot or kettle of water twenty-four hours; let it not boil, but be scalding hot; then strain it out, and make your jelly.

A Sack Posset without Eggs

Take a quart of cream, or new milk, and grate three Naples biscuits in it, and let them boil in the cream; grate some nutmeg in it, and sweeten it to your taste; let it stand a little to cool, and then put half a pint of sack a little warm in your basin, and pour your cream to it, holding it up high in the pouring; let it stand a little, and serve it.

A Sack Posset without Cream or Eggs

Take half a pound of Jordan almonds, lay them all night in water, blanch them and beat them in a stone mortar very fine, with a pint of orange-flower water, or fair-water a quart, half a pound of sugar, and a twopenny loaf of bread grated; let it boil till it is thick, continually stirring it; then warm half a pint of sack, and put to it; stir it well together, and put a little nutmeg and cinnamon in it.

To make a Posset with Ale (King William's Posset)

Take a quart of cream, and mix it with a pint of ale, then beat the yolks of ten eggs, and the whites of four; when they are well beaten, put them to the cream and ale; sweeten it to your taste, and slice some nutmeg in it; set it over the fire, and keep it stirring all the while; when it is thick, and before it boils, take it off, and pour it into the basin you serve it in to the table.

To make the Pope's Posset

Blanch and beat three quarters of a pound of almonds so fine that they will spread between your fingers like butter; put in water as you beat them, to keep them from oiling; then take a pint of sack or sherry, and sweeten it very well with double-refined sugar; make it boiling hot, and at the same time put half a pint of water to your almonds, and make them boil; then take both off the fire, and mix them very well together with a spoon; serve it in a China dish.

To make very fine Syllabubs

Take a quart and half a pint of cream, a pint of rhenish, half a pint of sack, three lemons, and near a pound of double-refined sugar; beat and sift the sugar, and put it to your cream; grate off the yellow rind of your three lemons, and put that in; squeeze the juice of the three lemons into your wine, and put that to your cream, then beat all together with a whisk just half an hour; then take it up all together with a spoon, and fill your glasses; it will keep good nine or ten days, and is best three or four days old; these are call'd the everlasting syllabubs.

To make an Oatmeal Sack Posset

Take a pint of milk, and mix in it two spoonfuls of flour of oatmeal, and one of sugar; put in a blade of mace, and let it boil till the rawness of the oatmeal is gone off; in the meantime have in readiness three spoonfuls of sack, three of ale, and two of sugar; set them over the fire till scalding hot, then put them to your milk; give one stir, and let it stand on the fire a minute or two, and pour it in your basin; cover your basin with a pie-plate, and let it stand a little to settle.

Preserves, Conserves, Syrups, &c.

To preserve Oranges whole

Take the best Bermudas oranges, pare them with a penknife very thin, and lay your oranges in water three or four days shifting them every day; then put them in a kettle with fair-water, putting a board on them, to keep them down in the water; have a skillet on the fire with water, that may be in readiness to supply the kettle with boiling water; as it wastes it must be fill'd up three or four times while the oranges are doing, for they will take up seven or eight hours in boiling, for they must be so tender that a wheat-straw may be thrust through them; then take them up, and scoop the seeds out of them, making a little hole on the top; then weigh them, and to every pound of orange take a pound and three quarters of double-refined sugar finely beaten and sifted; fill up your oranges with sugar, and strew some on them, and let them lie a little. Then make your jelly for them thus: take two dozen of pippins and slice them into water, and when they are boiled tender strain the liquor from the pulp, and to every pound of orange you must have a pint and half of this liquor, and put to it three quarters of the sugar you left in filling the oranges; set it on the fire, and let it boil, and skim it well, and put it in a clean earthen pan till it is cold; then put it in your skillet, and put in your oranges, and with a small bodkin jab the oranges as they are boiling, to let the syrup into them; strew on the rest of your sugar while they are boiling; and when they look clear, take them up and put them in your glasses, but in glasses just fit for them, and boil the syrup till it is almost a jelly; then fill up your oranges and glasses, and when they are cold paper them up, and put them in your stove.

Another

Take the best and largest Seville oranges, water them three days, shifting them twice a day, boiling them in a copper with a great deal of water till they are tender; they must be tied in a cloth and kept under water, the water must boil before you put them in; then take to every pound of orange, a pound and a half of double-refin'd sugar, beaten and sifted; then have in readiness apple-water made of John apples; take to every pint of that water a pound of sugar; then take a third part of the sugar and put to the water; boil it a while, and set it by to cool; then cut a little hole in the bottom of your orange, pick out all the seeds, and fill them up with what sugar is left; prick your oranges all over with a bodkin, put them into your syrup, boiling them so fast that the syrup may cover them, then put in your sugar that is left: when the syrup will jelly, and they look clear, they are enough; glass them with the holes uppermost, and pour in the syrup.

To preserve whole Quinces white

Take the largest quinces of the greenest colour, and scald them till they are pretty soft, then pare them, and core them with a scoop; then weigh your quinces against so much double-refined sugar, and make a syrup of one half, and put in your quinces and boil them as fast as you can; then you must have in readiness pippin liquor, let it be very strong of the pippins; and when it is strained out, put in the other half of your sugar, and make it a jelly; and when your quinces are clear put them into the jelly, and let them simmer a little – they will be very white; so glass them up, and when they are cold paper them, and keep them in a stove.

To preserve Gooseberries

Take of the best Dutch gooseberries before they are too ripe, stone them, and put them in a skillet with so much fair-water as will cover them; set them on a fire to scald, and when they are tender take them out of the liquor, and peel off the outer skin as you do codlins, and throw them into some double-refin'd sugar, powdered and sifted; put a handful more of gooseberries into that water, and let them boil a little, then run the liquor thro' a sieve; take the weight of your peel'd gooseberries in double-refin'd sugar, break the sugar in lumps, and wet the lumps in the liquor that the gooseberries were scalded in, and put your sugar in a preserving pan over a clear fire, let it boil up, and scum it well; then put in your gooseberries, and let them boil till they look clear; then place them in your glasses, and boil the liquor a little longer, and pour it on your gooseberries in the glasses; when they are cold paper them.

To preserve Raspberries in jelly

Take of the largest and best raspberries, and to a pound take a pound and a quarter of sugar made into a syrup, and boiled candy-high; then put in the raspberries, set them over a gentle fire, and as they boil shake them; when the sugar boils over them, take them off the fire, skim them, and set them by a little; then set them on again, and have half a pint of juice of currants by you, and at several times put in a little as it boils; shake them often as they grow nearer to be enough, which you may know by setting some in a spoon to try if it will jelly, for when they jelly they are enough; then lay them in your glasses and keep the jelly to cover them; but before you put it to them pick out all the seeds, and let the jelly cover them well.

To preserve Apricots

Take your apricots, stone and pare them; take their weight in double-refined sugar beaten and sifted, and put your apricots in a silver cup or tankard, and cover them over with the sugar, letting them stand so all night; the next day put them in a preserving pan, set them on a gentle fire, and let them simmer up a little while; then let them boil till they are tender and clear, taking them off sometimes to turn and skim; keep them under the liquor as they are doing, and with a small clean bodkin or great needle jab them sometimes that the syrup may penetrate into them; when they are enough take them and put them in glasses, boil and skim the syrup, and when it is cold put it on your apricots.

To preserve white Pear-Plums

Take pear-plums when they are yellow, before they are too ripe, give them a slit in the seam, and prick them behind; make your water almost scalding hot, and put a little sugar to it to sweeten it, and put in your plums, and cover them close; set them on the fire to coddle, and take them off sometimes a little, and set them on again; take care they do not break; have in readiness as much double-refined sugar boil'd to a height as will cover them, and when they are coddled pretty tender, take them out of the liquor, and put them into your preserving pan to your syrup, which must be but blood-warm when your plums go in; let them boil till they are clear, skim them, take them off, and let them stand two hours; then set them on again, and boil them, and when they are thoroughly preserved, take them up and lay them in glasses; boil your syrup till it is thick, and when 'tis cold put in your plums; a month after, if your syrup grows thin, you must boil it again, or make a fine jelly of pippins, and put on them. This way you may do the pimordian plum, or any white plum; and when they are cold paper them up.

To preserve Damsons whole

Take some damsons, cut them in pieces, and put them in a skillet over the fire, with as much water as will cover them; when they are boiled, and the liquor pretty strong, strain it out; having for every pound of your whole damsons wiped clean a pound of single-refined sugar, put the third part of the sugar in the liquor, and set it over the fire, and when it simmers put in your damsons; let them have one good boil, and take them off for half an hour, cover'd up close; then set them on again, and let them simmer over the fire, often turning them; then take them out, put them into a basin, and strew all the sugar that was left on them, and pour the hot liquor over them, cover them up, and let them stand till the next day; then boil them up again till they are enough; take them up, and put them in pots; boil the liquor till it jellies, and pour it on them when it is almost cold, so paper them up.

To parch Almonds

Take a pound of sugar, make it into a syrup, and boil it candy-high, then put in three quarters of a pound of Jordan almonds blanched; keep them stirring all the while till they are dry and crisp, then put them in a box, and keep them dry.

To dry Apricots

Take to a pound of apricots, a pound of double-refined sugar; stone them, pare them, and put them into cold water; when they are all ready, put them into a skillet of hot water, and scald them till they are tender; then drain them very well from the water, and put them into a silver basin; have in readiness your sugar boil'd to sugar again, and pour that sugar over your apricots; cover them with a silver plate, and let them stand all night; the next day set them over a gentle fire, and let them be scalding hot, turning them often; you must do them twice a day, till you see them begin to candy; then take them out, and set them in your stove in glasses to dry, heating your stove every day till they are dry.

To preserve Green Plums

Take green plums grown to their full bigness, but before they begin to ripen; let them be carefully gathered with their stalks and leaves, put them into cold spring-water over a fire, and let them boil very gently; when they will peel, take off the skins; then put the plums into other cold water, and let them stand over a very gentle fire till they are soft; put two pounds of double-refin'd sugar to every pound of plums, and make the sugar with some water into a thick syrup before the plums are put in; the stones of the plums are not to be grown so hard but that you may thrust a pin thro' them. After the same manner do green apricots.

To make Sugar Plates

Take a pound of double-refined sugar beaten and searced; blanch and beat some almonds and mix with it, and beat them together in a mortar, with gum-dragant dissolved in rose-water, till it is a paste; roll it out, and strew sugar on the papers or plate, and bake it after manchet; gild it if you please, and serve sweetmeats on it.

To clear Sugar

Take two or three whites of eggs, and put 'em into a basin of water, and with a very clean hand lather that as you do soap; take nothing but the froth, and when your syrup boils, with a ladle cover it with it; do this till your syrup is clear, making still more froth, and covering the syrup with it; it will make the worst sugar as clear as any, and fit to preserve any fruit.

To preserve Plums green

The plums that will be greenest are the white plums that are ripe in wheat harvest; gather them about the middle of July whilst they are green; when gathered, lay them in water twelve hours; then scald them in two several waters, let not the first be too hot, but the second must boil before you put the plums in; when they begin to shrivel, peel off the skin as you do codlins, keep them whole, and let a third water be made hot, and when it boils, put in your plums, and give them two or three walms; then take them off the fire, and cover them close for half a quarter of an hour, till you perceive them to look greenish and tender; then take them out and weigh them with double-refin'd sugar, equal weight; wet a quarter of a pound of your sugar in four spoonfuls of water, set it on the fire, and when it begins to boil, take it off, and put in your plums one by one, and strew the rest of your sugar upon them, only saving a little to put in with your perfume, musk or ambergris, which must be put in a little before they are done; let them boil softly on a moderate fire half an hour or more, till they are green and the syrup thickish, then put your plums in a pot or glasses; let the syrup have two or three walms more, and put it to them; when they are cold paper them up.

To preserve black Pear-Plums, or any black Plum

Take a pound of plums, give them a little slit in the seam; then take some of your worst plums, and put them in a gallipot close cover'd, and set them in a pot of boiling water, and as they yield liquor still pour it out. To a pint of this liquor, take a pound and a quarter of sugar; put them together, and give them a boil and a skim, after which take it off to cool a little; then take your pound of plums, and as you put them in, give every one of them a prick or two with a needle; so set them again on a soft fire a pretty while; then take them off, and let them stand till the next day, that they may drink up the syrup without breaking the skin; the next day warm them again once or twice, till you see the syrup grows thick, and the plums look of the right black, still skimming them, and when they will endure a boil, give them two or three walms, and skim them well, and put them in your glasses. Be sure you keep some of the syrup in a glass, that when your plums are settled and cold, you may cover them with it. The next day paper them up, and keep them for use.

To make white Jelly of Quinces

Pare your quinces, and cut them in halves; then core and parboil them; when they are soft, take them up and crush them through a strainer, but not too hard, only the clear juice. Take the weight of the juice in fine sugar; boil the sugar candy-high, and put in your juice and let it scald a while, but not boil; if any froth arise, skim it off, and when you take it up, have ready a white preserved quince cut in small slices, laying them in the bottom of your glasses, and pour your jelly to them; it will candy on the top and keep moist on the bottom a long time.

To make clear Cakes of the Jelly of any Fruit

To half a pound of jelly, take six ounces of sugar; wet your sugar with a little water, and boil it candy-high; then put in your jelly; let it boil very fast till it jelly; then put it into glasses, and when it is dried enough on one side, turn it into glass plates. Set them in a stove to dry leisurely; let your stove be hot against your cakes be turned.

To make clear Cakes of any sort

Take your gooseberries, or other fruit, and put them in an earthen pot stopped very close, and put them in a kettle of water, and let them boil till they break; then take them out, and run them through a cloth; take the weight of the liquor in sugar; boil the sugar candy-high; then put in your juice, and let it stand over a few embers to dry till it is thick like a jelly; if you fear it will change colour, put in three or four drops of juice of lemon; pour it out into clear cake glasses, and dry them with a little fire.

To make brown Sugar

Take gum-arabic, and dissolve it in water till it is pretty thick; then take as much double-refined sugar finely sifted and perfumed as will make the gum into a stiff paste; roll it out like jumballs, and set it in an oven exactly heated, that it may raise them and not boil, for if it boils it is spoiled; you may colour some of them.

To make Pastils

Take double-refined sugar beaten and sifted as fine as flour; perfume it with musk and ambergris; then have ready steeped some gum-arabic in orange-flower water, and with that make the sugar into a stiff paste; drop into some of it three or four drops of oil of mint, oil of cloves, oil of cinnamon, or what oil you like, and let some only have the perfume; then roll them up in your hand like little pellets, and squeeze them flat with a feel. Dry them in the sun.

To fricassee Almonds

Take a pound of Jordan almonds, do not blanch them, or but one half of them; beat the white of an egg very well, and pour it on your almonds, and wet them all over; then take half a pound of double-refined sugar, and boil it to sugar again; put your almonds in, and stir them till as much sugar hangs on them as will; then set them on plates, and put them into the oven to dry after bread is drawn, and let them stay in all night. They will keep the year round if you keep them dry, and are a pretty sweetmeat.

To make Almond Cakes

Boil a pound of double-refined sugar up to a thin candy; then have in readiness half a pound of almonds blanched, and finely beaten with some rose- or orange-flower water, the juice of one lemon, the peels of two grated into the juice; put all these together, stir them over a gentle fire till all the sugar is well melted, but be sure it does not boil after the lemon is in; then put it into your clear cake glasses: perfume them, and when they are a little dry, cut them into what shape you please.

To make Orange Cakes

Pare your oranges very thin, and take off the white rinds in quarters; boil the white rinds very tender, and when they are enough, take them up, scrape the black off, and squeeze them between two trenchers; beat them in a stone mortar to a fine pulp with a little sugar; pick the meat out of the oranges from the skins and seeds, and mix the pulp and meat together, and take the weight and half of sugar; boil the sugar to a candy-height, and put in the oranges, stir them well together, and when it is cold drop them on a pie-plate, and set them in a stove. You may perfume them. To the rinds of six oranges put the meat of nine lemons. Cakes are made the same way, only as many rinds as meat, and twice the weight of sugar.

To make Marchpane unboiled

Take a pound of almonds, blanch them and beat them in rose-water; when they are finely beaten, put to them half a pound of sugar, beat and searced, and work it to a paste; spread some on wafers, and dry it in an oven; when it is cold, have ready the white of an egg beaten with rose-water, and double-refined sugar. Let it be as thick as butter, then draw your marchpane thro' it, and put it in the oven; it will ice in a little time, then keep them for use.

If you have a mind to have your marchpane large, cut it when it is rolled out by a pewter-plate, and edge it about the top like a tart, and bottom with wafer-paper, and set it in the oven, and ice it as aforefaid: when the icing rises, take it out, and strew coloured comfits on it, or serve sweetmeats on it.

To preserve Cherries

Pick and stone your cherries; weigh them, and take their weight of single-refined sugar beaten fine; mix three parts of the sugar with juice of currants, put it in your preserving-pan, giving it a boil and a skim, and then put in your cherries; let them boil very fast, now and then strewing in some of the sugar that was left till all is in; skim it well, and when they are enough, which you may know by trying some in a spoon, and when it jellies, take it off, and fill your glasses, and when they are cold, paper them up.

To preserve Currants in Jelly

Take your currants, strip them, and put them in an earthen pot; tie them close down, set them in a kettle of boiling water, and let them stand three hours, keeping the water boiling; then take a clean flaxen cloth, and strain out the juice; when it has settled, take a pound of double-refined sugar, beaten and sifted, and put to a pint of the clear juice; have in readiness some whole currants stoned, and when the juice boils, put in your currants, and boil them till your syrup jellies, which you may know by taking up some in a spoon; then put it in your glasses. This way make jelly of currants, only leaving out the whole currants; when cold, paper them up.

To preserve Barberries

Take the largest barberries you can get, and stone them; to every pound of barberries take three pounds of sugar, and boil it till it is candy-high; then put in the barberries, and let them boil till the sugar boils over them all; then take them off, skim them, set them on again, and give them another boil, and put them in an earthen pan, cover them with paper, and set them by till the next day; then put them in pots, and pour the syrup over them; cover them with paper, and keep them in a stove. If the syrup grows thin you may make a little jelly of pippins, and put them in when it is ready, and give them one warm, and pour them again into glasses.

To preserve whole Pippins

Take Kentish pippins or apple-johns, pare them, and slice them into fair-water; set them on a clear fire, and when they are boiled to mash, let the liquor run through a hair sieve. Boil as many apples thus till you have the quantity of liquor you would have. To a pint of this liquor you must have a pound of double-refined sugar in great lumps, wet the lumps of sugar with the pippin liquor, set it over a gentle fire, let it boil, and skim it well, and while you are making the jelly, you must have your whole pippins boiling at the same time; they must be the fairest and best pippins you can get; scoop out the cores, and pare them neatly, and put them into fair-water as you do them; you must likewise make a syrup ready to put them into, the quantity as you think will boil them in clear; you must make that syrup with double-refined sugar and water; tie up your whole pippins in a piece of fine muslin severally, and when your sugar and water boils put them in; let them boil very fast, so fast that the syrup always boils over them; sometimes take them off, and then set them on again, and let them boil till they are clear and tender; then take off the tiffany or muslin they were tied up in, and put them into glasses that will hold but one in a glass; then see if your jelly of apple-johns be boiled to jelly enough; if it be, squeeze in the juice of two lemons, and put musk and ambergris in a rag, and let it have a boil; then strain it through a jelly-bag into the glasses your pippins were in; you must be sure to drain your pippins well from the syrup they were boiled in; before you put them in you glasses, you may if you please boil lemon-peel in little pieces in water till they are tender, and then boil them in the syrup your pippins were boiled in; then take them out, and lay them about the pippins before the jelly is put in; when they are cold, paper them up.

To make Pippin Jelly

Take fifteen pippins pared, cored and sliced, and put them into a pint and a half of water, let them boil till they are tender, then put them in a strainer, and let the thin run from them as much as it will; to a pint of liquor take a pound of double-refined sugar; wet your sugar, and boil it to sugar again; then cut some chips of candied orange- or lemon-peel, cut it as fine as threads, and put it into your sugar, and then your liquor, and let it boil till it is a jelly, which will be quickly; you may perfume it with ambergris if you please; pour the jelly into shallow glasses; when it is cold paper it up, and keep it in your stove.

To candy Angelica

Take angelica that is young, cut it in fit lengths, and boil it till it is pretty tender, keeping it close covered; then take it up and peel off the strings, then put it in again, and let it simmer and scald till it is very green; then take it up, dry it in a cloth, and weigh it, putting to every pound of angelica a pound of double-refined sugar beaten and sifted; put your angelica in an earthen pan, strew the sugar over it, and let it stand two days, then boil it till it looks very clear; put it in a colander to dry the syrup from it, and take a little double-refined sugar and boil it to sugar again; then throw in your angelica, and take it out in a little time, and put it on glass plates; it will dry in your stove, or in an oven after pies are drawn.

To make Jelly of white Currants

Take your largest currants, strip them into a basin; bruise and strain them, and to every pint of juice a pound of double-refined sugar; just wet your sugar with a little fair-water, and set it on a slow fire till it melts; then make it boil, and at the same time let your juice boil in another thing; skim them both very well, and when they have boiled a pretty while, take off your sugar, and strain the juice into it through a muslin; then set it on the fire and let it boil; if you please you may stone some white currants and put them in, and let them boil till they are clear; have a care you do not boil them too high; let them stand a while, then put them in glasses.

If you would make clear cakes of white currants, boil the juice just as this is; but this observe, that when you put your juice and sugar together, they must stand but so long on the fire till they are warm and well mixed, they must boil together; and when it is cold put it in flat glasses, and into your stove to dry them; turn them often.

To make white Marmalade

Take your quinces, scald them, pare them, and scrape the pulp clean from the cores, adding to every pound of pulp a pound of double-refined sugar; put a little water to your sugar to dissolve it, and boil it candy-high; then put in the quince-pulp, and set it on the fire till it comes to a body; let it boil very fast; when it is enough put it in gallipots.

To make red Quince Marmalade

Pare, core, and quarter your quinces, then weigh them, and to a pound of quince allow a pound of single-refined sugar beaten small, and to every pound of quince a pint of liquor. Make your liquor thus: put your parings and cores, and three or four quinces cut in pieces, into a large skillet, with water proportionable to the quantity of quinces you do; cover it and set it over the fire, and let it boil two or three hours; then put in a quart of barberries, and let them boil an hour, and strain all out; then put your quince, and liquor, and a quarter of your sugar, into a skillet or large preserving-pan, and let them boil together over a gentle fire; cover it close, and take care it does not burn; strew in the rest of your sugar by degrees, and stir it often from the bottom, but do not break the quince till it is near enough; then break it in lumps as small as you like it; when it is of a good colour and very tender, try some in a spoon; if it jellies it is enough, then take it off, and put it in gallipots; when it is cold paper it up.

To make Marmalade of Cherries

Take four pounds of cherries, stone them and put them in a preserving-pan, with a quart of juice of currants; set them on a charcoal fire, and let the fire draw away most of the juice; break or mash them, and boil three pounds of sugar candy-high, and put the cherries to it, and set it on the fire again, and boil it till it comes to a body; so put it in glasses, and when it is cold paper it up.

To make a Paste of green Pippins

Take pippins, scald them, and peel them till they are green; when you have peeled them, have fresh warm water ready to put them into, and cover them close, and keep them warm till they are very green; then take the pulp of them, but none of the core, and beat it in a mortar, and pass it through a colander, and to a pound of the pulp put a pound and an ounce of double-refined sugar; boil your sugar till it will ball between your fingers, put in your pulp, and take it off the fire to mix it well together; set it on the fire again, and boil it till it is enough, which you may know by dropping a little on a plate, and then put it in what form you please; dust it with sugar, and set in the stove to dry; turn it, and dust the other side.

To make white Quince Paste

Scald the quinces tender to the core, pare them, and scrape the pulp clean from the core; beat it in a mortar, and pulp it through a colander; take to a pound of pulp a pound and two ounces of sugar; boil the sugar till it is candy-high, then put in your pulp; stir it about constantly till you see it come clear from the bottom of the preserving-pan, then take it off and lay it on plates pretty thin; you may cut it in what shape you please, or make quince chips of it; you must dust it with sugar when you put it into the stove, and turn it on papers in a sieve, and dust the other side; when they are dry put them in boxes, with papers between; you may make red quince paste the same way as this, only colour the quince with cochineal.

To dry Pears or Apples

Take poppering pears, and thrust a picked stick into the head of them beyond the core; then scald them, but not too tender, and pare them the long way; put them in water, and take the weight of them in sugar; clarify it with water, a pint of water to a pound of sugar; strain the syrup, and put in the pears; set them on the fire and boil them pretty fast for half an hour; cover them with paper and set them by till the next day; then boil them again, and set them by till the next day; then take them out of the syrup, and boil it till it is thick and ropy; then put the syrup to them; if it will not cover them, add some sugar to them; set them over the fire and let them boil up, then cover them with paper and set them in a stove twenty-four hours; then lay them on plates, dust them with sugar, and set them in your stove to dry; when one side is dry, lay them on papers, turn them, and dust the other side with sugar; squeeze the pears flat by degrees; if it is apples, squeeze the eye to the stalk; when they are quite dry put them in boxes, with papers between.

To dry Pears or Pippins without Sugar

Take your pears or apples, wipe them clean, and take a bodkin and run it in at the head and out at the stalk; put them in a flat earthen pot and bake them, but not too much; you must put a quart of strong new ale to half a peck of pears, tie white paper over the pot, that they may not be scorched in baking; and when they are bak'd let them stand to be cold, and take them out to drain; squeeze the pears flat, and the apples the eye to the stalk; lay them on sieves with wide holes to dry, either in a stove or an oven that is not too hot.

To candy any sort of Flowers

Take your flowers, and pick them from the white part; then take fine sugar and boil it candy-high; boil as much as you think will receive the quantity of flowers you do, then put in the flowers, and stir them about till you perceive the sugar to candy well about them; then take them off from the fire, and keep them stirring till they are cold in the pan you candied them in; then sift the loose sugar from them, and keep them in boxes very dry.

To candy Orange Flowers

Take half a pound of double-refined sugar, finely beaten, wet it with orange-flower water, and boil it candy-high; then put in a handful of orange-flowers, keeping it stirring, but let it not boil; when the sugar candies about them, take it off the fire; drop it on a plate, and set it by till it is cold.

To make Syrup of any Flowers

Clip your flowers, and take their weight in sugar; then take a gallipot, and put a row of flowers and a strewing of sugar, till the pot is full; then put in two or three spoonfuls of the same syrup or still'd water; tie a cloth on the top of the pot, put a tile on that, set your gallipot in a kettle of water over a gentle fire, and let it infuse till the strength is out of the flowers, which will be in four or five hours; then strain it through a flannel, and when it is cold bottle it up.

To candy any sort of Fruit

After you have preserved your fruit, dip them suddenly into warm water, to take off the syrup; then sift on them double-refined sugar till they look white; then set them on a sieve in a warm oven, taking them out to turn two or three times; let them not be cold till they be dry, and they will look clear as diamonds; so keep them dry.

Another way to preserve Oranges

Take right Seville oranges, the thickest rind you can get, lay them in water, changing the water twice a day for two days, then rub them well with salt, wash them well afterwards, and put them in water, changing the water twice a day for two days more; then put them in a large pot of water to boil, having another pot of boiling water ready to throw them into, as the other grows bitter; change them often till they are tender; then take them up in a linen cloth, and a woollen over it, to keep them hot; take out one at a time, and make a little hole at the top, and pick out the seeds, but do not break the meat; pare them as thin as you can with a sharp penknife; take to a pound of oranges before they are open'd, a pound of double-refined sugar and a pint of fair-water, boil it and skim it, and let it be ready when you pare them, to throw them into; when they are all pared, set them on the fire, cover them close, and keep them boiling as fast as they can boil, till they look clear; then take them up into a deep gallipot, with the holes upward, fill them with syrup, and when they are almost cold, pour the rest of the syrup over them; let them stand a fortnight or three weeks in that syrup; then make a jelly of pippins, and when it is almost ready, take your oranges out of the gallipot, pour all the syrup out of them, put them into the jelly, and let them have a boil or two; then put them into your glasses, and when they are near cold fill them with jelly; the next day paper them.

To preserve Gooseberries in Hops

Take the largest Dutch gooseberries, and with a knife cut them across at the head and halfway down, picking out the seeds clean with a bodkin, but do not break them; then take fine long thorns, scrape them, and put them on your gooseberries, putting the leaf of the one to the cut of the other, and so till your thorn is full; then put them into a new pipkin with a close lid, cover them with water, and let them stand scalding till they are green; then take them up, and lay them upon a sieve to drain from the water; be sure they boil not in the greening, for if they have but one warm they are spoiled; and while they are greening make a syrup for them. Take whole green gooseberries and boil them in water till they all break, then strain the water through a sieve, and weigh your hops, and to a pound of hops put a pound and a half of double-refined sugar, put the sugar and hops into the liquor, and boil them open till they are clear and green, then take them up and lay them upon pie-plates, and boil your syrup longer; lay your hops in a pretty deep gallipot, and when the syrup is cold pour it on them; cover them with paper, and keep them in a stove.

To preserve Gooseberries whole without Stoning

Take the largest preserving gooseberries, and pick off the black eye, but not the stalk, then set them over the fire in a pot of water to scald, cover them very close, and let them scald, but not boil or break, and when they are tender take them up into cold water; then take a pound and a half of double-refined sugar to a pound of gooseberries, clarify the sugar with water, a pint to a pound of sugar; when the syrup is cold, put your gooseberries single into your preserving-pan, put the syrup to them, set them on a gentle fire, and let them boil, but not too fast, lest they break; when they are boiled, and you perceive the sugar has entered them, take them off, cover them with white paper, and set them by till the next day; then take them out of the syrup, and boil the syrup till it begins to be ropy, skim it, and put it to them again, and set them on a gentle fire, and let them preserve gently, till you perceive the syrup will rope; then take them off, and set them by till they are cold, covering them with paper; then boil some gooseberries in fair-water, and when the liquor is strong enough strain it out, let it stand to settle, and to every pint take a pound of double-refined sugar, make a jelly of it, and put the gooseberries in glasses; when they are cold cover them with the jelly; the next day paper them; wet and then half dry the paper that goes in the inside, it closes down better; and then put on the other papers, and put them in your stove.

To make Conserve of red Roses, or any other Flowers

Take rosebuds, pick them, and cut off the white part from the red; put the red flowers into a sieve and sift them to take out the seeds; then weigh them, and to every pound of flowers take two pounds and a half of loaf sugar; beat the flowers pretty fine in a stone mortar, then by degrees put the sugar to them, and beat it very well till it is well incorporated together; then put it into gallipots, and tie it over with paper, and over that leather; it will keep for seven years.

To Stew Apples

Take to a quart of water a pound of double-refined sugar beaten fine, boil and skim it, and put into it a pound of the largest and clearest pippins, pared, cut in halves, and cored; let them boil, cover'd with a continual froth, till they be as tender and clear as you would have them; then put in the juice of two lemons, and a little peel cut like threads; let them have five or six walms after the lemon is in, then put them in a China dish or salver you serve them in; they should be done two hours before used.

To dry Plums or Apricots

Take your plums or apricots and weigh them, and to every pound of fruit allow a pound of double-refin'd sugar; then scald your plums, stone them, and take off the skins, laying your plums on a dry cloth; then just wet your sugar, set it over the fire, and keep it stirring all one way till it boils to sugar again; take that sugar, laying some in the bottom of your preserving pan, and your plums on it; strew the rest of the sugar on the plums, and let it stand till it is melted; then heat it scalding hot twice a-day, but let it not boil; when the syrup is very thick, and candies about the pan, then take them out of the syrup, lay them on glasses to dry, and keep them continually warm, sifting a little sugar over them till they are almost dry; wet the stones in the syrup, and dry them with sugar, and put them at one end of the plum, and when they are thorough dry, keep them in boxes, with papers between.

To make Sugar of Roses

Clip off all the whites from the red rosebuds, and dry the red in the sun; to an ounce of that finely powder'd, you must have one pound of loaf sugar; wet the sugar with rose-water (but if in the season, juice of roses), boil it to a candy-height; then put in your powder of roses, and the juice of a lemon; mix it well together; then pour it on a pie-plate, and cut it into lozenges, or what form you please.

To preserve small Cucumbers green

Take small cucumbers, boil them, but not very tender; when you take them out of the water, make a hole through every one with a large needle; then pare and weigh them, and to every pound allow a pound of sugar, which make into syrup, with a pint of water to every pound of sugar; you must green them before you put them into the sugar; then let them boil, keeping them close cover'd; then put them by, and for three or four days boil them a little every day; put into the syrup the peel of a fresh lemon; then make a fresh syrup with double-refin'd sugar, you must have three quarters of a pound to a pound of cucumbers, and a quarter of a pint of fair-water, the juice of a lemon, and a little amber-grease boil'd in it; so do them for use; paper them when cold.

To preserve Mulberries whole

Set some mulberries over the fire in a skillet, and draw from them a pint of juice, when it is strained; then take three pounds of sugar beaten very fine, wet the sugar with the pint of juice; boil up your sugar and skim it, and put in two pounds of ripe mulberries, letting them stand in the syrup till they are thoroughly warm; then set them on the fire, and let them boil very gently; do them but half enough, so put them by in the syrup till next day; then boil them gently again, and when the syrup is pretty thick, and will stand in a round drop when it is cold, they are enough; put all together in a gallipot for use.

To make Rose Drops

The roses and sugar must be beat separately into a very fine powder, and both sifted; to a pound of sugar an ounce of red roses; they must be mixed together, and then wet with as much juice of lemon as will make it into a stiff paste; set it on a slow fire in a silver porringer, and stir it well, and when scalding hot quite through, take it off and drop it on a paper; set them near the fire, the next day they will come off.

Another way to candy Flowers

Gather your flowers when dry, cut off the leaves as far as the colour is good; according to your quantity, take of double-refined sugar, and wet it with fair-water, and boil it to a candy-height; then put in your flowers – of what sort you please, as primroses, violets, cowslips, or borage – with a spoon; take them out as quick as you can, with as little of the syrup as may be, and lay them in a dish over a gentle fire, and with a knife spread them, that the syrup may run from them; then change them upon another warm dish, and when they are dry from the syrup, have ready some double-refined sugar beaten and sifted, and strew some on your flowers; then take the flowers in your hand, and rub them gently in the hollow of your hand, and that will open the leaves, a stander-by strewing more sugar into your hand as you see convenient; so do till they are thoroughly open'd and dry; then put your flowers into a dry sieve, and sift all the sugar clean from them; they must be kept in a dry place; rosemary flowers must be put whole into your syrup; young mint leaves you must open with your fingers, but all blossoms rub with your hand as directed.

To make Cakes of Flowers

Boil double-refin'd sugar candy-high, and then strew in your flowers, and let them boil once up; then with your hand lightly strew in a little double-refined sugar sifted, and then as quick as may be put it into your little pans, made of card, and prick'd full of holes at bottom; you must set the pans on a pillow, or cushion; when they are cold, take them out.

To make Wormwood Cakes

Take one pound of double-refined sugar sifted, mix it with the whites of three or four eggs well beat, into this drop as much chymical oil of wormwood as you please; so drop them on paper; you may have some white and some marble, and some speckled with colour with the point of a pin; keep your colours severally in little gallipots: for red, take a drachm of cochineal, a little cream of tartar, as much of alum, tie them up severally in little bits of fine cloth, and put them to steep in one glass of water two or three hours when you use the colour, press the bags in the water, and mix some of it with a little of the white of egg and sugar. Saffron colours yellow, and must be tied in a cloth, as the red, and put in water. Powder blue mixed with the saffron-water makes a green; for blue, mix some dry powder blue with some water.

To candy Orange-Flowers

Take orange-flowers that are stiff and fresh pick'd, boil them in a good quantity of spring-water in a preserving pan; when they are tender, take them out, drain them in a sieve, and lay them between two napkins till they be very dry; take the weight of your flowers in double-refined sugar; if you have a pound, take half a pint of water and boil with the sugar, till it will stand in a drop, then take it off the fire, and when it is almost cold put it to the flowers, which must be in a silver basin; shake them very well together, and set them in a stove or in the sun, and as they begin to candy, take them out, and put them on glasses to dry, keeping them turning till they are dry.

Another

Take orange-flowers that are stiff and fresh, boil them in a good quantity of spring-water in a preserving-pan, and when they are tender take them up, drain them through a sieve, and dry them between napkins every day; take their weight in double-refined sugar, and to a pound put half a pint of water, boil it till it stands in a thick drop, and when it is almost cold put it to your flowers in a silver or China basin; shake them well together, and set them in a stove, or in the sun, and when they begin to candy take them out, and lay them on glasses to dry; sift sugar on them, and turn them every day till they are crisp.

Another

First pick your orange-flowers, and boil them quick in fair-water till they are very tender; then drain them through a hair sieve very clean from the water; to a pound of double-refined sugar take half a pint of fair-water, and as much orange-flower water, and boil it up to a thick syrup; then pour it out into broad flat glasses, and let the syrup stand in the glasses about an inch thick; when it is near cold, drop in your flowers, as many as you think convenient, and set your glasses in a stove with a moderate heat, for the flower they candy, the finer the rock will be; when you see it is well candied top and bottom, and that it glitters, break the candy at top in as great flakes as you can, and lay the biggest piece at the bottom on glass-plates, and pick out the rest, piling it up with the flowers to what size you please; after that it will presently be dry in a stove.

A fine way to preserve Raspberries

Take the juice of red and white raspberries and codlin jelly; to a pint and half, two pounds of double-refined sugar; boil it, and scum, and then put in three quarters of a pound of large pick'd raspberries; let them boil very fast, till they jelly and are clear; don't take them off the fire, that will make them hard; a quarter of an hour will do them when they begin to boil; then put your raspberries in the glass first, and strain the seeds from the jelly, and put it to them; and when they begin to cool, stir them gently, that they may not all lie on the top of the glass; and when they are cold, lay papers close on them; first wet the papers, and dry them in a cloth.

To make a Strong Apple-Jelly

Let your water boil in the pan you make it in, and when the apples are par'd and quarter'd, put them into your boiling water; let there be no more water than will just cover them, and let it boil as fast as possible; and when the apples are all to pieces, put in about a quart of water more, and let it boil half an hour longer, then run it thro' a jelly-bag, and use it as occasion for any sort of sweetmeat; in the summer codlins are best, in the winter golden rennets or winter pippins.

To preserve Raspberries whole

Take the full weight of your raspberries in double-refined sugar, beaten and sifted; lay your raspberries single in the bottom of your preserving-pan, and put all your sugar over them; set them on a slow fire, till there is some syrup in the bottom of the pan; then set them on a quick fire, till all the sugar be thoroughly melted; give them two or three walms, scum them, take them up, and put them in glasses.

To make Chocolate Almonds

Take a pound of chocolate finely grated, and a pound and a half of the best sugar finely sifted; then soak gum-dragant in orange-flower water, and work them into what form you please; the past must be stiff; dry them in a stove.

To make Lemon Puffs

Take a pound and a quarter of double-refin'd sugar beaten and sifted, and grate the rinds of two lemons, and mix well with the sugar; then beat the whites of three new-laid eggs very well, and mix it well with your sugar and lemon-peel; beat them together an hour and a quarter, then make it up in what form you please; be quick to set them in a moderate oven; don't take them off the papers till cold.

To make Almond Loaves

Blanch your almonds in hot water, and throw them into cold; then take their weight in double-refined sugar finely searced, beat them together until they come to a paste; make them up into little loaves, and ice them over with some white of egg and sugar; bake them on paper; if you please you may throw your almonds into orange-flower water instead of cold water.

To make Lemon Biscuit

Take six yellow rinds well beat with a pound of double-refin'd sugar and whites of four eggs till come to a paste; lay them on wafer-paper, so bake them on tins.

To make Orange Chips crisp

Pare your oranges very thin, leaving as little white on the peel as possible; throw the rinds into fair-water as you pare them off, then boil them therein very fast till they are tender, still filling up the pan with boiling water as it wastes away; then make a thin syrup with part of the water they were boil'd in, and put the rinds therein, and just let 'em boil; then take them off, and let them lie in the syrup three or four days; then boil them again, till you find the syrup begins to draw between your fingers; then take them off from the fire and let them drain through a colander; take out but a few at a time, because, if they cool too fast, it will be difficult to get the syrup from them, which must be done by passing every piece of peel through your fingers, and laying them single on a sieve, with the rind uppermost; the sieves may be set in a stove, or before the fire; but in summer the sun is hot enough to dry them; three pounds of sugar will make syrup to do the peels of twenty-five oranges.

To make Syrup of Orange-Peel

To every pint of the water in which the orange-peels were steep'd put a pound of sugar, boil it, and when it has boiled a little squeeze in some juice of lemon, making it more or less sharp to your taste; filter the lemon-juice thro' cap-paper; as it boils skim it clear; when boiled enough to keep, take it off the fire, and when cold bottle it; when your orange-peels are dried on one side, turn the other, and do so till they are crisp; brush the sugar from them, then take a cloth dipped in warm water and wipe off all that remains of sugar on the rind side; then lay them on the sieve again, and in an hour they will be dry enough to put into your boxes to keep.

To make Orange Marmalade

Take a pound of the best Seville oranges, pare off all the yellow rind very thin, quarter the peel, put them in water, cover them down close, and shift the water six or seven times as it boils, to take the bitterness out, and that they may look clear and be tender; then take them out, dry them in a cloth, take out all the strings, and cut them thin as palates; then take a pound of double-refin'd sugar beaten, and boil it with a little water to a candy-height; skim it clean and put in your peels, let them boil near half an hour; have in readiness your orange-meat all pick'd from the skins and seeds, and the juice of two large lemons, and put it into the peels, boiling all together a quarter of an hour longer; so glass it up, and paper it when cold.

To make Orange Cakes

Cut your oranges, pick out all their meat and juice free from the strings and seeds, and set it by; then boil it, and shift the water till your peels are tender; dry them in a cloth, mince them small, and put them to the juice; to a pound of that weigh a pound and a half of double-refined sugar; dip your lumps of sugar in water, and boil it to a candy-height; take it off the fire, and put in your juice and peel, stir it well, and when it is almost cold put it in a basin, and set it in a stove; then lay it thin on earthen plates to dry, and as it candies fashion it with your knife; and as they dry lay them on glass; when your plate is empty, put more out of your basin.

To make Lemon Cakes

Grate off the yellow rind of your lemon, and squeeze your juice to that peel; take two apples to every lemon, pare and core them, and boil them clear, then put them to your lemon; to a pound of this put two pounds of double-refined sugar, then order it as the orange.

To make clear Candy

Take six ounces of water, and four ounces of fine sugar searced, set it on a slow fire to melt without stirring, let it boil till it comes to a strong candy; then have ready your peel or fruit scalded hot in the syrup they were kept in, drain them very well from it, and put them into your candy, which you must rub on the sides of your basin with the back of your spoon till you see the candy pretty white; take out the fruit with a fork, touch it not with your fingers; if right, the candy will shine on your fruit, and dry in three or four hours in an indifferent hot stove; lay your fruit on sieves.

To keep Fruit in Syrup to candy

If you candy orange- or lemon-peels, you must first rub them with salt, then cut in what fashion you please, and keep them in water two days, then boil them tender, shifting the water you boil them in two or three times; you must have a syrup ready, a pint of water to a pound of sugar, scald your peels in it till they look clear. Fruit is done the same way, but not boil'd till you put them in your syrup; you must heat your syrup once a week, taking out your fruit, and putting them in again while the syrup is hot; the syrup will keep all the year.

To dry Apricots like Prunellos

Take a pound of apricots, being cut in halves or quarters, let them boil till they be very tender in a thin syrup; let them stand a day or two in the stove; take them out of the syrup, and lay them drying till they be as dry as prunellos, then box them; you may make your syrup red with the juice of red plums; if you please you may pare them.

To preserve green Cucumbers

Take gerkins, rub them clean, and green them in hot water; then take their weight in double-refin'd sugar, boil it to a thick syrup with a quarter of a pint of spring-water to every pound of sugar; then put in your cucumbers and set them over the fire, but not to boil fast – so do two or three days; the last day boil them till they are tender and clear, so glass them up.

To keep Artichokes all the year

In the latter end of the season boil them till they be half enough, and then dry them on a hair cloth upon a kiln the space of fifty hours, till they are very dry; lay them in a dry place; when you use them, soak them a night in water, and boil them till they are tender.

To keep Walnuts all the year

Almost in the latter end of the season, take off the green shell of your nuts, and dry them on a hair cloth on the kiln forty hours; when they are dry, keep them for use; when you would use them, soak them three days in water, shifting them three times a day.

To make clear Cakes of Gooseberries

Take your white Dutch gooseberries when they are thorough ripe, break them with your fingers, and squeeze out all the pulp into a fine piece of cambric or thick muslin, to run thro' clear; then weigh the juice and sugar one against the other; then boil the juice a little while; then put in your sugar and let it dissolve, but not boil; skim it and put it into glasses, and stove it in a warm stove.

Another way to make Orange Marmalade

Rasp your oranges, cut out all the meat, boil the rinds very tender, and cut them very fine; then take three pounds of double-refined sugar, and a pint of water, boil and skim it, and then put in a pound of rind; boil very fast till the sugar is very thick, then put in the meat of your oranges, the seeds and skins being pick'd out, and a pint of very strong pippin jelly; boil all together very fast half an hour, then put it in flat pots or glasses; when it is cold paper it up.

To preserve Cherries

Gather your cherries of a bright red, not too ripe, weigh them, and to every pound of cherries put three quarters of a pound of double-refin'd sugar beaten fine; stone them, and strew some sugar on them as you stone them; to keep their colour, wet your sugar with fair-water, near half a pint, and boil and skim it, then put in three small spoonfuls of the juice of currants that was infused with a little water; give it another boil and skim, and put in your cherries; boil them till they are tender, then pour them into a China basin; cover them with paper, and set them by twenty-four hours; then put them in your preserving pan and boil them till they look clear; put them in your glass clear from the syrup, and put the syrup on them strain'd thro' muslin.

To preserve green Apricots

Before the stones are hard, wet them and lay them in a coarse cloth, and put to them two or three handfuls of salt, rubbing them till the roughness is off; then put them in scalding water, and set them over the fire till almost boiled; then set them off till almost cold; do this two or three times; after this let them be close covered, and when they look green, let them boil till they begin to be tender; weigh them, and take their weight in double-refined sugar, to a pound of sugar half a pint of water; make the syrup, and when almost cold put in your apricots, boil them well till clear; warm the syrup two or three times till thick, or put them in cold jelly, or dry them as you use them.

Another

Take green apricots, about the middle of June, or when the stone is hard, put them on the fire in cold water three or four hours, cover them close, but first take their weight in double-refined sugar; then pare them nicely; dip your sugar in water, and boil the water and sugar very well; then put in your apricots, and let them boil till they begin to open; then take out the stone, and close it up again, and put them in the syrup, and let them boil till they are enough, skimming all the while; then put them in pots.

To preserve Apricots that are ripe

Gather your apricots about half ripe, before they look too yellow; weigh them, and to every pound put three quarters of a pound of treble-refined sugar, finely beaten and sifted; then pare them, and cut them in the parting to take out the stone; then make a fine syrup of the sugar, keeping a little out to strew on them whilst they are boiling; and after they are boiled a little, take them out of the pan and put them in a basin; cover them close with paper, and let them stand twenty-four hours; be careful not to break them in taking them out; the next day boil them up for good; put them into your glasses with care; strain your syrup over them through muslin.

To candy Orange Chips

Pare your oranges, and soak the peelings in water two days, shifting the water twice; but if you love them bitter, soak them not; tie your peels up in a cloth, and when your water boils put them in, and let them boil till they are tender; then take what double-refined sugar will do, break it small, wet it with a little water, and let it boil till it is near candy-high; then cut your peels of what lengths you please, and put them into the syrup; set them on the fire, and let them heat well through; then let them stand a while; heat them twice a day, but not boil; let them be so done till they begin to candy, then take them out and put them on plates to dry, and when dry keep them near the fire.

To scald Fruit for present use

Put your fruit into boiling water, as much as will almost cover them, set them over a slow fire and keep them in a scald till tender, turning the fruit where the water does not cover; when tender, lay paper close on it, let it stand till cold; to a pound of fruit put half a pound of sugar; let it boil, but not fast, till it looks clear; all fruit are done whole but pippins, and they in halves, with orange- or lemon-peel, and juice of lemon; cut your peel very thin, like threads, and strew them on your pippins.

To make Marmalade of Apricots

Gather your apricots just turn'd from the green, of a very pale yellow, pare them thin and weigh them, three quarters of a pound of double-refined sugar to a pound of apricots; then cut them in halves, take out the stones, and slice them thin; beat your sugar, and put it in your preserving pan with your sliced apricots, and three or four spoonfuls of water; boil and skim them, and when they are tender put them in glasses.

To make a Gooseberry Jam

Gather your gooseberries full ripe, but green, top and tail them, and weigh them, a pound of fruit to three quarters of a pound of double-refined sugar, and half a pint of water; boil them till clear and tender, then put them in pots.

To keep Orange-Flowers in Syrup

Pick off the leaves, and throw them in water boiling on the fire, and squeeze into it the juice of two or three lemons; let them boil half a quarter of an hour, and then throw them into cold water; then lay them on cloths to drain well; then beat and sift some double-refined sugar, lay some on the bottom of a gallipot, and then a layer of flowers, and then more sugar, till all is in; when the sugar melts put in more, till there is a pretty deal of syrup, so paper them up for use; you may put them in jelly, or what you please.

To make white Quince Marmalade

Scald your quinces tender, take off the skin, and pulp them from the core very fine, and to every pound of quince have a pound and a half of double-refined sugar in lumps, and half a pint of water; dip your sugar in the water, and boil and skim it till it is a thick syrup; then put in your quince, boil and skim it on a quick fire a quarter of an hour, so put it in your pots.

To make red Quince Marmalade

Pare and core a pound of quince, beat the parings and cores and some of your worst quinces, and strain out the juice; to every pound of quince take ten or twelve spoonfuls of that juice and three quarters of a pound of loaf sugar; put all into your preserving-pan, cover it close, and let it stew over a gentle fire two hours; when it is of an orange-red, uncover, and boil it up as fast as you can; when of a good colour, break it as you like it; give it a boil and pot it up.

To preserve Apricots ripe

Gather your apricots of a fine colour, but not too ripe; weigh them, and to every pound of apricots put a pound of double-refin'd sugar beaten and sifted; stone and pare your apricots; as you pare them put them into the pan you do them in, with sugar strew'd over and under them; let them not touch one another, but put sugar between; cover them up and let them lie till the next day, then stir them gently till the sugar is melted; then put them on a quick fire and let them boil half an hour, skimming exceeding well all the while; then take it off and cover it till it is quite cold, or till the next day; then boil it again, skimming it very well till it is enough; so put it in pots.

To preserve the great white Plum

To a pound of plums take three quarters of a pound of double-refined sugar in lumps; dip your sugar in water, and boil and skim very well; slit your plums down the seam, and put them into the syrup with the slit downward; let them stew over the fire a quarter of an hour; skim very well and take them off; and when cold turn them, and cover them up, and turn them in the syrup, every day, two or three times a day, for five days; then put them in pots.

To make Jelly of Currants

Strip your currants, put them in a jug, and infuse in water; strain out the juice upon sugar, sweeten to your taste, boil it a great while till it jellies, skimming all the while, and then put it in your glasses.

To make Apricot Chips

Pare your apricots, and part them in the middle; take out the stone, and cut them crossways pretty thin; as you cut them strew a very little sugar over them beaten and sifted, then set them on the fire, and let them stew gently a quarter of an hour; then take them off, cover them up, and set them by till the next day; then set them on the fire as long as before; take them out one by one and lay them on a sieve; strew sugar on the sieve, and over them; dry them in the sun or cool oven, turn them often; when they are dry put them in boxes.

All Sorts of
Made Wines,
&c.

To make Apricot Wine

Take three pounds of sugar and three quarts of water, let them boil together, and skim it well; then put in six pounds of apricots pared and stoned, and let them boil till they are tender; then take them up, and when the liquor is cold bottle it up; you may if you please, after you have taken out the apricots, let the liquor have one boil with a sprig of flower'd clary in it. The apricots make marmalade, and are very good for present spending.

To make Damson Wine

Gather your damsons dry, weigh them, and bruise them with your hand; put them into an earthen stein that has a saucet, put a wreath of straw before the saucet; to every eight pounds of fruit a gallon of water; boil the water, skim it, and put it to your fruit scalding hot; let it stand two whole days; then draw it off, and put it into a vessel fit for it, and to every gallon of liquor put two pounds and a half of fine sugar; let the vessel be full, and stop it close; the longer it stands the better; it will keep a year in the vessel; bottle it out; the small damson is the best: you may put a very small lump of double-refined sugar in every bottle.

To make Gooseberry Wine

Take to every four pounds of gooseberries a pound and a quarter of sugar, and a quart of fair-water; bruise the berries, and steep them twenty-four hours in the water, stirring them often; then press the liquor from them, and put your sugar to the liquor; then put it in a vessel fit for it, and when it has done working stop it up, and let it stand a month; then rack it off into another vessel, and let it stand five or six weeks longer; then bottle it out, putting a small lump of sugar into every bottle; cork your bottles well, and at three months end it will be fit to drink. In the same manner is currant and raspberry wine made; but cherry wine differs, for the cherries are not to be bruised, but stoned, and put the sugar and water together, and give it a boil and a skim, and then put in your fruit, letting it stew with a gentle fire a quarter of an hour; then let it run through a sieve without pressing, and when it is cold put it in a vessel, and order it as your gooseberry or currant wine. The only cherries for wine are the great bearers, murrey cherries, morellos, black Flanders, or the John Treduskin cherries.

Pearl Gooseberry Wine

Take as many as you please of the best pearl gooseberries, bruise them, and let them stand all night; the next morning press or squeeze them out, and let the liquor stand to settle seven or eight hours; then pour off the clear from the settling, and measure it as you put it into your vessel, adding to every three pints of liquor a pound of double-refined sugar; break your sugar in small lumps, and put it in the vessel, with a bit of isinglass, stop it up, and at three months' end bottle it out, putting into every bottle a lump of double-refined sugar. This is the fine gooseberry wine.

To make Caraway Brandy

Steep an ounce of caraway seeds and six ounces of sugar in a quart of brandy for nine days, and clear it off; it is a good cordial.

To make Cherry Brandy

Take six dozen pounds of cherries, half red and half black, mash or squeeze them with your hands to pieces, and put to them three gallons of brandy, letting them stand steeping twenty-four hours; then put the mashed cherries, and liquor a little at a time, into a canvas bag, and press it as long as any juice will run; sweeten it to your taste, put it into a vessel fit for it, let it stand a month, and bottle it out; put a lump of loaf sugar into every bottle.

Another

To every four quarts of brandy put four pounds of red cherries, two pounds of black, and one quart of raspberries, a few cloves, a stick of cinnamon, and a bit of orange-peel; let these stand a month close stopt, then bottle it off; adding a lump of sugar in every bottle.

To make Cherry Wine

Pull the stalks off the cherries, and mash them without breaking the stones; then press them hard thro' a hair bag, and to every gallon of liquor put a pound and a half of sixpenny sugar; the vessel must be full, and let it work as long as it makes a noise in the vessel; then stop it up close for a month or six weeks; when it is fine, draw it into bottles, put a lump of loaf sugar into each bottle, and if any of them fly, open them all for a moment, and cork them well again; it will not be fit to drink in less than a quarter of a year.

To make Currant Wine

Take four gallons of currants, not too ripe, and strip them into an earthen stein that has a cover to it; then take two gallons and a half of water, and five pounds and a half of double-refined sugar; boil the sugar, and water together, skim it, and pour it boiling hot on the currants, letting it stand forty-eight hours; then strain it through a flannel bag into the stein again, let it stand a fortnight to settle, and bottle it out.

To make Mead

To thirteen gallons of water put thirty-two pounds of honey, boil and skim it well, then take rosemary, thyme, bay-leaves and sweet-briar, one handful all together; boil it an hour, then put it into a tub with two or three good handfuls of the flour of malt; stir it till it is but blood warm, then strain it through a cloth and put it into a tub again; then cut a toast round a quartern loaf, spread it over with good ale-yeast, and put it into your tub; when the liquor has done fermenting put it up in your vessel; then take cloves, mace, nutmegs, an ounce and a half, ginger an ounce, sliced; bruise the spice, and tie all up in a rag, and hang it in the vessel; stop it up close for use.

To make Strong Mead

Take of spring-water what quantity you please, make it more than blood-warm, and dissolve honey in it till it is strong enough to bear an egg, the breadth of a shilling, then boil it gently, near an hour, taking off the scum as it rises; then put to about nine or ten gallons, seven or eight large blades of mace, three nutmegs quartered, twenty cloves, three or four sticks of cinnamon, two or three roots of ginger, and a quarter of an ounce of Jamaica pepper; put these spices into the kettle to the honey and water, a whole lemon, with a sprig of sweet-briar, and a sprig of rosemary; tie the briar and rosemary together, and when they have boiled a little while, take them out, and throw them away; but let your liquor stand on the spice in a clean earthen pot, till the next day; then strain it into a vessel that is fit for it, put the spice in a bag, hang it in the vessel, stop it, and at three months draw it into bottles: be sure that it is fine when it is bottled; after it is bottled six weeks, it is fit to drink.

To make small white Mead

Take three gallons of spring-water, make it hot, and dissolve in it three quarts of honey, and a pound of loaf sugar; let it boil about half an hour, and skim it as long as any rises; then pour it out into a tub, and squeeze in the juice of four lemons, put in the rinds but of two, twenty cloves, two races of ginger, a top of sweet-briar, and a top of rosemary; let it stand in a tub till it is but blood warm; then make a brown toast, and spread with two or three spoonfuls of ale-yeast; put it into a vessel fit for it; let it stand four or five days, then bottle it out.

To make Raisin Wine

Take two gallons of spring-water, and let it boil half an hour; then put into a stein-pot two pound of raisins stoned, two pounds of sugar, the rind of two lemons, and the juice of four; then pour the boiling water on the things in the stein, and let it stand cover'd four or five days; strain it out and bottle it up: in fifteen or sixteen days it will be fit to drink; it is a very cool and pleasant drink in hot weather.

Another

Take the best Malaga raisins, and pick the large stalks out, and have your water ready boil'd and cold; measure as many gallons as you design to make, and put it into a great tub, that it may have room to stir; to every gallon of water put six pounds of raisins, and let it stand fourteen days, stirring it twice a day; when you strain it off, or press it, you must do nothing to it, but leave enough to fill up your cask, which you must do as it wastes; it will be two months or more before it has done working; you must not stop it while you hear it hiss.

To make Shrub

Take two quarts of brandy, and put it in a large bottle, adding to it the juice of five lemons, the peels of two, and half a nutmeg; stop it up and let it stand three days, and add to it three pints of white wine, a pound and half of sugar; mix it, strain it twice through a flannel, and bottle it up; it is a pretty wine, and a cordial.

To make Orange Wine

Put twelve pounds of fine sugar and the whites of eight eggs well beaten into six gallons of spring-water; let it boil an hour, skimming it all the time; take it off, and when it is pretty cool put in the juice and rind of fifty Seville oranges, and six spoonfuls of good ale-yeast, and let it stand two days; then put it into your vessel, with two quarts of rhenish wine, and the juice of twelve lemons; you must let the juice of lemons and wine, and two pounds of double-refined sugar, stand close cover'd ten or twelve hours before you put it in the vessel to your orange wine, and skim off the seeds before you put it in; the lemon-peels must be put in with the oranges, half the rinds must be put into the vessel; it must stand ten or twelve days before it is fit to bottle.

To make Birch Wine

In March bore a hole in a birch tree, and put in a saucet, and it will run two or three days together without hurting the tree; then put in a pin to stop it, and the next year you may draw as much from the same hole; put to every gallon of the liquor a quart of good honey, and stir it well together; boil it an hour, skim it well, and put in a few cloves and a piece of lemon-peel; when it is almost cold put to it so much ale-yeast as will make it work like new ale; and when the yeast begins to settle, put it in a runlet that will just hold it; so let it stand six weeks, or longer if you please; then bottle it, and in a month you may drink it; it will keep a year or two; you may make it with sugar, two pounds to a gallon, or something more, if you keep it long; this is admirably wholesome as well as pleasant – an opener of obstructions, good against the phthisic, the spleen and scurvy, a remedy for the stone; it will abate heat in a fever or thrush, and has been given with good success.

To make Sugar Wine

Boil twenty-six quarts of spring-water a quarter of an hour, and when it is blood-warm put twenty-five pounds of Malaga raisins pick'd, rub'd, and shred into it, with half a bushel of red sage shred, and a porringer of ale-yeast; stir all well together, and let it stand in a tub covered warm six or seven days, stirring it once a day; then strain it out and put it in a runlet; let it work three or four days, and stop it up; when it has stood six or seven days put in a quart or two of Malaga sack, and when it is fine bottle it.

To make Cowslip Wine

To six gallons of water put fourteen pounds of sugar, stir it well together, and beat the whites of twenty eggs very well, and mix it with the liquor, and make it boil as fast as possible; skim it well, and let it continue boiling two hours; then strain it thro' a hair sieve, and set it a cooling; and when it is as cold as wort should be, put a small quantity of yeast to it on a toast, or in a dish; let it stand all night working; then bruise a peck of cowslips, put them into your vessel, and your liquor upon them, adding six ounces of syrup of lemons; cut a turf of grass and lay on the bung; let it stand a fortnight, and then bottle it; put your tap into your vessel before you put your wine in, that you may not shake it.

To make Raspberry Wine

Take your quantity of raspberries and bruise them, put them in an open pot twenty-four hours, then squeeze out the juice, and to every gallon put three pounds of fine sugar and two quarts of canary; put it into a stein or vessel, and when it hath done working stop it close; when it is fine bottle it: it must stand two months before you drink it.

To make Raspberry Wine another way

Pound your fruit and strain them through a cloth, then boil as much water as juice of raspberries, and when it is cold put it to your squeezings; let it stand together five hours, then strain it and mix it with the juice, adding to every gallon of this liquor two pounds and a half of fine sugar; let it stand in an earthen vessel close cover'd a week, then put it in a vessel fit for it, and let it stand a month, or till it is fine: bottle it off.

To make Morello-Cherry Wine

Let your cherries be very ripe, pick off the stalks, and bruise your fruit without breaking the stones; put them in an open vessel together; let them stand twenty-four hours; then press them, and to every gallon put two pounds of fine sugar; then put it up in your cask, and when it has done working stop it close; let it stand three or four months and bottle it; will be fit to drink in two months.

To make Quince Wine

Take your quinces when they are thorough ripe, wipe off the fur very clean; then take out the cores, bruise them as you do apples for cyder, and press them, adding to every gallon of juice two pounds and a half of fine sugar; stir it together till it is dissolved; then put it in your cask, and when it has done working, stop it close; let it stand till March before you bottle it. You may keep it two or three years, it will be the better.

Another sort of Raspberry Wine

Take four gallons of raspberries, and put them in an earthen pot; then take four gallons of water, boil it two hours, let it stand till it is blood-warm, put it to the raspberries, and stir them well together; let it stand twelve hours; then strain it off, and to every gallon of liquor put three pounds of loaf sugar, set it over a clear fire, and let it boil till all the scum is taken off; when it is cold, put it into bottles, and open the corks every day for a fortnight, and then stop them close.

To make Poppy Brandy

Take six quarts of the best and freshest poppies, cut off the black ends of them, put them in a glass jar that will hold two gallons, and press them in it, then pour over it a gallon of brandy, stop the glass very well, and set it in the sun for a week or more, then squeeze out the poppies with your hand, and sweeten it to your taste with double-refined sugar, adding to it an ounce and half of alkermes: mix it well together and bottle it up. This is in imitation of rosa folis.

To make Lemon Wine

Take six large lemons, pare off the rind, cut them, and squeeze out the juice; steep the rind in the juice, and put to it a quart of brandy; let it stand in an earthen pot close stopt three days; then squeeze six more, and mix with two quarts of spring-water, and as much sugar as will sweeten the whole; boil the water, lemons, and sugar together, letting it stand till it is cool; then add a quart of white wine, and the other lemon and brandy, and mix them together, and run it thro' a flannel bag into some vessel; let it stand three months and bottle it off; cork your bottles very well, and keep it cool; it will be fit to drink in a month or six weeks.

To make Elder Wine

Take twenty-five pounds of Malaga raisins, rub them and shred them small; then take five gallons of fair-water; boil it an hour, and let it stand till it is but blood-warm; then put it in an earthen crock or tub, with your raisins; let them steep ten days, stirring them once or twice a day; then pass the liquor thro' a hair sieve, and have in readiness five pints of the juice of elderberries drawn off as you do for jelly of currants; then mix it cold with the liquor, stir it well together, put it into a vessel, and let it stand in a warm place; when it has done working stop it close; bottle it about Candlemas.

To make Barley Water

Take of pearl barley four ounces, put it in a large pipkin and cover it with water; when the barley is thick and tender, put in more water and boil it up again, and so do till it is of a good thickness to drink; then put in a blade or two of mace, or a stick of cinnamon; let it have a walm or two and strain it out; squeeze in the juice of two or three lemons, and a bit of the peel, and sweeten it to your taste with fine sugar; let it stand till it is cold, and then run it through a bag, and bottle it up; it will keep three or four days.

To make Barley Wine

Take half a pound of French barley and boil it in three waters, and save three pints of the last water, and mix it with a quart of white wine, half a pint of borage-water, as much clary-water, a little red-rose water, the juice of five or six lemons, three quarters of a pound of fine sugar, and the thin yellow rind of a lemon; brew all these quick together, run it through a strainer and bottle it up; it is pleasant in hot weather, and very good in fevers.

To make Plum Wine

Take twenty pounds of Malaga raisins, pick, rub, and shred them, and put them into a tub; then take four gallons of fair-water, boil it an hour, and let it stand till it is blood-warm; then put it to your raisins; let it stand nine or ten days, stirring it once or twice a day; strain out your liquor, and mix with it two quarts of damson juice; put it in a vessel, and when it has done working stop it close; at four or five months bottle it.

To make Ebulum

To a hogshead of strong ale take a heap'd bushel of elderberries, and half a pound of juniper-berries beaten; put in all the berries when you put in the hops, and let them boil together till the berries break in pieces, then work it up as you do ale; when it has done working, add to it half a pound of ginger, half an ounce of cloves, as much mace, an ounce of nutmegs, as much cinnamon, grossly beaten, half a pound of citron, as much eryngo root, and likewise of candied orange-peel; let the sweetmeats be cut in pieces very thin, and put with the spice into a bag, and hang it in the vessel when you stop it up; so let it stand till it is fine, then bottle it up, and drink it with lumps of double-refined sugar in the glass.

To make Cock Ale

Take ten gallons of ale and a large cock, the older the better; parboil the cock, flay him and stamp him in a stone mortar till his bones are broken (you must craw and gut him when you flay him), then put the cock into two quarts of sack, and put to it three pounds of raisins of the sun stoned, some blades of mace, and a few cloves; put all these into a canvas bag, and a little before you find the ale has done working, put the ale and bag together into a vessel; in a week or nine days' time bottle it up; fill the bottle but just above the neck, and give it the same time to ripen as other ale.

To make Elder Wine at Christmas

Take twenty pounds of Malaga or Lipara raisins, rub them clean, and shred them small; then take five gallons of water, boil it an hour, and when it is near cold put it in a tub with the raisins; let them steep ten days, and stir them once or twice a day; then strain it thro' a hair sieve, and by infusion draw three pints of elder-juice, and one pint of damson-juice; make the juice into a thin syrup, a pound of sugar to a pint of juice, and not boil it much, but just enough to keep; when you have strained out the raisin-liquor, put that and the syrup into a vessel fit for it, and two pounds of sugar; stop the bung with a cork till it gathers to a head, then open it, and let it stand till it has done working; then put the cork in again, and stop it very close, and let it stand in a warm place two or three months, and then bottle it; make the elder- and damson-juice into syrup in its season, and keep it in a cool cellar till you have convenience to make the wine.

To make fine Milk Punch

Take two quarts of water, one quart of milk, half a pint of lemon-juice, and one quart of brandy, sugar to your taste; put the milk and water together a little warm, then the sugar, then the lemon-juice, stir it well together, then the brandy; stir it again, and run it through a flannel bag till it is very fine, then bottle it; it will keep a fortnight, or more.

Sage Wine another way

Take thirty pounds of Malaga raisins picked clean and shred small, and one bushel of green sage shred small; then boil five gallons of water, let the water stand till it is lukewarm, then put it in a tub to your sage and raisins; let it stand five or six days, stirring it twice or thrice a day; then strain and press the liquor from the ingredients, put it in a cask, and let it stand six months, then draw it clean off into another vessel; bottle it in two days; in a month or six weeks it will be fit to drink, but best when it is a year old.

To make Palermo Wine

Take to every quart of water a pound of Malaga raisins, rub and cut the raisins small, and put them to the water, and let them stand ten days, stirring once or twice a day; you may boil the water an hour before you put it to the raisins, and let it stand to cool; at ten days' end strain out your liquor, and put a little yeast to it; and at three days' end put it in the vessel, with one sprig of dried wormwood; let it be close stopt, and at three months' end bottle it off.

To make Clary Wine

Take twenty-four pounds of Malaga raisins, pick them and chop them very small, put them in a tub, and to each pound a quart of water; let them steep ten or eleven days, stirring it twice every day; you must keep it covered close all the while; then strain it off, and put it into a vessel with about half a peck of the tops of clary, when it is in blossom; stop it close for six weeks, and then bottle it off; in two or three months it is fit to drink. It is apt to have a great settlement at bottom; therefore it is best to draw it off by plugs, or tap it pretty high.

The fine Clary Water

Take a quart of borage water, put it in an earthen jug, and fill it with two or three quarts of clary flowers fresh gather'd; let it infuse an hour over the fire in a kettle of water, then take out the flowers and put in as many fresh flowers, and so do for six or seven times together; then add to that water two quarts of the best sack, a gallon of fresh flowers, and two pounds of white sugar-candy beaten small, and distil it all off in a cold still; mix all the water together, and sweeten it to your taste with the finest sugar. This is a very wholesome, and fine entertaining water. Cork the bottles well and keep it cool.

To recover Wine that is turned sharp

Rack off your wine into another vessel, and to ten gallons put the following powder: take oyster-shells, scrape and wash off the brown dirty outside of the shell, then dry them in an oven till they will powder; a pound of this powder to every nine or ten gallons of your wine; stir it well together, and stop it up, and let it stand to settle two or three days, or till it is fine; as soon as it is fine, bottle it off, and cork it well.

To fine Wine the Lisbon way

To every twenty gallons of wine, take the whites of ten eggs, and a small handful of salt; beat these together to a froth, and mix it well with a quart or more of the wine; then pour it into the vessel, and in a few days it will be fine.

To clear Wine

Take half a pound of hartshorn, and dissolve it in cyder, if it be for cyder, or rhenish wine for any liquor. This is enough for a hogshead.

To make Orange Wine with Raisins

Take thirty pounds of new Malaga raisins, pick them clean, and chop them small; you must have twenty large Seville oranges, ten of them you must pare as thin as for preserving. Boil about eight gallons of soft water, till a third part be consumed; let it cool a little, then put five gallons of it hot upon your raisins and orange-peel; stir it well together, cover it up, and when it is cold, let it stand five days, stirring it up once or twice a day; then pass it through a hair sieve, and with a spoon press it as dry as you can, and put it in a runlet fit for it, and put to it the rinds of the other ten oranges, cut as thin as the first; then make a syrup of the juice of twenty oranges with a pound of white sugar. It must be made the day before you tun it up; stir it well together, and stop it close; let it stand two months to clear, then bottle it up; it will keep three years, and is better for keeping.

To make Cherry Wine

Pull off the stalks of the cherries, and mash them without breaking the stones; then press them hard through a hair bag, and to every gallon of liquor put two pounds of eightpenny sugar. The vessel must be full, and let it work as long as it makes a noise in the vessel, then stop it up close for a month or more, and when it is fine, draw it into dry bottles, and put a lump of sugar into every bottle. If it makes them fly, open them all for a moment, and stop them up again; it will be fit to drink in a quarter of a year.

Another way to make Gooseberry Wine

Boil eight gallons of water, and one pound of sugar an hour; skim it well, and let it stand till it is cold; then to every quart of that water allow three pounds of gooseberries, first beaten or bruised very well; let it stand twenty-four hours; then strain it out, and to every gallon of this liquor put three pounds of sevenpenny sugar; let it stand in the vat twelve hours; then take the thick scum off, and put the clear into a vessel fit for it, and let it stand a month; then draw it off, and rinse the vessel with some of the liquor; put it in again, and let it stand four months, and bottle it.

To make Frontiniac Wine

Take six gallons of water, twelve pounds of white sugar, and six pounds of raisins of the sun cut small; boil these together an hour; then take of the flowers of elder, when they are falling, and will shake off, the quantity of half a peck; put them in the liquor when it is almost cold; the next day put in six spoonfuls of syrup of lemons, and four spoonfuls of ale-yeast, and two days after put it in a vessel that is fit for it; and when it has stood two months, bottle it off.

To make English Champaign, or the fine Currant Wine

Take to three gallons of water nine pounds of Lisbon sugar; boil the water and sugar half an hour, skim it clean, then have one gallon of currants pick'd, but not bruised; pour the liquor boiling-hot over them; and when cold, work it with half a pint of balm two days; then pour it through a flannel or sieve; then put it into a barrel fit for it, with half an ounce of isinglass well bruised; when it has done working, stop it close for a month; then bottle it, and in every bottle put a very small lump of double-refined sugar; this is excellent wine, and has a beautiful colour.

To make Saragosa Wine or English Sack

To every quart of water put a sprig of rue, and to every gallon a handful of fennel-roots; boil these half an hour, then strain it out, and to every gallon of this liquor put three pounds of honey, boil it two hours, and skim it well; when it is cold, pour it off, and turn it into the vessel, or such cask as is fit for it; keep it a year in the vessel, and then bottle it; is a very good sack.

To make Cyder

Pull your fruit before it is too ripe, and let it lie but one or two days, to have one good sweat; your apples must be pippins, pearmains or harveys (if you mix winter and summer fruit together, it is never good); grind your apples, and press them; when your fruit is all press'd, put it immediately into a hogshead, where it may have some room to work, but no vent but a little hole between the hoops; it must be close bung'd; put three or four pounds of raisins into a hogshead, and two pounds of sugar, it will make it work better; often racking it off is the best way to fine it, and always rack it into small vessels, keeping them close bung'd, and only a small vent hole; if it should work after racking, put into your vessel some raisins for it to feed on; and bottle it in March.

To make the fine Clary Wine

To ten gallons of water put twenty-five pounds of sugar, and the whites of twelve eggs well beaten; set it over the fire, and let it boil gently near an hour; skim it clean, and put it in a tub; and when it is near cold, then put into the vessel you keep it in about half a strike of clary in the bossom, stripped from the stalks, flowers and little leaves together, and a pint of new ale-yeast; then put in the liquor, and stir it two or three times a day for three days; when it has done working, stop it up; and bottle it at three or four months old, if it is clear.

To make Currant Wine

Gather your currants full ripe, strip them and bruise them in a mortar, and to every gallon of the pulp put two quarts of water, first boiled, and cold; you may put in some rasps, if you please; let it stand in a tub twenty-four hours to ferment, then let it run through a hair sieve; let no hand touch it; let it take its time to run; and to every gallon of this liquor put two pounds and a half of white sugar; stir it well, and put it in your vessel, and to every six gallons put in a quart of the best rectified spirit of wine; let it stand six weeks, and bottle it; if it is not very fine, empty it into other bottles, or at first draw it into large bottles and then, after it has stood a fortnight, rack it off into smaller.

To make Elderflower Water

Take two large handfuls of dried elder-flowers, and ten gallons of spring-water; boil the water, and pour it scalding hot upon the flowers; the next day put to every gallon of water five pounds of Malaga raisins, the stalks being first pick'd off, but not wash'd; chop them grossly with a chopping-knife, then put them into your boiled water, and stir the water, raisins and flowers well together; and so do twice a day for twelve days; then press out the juice clear, as long as you can get any liquor out; put it in your barrel fit for it, and stop it up two or three days till it works; and in a few days stop it up close, and let it stand two or three months, till it is clear; then bottle it.

Another way to make Elder Wine

Take spring-water, and let it boil half an hour; then measure five gallons, and let it stand to cool; then have in readiness twenty pounds of raisins of the sun, well picked and rubbed in a cloth, and hack them so as to cut them, but not too small; then put them in, the water being cold, and let them stand nine days, stirring them two or three times a day; then have ready six pints of the juice of elderberries full ripe, which must be infused in boiling water, or baked three hours; then strain out the raisins, and when the elder liquor is cold, mix that with it; but it is best to boil up the juice to a syrup, a pound of sugar to every pint of juice; boil and skim it, and when cold mix it with your raisin liquor, and three or four spoonfuls of good ale-yeast; stir it well together; then put it into a vessel fit for it; let it stand in a warm place to work, and in your cellar five or six months.

Another way to make Gooseberry Wine

Take twenty-four quarts of gooseberries full ripe, and twelve quarts of water, after it has boiled two hours; pick and bruise your gooseberries one by one in a platter with a rolling-pin, as little as you can, so they be all bruised; then put the water, when it is cold, on your mash'd gooseberries and let them stand together twelve hours; when you drain it off, be sure to take none but the clear; then measure the liquor, and to every quart of that liquor put three quarters of a pound of fine sugar, the one half loaf sugar; let it stand to dissolve six or eight hours, stirring it two or three times; then put it in your vessels, with two or three spoonfuls of the best new yeast; stop it easy at first, that it may work if it will; when you see it has done working, or will not work, stop it close, and bottle it in frosty weather.

Mountain Wine

Pick out the big stalks of your Malaga raisins then chop them very small, five pounds to every gallon of cold spring-water; let them steep a fortnight or more, squeeze out the liquor, and barrel it in a vessel fit for it; first fume the vessel with brimstone; don't stop it up till the hissing is over.

To make Citron Water

To a gallon of brandy take ten citrons, pare the outside rinds of the citrons, dry the rinds very well, then beat the remaining part of the citrons all to mash in a mortar, and put it into the brandy; stop it close and let it stand nine days, then distil it; take rinds that are dry and beat them to powder, infuse them nine days in the spirit, and distil it over again; sweeten it to your taste with double-refined sugar; let it stand in a large jug for three weeks, then rack it off into bottles This is the true Barbadoes receipt for citron water.

Lemon Wine – or what may pass for Citron Water

Take two quarts of brandy, one quart of spring-water, half a pound of double-refined sugar, and the rinds of sixteen lemon; put them together in an earthen pot; pour into it twelve spoonfuls of milk boiling hot; stir it together, and let it stand three days; then take off the top, and pass the other two or three times through a jelly-bag; bottle it; it is fit to drink, or will keep a year or two.

To make Strong Beer

To a barrel of beer take two bushels of malt, and half a bushel of wheat, just crack'd in the mill, and some of the flour sifted out of it; when your water is scalding hot, put it into your mashing vat; there let it stand till you can see your face in it; then put your malt upon it; then put your wheat upon that, and do not stir it; let it stand two hours and a half; then let it run into a tub that has two pounds of hops in it, and a handful of rosemary-flowers; when it is all run, put it in your copper, and boil it two hours; then strain it off, setting it a-cooling very thin, and set it a-working very cool; clear it very well before you put it a-working; put a little yeast to it, and when the yeast begins to fall, put it into your vessel; and when it has done working in the vessel, put in a pint of whole wheat, and six eggs; then stop it up; let it stand a year, and then bottle it; then mash again; stir the malt very well in, and let it stand two hours, and let that run and mash again, and stir it as before; be sure you cover your mashing vat well up; mix the first and second running together, it will make good household beer.

To make Elder Ale

Take ten bushels of malt to a hogshead; then put two bushels of elderberries, pick'd from the stalks, into a pot or earthen pan, and set it in a pot of boiling water till the berries swell; then strain it out, and put the juice into the guile-vat, and beat it often in; and so order it as the common way of brewing.

All Sorts of
Remedies

Medicinal Cordial Waters

The great Palsey Water

Take of sage, rosemary, and betony-flowers, of each a handful; borage, and bugloss-flowers, of each a handful; of lily of the valley and cowslip flowers, of each four or five handfuls; steep these in the best sack; then put to them balm, spike-flowers, mother-wort, bay-leaves, leaves of orange tree, with the flowers, of each one ounce; citron-peel, peony seeds, and cinnamon, of each half an ounce; nutmegs, cardamums, mace, cubebs, yellow sanders, of each half an ounce; lignum aloes, one dram; make all these into powder; then add jujubes, the stones taken out, and cut in pieces, half a pound; pearl prepared, smaragdes, musk and saffron, of each ten grains; ambergris one scruple, red roses dried one ounce; as many lavender flowers as will fill a gallon glass; steep all these a month, and distil them in an alembic very carefully; then take pearl prepared, smaragdes, musk and saffron, of each ten grains; ambergris, one scruple; red roses dried, red and yellow sanders, of each one ounce; hang these in a white farcenet bag in the water; stop it close. This water is of excellent use in all swoonings, in weakness of heart and decay of spirits; it restores speech in apoplexies and palsies; it helps all pains in the joints from cold or bruises, bathing the place outwardly, and dipping cloths and laying on it; it strengthens and comforts the vital spirits, and helps the memory; restoreth lost appetite, helpeth all weakness of the stomach; taken inwardly, or bathed outwardly, it taketh away giddiness of the head, and helpeth hearing; it makes a pleasant breath, it is good in the beginning of dropsies; none can sufficiently express the virtues of this water. When it is taken inwardly, drop ten or twelve drops on a lump of sugar, a bit of bread, or in a dish of tea; but in a fit of the palsey give so much every hour to restore speech. Add to the rest of the flowers single wallflowers, and the roots and flowers of single peonies, and misletoe of the oak, of each a good handful.

The Lady Hewet's Water

Take red sage, betony, spearmint, unset hyssop, thyme, balm, pennyroyal, celandine, watercresses, heartsease, lavender, angelica, germander, calamint, tamarisk, coltsfoot, avens, valerian, saxifrage, pimpernel, vervain, parsley, rosemary, savory, scabious, agrimony, mother-thyme, wild marjoram, roman wormwood, carduus benedictus, pellitory of the wall, field daisies, flowers and leaves, of each a handful, after they are pick'd and wash'd; of rue, yarrow, comfry, plantain, camomile, maidenhair, sweet-marjoram, and dragons, of each a handful, before they are wash'd or pick'd; red-rose leaves and cowslip flowers, of each half a peck, rosemary flowers a quarter of a peck, hartshorn two ounces, juniper berries one drachm, china roots an ounce, comfry roots slic'd, aniseeds, fennel seeds, caraway seeds, nutmegs, ginger, cinnamon, pepper, spikenard, parsley seeds, cloves and mace, of each three drachms, sassafras slic'd half an ounce, elecampane roots, melilot flowers, calamus-aromaticus, cardamums, lignum aloes, rhubarb sliced thin, galingal, veronica, and cubebs, of each two drachms, musk twenty-four grains, ambergris twenty grains, powder of coral two drachms, powder of amber one drachm, powder of pearl two drachms, white sugar-candy one pound; wash the herbs, and swing them in a cloth till they are dry, then cut them and bruise the drugs, putting them into an earthen pot; then put thereto such a quantity of sherry sack as will cover them, let them steep twenty-four hours; then distil it twice in an alembic, drawing from each three pints of water; mix it all together, put it into quart bottles, and divide the cordials into three parts, putting into each bottle of water a like quantity; shake it often together at the first; the longer you keep it the better it will be; there never was a better cordial in cases of the greatest illness, two or three spoonfuls almost revive from death.

The Lady Allen's Water

Take of balm, rosemary, sage, carduus, wormwood, dragons, scordium, mugwort, scabious, tormentil roots and leaves, angelica roots and leaves, marigold flowers and leaves, betony flowers and leaves, centaury tops, pimpernel, wood-sorrel, rue, agrimony, rosa folis, of each half a pound, liquorice four ounces, elecampane roots, two ounces; wash the herbs, shake and dry them in a cloth, then shred them, slice the roots, put all into three gallons of the best white wine, and let them stand close covered two days and two nights, stirring them morning and evening; then take out some of the herbs, lightly squeezing them with your hands, and fill a still full; let them still twelve hours in a cold still with a reasonable quick fire; then put the rest of the herbs and the wine in an alembic, and distil them till all the strength is out of the herbs and wine: mix all the water in both stills together, sweeten some, but not all; for cases of great illness, warm some of that unsweeten'd, blood-warm, and put in it a little syrup of gilliflowers, and go to bed, covering warm: it is a very excellent water.

Plague Water

Take rosa folis, agrimony, betony, scabious, centaury tops, scordium, baum, rue, wormwood, mugwort, celandine, rosemary, marigold leaves, brown sage, burnet, carduus, and dragons, of each a large handful, angelica roots, peony roots, tormentil roots, elecampane roots and liquorice, of each an ounce; cut the herbs, slice the roots, put them all into an earthen pot, adding to them a gallon of white wine, and a quart of brandy, and let them steep two days close cover'd, then distil it in an ordinary still with a gentle fire; you may sweeten it, but not much.

Dr Stevens's Water

Take a gallon of the best Gascoigne wine or sack, then take of ginger, galingal, cinnamon, nutmegs, cloves, mace, aniseeds, caraway seeds, coriander seeds, of every of these a drachm; then take sage, mint, camomile, thyme, pellitory of the wall, pot marjoram, rosemary flowers, pennyroyal, wild thyme, common lavender, of each of these a handful; bruise the spice and seeds, stamp the herbs, put them all into the wine, and let it stand close cover'd twelve hours, stirring it often; then distil it in an alembic, and mix it as you please.

To make Aqua Mirabilis

Take cubebs, cardamums, galingal, cloves, mace, nutmegs, cinnamon, of each two drachms, bruised small; then take of the juice of celandine a pint, the juice of spearmint half a pint, the juice of balm half a pint; the flowers of melilot, cowslip, rosemary, borage, bugloss, and marigolds, of each three drachms; seeds of fennel, coriander and caraway, of each two drachms; two quarts of the best sack, a quart of white wine, of brandy, the strongest angelica-water, and red-rose water of each one pint; bruise the spices and seeds, and steep them with the herbs and flowers in the juices, waters, sack, white wine and brandy all night; in the morning distil it in a common still pasted up; from this quantity draw off a gallon at least; sweeten it to your taste with sugar candy; bottle it up and keep it in sand, or very cool.

A Tincture of Ambergris

Take ambergris and musk, of each an ounce, and put to them a quarter of a pint of spirit of wine; stop it close, tie it down with leather, and set it in horse dung ten or twelve days.

To make Orange or Lemon Water

To the outer rind of an hundred oranges or lemons, put three gallons of brandy and two quarts of sack; and let them steep in it one night; the next day distil them in a cold still; a gallon, with the proportion of peels, is enough for one still, and of that you may draw off between three and four quarts; draw it off till you taste it begin to be sourish; sweeten it to your taste with double-refin'd sugar; mix the first, second and third running together; if it is lemon water, it should be perfumed; put two grains of ambergris, and one of musk, ground fine, tie it in a rag, and let it hang five or six days in a bottle, and then put it in another, and so for a great many if you please, or else you may put three or four drops of tincture of ambgris in it; cork it very well: the orange is an excellent water for the stomach, and the lemon is a fine entertaining water.

King Charles II's Surfeit Water

Take a gallon of the best aqua vitae, a quart of brandy, a quart of aniseed water, a pint of poppy water, and a pint of damask-rose water; put these in a large glass jar, adding to it a pound of fine powder'd sugar, a pound and a half of raisins stoned, a quarter of a pound of dates stoned and sliced, one ounce of cinnamon bruised, cloves one ounce, four nutmegs bruised, one stick of liquorice scrap'd and slic'd; let all these stand nine days close cover'd, stirring it three or four times a day; then add to it three pounds of fresh poppies, or three handfuls of dry'd poppies, a sprig of angelica, two or three of balm; so let it stand a week longer, then strain it out and bottle it.

The Walnut Water

Take a peck of walnuts in July, and beat them pretty small, adding to them of clove-gilliflowers, poppy flowers, cowslip flowers dried, marigold flowers, sage flowers, and borage flowers of each two quarts; then put to them two ounces of mace beaten, two ounces of nutmegs bruised, and one ounce of cinnamon bruised; steep all these in a pot with a gallon of brandy, and two gallons of the strongest beer; let it stand twenty-four hours, and still it off.

To make Orange-Flower Brandy

Take a gallon of French brandy, and boil a pound of orange-flowers a little while, and put them to it; save the water, and with that make a syrup to sweeten it.

A Cordial Water that may be made in Winter

Take three quarts of brandy or sack, put two handfuls of rosemary and two handfuls of baum to it chopped pretty small, one ounce of cloves, two ounces of nutmegs, three ounces of cinnamon; beat all the spices grossly, and steep them with the herbs in the wine; then put it in a still pasted up close; save near a quart of the first running, and so of the second, and of the third; when it is distilled mix it all together, and dissolve about a pound of double-refin'd sugar in it, and when it is settled bottle it up.

The Golden Cordial

Take two gallons of brandy, two drachms and a half of alkermes, a quarter of a drachm of oil of cloves, an ounce of the spirit of saffron, three pounds of double-refin'd sugar powder'd, and a book of leaf gold. First put your brandy into a large bottle, then put three or four spoonfuls of brandy in a China cup, mix your alkermes in it; then put in your oil of cloves, and mix that, and do the like to the spirit of saffron; pour all into your bottle of brandy; then put in your sugar, cork your bottle, and tie it down close; shake it well together for two or three days, and let it stand about a fortnight; you must set the bottle so, that when it is rack'd off into other bottles it must only be gently tilted; put into every bottle two leaves of gold cut small; you may put one or two quarts to the dregs and it will be good, though not so good as the first.

The Fever Water

Take of Virginia snake-root six ounces, carduus seeds and marigold flowers, of each four ounces, twenty green walnuts, carduus water, poppy water, of each two quarts, two ounces of hartshorn; slice the walnuts, and steep all in the waters a fortnight; then add to it an ounce of London treacle, and distil it all in an alembic pasted up; three drops of spirit of amber in three spoonfuls of this water will deliver a woman of a dead child.

To make the first Liquid Laudanum

Take a quart of sack, half a pint of spirit of wine, four ounces of opium, and two ounces of saffron; slice the opium, pull the saffron, and put it in a bottle with the sack and spirit of wine; adding to it cinnamon, cloves and mace, of each a drachm; cork and tie down the bottle, and set it in the sun or by the fire twenty days; pour it off the dregs and it is fit to use; ten, fifteen, twenty, or twenty-five drops.

A fine Cordial Water

Beat two pounds of double-refined sugar very well, and put to it a gallon of the best brandy, stirring it a good while; then add confection of alkermes and oil of cloves of each one drachm, spirit of saffron an ounce; stir it a quarter of an hour; then add three sheets of leaf gold, and bottle it up; it will keep as long as you please.

To make Spirit of Caraways

Take of caraway comfits two pounds, put them into a glass bottle with a wide mouth, put upon the caraways spirit of wine as much as will cover them, one drachm of ambergris rub'd to powder, with as much fine sugar, and tied up in a rag; let this stand three months close stopt, then pour off the spirit clear from the seeds; take a little of this dropt in beer or ale for wind or pain in the bowels.

To cure the Spleen or Vapours

Take an ounce of the filings of steel, two drachms of gentian sliced, half an ounce of carduus seeds bruised, half a handful of centaury tops; infuse all these in a quart of white wine four days; drink four spoonfuls of the clear every morning, fasting two hours after it, and walking about; if it binds too much, take once or twice a week some little purging thing to carry it off.

Hysteric Water

Take zedoary, roots of lovage, seeds of wild parsnips, of each two ounces, roots of single peony four ounces, of misletoe of the oak three ounces, myrrh a quarter of an ounce, castor half an ounce; beat all these together, and add to them a quarter of a pound of dried millipedes; pour on these three quarts of mugwort-water, and two quarts of brandy; let them stand in a close vessel eight days, then distil it in a cold still pasted up; you may draw off nine pints of water; sweeten it to your taste and mix all together. This is an excellent water to prevent fits, or to be taken in faintings.

A Stone Water

Take beans in pod, and cut them in small pieces, fill a good part of an ordinary still with them, and put to them two good handfuls of yarrow, and distil them together in a cold still; let the party drink a glass when in pain, and at the changes of the moon.

Stitch Water

Take a gallon of new ale wort and put to as much stone-horse dung as will make it pretty thick; add to this a pound of London treacle, two pennyworth of ginger sliced, and six pennyworth of saffron, mix these together, and distil off in a cold still: take three or four spoonfuls at a time.

The Saffron Cordial

Fill a large still with marigold flowers, adding to them of nutmegs, mace, and English saffron, of each an ounce; then take three pints of muscadine, or tent, or Malaga sack, and with a sprig of rosemary dash it on the flowers; then distil it off with a slow fire, and let it drop on white sugar-candy; draw it off till it begins to be sour; save a pint of the first running to mix with other waters on an extraordinary occasion; mix the rest together to drink it by itself. This cordial is excellent in fainting, and for the smallpox or ague; take five or six spoonfuls at a time.

To make Spirit of Saffron

Take four drachms of the best saffron, put it in a quart bottle, pour on it a pint of the ordinary spirit of wine, and add to it half a pound of white sugar-candy beaten small; stop it close with a cork, and a bladder tied over it; set it in the sun and shake it twice a day, till the candy is dissolv'd, and the spirit of a deep orange colour; let it stand two days longer to settle, clear it off in another bottle, and keep it for use; give a small spoonful to a child, and a large one to a man or woman; it is excellent in any pestilential disease; it is good against colds, or the consumptive cough.

Black Cherry Water for Children

Take six pounds of black cherries and bruise them small, then put to them the tops of rosemary, sweet-marjoram, spearmint, angelica, baum, marigold flowers, of each a handful, dried violets an ounce, aniseeds and sweet fennel seeds, of each half an ounce bruised; cut the herbs small, mix them together, and distil them off in a cold still. This water is excellent for children, and may be given two or three spoonfuls at a time.

To make Gripe Water

Take of pennyroyal ten handfuls, coriander seeds, aniseeds, sweet fennel seeds, caraway seeds, of each one ounce; bruise them and put them to the herbs in an earthen pot; sprinkle on them a pint of brandy; let them stand all night, the next day distil it off, and take six, seven, or eight spoonfuls of this water, sweetened with syrup of gilliflowers warm, and go to bed; cover very warm to sweat if you can, and drink some of it as long as the gripes continue.

To make the Dropsy Water

Take a bushel of picked elderberries, put them in a large tub, with as much water or strong beer as will cover them, a quart of ale-yeast, and a piece of leaven as big as a penny loaf; break it to pieces, and stir it together once or twice a day for eight days together; then put it in a pot, and distil off a gallon in an alembic. It must be drunk three times a day – in the morning fasting, before dinner, and last at night – till you have drunk up the quantity.

Lily of the Valley Water

Take the flowers of lily of the valley, distil them in sack, and drink a spoonful or two as there is occasion; it restores speech to those who have the dumb palfy or apoplexy, it is good against the gout, it comforts the heart, and strengthens the memory; it helps the inflammation of the eyes, being dropt into them. Take the flowers, put them into a glass close stopt, and set it into a hill of ants for a month; then take it out, and you will find a liquor that comes from the flowers, which keep in a phial; it easeth the pains of the gout, the place affected being anointed therewith.

To make Vertigo Water

Take the leaves of red sage, cinquefoil, and wood betony, of each a good handful, boil them in a gallon of spring-water till it comes to a quart; when it is cold put into it a pennyworth of roachalum, and bottle it up; when you use it put a little of it in a spoon, or in the palm of your hand, and snuff it up; go not into the air presently.

Dr Burgess's Antidote against the Plague

Take three pints of muscadine, and boil therein one handful of sage, as much rue, angelica roots one ounce, zedoary roots one ounce, Virginia snake-root half an ounce, saffron twenty grains; let all these boil till a pint be consumed, then strain it and set it over the fire again, and put therein two pennyworth of long pepper, half an ounce of ginger, as much nutmegs; beat all the spice, and let them boil together a little, and put thereto a quarter of an ounce of mithridate, as much Venice treacle, and a quarter of a pint of the best angelica water; take it warm both morning and evening, two spoonfuls if already infected; if not infected, one spoonful is enough for a day, half a spoonful in the morning, and as much at night. This had great success, under God, in the plague; it is good likewise against the smallpox, or any other pestilential disease.

The Lady Onslow's Water for the Stone

Take as much saxifrage as, being distill'd, will yield two quarts of water, add to this a peck of hogs haws bruised; filipendula and parsley, of each three handfuls; parsley of break-stone and mother-thyme, of each two handfuls; marshmallow roots and parsley roots, of each one handful; four large horseradish roots; red nettle seed and burdock seed, of each an ounce; bruise the seeds, cut the herbs, and slice the roots; mix them well together with three quarts of white wine, and as much new milk from the cow; distil them and the saxifrage water together in a cold still, and draw it off as long as any water will come; the saxifrage must be distill'd in May, and the other water the latter end of September or October, when the haws are ripe. Let the person, when the fit of the stone cometh, take three or four spoonfuls of white wine, and as much of this water mixed together. If the distemper abate not, take six spoonfuls of this water once in six hours, till it is removed. You may sweeten it with syrup of marshmallows.

Centaury Water

Take one pound of gentian and six pounds of green centaury, beat the gentian, shred the centaury, and put them into an earthen pot, with as much white wine as will cover them; let it stand five days, and distil it in an ordinary still. This is an excellent water; take three or four spoonfuls at a time in a morning, and fast two hours after it, and use exercise; likewise take it at night, an hour or two before you go to bed.

To make Tincture of Hiera-picra

Take a drachm of hiera-picra, a drachm of cochineal, and two drachms of aniseeds, and put them into a bottle, with a pint of the best sack and a pint of brandy; shake them well together five or six days, then let it stand to settle twelve hours, pour it off into another bottle clear from the dregs, and keep it for use; it is very good against the colic or stomach-ache, and removes anything that offends the stomach; take four spoonfuls of it fasting, and fast two hours after it; you must take it constantly three weeks or a month, and it is well to drink the following drink after it.

Take new-laid eggs and break them, save the shells, and pull off the skin that is in the inside; dry the shells, and beat them to powder; sift them, and put six spoonfuls of this powder into a quart of the following waters: take a fennel water, parsley water, mint water, and black-cherry water, of each half a pint; take a quarter of a pint at a time, shaking the glass when you pour it out, three times a day – at eleven in the morning, at three in the afternoon, and eight at night; and you should take it as long as you take the hiera-picra.

Another way

Put an ounce of hiera-picra into a quart of brandy; let your bottle hold more than a quart, that you may have room to shake it; let it stand five days near the fire, shaking it often, and stop it close. This is a good purge; take half a quarter of a pint going to bed, drink a draught of warm ale or broth a little while after it; you may take it nine or ten days together; it opens the stomach, causes digestion, prevents green sickness, and kills worms in children.

To make Lime Water

Take a pound of unslack'd lime, put it into an earthen jug well glaz'd, adding to it a gallon of spring-water boiling hot; cover it close till it is cold, then skim it clean, let it stand two days, pour it clear off into glass bottles, and keep it for use; the older the better. The virtues are as follow.

For a sore, warm some of the water and wash the sore well with it for half an hour, then lay a plaister on the sore of some gentle thing, and lay a cloth over the plaister four or five double, wet with this water, and as it dries wet it again, and it will heal it.

For a flux or looseness, take two spoonfuls of it cold in the morning, and two at night as you go to bed; do this seven or eight days together for a man or woman; but if for a child, one spoonful at a time is enough; and if very young, half a spoonful at a time; it will keep twenty years, and no one who has not experienced it knows the virtues of it.

A Milk Water for a cancerous Breast

Take six quarts of new milk, four handfuls of cranesbill, and four hundred of woodlice; distil this in a cold still with a gentle fire; then take an ounce of crabs' eyes, and half an ounce of white sugar-candy, both in fine powder; mix them together, and take a drachm of the powder in a quarter of a pint of the milk water in the morning, at twelve noon, and at night; continue taking this three or four months, it is an excellent medicine.

Cock Water for a Consumption

Take an old cock, kill him and quarter him, and with clean cloths wipe the blood from him; then put the quarters into a cold still with part of a leg of veal, two quarts of old Malaga sack, a handful of thyme, as much sweet-marjoram and rosemary, two handfuls of pimpernel, four dates stoned and sliced, a pound of currants, as many raisins of the sun stoned, a pound of sugar-candy finely beaten; when all is in, paste up the still, let it stand all night, the next morning distil it, mix the water together, and sweeten it to your taste with white sugar-candy; drink three or four spoonfuls an hour before dinner and supper.

Another Water against a Consumption

Take a pound of currants, and of hart's-tongue, liverwort and speedwell, of each a large handful; then take a peck of snails, lay them all night in hyssop, the next morning rub and bruise them, and distil all in a gallon of new milk; sweeten it with white sugar-candy, and drink of this water two or three times a day, a quarter of a pint at a time; it has done great good.

Another Water against a Consumption

Take three pints of the best canary and a pint of mint water, of candied eryngo roots, dates, China roots, and raisins stoned, of each three ounces; of mace a quarter of an ounce; infuse these twelve hours in an earthen pot close cover'd over a gentle fire; when it is cold strain it out, and keep it in a clean pan or glass jar for use; then make about a quart of plain jelly of hartshorn, and drink a quarter of a pint of this liquor with a large spoonful of jelly night and morning for two or three months together.

A Water to Strengthen the Sight

Take rosemary flowers, sage, betony, rue, and succory, of each a handful; infuse these in two quarts of sack, and distil them in an alembic; the dose is a spoonful in the morning fasting till the water is done.

Rue Water good for Fits of the Mother

Take of rue and green walnuts, of each a pound, figs a pound and a half; bruise the rue and walnuts, slice the figs, lay them between the rue and walnuts, and distil it off; bottle it up and keep it for use: take a spoonful or two when there is any appearance of a fit.

An opening Drink

Take pennyroyal, red sage, liverwort, horehound, maidenhair, hyssop, of each two handfuls, figs and raisins stoned, of each a pound, blue currants half a pound, liquorice, aniseeds, coriander seeds, of each two ounces; put all these in two gallons of spring-water, and let it boil away two or three quarts; then strain it, and when it is cold put it in bottles: drink half a pint in the morning, and as much in the afternoon; keep warm and eat little.

For a Distemper got by an Ill Husband

Take two pennyworth of gum-dragant, pick and clean it, and put it in an earthen pot; put to it as much red-rose water as it will drink up, stir it two or three times a day, till it is all dissolv'd into a jelly; then put in three grated nutmegs, a little double-refin'd sugar, finely powder'd, and a little cinnamon water, no more than will leave it in a jelly; take the quantity of a nutmeg in the morning fasting, and last at night, but first prepare the body for it by taking six pennyworth of *pulvis sanctus* in posset-drink, and drink broth in the working.

For a Cough settled on the Stomach

Take half a pound of figs, as many raisins of the sun stoned, a stick of liquorice scrap'd and sliced, a few aniseeds, and sweet fennel seeds, with some hyssop wash'd; boil all these in a quart of spring-water till it comes to a pint; strain it, and sweeten it very well with white sugar-candy; take two or three spoonfuls of it morning and night, or when you please.

To make Hungary Water

Take four ounces of rosemary-flowers, and a pint of spirits of wine, infuse it twelve hours, and draw it off in a glass still.

A Drink to preserve the Lungs

Take three pints of spring-water, put it to an ounce of flour of sulphur, and let it boil on a slow fire till half is consumed; let it stand to settle and strain it out; then pour it on one ounce of liquorice scrap'd, and a drachm of coriander seeds, and as many aniseeds bruised; let it stand to settle, and drink a quarter of a pint morning and night.

An excellent Snail Water

Take of comfry and succory-roots, of each four ounces, liquorice three ounces, the leaves of hart's-tongue, plantain, ground-ivy, red nettle, yarrow, brooklime, watercresses, dandelion, and agrimony, of each two large handfuls; gather these herbs in dry weather, and do not wash them, but wipe them clean with a cloth; then take five hundred of snails, cleansed from their shells, but not scoured, and of whites of eggs beaten up to a water, a pint, four nutmegs grossly beaten, the yellow rind of one lemon and one orange; bruise all the roots and herbs, and put them together with the other ingredients in a gallon of new milk and a pint of canary; let them stand close covered forty-eight hours, and then distil them in a common still with a gentle fire; this quantity will fill your still twice; it will keep good a year, and is best when made spring or fall, but it is the best when new; you must not cork up the bottles in three months, but cover them with paper; it is immediately fit for use; and when you use it take a quarter of a pint of this water, and put to it as much milk warm from the cow, and drink it in the morning, and at four o'clock in the afternoon, and fast two hours after it; to take powder of crabs' eyes with it, as much as will lie on a sixpence, mightily assists to sweeten the blood. When you drink this water, be very regular in your diet, and eat nothing salt or sour.

Eye Water

Take orrice-root slic'd two ounces, white copperas finely beaten an ounce, put them in three pints of running water, shake it well together three or four days, and then use it; if a watery eye, you may add a bit of bole-armoniac.

To make Briony Water

Take twelve pounds of briony root, pound it to mash, then take a quart of the juice of rue, a quart of the juice of mugwort leaves, of savin three handfuls, sweet basil two handfuls, mother of thyme, nepp, and pennyroyal, of each three handfuls; dittany of Crete and dry orange-peel of each four handfuls; myrrh two ounces, castor an ounce, both powder'd, and likewise the orange-peel; distil this off in an alembic; first cut your herbs, and put them in the bottom of your still, then put in your briony root, then mix your powders in a China dish with some sack, then pour in six quarts of sack; close up your still and draw it off.

A Water to take after taking Balsam of Tolu

Take a pint of whites of eggs beaten to a froth, five nutmegs bruised, two handfuls of dried spearmint, two handfuls of unset hyssop; add to these a gallon of new milk, and distil it off in a cold still; you may draw off about three pints; take six spoonfuls of this water at a time, with sugar-candy in it.

To make the true Daffy's Elixir

Take five ounces of aniseeds, three ounces of fennel seeds, four ounces of parsley seeds, six ounces of Spanish liquorice, five ounces of senna, one ounce of rhubarb, three ounces of elecampane, seven ounces of jalap, twenty-one drachms of saffron, six ounces of manna, two pounds of raisins, a quarter of an ounce of cochineal, two gallons of brandy; stone the raisins, slice the roots, bruise the jalap; put them all together, keep them close cover'd fifteen days; then strain it out.

Milk Water

Take two good handfuls of wormwood, as much carduus, as much rue, four handfuls of mint, as much baum, half as much angelica; cut these a little, put them in a cold still, with three quarts of milk; let your fire be quick till your still drops, then a little slower; you may draw off two quarts; the first quart will keep all the year: this is extraordinary good in fevers, sweetened with sugar or syrup of cloves.

A Powder to cure a Rupture

Take half a pound of knots of scurvy-grass before they are quite blown, one pound of comfry roots, half a pound of fern roots, one ounce of juniper berries, one ounce of dragon's blood, half a pound of the roots of solomon-seal, a quarter of an ounce of nutmegs, a quarter of an ounce of mace; scrape your roots very clean, slice them thin, and put every sort by themselves in a clean paper bag; lay them on a clean earthen dish, and let them be put in a slow oven till they are dry enough to powder; you must do the like to your scurvy-grass, that they may be all finely powder'd and mix'd together, and kept close in a glass with paper round it. You may in any liquor give as much of this powder to a young child as will lie on a sixpence, morning and night; to one of seven years more; to a man or woman as much as will lie on a shilling; put the powder in a spoon, and wet it to mix, and take it three weeks.

A good Remedy for a hollow aching Tooth

Take of camphire and crude opium, of each four grains, make them into three pills with as much oil of cloves as is convenient; roll them in cotton, apply one of them to the aching tooth, and repeat it if there is occasion.

A successful Method to cure the Jaundice

In the first place give the patient a vomit of the infusion of crocus-metallorum, or oxymel of squills, according to his constitution; then take of aloes and rhubarb, of each two scruples, of prepar'd steel a drachm, tartar vitriolated a scruple; make pills with syrup of horehound, of which give four every night.

Take of the roots of turmeric half an ounce, tops of centaury the lesser, roman wormwood and horehound, of each a handful, roots of the greater nettle two ounces; boil them in three pints of water to the consumption of half; when it is almost boiled enough, add to it juniper berries an ounce, yellow sanders and goose dung made into a nodulus, of each three drachms, saffron two scruples, rhenish wine a pint; when it is boil'd enough strain it, and add to it compound water of snails and earthworms, of each two ounces; take three ounces of it after each time of taking the following electuary.

Take of the conserve of sea wormwood and outward rind of orange-peels, of each two ounces; of species of diacurcumae and prepared steel, of each three drachms; of prepared earthworms and rhubarb, of each two drachms; flowers of sal-armoniac and salt of amber, of each two scruples; of saffron powder'd one scruple; with a sufficient quantity of syrup of horehound, make an electuary, of which take the quantity of a large nutmeg twice a day, drinking three ounces of the bitter tincture after it.

For a Rheumatism, or Pain in the Bones

Take a quart of milk, boil it, and turn it with three pints of small-beer; then strain the posset on seven or nine globules of stone-horse dung tied up in a cloth, and boil it a quarter of an hour in the posset-drink; when it is taken off the fire press the cloth hard, and drink half a pint of this morning and night hot in bed; if you please you may add white wine to it. This medicine is not good if troubled with the stone.

To make Treacle Water

Take juice of green walnuts four pounds, of rue, carduus, marigolds, and baum, of each three pounds, roots of butter-bur half a pound, roots of burdock a pound, angelica and master-wort, of each half a pound, leaves of scordium six handfuls, Venice treacle and mithridate, of each half a pound, old canary wine a pound, white-wine vinegar six pounds, juice of lemon six pounds; distil this in an alembic, and on any illness take four spoonfuls going to bed.

To make Usquebaugh

To three gallons of brandy put four ounces of aniseeds bruised, the next day distil it in a cold still pasted up, then scrape four ounces of liquorice and pound it in a mortar, dry it in an iron-pan, do not burn it, put it in the bottle to your distill'd water, and let it stand ten days, then take out the liquorice, and to every six quarts of the spirits put in cloves, mace, nutmegs, cinnamon and ginger, of each a quarter of an ounce, dates ston'd and slic'd four ounces, raisins stoned half a pound; let these infuse ten days, then strain it out, tincture it with saffron, and bottle it and cork it well.

Mr Denzil Onslow's Surfeit Water

Take a gallon and a half of the best brandy, half a bushel of poppies, half a handful of rue, and as much wormwood; of sage, baum, hyssop, mint, and sweet-marjoram, of each one handful; half a pound of rosa folis; wash, pick, and dry these herbs in a coarse cloth; then shred them very fine. Take half a pound of liquorice scraped; of coriander seeds, and aniseeds, of each an ounce; a few cloves all bruised; a pound of raisins stoned, a pound of loaf sugar; put all these in an earthen jar, cover'd very close, and set it in a cool cellar, stirring them twice a day, till the poppies look pale; put a little saffron in with the other ingredients, strain it off into another jar, and in a fortnight, when it is settled, bottle it; mix the herbs that are strained from it with milk; it is a cordial milk-water.

An excellent Medicine for the Dropsy

Take of the leaves that grow upon the stem or stalk of the artichoke, bruise them in a stone mortar, then strain them thro' a fine cloth, and put to each pint of the juice a pint of Madeira wine; take four or five spoonfuls the first thing in the morning, and the same quantity going to bed, shaking the bottle well every time you use it.

Another Medicine for the Dropsy

Take about three spoonfuls of the best mustard seed, and about half a handful of bay berries, the like quantity of juniper berries, an ounce of horseradish, and about half a handful of sage of virtue, as much wormwood-sage, half a handful of scurvy-grass, a quarter of a handful of stinking orach, a little sprig of wormwood, a sprig of green broom, and half an ounce of gentian root; scrape, wipe, and cut all these, and put them into a bottle that will hold a gallon; then fill the bottle with the best strong beer you can get, stop it close, let it stand three or four days, and drink every morning fasting half a pint.

A Remedy for Rheumatic Pains

Take of senna, hermodactils, turpethum, and scammony, of each two drachms; of zedoary, ginger, and cubebs, of each one drachm, mix them and let them be powdered; the dose is from one drachm to two in any convenient vehicle. Let the parts affected be anointed with a liniment made thus: take palm oil two ounces, oil of turpentine one ounce, volatile salt of hartshorn two drachms; afterwards lay on a mucilaginous plaister. Some that have been very much troubled with rheumatic pains have by taking of hartshorn in compound water of earthworms found mighty benefit.

An excellent Medicine for the Spotted and all other Malignant Fevers

Take of the best Virginia snakeweed, root of contrayerva finely powdered and Goa stone, of each half a scruple, castor and camphire, of each five grains, and make them into a bolus with a scruple of Venice treacle and as much syrup of peony as is sufficient; repeat the bolus every six hours, drinking a draught of the following julep after it.

Take of scorzonera roots two ounces, of butter-burroots half an ounce, of baum and scordium, of each a handful, of coriander seeds three drachms, of liquorice, figs, and raisins, of each an ounce; let them boil in three pints of spring-water to a quart, then strain it, and add to it compound peony water three ounces, syrup of raspberries an ounce and a half: let the patients drink of it plentifully.

A specific Cure for stopping Blood

Take two ounces of clarified roch-alum, finely powdered, and melt it in a ladle, adding to it half an ounce of dragon's blood in powder, and mix them well together; then take it off the fire, keeping it stirring till it comes to the consistence of a soft paste, fit for making up into pills; make your pills of the bigness of a large pea, and as the paste cools, warm it again to such a degree as the whole quantity may be made into pills; this medicine is proper in all cases of violent bleedings, without exception; the ordinary or usual dose is half a grain, to be taken once in four hours till the bleeding stops, taking a glass of water or ptisan after it, and after every dose, and another of the same liquor a quarter of an hour after; in violent cases give half a drachm for a dose.

To make Stoughton's Elixir

Pare off the rinds of six Seville oranges very thin, and put them in a quart bottle, with an ounce of gentian scraped and sliced, and six pennyworth of cochineal; put to it a pint of the best brandy; shake it together two or three times the first day, and then let it stand to settle two days, and clear it off into bottles for use; take a large teaspoonful in a glass of wine in the morning, and at four in the afternoon; or you may take it in a dish of tea.

An excellent Medicine for a Pain in the Stomach

Take of *tinctura sacra* (or tincture of hiera-picra) one ounce in the morning, fasting an hour; then drink a little warm ale; do this two or three times a week, till you find relief.

For a Pain in the Stomach

Take a quarter of a pound of blue currants, wipe them clean, and pound them in a mortar, with an ounce of aniseeds bruised; before you put them to the currants, make this into a bolus with a little syrup of clove-gilliflowers; take every morning the quantity of a walnut, and drink rosemary-tea, instead of other tea, for your breakfast; if the pain returns, repeat it.

For a Stitch in the Side

Take rosin, pound and sift it, and with treacle mix it into an electuary, and lick it up often in the day or night.

To cure an intermitting Ague and Fever, without returning

Take Jesuits' bark in fine powder one ounce; salt of steel and Jamaica pepper, of each a quarter of an ounce; treacle or molasses, four ounces; mix these together, and take the quantity of a nutmeg three times a day when the fit is off, and a draught of warm ale, or white wine after it.

Dr Hall's Plaister for an Ague

Take a pennyworth of black soap, one pennyworth of gunpowder, one ounce of tobacco-snuff, and a glass of brandy; mix these in a mortar very well together; spread plaisters on leather for the wrists, and lay them on an hour before you expect the fit.

Excellent for a Burn or Scald

Take of oil-olive three ounces, white wax two ounces, sheep suet an ounce and half, minium and Castile soap, of each half an ounce; dragon's blood and camphire, of each three drachms; make them into a salve by melting them together; anoint with oil to take out the fire; then put the plaister on; dress it every day.

Water in a Consumption, or in Weakness after Sickness

Take a calf's-pluck fresh killed, but do not wash it; cut it in pieces, and put it in a cold still; but first put at the bottom of your still a sheet of white paper well butter'd; then put in your pluck, with mint, baum, borage, hyssop, and oak lungs, of each about two handfuls; wipe and cut the herbs, but do not wash them; put in a gallon of new milk warm from the cow, paste up the still, and let it drop on white sugar-candy; it will draw off about seven pints; mix it together, and bottle it for use: drink a quarter of a pint in the morning, and as much at four in the afternoon.

A Stay to prevent a Sore Throat in the Smallpox

Take rue, shred it very fine, and give it a bruise; mix it with honey and album Graecum, and work it together; put it over the fire to heat; sew it up in a linen stay, and apply it to the throat pretty warm; as it dries repeat it.

To prevent Pitting, and to take off Redness

Take rue, and chop it, boil it in hog's-lard till it is green; strain it out, and keep it for use; warm a little in a spoon, and with a feather anoint the face as they begin to shell off; do it as often as convenient.

An admirable Cerecloth

Take a pound of frankincense beaten fine, and a pound of rosin beaten, a pound of black pitch, and four ounces of cummin seeds powder'd, of saffron dried and powder'd, mace beaten and sifted, and cloves beaten fine, of each four pennyworth; an ounce of liquid laudanum, and a pound of deer-suet.

Season a new pipkin; first lay it in cold water; then boil water in it, and set it by till it is cold; then dry it, and put in your deer-suet, and let it melt, shaking it about as you do for melting butter; then put in your other ingredients, and set over the fire to boil; then take it off, and sprinkle in your liquid laudanum; let it simmer a little; take it off, and when it is fit to spread, spread it on the thickest brown paper, and use it on occasion: it is good for bruises, aches, pains, burns, scalds, and sore breasts; wipe the plaister every day, and put it on again: one or two plaisters will do.

For the Colic

Take of camomile flowers and mallow leaves, of each a handful; juniper berries and fenugreek seeds, of each half an ounce; let the seeds and berries be bruised; boil them in a pint of water; add to it strained, of turpentine dissolved, with the yolk of an egg, and oil of camomile, of each an ounce; diacatholicon six drachms, hiera-picra two drachms; mix, and give it. After the operation of the clyster, give the patient the following mixture: take of rue and camomile water, of each an ounce; cinnamon water an ounce, liquid laudanum twenty drops, syrup of white poppies an ounce.

How to make the Lime Drink, famous for curing the Stone

Take half a peck of limestones new burnt, and put them into four gallons of water; stir it well at the first putting in; then let it stand, and stir it again; as soon as it is very well settled, strain off the clear into a large pot, and put to it four ounces of saxifrage, and four ounces of liquorice, sliced thin, raisins of the sun stoned one pound, half a pound of blue currants, mallows, and mercury, of each a handful; coriander, fennel, and aniseeds, of each an ounce; let the pot stand close covered for nine days; then strain it and, being settled, pour the clearest of it into bottles; you may drink half a pint of it at a time, as often as you please; in your morning's draught, put a drachm of winter cherries powder'd. This has cured some who have been so tormented with the stone in the bladder that they could not make water, although they had in vain tried abundance of other remedies.

A Receipt for the Cure of the Stone and Gravel, whether in the Kidneys, Ureters or Bladder

Take marshmallow leaves, the herb mercury, saxifrage, and pellitory of the wall, of each, fresh gathered, three handfuls; cut them small, mix them together, and pound them in a clean stone mortar, with a wooden pestle, till they come to a mash; then take them out, spread them thin in a broad glazed earthen pan, and let them lie, stirring them about once a day, till they are thoroughly dry (but not in the sun), and then they are ready, and will keep good all the year. Of some of these ingredients so dried, make tea, as you do common tea, with boiling water, as strong as you please, but the stronger the better; and drink three, four, or more teacups full of it blood-warm, sweetened with coarse sugar, every morning and afternoon, putting into each cup of it half a spoonful, or more, of the expressed oil of beach nuts, fresh drawn (which in this case has been experienced to be vastly preferable to oil of almonds, or any other oil), stirring them about together, as long as you see occasion.

This medicine, how simple soever it may seem to some, is yet a fine emollient remedy, is perfectly agreeable to the stomach (unless the beach oil be stale or rancid), and will sheath and soften the asperity of the humours in general, particularly those that generate the gravel and stone, relaxing and suppling the solids at the same time; and it is well known by all physicians, that emollient medicines lubricate, widen, and moisten the fibres, so as to relax them into their proper dimensions, without forcing the parts; whereupon obstructions of the reins and urinary passages are opened, and cleared of all lodgments of sandy concretions, gravel and passable stones, and made to yield better to the expulsion of whatever may stop them up; and likewise takes away, as this does, all heat and difficulty of urine and stranguries; and withal, by its soft mucilaginous nature, cools and heals the reins, kidneys, and bladder, giving present ease in the stone-colic; breaks away wind, and prevents its return, as it always keeps the bowels laxative.

An excellent Vomit

Take a quarter of a pound of clear alum, beaten and sifted as fine as flour, divide it into three parts, the first the biggest; put a quarter of a pint of water in a saucepan, and put in your biggest paper of alum, and let it simmer over the fire, but not boil; take it off, cool it to blood-warm; drink it off, but take nothing after it; sit still till it has worked once; keep very warm, and take nothing in the working; but you may walk about after it has worked once; take it three mornings together, or more, if there be occasion, till the stomach is clear. There is no case where a vomit is proper, but this is good.

A fine Purge

Take an ounce of liquorice, scrape it and slice it thin, and a spoonful of coriander seeds bruised; put these into a pint of water, and boil it a little; and strain this water into an ounce of senna; let it stand six hours; strain it from the senna, and drink it fasting.

A Purging Diet-Drink in the Spring

Take six gallons of ale, three ounces of rhubarb, senna, madder-roots, and dock-roots, of each twelve ounces; twelve handfuls of scabious, and as much agrimony, three ounces of aniseeds; slice and cut these, put them in a bag, and let them work in the ale; drink of it three or four times a day.

For a Sore Mouth in Children

Take half a pint of verjuice, strain into it four spoonfuls of the juice of sage; boil this with fine sugar to a syrup, and with a feather anoint the mouth often; touch it not with a cloth, or rub it; the child may lick it down, it will not hurt it.

To create a good Appetite and strengthen the Stomach

Take of the stomachic pill with gums, *extractum rudii*, of each a drachm, refin of jalap half a scruple, tartar vitriolated one scruple, oil of aniseeds four drops; mix with syrup of violets, and make into pills, of which take four or five overnight; they are of excellent use in the megrims and vertigo, by reason they carry the humour off from the stomach, which fumes up into the head.

A very good Medicine for the Bloody-Flux

Take of the best rhubarb, finely powder'd, half an ounce, of red saunders two drachms, cinnamon one drachm, crocus martis astringent three drachms, of Lucatellus's balsam what suffices; make a mass of pills, of which take three every night and morning for a fortnight. This has cured some who have loft a vast quantity of blood, after other remedies have proved ineffectual.

For red or sore Eyes

Take a quarter of an ounce of white copperas, and an ounce of bole-armoniac; beat them to a fine powder, adding an ounce of camphire; set two quarts of spring-water on the fire; when it boils, take it off, and let it stand till it is lukewarm; then put in your ingredients, stirring till cold; drop the clear into the eye.

For a Pain in the Stomach, or Heaviness of Heart

Take a pint of rose-water, put to it some double-refined sugar, and a pennyworth of saffron tied up in a piece of lawn; let it stand two or three days, and then at any time take three spoonfuls.

For Fits from Wind or Cold

Take three drops of oil of amber in some burnt wine, or mace ale. If it is given in black-cherry water, it is good to forward labour in child-bed.

To make the Red Balls

Take rue, dragon, rosemary, sage, baum, betony, plantain, pimpernel, dandelion, scabious, wormwood, mugwort, saxifrage, red bramble-tops, tormentil, shepherd's purse, lovage, carduus, centaury, angelica, agrimony, fumitory, scordium, of each a handful; gather these in dry weather, pick and chop them, put them in a broad pan, pour on them a pint of white wine, and let it stand nine or ten days in the sun, stirring it sometimes; then strain it out, squeezing it with your hand; wipe your pan clean, and put in your juice, with half an ounce of powder of pearl prepared, half an ounce of Venice treacle, half an ounce of powder of coral, powder of crabs' claws two ounces, one ounce of confection of alkermes, and of bole-armoniac powder'd, as much as will make it the thickness of a syrup; let it stand in the sun to dry two or three days, or till it will roll up into balls, what size you please; if it is too thin, use more bole-armoniac; dry them well, and keep them for use: scrape as much as will lie on a sixpence, and take it in a glass of sack, or small cordial, going to bed.

To make Elixir Proprietatis

Take of myrrh, aloes, and saffron, of each four drachms, infuse them in a pint of the best brandy; first put in the myrrh, and let it stand twelve hours; then the saffron and aloes; set it by the fire three or four days, shaking it very often; then strain it off. Take sixty or seventy drops, more or less, in a little white wine, in a morning fasting, for a week or ten days together; it is good for any illness in the stomach, or in the bowels: it is the best of physic for children.

To cure a Pimpled Face

Take an ounce of live brimstone, as much roch-alum, as much common salt; white sugar-candy, and spermaceti, of each two drachms; pound and sift all these into a fine powder, and put it in a quart bottle; then put to it half a pint of brandy, three ounces of white-lily water, and three ounces of spring-water; shake all these well together, and keep it for use. When you use it, shake the bottle, and bathe the face well; and when you go to bed, dip rags in it, and lay it all over the face; in ten or twelve days it will be perfectly cured.

A Purge for Hoarseness or any Illness on the Lungs

Take four ounces of the roots of sorrel, of hyssop and maidenhair, of each half a handful; raisins stoned a quarter of a pound, senna half an ounce, barley water two quarts; put all these in a jug, and infuse them in a kettle of water two hours; strain it out, and take a quarter of a pint morning and night.

An Electuary for a cold or windy Stomach

Take gum-guaiacum one ounce, cubebs and cardamums of each a quarter of an ounce; beat and sift all these, and mix it with syrup of gilliflowers into an electuary. Take night and morning the quantity of a nutmeg; drink a little warm ale after it.

An Electuary for a Pain in the Stomach

Take conserve of wood-sorrel and mithridate an equal quantity; mix it well together, and take night and morning the quantity of a nutmeg; so do for fifteen days together.

To make Syrup of Marshmallows

Take of marshmallow roots four ounces, grass root, asparagus roots, liquorice, ston'd raisins, of each half an ounce; the tops of marshmallows, pellitory, pimpernel, saxifrage, plantain, maiden-hair white and black, of each a handful, red chickes an ounce; the four greater and four lesser cold seeds, of each three drachms; bruise all these, and boil them in three quarts of water till it comes to two; then put to it four pounds of white sugar, till it comes to a syrup.

To make Syrup of Saffron

Take a pint of the best canary, as much baum water, and two ounces of English saffron; open and pull the saffron very well, and put it into the liquor to infuse; let it stand close cover'd (so as to be hot, but not boil) twelve hours; then strain it out as hot as you can, and add to it two pounds of double-refined sugar; boil it till it is well incorporated, and when it is cold bottle it, and take one spoonful in a little sack or small cordial, as occasion serves.

A Syrup for a Cough or Asthma

Take of hyssop and pennyroyal water, of each a quarter of a pint, slice into it a small stick of liquorice, and a few raisins of the sun stoned; let it simmer together a quarter of an hour and then make it into a syrup with brown sugar-candy; boil it a little, and then put in four or five spoonfuls of snail-water; give it a walm, and when it is cold, bottle it; take one spoonful morning and night, with three drops of balsam of sulphur in it; you may take a little of the syrup without the drops once or twice a day; if the party is short-breath'd, a blister is very good.

To make Syrup of Balsam for a Cough

Take one ounce of balsam of Tolu, and put to it a quart of spring-water, let them boil together two hours; then put in a pound of white sugar-candy finely beaten, and let it boil half an hour longer; take out the balsam, and strain the syrup thro' a flannel bag twice; when it is cold, put it in a bottle. This syrup is excellent for a cough; take a spoonful of it as you lie down in your bed, and a little at any time when your cough troubles you; you may add to it two ounces of syrup of red poppies, and as much of raspberry syrup.

A Syrup for a Cough

Take of oak-lungs, French moss, and maidenhair, of each a handful; boil all these in three pints of spring-water, till it comes to a quart; then strain it out, and put to it six-pennyworth of saffron tied up in a rag, and two pounds of brown sugar-candy; boil it up to a syrup, and when it is cold bottle it; take a spoonful of it as often as your cough troubles you.

Another

Take of unset hyssop, coltsfoot flowers, and black maidenhair, of each an handful; of white horehound two handfuls; boil these herbs together in three quarts of water till it come to three pints; then take it off, and let the herbs stand in it till it is cold; then squeeze them out very dry, and strain the liquor, and let it boil a quarter of an hour, skim it well; to every pint put in half a pound of white sugar, and let it boil, and skim it, till it comes to a syrup; when it is cold bottle it; take two spoonfuls night and morning, and at any time when the cough is troublesome take one spoonful; don't cork the bottles, but tie them down with a paper.

For a Cough

Take three quarts of spring-water, and put it in a large pipkin, with a calf's foot, and four spoonfuls of barley, and a handful of dried poppies; boil it together till one quart be consumed; then strain it out, and add a little cinnamon, and a pint of milk, and sweeten it to your taste with loaf sugar; warm it a little, and drink half a pint as often as you please.

Another

Take two ounces of raisins of the sun stoned, one ounce of brown sugar-candy, one ounce of conserve of roses, add to these a little flour of brimstone, mix all well together in a mortar, and take the quantity of a nutmeg night and morning.

To make Conserve of Hips

Gather the hips before they grow soft, cut off the heads and stalks, slit them in halves, and take out all the seed and white that is in them very clean; then put them in an earthen pan, and stir them every day, else they will grow mouldy; let them stand till they are soft enough to rub thro' a coarse hair sieve; as the pulp comes, take it off the sieve; then add its weight in sugar, and mix it well together without boiling, keeping it in deep gallipots for use.

Medicines and Salves

To make the Drink

Take a quart of spring-water, of liverwort one handful, liquorice, aniseeds, coriander seeds, sweet fennel seeds, and hartshorn, of each an equal quantity; forty raisins of the sun stoned; fourteen figs: boil all these together till one half is consumed; then put in three spoonfuls of honey, and boil it a little more; let it stand till it is cold, strain it out, put in two spoonfuls of syrup of gilliflowers, and bottle it up; take two or three spoonfuls morning and evening.

The Green Ointment

Take rue, camomile, hyssop, hog's fennel, red fennel, rosemary, bays, ladies' mantle, Paul's betony, water-betony, balm, nepp, valerian, mallows, nightshade, plantain, comfry, adder's tongue, Roman wormwood, common wormwood, vervain, clary, agrimony, red sage, ground-ivy, feverfew, self-heal, melilot, bramble-tops, marshmallows, fanicle, ribwort, may-weed, of each two large handfuls; pick and chop them; then take four pounds of butter unwash'd, and three pounds of boar's grease; melt them together, put in the herbs, and let it boil two hours; then strain it out; let it stand a little, and put it into pots for use.

To cure the Rickets

Open a vein in both ears between the junctures, mix a little aqua vitae with the blood, and with it anoint the breast, sides, and neck; then take three ounces of the green ointment, warm a little of it in a spoon, and anoint the wrists and ankles as hot as it may be endured; do this for nine nights just before bedtime; shift not the shirt all the time. If the veins do not appear, rub it with a little lint dipped in aqua vitae, or else cause the child to cry, and that will make the veins more visible, and bleed the better.

Another way to cure the Rickets

Make the drink thus: Take polypodium of the oak, three ounces, of liverwort, and hart's tongue, of each a good handful; betony twenty leaves; white horehound and nepp, of each four tops: boil these all together in three quarts of sweet-wort till it come to two; then strain it, and when it is cold, put to it two quarts of middling-wort; let it work together; then put it in a little vessel; and when it has done working take half a quarter of an ounce of rhubarb sliced very thin; put it in a little linen bag, with a stone in it to keep it from swimming, and hang it in the vessel; when it is three days old, let the child drink of it a quarter of a pint in the morning, and as much in the afternoon at four o'clock, or when the child will take it. You must likewise anoint the child morning and night with this following ointment. Take butter in the month of May, as soon as it is taken out of the churn, and wash it with the dew of wheat; to a pound of butter take a handful of red sage, as much of rue, camomile, and hyssop; boil all these in the butter, and skim it till it is boiled clear; then strain it out, and keep it in a gallipot for use; you must anoint the reins of the back and the ribs, stroaking it downwards, and upon the small of the belly, and swing the child often with the heels upwards.

To make Charity Oil

Take poplar buds in the beginning of May one handful, and put them into a pint and a half of oil, and half a pint of aqua vitae, cover them close, and let them stand till the following herbs are in season, then add them to your buds: betony, charity, fanicle, the tops of St John's wort when blown, adder's tongue, comfry, self-heal, beam, southernwood, pennyroyal, flowers of red sage, parsley, clowns' all-heal, balsam, knotgrass, sweet-marjoram, lavender-cotton, red rosebuds, camomile, lavender-tops when blown, of each a small handful; but of poplar-buds, red rosebuds, and adder's tongue double the quantity; gather the herbs in dry weather, and wipe them clean with a cloth; shred them pretty grossly before you put them in; let them steep in a stone pot cover'd very close; then set them on the fire in a skillet; let them simmer with a slow fire five or six hours, then strain it out. This oil is good for any green wound, bruise, burn, or ache; and for inward bruises, taking a spoonful in a little warm sack; and for any outward swelling, warm it and anoint the part affected.

An excellent Plaister for any Pain occasioned by a Cold or Bruise

Take of the plaister of red lead and oxycroceum, of each equal parts; of the best Thebian opium one scruple; spread it on leather, and lay it to the part affected, after you have well anointed it with the following ointment. Take of ointment of marshmallows one ounce, oil of Exeter half an ounce, oil of spike, and spirit of hartshorn, of each a drachm.

For a Dropsy

Take of horseradish roots sliced thin, and sweet fennel seeds bruised, of each two ounces; smallage and fennel roots sliced, of each an ounce; of the tops of thyme, winter-savory, sweet-marjoram, watercresses, and nettles, of each a handful; bruise the herbs, and boil them in three pints of sack, and three of water, to the consumption of half; let it stand close covered for three hours; then strain it, and drink a draught of it twice a day sweetened with syrup of fennel, fasting two hours after it.

For the Gripes

Take a glass of sack warmed, and dissolve in it one drachm of Venice treacle, or Diascordium; drink it off going to bed; cover warm.

To stay a Looseness

Take a very good nutmeg, prick it full of holes, and toast it on the point of a knife; then boil it in milk till half be consumed; then eat the milk with the nutmeg powdered in it; in a few times it will stop.

For the Strangury

Take half a pint of plantain water, one ounce of white sugar-candy finely powder'd, two spoonfuls of salad oil, and the juice of a lemon; beat all these together very well, and drink it off.

For a Drought in a Fever

Take of sal-prunella one ounce, dissolve it in spring-water, and put as much sugar to it as will sweeten it; simmer it over the fire till it is a syrup; put some into posset-drink, and take it two or three times a day, or when very thirsty.

A Plaister for an Ague

Take Venice turpentine, and mix with it the powder of white hellebore roots, till it is stiff enough to spread on leather. It must be laid all over the wrist, and over the ball of the thumb, six hours before the fit comes.

For a Chin-Cough

Take a spoonful of woodlice, bruise them, mix them with breast-milk, and take them three or four mornings according as you find benefit. It will cure; but some must take it longer than others.

An admirable Tincture for green Wounds

Take balsam of Peru one ounce, storax calamita two ounces, benjamin three ounces, succotrine aloes, myrrh, and frankincense, of each half an ounce, angelica roots and flowers of St John's wort, of each half an ounce, spirit of wine one pint; beat the drugs, scrape and slice the roots, and put it into a bottle; stop it well, and let it stand in the sun throughout July, August, and September; then strain it through a fine linen cloth, put it in a bottle, stop it close, and keep it for use. Apply it to a green wound by anointing it with a feather; then dip lint in it, and put it on, binding it up with a cloth; but let no plaister touch it; twice a day wet the lint with a feather, but do not take it off till it is well.

To take off Blackness by a Fall

Rub it well with a cold tallow candle, as soon as it is bruised, and this will take off the blackness.

To break a Bile

Take the yolk of a new-laid egg, some honey and wheat-flour; mix them well together, spread it on a rag, and lay it on cold.

A Poultice for a hard Swelling

Boil the finest wheat-flour in cream, till it is pretty thick; then take it off, and put in mallows chopped; stir it, and apply it as hot as can be endured; dress it twice a day, and make fresh every time.

To stay Vomiting

Take ash leaves, boil them in vinegar and water, and apply them hot to the stomach; do this often.

A Poultice for a sore Breast, Leg, or Arm

Boil wheat-flour in strong ale very well, and pretty thick; then take it off the fire, and scrape in some boar's grease, stir it well and apply it hot.

A Salve for a Blast, Burn, or Scald

Take May butter fresh out of the churn, neither washed nor salted, put into it a good quantity of the green inner rind of elder, put it in a pipkin, and set that in a pot of boiling water; let it infuse a day or two; then strain it out and keep it in a pot for use.

An excellent Remedy for Agues, which has been often tried with very great success

Take of black soap, gunpowder, tobacco and brandy, of each an equal quantity; mix them well together, and three hours before the fit comes, apply to the patient's wrist; let this be kept on for a fortnight.

To cure the Bite of a Mad Dog

Take two quarts of strong ale, two pennyworth of treacle, two garlic-heads, a handful of cinquefoil, sage and rue; boil them all together to a quart; strain it, and give the patient three or four spoonfuls twice a day. Take dittany, agrimony, and rusty bacon, beaten well together, and apply to the sore, to keep it from festering.

Another cure for the Biting of a Mad Dog

Primrose roots stamped in white wine, and strained; let the patient drink a good draught of it.

Dr Mead's Receipt for the Bite of a Mad Dog

Let the patient bleed at the arm nine or ten ounces; take of the herb called in Latin *lichen cinerus terrestris*, in English ash-coloured ground liverwort, cleaned, dried and powdered, half an ounce; of black pepper powdered, two drachms: mix these well together, and divide the powder into four doses, one of which must be taken every morning fasting, for four mornings successively, in half a pint of cow's milk warm; after these four doses are taken, the patient must go into the cold bath, or a cold spring or river, every morning fasting, for a month; he must be dipped all over, but not stay in (with his head above water) longer than half a minute, if the water be very cold; after this he must go in three times a week for a fortnight longer. The *lichen* is a very common herb, and grows generally in sandy and barren soils all over England; the right time to gather it is in the months of October and November.

Another for the Bite of a Mad Dog, which has cured when the Person was disordered, and the salt Water failed

Take of tormentil-roots an ounce, assa foetida as much as a bean, castor four pennyworth, lignum aloes two pennyworth; steep these in milk twelve hours; boil the milk, and drink it fasting, before the change or full moon, or as oft as occasion.

An infallible cure for the Bite of a mad Dog

Of all the diseases incident to mankind, there is none so shocking to our nature as the bite of a mad dog; and yet as terrible as it is, we have known instances of those who chose rather to hazard the worst effects of it, and to die the worst of deaths, than to follow the advice of their physicians, by making use of the known specific of dipping in the sea, or salt-water. It is for the sake of people of this unhappy temper, who may have the misfortune to be bit, and of those who may have cattle that are so, that we publish the following receipt, which has been frequently made use of in a neighbouring country, and (as the gentleman who communicated it says) was never known to fail.

Take the leaves of rue, picked from the stalks and bruised, six ounces; garlic picked from the stalks and bruised, Venice treacle or mithridate, and scrapings of pewter, of each four ounces; boil all these over a slow fire in two quarts of ale, till one pint is consumed; keep it in a bottle close stopped, and give of it nine spoonfuls to the person warm seven mornings successively, and six to a dog, to be given nine days after the bite; apply some of the ingredients to the part bitten.

Note This receipt was taken out of Cathorp church in Lincolnshire, the whole town almost being bitten, and not one person who took this medicine but was cured.

Another for the same

Take the shells of oysters, and calcine the white or inner part of them; when thoroughly calcined, which may be done either in an oven or a crucible, beat them to a fine powder in a mortar; that powder must also be sifted through a fine sieve; when all this is done, put six gros (eight gros makes a French ounce, which our apothecaries know how to adjust to their own) of the powder into a pint of right neat white wine; and let the patient drink it off, without taking any other thing, of any kind whatever, until at least three hours afterwards; and by all means not to touch butter, or anything that is oily, during the time of cure. The next day he must take four gros of the same powder in the aforesaid quantity of wine, and the third day two gros, still fasting three hours afterwards; and then the cure is completed.

A Receipt for Colds

Take of Venice treacle half a drachm, powder of snake-root twelve grains, powder of saffron six grains, volatile salt of hartshorn four grains, syrup of cloves a sufficient quantity to make it into a bolus; to be taken going to rest, drinking a large draught of warm mountain whey after it.

Note Those who cannot afford mountain whey may drink treacle posset To such constitutions as cannot be provoked to sweat, opening a vein, or a gentle purge, will be of great service.

For spitting Blood

Take of cinnabar of antimony one ounce, and mix it with two ounces of conserve of red roses; take as much as a nutmeg night and morning.

To know if a Child has Worms or not

Take a piece of white leather, prick it full of holes with your knife, rub it with wormwood, spread honey on it, and strew the powder of succotrine aloes on it; lay it on the child's navel when it goes to bed; and if it has worms, the plaister will stick fast; and if it has not, it will fall off.

Another wey to Stop Vomiting

Take half a pint of mint-water, an ounce of syrup of violets, a quarter of an ounce of mithridate, and half an ounce of syrup of roses; mix all these well together, and let the party take two spoonfuls first, and then one spoonful after every vomiting, till it is stayed.

To cure the Toothache

Let the party that is troubled with the toothache lie on the contrary side, drop three drops of the juice of rue into the ear on that side the tooth acheth, let it remain an hour or two. It will remove the pain.

A rare Mouth Water

Take rosemary, rue, celandine, plantain, bramble leaves, woodbine leaves, and sage, of each a handful; beat them, and steep them in a quart of the best white-wine vinegar two days and nights; then press it well, strain it, put to it six ounces of alum, and as much honey, boil them a little together softly, till the alum is dissolved; when it is cold, keep it for use.

To make Lozenges for the Heartburn

Take of white sugar-candy a pound, chalk three ounces, bole-armoniac five scruples, crab's eyes one ounce, red coral four scruples, nutmegs one scruple, pearl two scruples; let all these be beaten and sifted, and made all into a paste with a little spring-water; roll it out, and cut your lozenges out with a thimble; lay them to dry; eat four or five at a time, as often as you please.

To make Syrup of Garlic

Take two heads of garlic, peel it clean, and boil it in a pint of water a pretty while; then change your water and boil it till the garlic is tender; then, straining it off, add a pound of double-refined sugar to it, and boil it till it is a thick syrup; skim it well, and keep it for use; take a spoonful in a morning fasting, another last at night, for a short breath.

To prevent Afterpains

Take nine single peony seeds powdered, the same quantity of powder of borax, and a little nutmeg; mix all these with a little white aniseed water in a spoon, and give it the woman; and a little aniseed water after it, as soon as possible after she is laid in bed.

Another way to cure the Toothache

Take half an ounce of conserve of rosemary overnight, and half a drachm of extract of rudium in the morning; do this three times together; keep warm.

To Stop Bleeding at Mouth, Nose or Ears

In the month of May take a clean cloth, and wet it in the spawn of frogs, nine days, drying it every day in the wind; lay up that cloth, and when you have need, hold it to the place where the blood runs, and it will stop.

Another to Stop Bleeding

Take two handfuls of the tops of bramble-wood and boil it in a quart of old claret till it comes to a pint; give six spoonfuls once in half an hour; in the winter the roots will do.

To cure the Dropsy

Take six gallons of ale pretty strong, but little hopped; alexander, red sage, scurvy-grass, ground-ivy, and the long green leaves of flower-deluce, of each two handfuls; bruise these well, and boil them well in the ale; then strain it out, and when it is cool, work it as other ale; put it in your vessel, and when it is clear, drink of it in a morning fasting; use no other drink except white wine; sometimes drink good draughts of it at a time.

An excellent Medicine for Shortness of Breath

Take half an ounce of flour of brimstone, a quarter of an ounce of beaten ginger, and three quarters of an ounce of beaten senna; mix all together in four ounces of honey; take the bigness of a nutmeg night and morning for five days together; then once a week for some time; then once a fortnight.

Another for Shortness of Breath

Take two quarts of elderberry juice when very ripe, put one quart in a pipkin to boil, and as it consumes, put in the rest by a little at a time; boil it to a balsam; it will take five or six hours in boiling. Take a little of it night and morning, or any time.

To cure a pimpled Face, and sweeten the Blood

Take senna one ounce, put it in a small stone pot, and pour a quart or more of boiling water on it, then fill it up with prunes; cover with paper, and set it in the oven with household-bread; take every day, one, two, three, or more, of the prunes and liquor, according as it operates; continue this always, or at least half a year.

To cure the Dropsy, Rheumatism, Scurvy, and Cough of the Lungs

Take English orrice roots, squills, and elecampane roots, each one ounce, hyssop and horehound leaves, each one handful, the inner rind of green elder and dwarf-elder, of each one handful, senna one ounce and a half, agaric two drachms, ginger one drachm; cut the roots thin, bruise the leaves, and put them into two quarts of the best Lisbon wine; let these boil an hour and a half on a gentle fire in an earthen mug, very close stopt with a cork, and tied down with a bladder, that no air come to it, and set it in a large pot of boiling water; set it so that no water get into the mug, which must hold three quarts, that all the ingredients may have room to go in; when it is almost cold, strain it out very hard; take this for a week together if you can, and then miss a day; and if that does not do, go on with your other bottle of the same; take it in a morning fasting, ten spoonfuls at a time, without any posset drink; it will both vomit and purge you; it is of an unpleasant taste; therefore take a lump of sugar after it; when it is quite cold, after it is strain'd off, let it stand in a flagon to settle a night and a day; then bottle it up clear and fine for use: it is an admirable medicine.

Another to Stop Bleeding

Take a pint of plantain water, put to it two ounces of isinglass, and let it stand twenty-four hours to dissolve; pour it from the dregs, and put in a pint of red port wine, and add to it three or four sticks of cinnamon, and two ounces of double-refined sugar; give it a boil or two, and pour it off: let the party take two or three spoonfuls two or three times a day.

To cure a Cancer

Take a drachm of the powder of crabs' claws finely searced, and made into a paste with damask-rose water, and dried in pellets or lozenges; powder the lozenges as you use them, and drink the powder in whey every morning fasting; if there be a sore, and it is raw, anoint it with a salve made of dock-roots and fresh butter; keep a low diet, and abstain from anything that is salt, sour or strong.

To cure the Joint Evil

Take good store of elder leaves, and distil them in a cold still; let the person drink every morning and evening half a pint of this water, and wash the sores with it morning and evening, first warming it a little; lay fresh elder leaves on the sores, and in a little time you will find they will dry up; but be sure to follow it exactly. It has cured, when all other remedies have failed.

For the Green Sickness

Take centaury the less, wormwood, and rosemary flowers, of each a handful, gentian root a drachm, coriander seeds two drachms; boil these in a quart of water; sweeten it with syrup of steel; take four or five spoonfuls in the morning, and as much in the afternoon.

To take off Freckles

Take either bean-flower water, elder-flower water, or May-dew gathered from corn, four spoonfuls, and add to it one spoonful of oil of tartar *per deliquium*; mix it well together, and often wash the face with it; let it dry on.

A Salve for a Sprain

Take a quarter of a pound of virgin wax, a quarter of a pound of frankincense, half a pound of Burgundy pitch; melt them well together, stirring them all the while till they are melted; then give them a good boil, and strain them into water; work it well into rolls, and keep it for use; the more it is worked, the better it is; spread it on leather.

A rare green Oil for Aches and Bruises

Take a pot of oil of olives, and put it into a stone pot of a gallon, with a narrow mouth; then take southernwood, wormwood, sage, and camomile, of each four handfuls; a quarter of a peck of red rosebuds, the white cut from them; shred them together grossly, and put them into the oil; and once a day, for nine or ten days, stir them well; and when the lavender spike is ripe, put four handfuls of the tops in, and let it stand three or four days longer, covered very close; then boil them an hour upon a slow fire, stirring it often; then put to it a quarter of a pint of the strongest aqua vitae, and let it boil an hour more; then strain it through a coarse cloth, let it stand till it is cold, and keep it in glasses for use; warm a little in a spoon or saucer and bathe the part affected.

To take out Spots of the Smallpox

Take half an ounce of oil of tartar, and as much oil of bitter almonds; mix it together, and with a fine rag daub it often on the face and hands, before the air has penetrated into the skin or flesh.

For the Colic

Take a drachm and a half of Dr Holland's powder, mix it with a little sack, and take it, drinking a glass of sack after it; gives present ease.

An approved remedy against Spitting of Blood

Take of the tops of stinging-nettles, and plantain leaves, of each a like quantity; bruise them, strain the juice out, and keep it close stopt in a bottle; take three or four spoonfuls every morning and evening, sweetened with sugar of roses; the juice of comfry roots drunk with wine is also very good; let the patient be blooded at first, and sometimes gently purged; but if there happens to be any inward soreness, occasioned by straining, this electuary will be very convenient – viz. take an ounce of Lucatellus's balsam, of conserve of roses two ounces, twelve drops of spirit of sulphur, to be made into a soft electuary with syrup of white poppies; the dose is the quantity of a nutmeg every morning and evening.

A receipt that cured a gentleman, who had a long time Spit Blood in a great quantity, and was wasted with a Consumption

Take of hyssop water, and of the purest honey, of each a pint; of agrimony and coltsfoot of each a handful; a sprig of rue, brown sugar-candy, liquorice sliced, shavings of hartshorn, of each two ounces; aniseeds bruised one ounce; of figs sliced, and raisins of the sun stoned, of each four ounces; put them all into a pipkin with a gallon of water, and boil it gently over a moderate fire, till half is consumed; then strain it, and when it is cold, put it into bottles, keep it close stopt, and take four or five spoonfuls every morning, at four in the afternoon, and at night the last thing; if you add fresh water to the ingredients, after the first liquor is strained off, you will have a pleasant drink, to be used at any time when you are dry.

An infallible Cure for the galloping Consumption

Take half a pound of raisins of the sun stoned, of figs and honey, of each a quarter of a pound; of Lucatellus's balsam, powder of steel, and flour of elecampane, of each half an ounce; a grated nutmeg, one pound of double-refined sugar pounded; shred and pound all these together in a stone mortar; pour on it a pint of salad oil by degrees; eat a bit of it four times a day the bigness of a nutmeg; every morning drink a glass of old Malaga sack, with the yolk of a new-laid egg, and as much flour of brimstone as will lie upon a sixpence; the next morning as much flour of elecampane, alternately.

For the Scurvy

Take a pound of guaiacum bark, half a pound of sassafras, and a quarter of a pound of liquorice; boil all these in three quarts of water, till it comes to three pints; and when it is cold, put it in a vessel with two gallons of ale; in three or four days it is fit to drink; use no other drink for six or twelve months, according to the violence of the distemper; it will certainly cure.

For the Jaundice

Take some tares, dry them in an oven, and beat them to powder; sift them, and take a spoonful of that powder in a morning fasting, and drink half a pint of white wine after it; do this for three mornings together, and it will cure though very far gone.

For Corns on the Feet

Take the yeast of beer (not of ale) and spread it on a linen rag, and apply it to the part affected; renew it once a day for three or four weeks; it will cure.

For Chilblains

Roast a turnip soft; beat it to mash, and apply it as hot as can be endured to the part affected; let it lie on two or three days, and repeat it two or three times.

To Stop Bleeding inwardly

Take two drachms of henbane seed, and the like of white poppy seed; beat them up with conserve of roses, and give the quantity of a nutmeg at a time; or take twelve handfuls of plantain leaves, and six ounces of fresh comfry roots; beat these, and strain out the juice, adding to it some fine sugar, and drink it off.

To Stop Vomiting

Take a large nutmeg, grate away half of it and toast the flat side till the oil ouze out; then clap it to the pit of the stomach; let it lie so long as it is warm; repeat it often till cured.

To kill a Tetter

Take flour of brimstone, ginger, and burnt alum, a like quantity; mix it with unsalted butter, anoint, as hot as can be endured, at bedtime; in the morning wash it off with celandine water heated; while this is continued, the party must sometimes take cordials, to keep the humour from going inward.

An Ointment for a Blast

Take velvet-leaves, wipe them clean, chop them small, put them to unsalted butter out of the churn, and boil them gently, till they are crisp; then strain it into a gallipot, and keep it for use; lay velvet-leaves over the part, after it is anointed.

A Poultice to ripen Tumours

Take half a pound of figs, white-lily roots, and bean-flour or meal, of each two ounces; boil these in water till it comes to a poultice; spread it thick on a cloth, apply it warm, and shift it as often as it grows dry.

For the Teeth

Take a pint of spring-water, put to it six spoonfuls of the best brandy; wash the mouth often with it, and in the morning roll a bit of alum a little while in the mouth.

For a Drought in a Fever

Make barley water, sweeten it with syrup of violets, and tincture it with spirit of vitriol; let them drink sometimes of this; put sal-prunella in beer or posset-drink, and sometimes drink of that; and if they are sick and faint, give a spoonful of cordial in a dish of tea.

A Powder that has restored Sight when almost lost

Take of betony, celandine, saxifrage, eyebright, pennyroyal, and levisticum, of each a handful; of aniseeds and cinnamon, of each half an ounce; grains of paradise, ginger, hyssop, parsley, origany, osier of the mountain, of each a drachm; galangal and sugar, of each an ounce; make all into a fine powder, and eat of it every day with your meat such a quantity as you used to eat of salt, and instead of it; the osier you must have at the physic-garden.

For a Cough settled on the Stomach

Take half a pound of figs sliced, raisins of the sun stoned as many, and a stick of liquorice scraped and sliced, a few aniseeds, and some hyssop washed clean; put all these into a quart of spring-water; boil it till it comes to a pint; then strain it, and sweeten it with white sugar-candy; take two or three spoonfuls morning and night, and when the cough troubles you.

Another way to cure a Dropsy

Take of horseradish roots slic'd two ounces, sweet fennel roots sliced two ounces, sweet fennel seeds beaten two ounces, the tops of thyme, winter-savory, sweet-marjoram, watercresses and nettle-tops, of each one handful, wiped and shred small; boil these in three pints of spring-water, a quart of sack, and a pint of white wine; cover it close, and let it boil till half be consumed; then take it off the fire, and let it stand to settle three hours; then strain it out, and to every draught put in an ounce of the syrup of the five opening roots. Take this in the morning fasting, and at three o'clock in the afternoon, fasting three hours after it. If the party have the scurvy (which usually goes with the dropsy) then add a spoonful of the juice of scurvy-grass to each draught.

An excellent Method to cure the Dropsy

Take a good quantity of black snails, stamp them well with bay-salt, and lay to the hollow of the feet, putting fresh twice a day; take likewise a handful of spearmint and wormwood, bruise them, and put them in a quart of cream, which boil till it comes to an oil; then strain and anoint those parts which are swelled. Take of the tops of green broom, which, after you have dried in an oven, burn upon a clean hearth to ashes, which mingle very well with a quart of white wine; let it stand all night to settle, and in a morning drink half a pint of the clearest; at four in the afternoon, and at night going to bed, do the same. Continue laying the poultice to your feet, and drinking the white wine for three weeks together: this method has been often used with success.

An experienced Eye-Water to strengthen the Sight, and prevent Cataracts

Take of eyebright tops, two handfuls, of celandine, vervain, betony, dill, ground-pine, clary, avens, pimpernel, and rosemary flowers, of each a handful; of capons, gall and aloes bruised, of each half an ounce; of long pepper, a drachm; infuse twenty-four hours in two quarts of white wine, then draw it off in a glass still; drop the water with a feather into the eye often.

For Stuffing in the Lungs

Take white sugar-candy powdered and sifted, two ounces; China roots powdered and sifted, one ounce; flour of brimstone, one ounce; mix these with conserve of roses, or the pap of an apple; and take the bigness of a walnut in the morning, fasting an hour after it; and the last at night, an hour after you have eaten or drunk.

To cure Spitting of Blood, if a Vein is Broken

Take mice-dung beaten to powder, as much as will lie on a sixpence, and put in a quarter of a pint of the juice of plantain, with a little sugar; give it in the morning fasting, and at night going to bed. Continue this some time, and it will make whole, and cure.

To give Ease in a violent Fit of the Stone

Take a quart of milk, and two handfuls of dried sage, a pennyworth of hemp seed, and one ounce of white sugar-candy; boil all these together a quarter of an hour, and then put in half a pint of rhenish wine. When the curd is taken off, put the ingredients in a bag, and apply it to the grieved part; and of the liquor drink a good glass full. Let both be as hot as can be endured. If there is not ease the first time, warm it again, and use it. It seldom fails.

For the Strangury

Take three spoonfuls of the juice of camomile, in a small glass of white wine, thrice a day, for three days together.

To procure easy Labour

Take of figs, and raisins of the sun stoned, of each half a pound, four ounces of liquorice scraped and sliced, one spoonful of aniseeds bruised; boil all these in two quarts of spring-water, till one pint is wasted; then strain it out, and drink a quarter of a pint of it morning and evening six weeks before the time.

To procure speedy Delivery when the Throws are great

Take half a drachm of borax powder'd, and mixed with a glass of white wine, some sugar, and a little cinnamon water; if it does no good the first time, try it again two hours after; so likewise the third time.

To bring away the Afterbirth

Give thirty or thirty-five drops of oil of juniper in a good glass of sack.

To prevent Afterpains

Take half an ounce of large nutmegs and toast them before the fire, and one ounce of the best cinnamon, and beat them together; then mix it with the whites of two eggs, beating it together in a porringer; take every morning in bed as much as will lie on the point of a knife, and so at night, drinking after it the following caudle. Take of Alicant wine or tent, red-rose water, and plantain water, of each a quarter of a pint; mingle them together, and beat three new-laid eggs, yolks and whites, making a caudle of them; put into it two ounces of double-refined sugar, and a quarter of an ounce of cinnamon; you must boil the cinnamon in the wine and water before the eggs are in; and after all is mixed, put to it half a drachm of the powder of knotgrass; take of this six spoonfuls morning and evening after the electuary.

Another for the same

Take a small quantity of bole-armoniac, and boil it in new milk. Let the party drink of it morning and evening, if it be either a woman with child, or in child-bed.

Take also some hog's dung, and wrap it in a fine linen-rag; warm it well, and put it to the lower part of the belly, and it will stop immediately.

To stop Floodings

Take the white of an egg, and beat it well with four or five spoonfuls of red-rose water, and drink it off morning and night nine mornings together; it has cured, when all other things have failed.

Let the party often take isinglass boil'd or dissolved in warm new milk, a pint at a time.

A Plaister for a Weakness in the Back

Take plantain, comfry, knotgrass, and shepherd's purse, of each a handful; stamp them small, and boil them in a pound of oil of roses, and a little vinegar; when it is well boiled, strain it, and set it on the fire again, adding to it of wax four ounces, chalk, bole-armoniac and terra-figillata, of each one ounce; boil all well, keeping it constantly stirring; then cool it, make it into rolls, and keep it for use; spread it on leather when you lay it to the back.

A Drink for the same

Take four roots of comfry, and of knotgrass and clary one handful, a sprig of rosemary, a little galangal, a good quantity of cinnamon and nutmeg sliced, and the pith of the chine of an ox. Stamp and boil all these in a quart of muscadine; then strain it, and put in six yolks of eggs; sweeten the caudle to your taste with double-refined sugar, and drink a good draught morning and evening. Take of crocus martis and conserve of red roses, mixed together, three or four times in a day.

For the Dysentery or Bloody-Flux

Take an iron ladle; anoint it with fine wax; put into it glass of antimony, what amount you please; set it on a slow fire without flame half an hour, still stirring it with a spatula; then pour it on a clean linen cloth, and rub off all the wax. Grind it to powder.

This is the receipt as I had it; but I kept it three quarters of an hour on the fire, and could not rub off any wax. The dose of a boy of seven or eight years is three grains; for a weak adult five grains; for a strong woman twelve or fourteen grains; for a very strong man eighteen or twenty grains. I never gave above fourteen grains; and in the making of it put about a drachm of wax to an ounce of the glass. It sometimes vomits, always purges, and seldom fails of success. I always intermit one day at least betwixt every dose.

For a Flux

Take a pint of new milk, and dissolve in it half a quarter of a pound of loaf sugar, and two drachms of mithridate; give this for a clyster moderately warm; repeat it once or twice, if there be occasion.

For the Falling Down of the Fundament

Take ginger, slice it, and put it in a little pan; heat it by clear well-kindled coals, and put it in a close-stool. Let the party sit over it, and receive the fume; cast in the ginger by little and little, and keep it warm.

To increase Milk in Nurses

Make gruel with lentils, and let the party drink freely of it; or else boil them in posset-drink, which they like best.

A good Purge

Infuse an ounce of senna in a pint of water, till half be consumed; when it is cold, add to it one ounce of syrup of roses, and one ounce of syrup of buckthorn; mix them well together. This quantity makes two strong purges for either man or woman, and four for a child.

To prevent Miscarrying

Take of dragon's blood the weight of a silver two-pence, and a drachm of red coral, the weight of two barley-corns of ambergris; make all these into a very fine powder, mix them well together, and keep them close in a box; if you are frighted, or need it, take as much at a time as will lie on a penny, and keep very still and quiet. Take it in a caudle made with muscadine or tent, and the husks of almonds dried and beaten to powder, and thicken it with the yolks of eggs. Take it in the morning fasting, and at night going to bed; this do till you are out of danger, and lay the following plaister to the back.

Take Venice turpentine, and mix it with bole-armoniac, and spread it on black-brown paper, the length and breadth of a hand, and lay it to the small of the back, keeping bed.

For the Green-Sickness

Take an ounce of the filings of steel, or rusty iron beaten to powder, and mix it with two ounces of flour of brimstone; then mix it up into an electuary with treacle; the party must take the quantity of a nutmeg in the morning fasting, and at four in the afternoon, continuing it till cured.

To procure a Good Colour

Take germander, rue, fumitory, of each a good handful, one pennyworth of saffron tied up in a rag, half a pound of blue currants bruised; stamp the herbs, and infuse all the ingredients in three pints of sack over a gentle fire till half be consumed; drink a quarter of a pint morning and evening, and walk after it; repeat this quantity once or twice.

You may add a spoonful of the following syrup to every draught: Take three ounces of the filings of steel, and put it in a glass bottle with a drachm of mace, and as much cinnamon; pour on them a quart of the best white wine; stop it up close, and let it stand fourteen days, shaking the bottle every day; then strain it out into another bottle, and put two pounds of fine loaf sugar to it finely beaten; let it stand till the sugar is dissolved, without stirring it; then clear it into another bottle, and keep it for use.

A Receipt for the Gout

The following prescription of the celebrated Messrs Boerhave and Ofterdyke, for the cure of the gout, has been tried with so much success by a gentleman who was afflicted with that distemper from the age of fifteen to upwards of forty, and is now, as he hopes, perfectly cured of it, and is returning (with all proper caution) to his usual (temperate) manner of living; and it has besides done so much good to several others to whom the salutary regimen has been communicated, that he thinks he cannot do a more acceptable service to the public, nor make a better acknowledgment for the benefit he has received by it, than to publish the same for the general good of his fellow-creatures; and though he cannot answer for it, that it may have the same happy effects on every constitution that it has had with him; yet he doubts not that the innocence of the method prescribed, and the disinterested manner in which he offers it to the public, will be a sufficient justification of his good intentions, and a better recommendation of its genuineness and efficacy, than anything he can say further on this subject.

Professors Boerhaave and Osterdyke's Regimen prescribed for the Gout

They are of opinion, that the gout is not to be cured by any other means but by milk, a diet which will in twelve months' time alter the whole mass of blood; and in order thereto, the following directions must be strictly observed and followed:

1 You must not taste any liquor, only a mixture of one third milk, and two thirds water, your milk as new as you can get it, and to drink it as often as you have occasion, without adding any other to it. A little tea and coffee is likewise permitted, with milk.

2 In the morning as soon as awake, and the stomach has made a digestion, you must drink eight ounces of spring-water, and fast two hours after; eat milk and bread, milk-pottage, or tea with milk, with a little bread, and fresh butter.

3 At dinner you must not eat anything but what is made of barley, oats, rice, or millet seed, carrots, potatoes, turnips, spinage, beans, pease, &c. You may likewise eat fruit when full ripe, baked pears or apples, apple-dumplings; but above all, milk and biscuit is very good, but nothing salt or sour, not even a Seville orange.

4 At supper you must eat nothing but milk and bread.

5 It is necessary to go to bed betimes, even before nine o'clock, to accustom yourself to sleep much, and use yourself to it.

6 Every morning before you rise, to have your feet, legs, arms, and hands well rubbed with pieces of woollen cloth for half an hour, and the same going to bed. This article must be strictly

observed; for by this means the humours, knobs, and bunches will be dissipated, and prevent their fixing in the joints, by which they become useless.

7 You must accustom yourself to exercise, as riding on horse-back, which is best, or in any coach, chaise, &c., the more the better; but take care of the cold weather, winds and rain.

Lastly, in case a fit of the gout should return, and be violent, which they are of opinion will not, then a little dose of opium, or laudanum, may be taken to compose you; but no oftener than necessity requires. They are of opinion that your father or mother having the gout is of no consequence if you will resolve to follow the foregoing directions strictly.

Another remedy for the Gout

Take a pound of beeswax, and half a pound of rosin, of olibanum four ounces, of litharge of gold finely powdered, and white lead, of each twelve ounces, of neat's-foot oil a pint. Set the oil, together with the beeswax and rosin, over the fire; as soon as they are melted, put in the powders, keeping it continually stirring with a stick; as soon as it is boiled enough, take it off the fire, and pour it on a board anointed with neat's-foot oil, and make it into rolls; apply this plaister, spread on sheep's-leather, to the part affected; once a week take of caryocostinum four drachms dissolved in white wine, keeping yourself warm after it; by applying this plaister, and taking the caryocostinum, there are many which have found very great benefit.

Another for the same

Take as much Venice treacle as a hazelnut, mixed up with a scruple of Gascoign's powder, three or four nights together, when the fit is either on you, or coming on.

For the Hiccup

Take three or four preserved damsons in your mouth at a time, and swallow them by degrees.

For the Piles

Take of the tops of parsley, of mullet, and of elder buds, of each one handful; boil in a sufficient quantity of fresh butter till it looks green, and has extracted the smell of the herbs; strain, and anoint the place with it three or four times a day.

A bitter Draught

Take of the leaves of Roman wormwood, tops of centaury, and St John's wort, of each a small handful, roots of gentian sliced two drachms, caraway seeds half an ounce; infuse these in half a pint of rhenish and three pints of white wine for four or five days; take a quarter of a pint in the morning, filling up the bottle, and it will serve two or three months.

Another Remedy for the Piles

Mix calcined oyster-shells with honey, and anoint the part tenderly night and morning.

Another for the same

Take a sheet of lead, and have a piece of lead made like a flick-stone; then between them grind white lead and salad oil till it is very fine; put it in a gallipot for use. If the piles are inward, cut a piece of old tallow-candle, and dip it in this ointment, and put it up; if outward, put some on a fine rag, and put it to them.

For the Haemorrhoids inflamed

Let the party dip their finger in balsam of sulphur, made with oil of turpentine, and anoint the place two or three times a day.

For Costiveness

Take virgin-honey a quarter of a pound, and mix it with as much cream of tartar as will bring it to a pretty thick electuary, of which take the bigness of a walnut when you please; and for your breakfast eat

water-gruel with common mallows boiled in it, and a good piece of
butter; the mallows must be chopped small, and eaten with the gruel.

To raise a Blister

The seeds of *Clematis peregrina*, being bound hard on any place, will
in an hour or two raise a blister, which you must cut and dress with
melilot plaister, or colewort leaves, as other blisters.

Likewise, leaven mixed with a little verjuice, and about half a
pennyworth of cantharides, and spread on leather the bigness you
please, will in nine or ten hours raise a blister; which dress as usual.

A Plaister for the Feet in a Fever

Take of briony roots one pound, tops of rue a handful, black soap
four ounces, and bay-salt two ounces; beat all this in a mash, and
out of this spread on a cloth for both feet; apply it warm, and few
cloths over them, and let them lie twelve hours; if there be
occasion, renew them three times.

A Drink for a Fever

Take a quart of spring-water, an ounce of burnt hartshorn, a
nutmeg quartered, and a stick of cinnamon; let it boil a quarter of
an hour; when it is cold sweeten it to your taste with syrup of
lemons, or fine sugar, with as many drops of spirit of vitriol as will
just sharpen it. Drink of this when you please.

A Vomit

Take seven or eight daffodil roots, and boil them in a pint of
posset-drink, and in the working drink carduus water, a gallon or
more; your posset must be cold when you drink it, and your
carduus tea must be blood-warm; if it works too much, put some
salt in a dish of posset, and drink it off.

For the Cramp

Take of rosemary leaves, chop them very small, sew them in fine linen, make them into garters, and wear them night and day; lay a down pillow on your legs in the night.

For Weakness in the Hands after a Palsey

Take of the tops of rosemary, bruise it, and make it up into a ball as big as a great walnut, and let the party roll it up and down in their hand very often, and grasp it in the hand till it is hot; do this very often.

For an old Ache or Strain

Take an ounce of Lucatellus's balsam, and mix it with two drachms of oil of turpentine; gently heat it; anoint the place, and put new flannel on it.

A new Method for curing the Venereal Disease

It need not be said what direful accidents daily happen to people by salivations, as the loss of teeth, of hearing, of a healthful constitution, and often even of life itself; and what makes this case still more deplorable is that it hath been generally thought that nothing but a high salivation is the proper and adequate cure for this distemper; but the learned Dr Chicoyneau has happily discovered and proved the contrary. His method, which is sometimes called The Montpelier Method, and sometimes The New French Method, and which is attended with very little pain, and no danger at all, is as follows.

The doctor, according as he finds the patient's case to be, sometimes orders a little blood to be taken away, sometimes a gentle purge or two to be taken; but always makes him bathe five or six times, and always an hour at each time; after which the whole operation consists in nothing more than rubbing his feet, legs, and arms, four, five, or six times, as the case requires, with a mercurial ointment, in such quantities, and at such proper intervals of time, that no high salivation may be raised thereby; sometimes indeed, but not always, a gentle, moderate spitting will ensue, nor is it possible, in some constitutions, to prevent it; but then it is never carried high nor encouraged, it is neither troublesome nor dangerous; the patient during this time keeps his chamber, and observes a regular diet; and all he suffers is only a little feverish heat and restlessness, sometimes for a day or two, when the operation is at the height.

After this manner only, without any further trouble or danger, does Dr Chicoyneau cure the most inveterate pox, with all its symptoms and attendants; it is therefore greatly to be wished that all our surgeons, and others who undertake the cure of this disease, could be prevailed on, out of regard to the ease and safety of mankind, wholly to lay aside the old pernicious way of salivation, and embrace this new and safe method.

There are some hundreds of gentlemen in England, that can, from their own experience, bear witness to the excellency and efficacy of it: three have lately been cured by it, two by Dr Chicoyneau himself, in France, and the other here in London.

If any person is desirous to be further informed as to this practice, he may consult a book written by Dr Chicoyneau, and translated into English by Dr Willoughby, entitled *The Practice of Salivation Shown to be of No Use or Efficacy in the Cure of the Venereal Disease, but Greatly Prejudicial to It*; or else a treatise published by Dr Didier, one of the professors at Montpelier; or lastly, a pamphlet lately published here, entitled, 'A Letter from a Physician in London, to his Friend in the Country', giving an account of the Montpelier practice in curing the venereal disease, &c.

For the Jaundice

Take half an ounce of rhubarb powdered and beat it well with two handfuls of good currants well cleansed; and of this electuary take every morning a piece as big as a nutmeg, for fourteen or fifteen mornings together, or longer if need require.

Another Remedy for the Colic

Take half a pint of Dr Stephens's water, as much plague water, as much juniper-berry water, and an ounce of powder of rhubarb; shake the bottle, and take four or five spoonfuls at a time when the fit is on you, or likely to come.

For a Burn

Mix lime water with linseed-oil, beat it together, and with a feather anoint the place, and put on a plaister to defend it.

To cure a Place that is Scalded

Take linseed-oil, and put to it as much thick cream; beat them together very well, and keep it for use; anoint the place that is scalded twice a day, and it will cure it; put on it soft rags, and let nothing press it.

The Bitter Draught

Take of gentian root three drachms, of camomile flowers one ounce, of rosemary flowers one ounce, tops of centaury, tops of Roman wormwood, tops of carduus, of each one handful; boil all these in two quarts of spring-water till it comes to a quart; you may add a pint of white wine to it; strain it out, and when it is cold, bottle it; drink a quarter of a pint in the morning, and as much at four o'clock in the afternoon.

To draw out a Thorn

Take the roots of comfry, and bruise them in a mortar with a little boar's grease, and use this as a plaister.

For a Scalded Head

Take three spoonfuls of juice of comfry, two pennyworth of verdigris, and half a pound of hog's lard; melt it together, but let it not boil; cut off the hair, and anoint the place; it will cure it.

For the Falling-Sickness

Take the afterbirth of a woman, and dry it to powder, and drink half an ounce thereof in a glass of white wine for six mornings . If the patient be a man, it must be the afterbirth of a female child; if a woman, the contrary.

For the Trembling at the Heart

Make a syrup of damask roses, and add thereto a small quantity of red coral, pearl, and ambergris, all finely beaten and powdered; take this so long as your pains continue, about a spoonful at a time.

For a Pleurisy, if the person cannot be blooded

Take of carduus, the seeds or leaves, a large handful; boil them in a pint of beer till half is consumed; then strain it, and give it the party warm; they must be fasting when they take it, and fast six hours after it, or it will do them harm.

To draw a Rheum from the Eyes

Roast an egg hard; then cut out the yolk, and take a spoonful of cummin seed, and a handful of bear's foot; bruise them, and put them into the white of the egg; lay it on the nape of the neck, bind it on with a cloth, and let it lie twenty-four hours, and then renew it: it will cure in a little time.

To clear the Eyes

Take the white of hen's dung, dry it very well, and beat it to powder; sift, and blow it into the eyes when the party goes to bed.

For a Pin or Webb in the Eye

Take the gall of a hare, and honey, of each a like quantity; mix them together, take a feather, and put a little into the eye; it will cure in two or three days.

If a hair or fish-bone stick in the throat, immediately swallow the yolk of a raw egg: it is a very good thing.

An extraordinary Ointment for Burns and Scalds

Take of red dock-leaves and mallow-leaves, of each a large handful, two heads of houseleek, of green elder, the bark being scraped from it, a small handful; wash the herbs, and the elder; which being cut small, boil in it a pint and a half of cream; boil till it comes to an oil, which, as it rises up, take off with a spoon; afterwards strain, and put to it three drachms of white lead powdered fine.

A very good Drink to be used in all Sorts of Fevers

Take two ounces of burnt hartshorn; boil it with a crust of bread in three pints of water to a quart; strain, and put to it of barley, cinnamon water, two ounces, cochineal half a drachm; sweeten it with fine sugar, and let the patient, as often as he is thirsty, drink plentifully of it; rub the cochineal in a mortar together with the sugar.

To cure the Yellow or Black Jaundice

Take a quart of white wine, a large red dock-root, a bur-root, that which bears the small bur, two pennyworth of turmeric, a little saffron, a little of the white goose-dung; boil all these together a little while; then let it run through a strainer; drink it morning and evening three days.

A Plaister for the Sciatica

Take of yellow wax a pound, the juice of marjoram and red sage, of each six spoonfuls, juice of onions two spoonfuls: let all these boil together till the juice is consumed; and when it is cold, put in two ounces of turpentine, and of nutmegs, cloves, mace, aniseeds, and frankincense, of each a pennyworth finely powdered; stir it well together, and make a plaister.

A Salve for the King's Evil

Take a burdock root, and a white-lily root, wash, dry, and scrape them; wrap them in brown paper, and roast them in the embers;

when they are soft, take them out, and cut off the burn or hard, and beat them in a mortar with boar's grease and bean-flour; when it is almost enough, put in as much of the best turpentine as will make it smell of it; then put it in a pot for use.

The party must take inwardly two spoonfuls of lime water in the morning, and fast two hours after it, and do the same at four o'clock in the afternoon; if there be any swelling of the evil, they must bathe it with this water a quarter of an hour together, a little warmed, and wet a cloth, and bind it on the place; but if the skin be broken, only wash it in the water, and spread a thin plaister of the salve, and lay on it; shift it once a day; if very bad, you must dress it twice a day.

To make the lime water: Take a limestone as big as a man's head, it must be well burnt; put it into six quarts of boiling water, cover it close, but sometimes stir it; the next day, when it is settled, pour off the clear water, and keep it in bottles for use.

To cure Burstenness

Take hemlock, and bruise it a little; heat it pretty well, and apply it twice a day, without any truss, and keep the party as still as may be; this has cured, when many other things have failed.

A Powder for Burstenness

Take a good quantity of wild musk, roots and all; pick, wash, and dry them; then take of currant leaves, vine leaves and strings an equal quantity; then take a quart of hemp seed; you must lay the seed at the bottom of a pot, and the leaves and roots on the top; then put it into an oven, dry them, rub them to powder, and sift them together; the party must take as much of this powder as will lie on a sixpence in a little ale in the morning, and at four in the afternoon, and continue it five or six weeks. The powder should be made in May, if possible.

Another Remedy for the Chin-Cough

Take a spoonful of the juice of pennyroyal, mixed with sugar-candy beaten to powder; take this for nine mornings together.

To cure the Itch without Sulphur

Take a handful of elecampane-root, and as much sharp-pointed dock, shred them small, and boil them in two quarts of spring-water till it comes to a pint; strain the liquor, and with it let the party wash his hands and face two or three times a day.

For the Itch

Take of camomile and velvet-leaves, scurvy-grass and capons' feathers, of each one handful; boil these in half a pound of butter out of the churn, till it is an ointment; then strain it out, and mix it with half an ounce of black pepper beaten fine; stir it in till it is cold, and anoint the party with it all over; keep on the same linen for a week; then wash with warm water and sweet herbs, and put on clean linen. Before you begin to use this, you must take brimstone and milk for three mornings; keep warm, and purge well after it is over.

For the Scurvy or Dropsy

Stamp the leaves of elder, and strain the juice, and to a quarter of a pint of juice put so much white wine; warm it a little, and drink it off; do this four or five mornings together; if it purge you, it will certainly do good; take this in the spring.

For a Looseness

Boil a good handful of bramble leaves in milk, sweetened with loaf sugar; drink it night and morning.

For an Ague

Give as much Virginia snake-root, dried and powdered, as will lie upon a shilling, in a glass of sherry or sack, just before the cold fit begins; use this two or three times till the ague is gone.

Another

Take an ounce and a half of the best refined aloes, and steep it in a quart of brandy; infuse it forty-eight hours, and take four spoonfuls just before the fit comes.

Another

Take a pint of red-rose water, and put to it an ounce of white sugar-candy, and the juice of three Seville oranges; mix all together, and drink it off an hour before you expect the fit; it cures at once or twice taking.

An Ointment for a Burn or Scald

Take a pound of hog's lard, two good handfuls of sheep's dung, and a good handful of the green bark of the elder, the brown bark being first taken off; boil all these to an ointment: you must first take out the fire with salad oil, a bit of an onion, and the white of an egg, beaten well together; then anoint with the ointment, and in less than a week it will be well.

A Cerecloth

Take three pounds of oil-olive, of red lead and white lead, of each half a pound, both powdered and sifted; then take three ounces of virgin wax, two ounces of Spanish soap, and as much deer's suet; put all these into a brass kettle, setting it over the fire, stirring it continually till it comes to the height of a salve, which you may know by dropping a little on a trencher; and if it neither hangs to the trencher, nor your fingers, it is enough; then dip your cloths in, and when you take them out, throw them into a pail of water; as they cool, take them out, lay them on a table, and clap them; when you have done, roll them up with papers between, and keep them for use; they must be kept pretty cool. This cerecloth is good for any pain, swelling, or bruise.

The Yellow Balsam

Take eight ounces of burgundy-pitch, three ounces and half of yellow beeswax sliced, one pound of deer's suet, one ounce of Venice turpentine beaten up in plantain water, half a pint of red roses, a quarter of a pint of vinegar of red roses, twenty-four cloves of garlic, and of saltpetre dried before the fire half the quantity of a nutmeg: bruise the garlic in a stone mortar, and set the oil, vinegar, and garlic, in an earthen pipkin over the fire; let it boil gently half an hour; then put in the pitch and wax, and when that is melted, put in the suet, and one ounce of palm-oil; let it boil a quarter of an hour longer; then take it off the fire, and put in the turpentine and saltpetre; set it over the fire again for a little while; then take it off, and let it stand to cool; then pour it gently into your gallipots; be sure you put in no dregs; the vinegar will fall to the bottom; tie the gallipots down with leather; it is an excellent salve for sore legs, biles, whitloes, sore breasts, and may be safely used to draw corruption out of any sore; put a little of it on lint, and put a plaister of the following black salve over it.

The Black Salve

Take a pint of oil-olive, three quarters of a pound of yellow wax, of frankincense finely beaten and searced, the best mastic, olibanum and myrrh, of each two ounces, half a pound of white lead finely ground, and two drachms of camphire; boil these till they are black; then let it stand a little; oil a board, and pour it on; oil your hand, and make it up in rolls for use.

Another Remedy for the Falling-Sickness

Take of the powder of a man's skull, of cinnabar, and antimony, of each a drachm; of the root of the male peony, and frog's liver dried, of each two drachms; of the salt of amber half a drachm, conserve of rosemary two ounces, syrup of peonies enough to make it into a soft electuary, of which give the quantity of a large nutmeg every morning and evening, drinking after it three ounces of the water of the lilies of the valley; take it three days before the new moon, and three days before the full moon; to bring the patient quickly out of the fit, let the nostrils and temples be rubbed with the oil of amber.

For an Ague

Take a quart of strong beer, and a good quantity of the youngest artichoke-leaves; shred them, and boil them very well together; when you think it almost enough, put a spoonful of mustard seed bruised, and give it one boil; then strain it, and bottle it; take half a pint, as hot as you can, half an hour before the fit comes.

A calcined Water to dry up Ulcers and old Sores

Take of the best Roman vitriol three ounces, camphire one ounce; beat them into fine powder, put them into the bottom of a crucible, and fix it in hot embers; cover it with white paper, and put a little tile on it; let it be well calcined, but not too much; when it is cold beat it into fine powder, and sift it; then add to it three ounces of bole-armoniac, beaten and sifted; mix all together, and to half an ounce of this powder put a quart of spring or plantain water; boil the water, and when it is blood-warm, put in your half ounce of powder, and stir it together in a pewter basin till it is quite cold; then put it in a bottle for use; when you use it, shake the bottle, and pour some out, and use it as hot as can be endured, either by syringe or washing the place twice or thrice a day; and use the following plaister or salve.

The Leaden Plaister

Take of white lead three ounces, of red lead seven ounces, of bole-armoniac nine ounces; beat all into fine powder, and put to them a pint of the best oil-olive; incorporate them over the fire, and let them boil gently half an hour, putting in one ounce of oil of Exeter; stir it continually, and when it is enough, make it up in rolls. This is a drying plaister.

A Salve for a Burn or Scald

Take a pound of mutton-suet shred small, melt it, and put into it thyme, sweet-marjoram, melilot, pennyroyal, and hyssop, of each a good handful chopped small; let it stand together four days; then heat it, and strain it out, and put in the same quantity of herbs again, and let it stand four days longer; then heat it, and strain it out, and to that liquor put five pounds of white rosin, and two pounds of beeswax sliced, and boil it up to a salve; when it is cold enough, oil a board, pour it on it, and make it up in rolls. This is an admirable salve, when the fire is taken out; you must take out the fire with oil, then lay on the plaister: it is good for a small cut, or tissue inflamed.

A Green Salve

Take five handfuls of clowns' all-heal, stamp it, and put it in a pot, adding to it four ounces of boar's grease, half a pint of oil-olive, and wax three ounces sliced; boil it till the juice is consumed, which is known when the stuff doth not bubble at all; then strain it, and put on the fire again, adding two ounces of Venice turpentine; let it boil a little, and put it in gallipots for use; melt a little in a spoon, and if the cut or wound be deep, dip your tents in it; if not, dip lint, and put on it, defending the place with a leaden plaister; dress it once a day.

For a sore Breast, when it is broken

Take a quarter of a pound of raisins of the sun stoned, and beat them very small; then add to it near as much honey, and beat it together into a salve; spread it on a cloth, and make tents, if occasion; dress it once a day; when it is well drawn, use the yellow balsam, and black or leaden plaister.

A Poultice for a sore Breast, before it is broken

Boil white bread and milk to a poultice; then put to it oil of lilies, and the yolk of an egg; set it over the fire again to heat, and apply it as hot as can be endured; dress it morning and night till it is broke: then dress it with the poultice of raisins.

To disperse Tumours

Take of yellow wax, frankincense, and rosin, of each four ounces; melt them together, strain it out, and when it is cold, make it into a roll, and keep it for use.

To keep a Cancer in the Breast from increasing

Take of lapis calaminaris four ounces, all in one piece; and having made it red hot in a crucible nine times, quench it every time in a pint of white wine; then take two ounces of lapis tutty, and having burnt that red hot in a crucible three times, quench that every time in a pint of red-rose water; then beat the tutty and the calaminaris stone together in a mortar very fine, and put in a glass bottle, with the rose-water and white wine; shake it three or four times a day for nine days before you begin to use it; you must keep the wine and the rose-water close covered when you quench the stone, that the steam does not go out; when you use it, shake it well, dip rags in it, and lay them to the breast; let the rags remain on till it is dressed again; it must be dressed twice a day, night and morning; the clear water is excellent for weak or sore eyes.

For a Swelling in the Face

Take a handful of damask rose leaves; boil them in running water till they are tender; stamp them to a pulp, and boil white bread and milk till it is soft; then put in your pulp, with a little hog's lard, and thicken it with the yolk of an egg, and apply it warm.

For a Sore Throat

Make a plaister of Paracelsus four inches broad, and so long as to come from ear to ear, and apply it warm to the throat; then bruise houseleek, and press out the juice; add an equal quantity of honey, and a little burnt alum; mix all together, and let the party often take some on a liquorice stick.

A Purging Diet drink

Take of garden scurvygrass six handfuls, watercresses, brooklime, and peach-blossoms, of each four handfuls, nettle-tops and fumitory of each three handfuls, monk's rhubarb, and senna of each four ounces, china two ounces, sarsaparilla three ounces, rhubarb one ounce, coriander and sweet-fennel seed, of each half an ounce; cut the herbs, slice the roots, bruise the seeds; put them in a thin bag, and hang them in four gallons of small ale; after three days drink a pint of it every morning; be regular in diet, eat nothing salt or sour.

Pills to purge the Head

Take of the extract of rudium two drachms, and pill foetida one drachm; mix these well together, and make into twelve pills; take two, or, if the constitution be strong, three of them, at six o'clock in the morning; drink warm gruel, thin broth, or posset-drink, when they work.

For a Canker in the Mouth

Take celandine, columbine, sage and fennel, of each one handful; stamp and strain them, and to the juice put a spoonful of honey, half a spoonful of burnt alum, and as much bole-armoniac beaten fine; mix and beat all these together very well, and wrap a little flax about a stick, and rub the canker with it; if it bleeds, it is the better.

A Water for Sore or Weak Eyes

Take ground-ivy, celandine and daisies, of each a like quantity, stamped and strained; add to the juice a little sugar and white-rose water, shake this together, and with a feather drop it into the eyes; this takes away all manner of inflammations, spots, itching, smarting, or webb, and is an excellent thing for the eyes.

An excellent Prescription for the Cure of Worms

The following receipt is an extraordinary remedy for the worms which breed in human bodies, and with which vast numbers of people of all ages and both sexes are afflicted, and some of them very severely, especially children, and other young persons, of whom abundance are carried off yearly by being thrown thereby into convulsions, epileptic fits, vomitings, loosenesses, white or green sickness, and other disorders, which had been judged to have proceeded from other causes, when the occasion thereof was worms. But as there is such a variety of disorders proceeding from those intestine animals, representing other diseases, I shall, for the information of such as may little imagine their malady to be occasioned by worms, when it appears so plain to themselves and their physicians that it is this or that other disease, first set down some of the many signs and symptoms of worms, and then prescribe the remedy to destroy, expel, and rid the patient's body of them; and this is a medicine so effectually adapted, and so innocent withal, that if it be pursued as directed, they that take it may depend it will not fail utterly and safely to do it, be the worm of any kind, or situated in any part of the body.

It is to be noted that there are divers sorts of worms that breed in the body, and take up their residence therein, either in the stomach or bowels, and sometimes near the sphincter ani, or fundament, and often knit themselves together, and appear like a bag of worms, and are supposed to be bred from the ova or eggs of those animals swallowed down with the food, and encouraged and fed by viscidities in the passages; and according as they reside, or have placed themselves in the body, the symptoms and complaints which such people make are different both in kind and degree: in some to occasion looseness, in others costiveness, or frequent desires to go to stool, but cannot; in some to cause a fetid or stinking breath, which is a shrewd sign of worms, as is also a hard or inflamed belly, especially in children, with a voracious appetite, and almost continual thirst, feverishness by fits, and intermitting pulse, and glowing cheeks; in some, a heaviness or pain in the head, startings in sleep, with frightful terrifying dreams; in some, a sleepiness representing a lethargy; in others, a nausea, or loathing of food, with or without motion to vomit, a pain and weight with a gnawing in the stomach, gripings and rumblings in the bowels, like the colic; in children, a dry cough, and sometimes screaming fits and convulsions, with white lips and white urine; and in both old and young a weakened or lost appetite, giddiness in the head, paleness of countenance, with faintings and cold sweats of a sudden, indigestions, abatement of the strength, and falling away of flesh, as if dropping into a consumption; with many other symptoms, but these are the chief, whichever more or less, some or other of them always affect where worms are the cause; and for remedy of which the following receipt may be depended on, and very innocent, as well as powerful and effectual, as everyone, when they read what it is, will believe, and when they try it, will find.

Take tops of carduus, tops of centaury, Roman wormwood, and flowers of camomile (all of them dried, and of the latest year's growth that you use them in), of each a small handful; cut the herbs small, but not the flowers, put them with an ounce of worm-seed bruised small into an earthen jar or pickling-pot, and pour upon them a quart of spring-water cold; stir all about, and then tie the pot over with a double paper, and let it stand forty-eight hours, opening and stirring it about five or six times in that space; at the end of forty-eight hours strain it through a cloth, squeezing the herbs as dry as you can; fling away the latter, and of the liquor give to a child from two to four or five years old half a spoonful, more or less, mixed with a quarter of a spoonful of the oil of beechnuts, every morning upon an empty stomach, and to fast for about an hour after it; and also the same dose about four or five in the afternoon every day, for a week or ten days together; by which time, if the case be worms, and you make but observation, you will find them to come away either dead or alive; older children must take more, in proportion to their ages; and grown persons from three or four to six or eight spoonfuls, or more, with always half the quantity of the said oil mixed with each dose, and it will keep the body soluble, and sometimes a little loose.

This medicine has cured in supposed incurable cases, when it has proved at last to be from worms, when neither the physician or patient have before thought it to be so; but if it be not worms, it cannot hurt, but may cure in cases similar to worms, especially where the stomach and bowels are disordered.

Note The beechnut oil may be had at most oil shops; and the reason that oil before any other is advised is that it has a property, as has been often tried, of killing worms of itself, when olive oil and oil of almonds would not do it; and as a confirmation of it, Dr Baglivi says, in a book of experiments upon live worms from human bodies, that he put worms into divers liquors, which were reputed would kill them, but did not under a great many hours; and that towards night he put others into oil of sweet almonds, and found them alive the next morning; then, after many other experiments, he put one into oil of nuts, where it died presently; and Malpighi, another noted physician, says that of all common oils, oil of nuts is the best against worms; and that at Milan, mothers have a custom to give their little children once or twice a week toasts dipped in oil of nuts, and to grown people some spoonfuls of it fasting; and many other authors say the same, particularly Dr Nicolas Andry, of the faculty of physic at Paris, in his treatise on worms; who also says, if you dip a pencil in oil of nuts, and anoint the bodies of live worms that anyone voids, tho' you never touch their heads, they will presently grow motionless, and die beyond recovery; the reason, he says, they die so suddenly, when anointed, is because they breathe only by the means of certain little windpipes that run through their bodies; so that if you stop up those pipes with nut-oil, which hinders the commerce of the air (for that the parts of oil of almonds are more porous than nut-oil, and consequently less able to hinder the entrance of the air into the worms), of necessity the creatures must die for want of respiration, though neither the head, nor any other part where the pipes are not, be anointed. This is so true, says Malpighi, that if you put nut-oil upon a worm in any other part but where the pipes are, though the head be not spared, yet the worm will live, and have its natural motion; and if you put the oil upon some of the pipes only, you shall see the parts where those pipes are become immoveable; but if you put it, says he, upon all the tracheas or pipes, the whole worm becomes motionless, and dies in an instant; and I do assure the public that the same has been many times tried, and found, both by myself and others, that no other oil whatever would do what this will. The late Dr Radcliffe, in many of his prescriptions I have seen, ordered that oil preferable to all others, where he had reason to suspect the patient had worms; and in one very remarkable case of a young lady of thirteen I could name, who was at death's door with the green-sickness, as supposed, and who, by the use of this very oil, and such bitters as he believed the case then indicated, once or twice a day repeated, was cured perfectly, upon her voiding clusters of small worms for several days together, some of which were enclosed in a cystis or bag.

This I was willing to observe, that people may be sure to get the oil of nuts and not any other oil.

Another Remedy for the Worms

Take of wormwood, rue, whitewort, and young leeks of each one a handful; chop and strip these herbs very small, and fry them in lard; put them on a piece of flannel, and apply them to the stomach, as hot as can be borne; and let them lie forty-eight hours, changing the herbs when they are dry.

A Plaister for Worms in Children

Take two ounces of yellow wax, and as much rosin; boil them half an hour, stirring them all the while; skim them well, and take it off, and put to it three drachms of aloes, and two spoonfuls of treacle, and boil it up again; rub a board with fresh butter, and pour the salve thereon; work it well, and make it up in rolls; when you make the plaister, sprinkle it with saffron, and cut a hole against the navel.

A Clyster for the Worms

Take of rue, wormwood, lavender cotton, three or four sprigs of each; a spoonful of aniseeds bruised; boil these in a pint of milk, let the third part be consumed; then strain it out, and add to it as much aloes finely powdered as will lie on a threepence; sweeten it with honey, and give it pretty warm; it should be given three mornings together, and the best time is three days before the new or full moon.

Lucatellus's Balsam

Take of yellow wax one pound, melt it in a little Canary wine, then add to it oil of olives and Venice turpentine of each one pound and a half. Boil them till the wine is evaporated, and when it is almost cold, stir in of red saunders two ounces, and keep it for use.

A Salve for a Cerecloth for Bruises or Aches

Take a pint of oil, nine ounces of red lead, two ounces of beeswax, an ounce of spermaceti, two ounces of rosin beaten and sifted; set all these on a soft fire in a bell-skillet, stirring till it boils; and then try it on a rag, whether it firmly stick upon it; when it does stick, take it off; and when you have made what cerecloths you please, pour the rest on an oiled board, and make it up in rolls; it is very good for a cut or green wound.

An excellent Recipe to cure a Cold

Take of Venice treacle half a drachm, powder of snake-root twelve grains, powder of saffron six grains, volatile salt of hartshorn four grains, syrup of cloves a sufficient quantity to make it into a bolus, to be taken going to rest, drinking a large draught of mountain whey after it; those who cannot afford mountain whey, may drink treacle posset.

To such constitutions as cannot be provoked to sweat, open a vein, or a gentle purge will be of great service.

An Ointment for a Cold on the Stomach

Take an ounce and a half of the oil of Valentia scabiofa, oil of sweet almonds a quarter of an ounce, a quarter of an ounce of man's fat, and four scruples of the oil of mace; mix these together, and warm a little in the spoon, and night and morning anoint the stomach; lay a piece of black or lawn-paper on it.

To make Gascoign's Powder

Take pearls, crabs' eyes, red coral, white amber, burnt hartshorn, and oriental bezoar, of each half an ounce; the black tips of crabs' claws three ounces; make all into a paste, with a jelly of vipers, and roll it into little balls, which dry and keep for use.

A Water to cure Red or Pimpled Faces

Take a pint of strong white-wine vinegar, and put to it powder of the roots of orrice three drachms, powder of brimstone half an ounce, and camphire two drachms; stamp with a few blanched almonds, four oak apples cut in the middle, and the juice of four lemons, and a handful of bean-flowers; put all these together in a strong double-glass bottle, shake them well together, and set it in the sun for ten days; wash the face with this water; let it dry on, and do not wipe it off; this cures red or pimpled faces, spots, heat, morphew, or sunburn; but you must eat the following diet for three weeks or a month.

Take cucumbers, and cut them as small as herbs to the pot; boil them in a small pipkin with a piece of mutton, and make it into pottage with oatmeal; so eat a mess morning, noon, and night, without intermission, for three weeks or a month; this diet and the water have cured when nothing else would do.

A good thing to wash the Face in

Take a large piece of camphire, the quantity of a goose-egg, and break it so that it may go into a pint bottle, which fill with water; when it has stood a month, put a spoonful of it in three spoonfuls of milk, and wash in it. Wear a piece of lead beaten exceeding thin, for a forehead-piece, under a forehead-cloth; it keeps the forehead smooth and plump.

The Stomach Plaister

Take of Burgundy pitch, frankincense, and beeswax, of each an ounce; melt them together; then put in an ounce of Venice turpentine, and an ounce of oil of mace; melt it together, and spread your plaister on sheep's-leather; grate on it some nutmeg when you lay it on the stomach.

To make a Quilt for the Stomach

Take a fine rag four inches square, and spread cotton thin over it; take mint and sweet-marjoram dried and rubbed to powder, and strew it over the cotton, pretty thick; then take nutmeg, cloves and mace, of each a quarter of an ounce beaten and sifted, and strew that over the herbs, and on that strew half an ounce of galangal finely powder'd, then a thin row of cotton, and another fine rag, and quilt it together; when you lay it on the stomach, dip it in hot sack, and lay it on as warm as can be endured. This is very good for a pain in the stomach.

For the Pains of the Gout

Mix Barbadoes tar and palm-oil, an equal quantity; just melt them together, and gently anoint the part affected.

A present Help for the Colic

Mix a drachm of mithridate in a spoonful of dragon-water, and give it the party to drink in bed, laying a little suet on the navel.

A Plaister for the Colic

Spread the whites of four or five eggs well beaten on some leather, and over that strew on a spoonful of pepper, and as much ginger finely beaten and sifted; then put this plaister on the navel; it often gives speedy ease.

For the Ague

Take smallage, ribwort, rue, plantain, and olibanum, equal parts; beat all these well together with a little bay-salt, and put them in a thin bag, and lay it to the wrist a little before the cold fit comes.

A Powder for Convulsion-Fits

Take a drachm and a half of single-peony seed, of misletoe of the oak one drachm, pearl, white amber and coral, all finely powdered, of each half a drachm, bezoar two drachms, and five leaves of gold; make all these up in a fine powder, and give it in a spoonful of black-cherry water, or, if you please, hysteric water; you may give to a child newborn, to prevent fits, as much as will lie on a threepence, and likewise at each change of the moon; and to older people as much as they have strength and occasion.

To prevent Fits in Children

Take saxifrage, bean pods, black-cherry, groundsel and parsley waters; mix them together with syrup of single peony; give a spoonful very often, and especially observe to give it at the change of the moon.

Another

Take a quart of ale, and as much small beer; put into it a handful of southernwood, as much sage, and as much pennyroyal; let it boil half an hour, strain it out, and let the child drink no other drink.

For a Hoarseness with a Cold

Take a quarter of a pint of hyssop water; make it very sweet with sugar-candy; set it over the fire, and when it is thorough hot, beat the yolk of an egg, brew it in it, and drink it morning and night.

A Remedy for a Cough

Take the yolk of a new-laid egg, and six spoonfuls of red-rose water; beat them well together, and make it very sweet with white sugar-candy; drink it six nights, going to bed.

An excellent Remedy for Whooping-Coughs

Take dried coltsfoot leaves a good handful, cut them small, and boil them in a pint of spring-water till half a pint is boil'd away; then take it off the fire, and when it is almost cold, strain it thro' a cloth, squeezing the herb as dry as you can, and then throw it away; dissolve in the liquor an ounce of brown sugar-candy finely powdered, and give the child (if it be about three or four years old, and so in proportion) one spoonful of it, cold or warm, as the season proves, three or four times a day (or oftener, if the fits of coughing come frequently) till well, which will be in two or three days; but it will presently almost abate the fits of coughing.

This herb seems to be a specific for those sorts of coughs, and indeed for all others, in old as well as young; the Latin name *tuffilago*, from *tuffis*, the cough, denotes as much; as does also the Latin word *bechium*, from the Greek word βήχιον, a cough; these are the names given it by the ancients, perhaps some thousand years ago. It has wonderfully eased them, when nothing else would do it, and greatly helps in shortness of breath; and in the asthma and phthisic I have not known anything to exceed it; likewise in wastings or consumptions of the lungs it has been found of excellent use, by its smooth, softening, healing qualities, even where there has been spitting of blood, rawness and soreness of the passages, with hoarseness, &c., in blunting the acrimonious humours which, in such cases, are almost continually dripping upon them; it is to be questioned whether for those purposes there is to be had, in the whole *Materia Medica*, a medicine so innocent, so safe, and yet so pleasant and effectual, or that can afford relief so soon as this will; grown people may make it stronger than for children. Get the herb of the same year's growth and drying that you use; and the larger the leaves, as being the fuller grown, the better; it is best to be made fresh, and fresh as you want it, and not too much at a time, especially in warm weather.

Pills to purge off a Rheum in the Teeth

Take four drachms of mastic, ten drachms of aloes, three drachms of agaric; beat the mastic and aloes, and grate the agaric; searce them, and make them into pills with syrup of betony; you may make but a quarter of this quantity at a time, and take it all out, one pill in the morning, and two at night; you may eat or drink anything with these pills, and go abroad, keeping yourself warm; and when they work, drink a draught or two of something warm.

To make Daffy's Elixir

Take elecampane roots sliced, and liquorice sliced, aniseeds, coriander seeds, and caraway seeds, oriental senna, guaicum bruised, of each two ounces; rhubarb an ounce, saffron a drachm; raisins of the sun stoned a pound; put all these into a glass bottle of a gallon, adding to it three quarts of white aniseed water; stop the bottle, and let it stand infusing four days, stirring it strongly three or four times a day; then strain it off, and put it into bottles cork'd very well; you must take it morning and night, three spoonfuls going to bed, and as much in the morning, according as you find it work; it requires not much care in diet, nor keeping within; but you must keep warm, and drink something hot in the morning after it has work'd. This elixir is excellent good for the colic, the gravel in the kidneys, the dropsy, griping of the guts, or any obstructions in the bowels; it purgeth two or three times a day.

An Ointment to cause Hair to grow

Take of boar's grease two ounces, ashes of burnt bees, ashes of southernwood, juice of white-lily root, oil of sweet almonds, of each one drachm; six drachms of pure musk; and according to art make an ointment of these; and the day before the full moon shave the place, anointing it every day with this ointment; it will cause hair to grow where you will have it. Oil of sweet almonds, or spirit of vinegar, is very good to rub the head with, if the hair grows thin.

To preserve and whiten the Teeth

Take a quarter of a pound of honey, and boil it with a little roach alum; skim it well, and then put in a little ginger finely beaten; let it boil a while longer, then take it off; and before it is cold, put to it as much dragon's blood as will make it of a good colour; mix it well together, and keep it in a gallipot for use; take a little on a rag and rub the teeth – you may use it often.

To make Lip Salve

Take a quarter of a pound of alkanet root bruised, and half a quarter of a pound of fresh butter, as much beeswax, and a pint of claret; boil all these together a pretty while; then strain it, and let it stand till it is cold; then take the wax off the top, and melt it again, and pour it clear from the dregs into your gallipots or boxes; use it when and as often as you please.

To make Paste for the Hand

Take a pound of bitter almonds blanched, and two handfuls of stoned raisins, beat them together till they are very fine; then take three or four spoonfuls of sack or brandy, as much ox-gall, three or four spoonfuls of brown sugar, and the yolks of three eggs; beat it well together, set it over the fire, and give it two or three boils; when it is almost cold, mix it with the almonds; put it in gallipots; the next day cover it close, and keep it cool, and it will be good five or six months.

To clean and soften the Hands

Set half a pint of milk over the fire, and put into it half a quartern of almonds blanch'd and beaten very fine; when it boils take it off, and thicken it with the yolk of an egg; then set it on again, stirring it all the while both before and after the egg is in; then take it off, and stir in a small spoonful of sweet oil, and put it in a gallipot; it will keep about five or six days; take a bit as big as a walnut, and rub about your hands, and the dirt or soil will rub off, and it will make them very soft; draw on gloves just as you have used it.

A Remedy for Pimples

Take half a quarter of a pound of bitter almonds, blanch, stamp them, and put them into half a pint of spring-water; stir it together, and strain it out; then put to it half a pint of the best brandy, and a pennyworth of the flour of brimstone; shake it well when you use it, which must be often; dab it on with a fine rag.

Another to take away Pimples

Take wheat-flour mingled with honey and vinegar, and lay the mixture on the pimples going to bed.

A Water to wash the Face

Boil two ounces of French barley in three pints of spring-water, shift the water three times; the last water use, adding to it a quartern of bitter almonds blanched, beat, and strained out; then add the juice of two lemons, and a pint of white wine; wash with it at night; put a bit of camphire in the bottle.

To whiten and clean the Hands

Boil a quart of new milk, and turn it with a pint of aqua vitae, and take off the curd; then put into the posset a pint of rhenish wine, and that will raise another curd, which take off; then put in the whites of six eggs well beaten, and that will raise another curd, which you must take off, and mix the three curds together very well, and put them into a gallipot, and put the posset in a bottle; scour your hands with the curd, and wash them with the posset.

A Water for the Scurvy in the Gums

Take two quarts of spring-water, a pound of flower-de-luce root, a quarter of a pound of roch-alum, two ounces of cloves; of red-rose leaves, woodbine leaves, columbine leaves, brown sage, of each two handfuls, and one of rosemary, eight Seville oranges, peel and all, only take out the seeds; set these over the fire, and let them boil a quart away; then take it off, strain it, and set it over the fire again, adding to it three quarts of claret, and a pint of honey; let them boil half an hour, skim it well, and when it is cold, bottle it for use; wash and gargle your mouth with it two or three times a day.

To take away Morphew

Take briony roots, and wake-robin; stamp them with brimstone, and make it up in a lump; wrap it in a fine linen rag, dip it in vinegar, and rub the place pretty hard with it; will take away the morphew spots.

The Italian Wash for the Neck

Take a quart of ox-gall, two ounces of roch-alum, and as much white sugar-candy, two drachms of camphire, half an ounce of borax; beat all these in a mortar, and sift them through a fine sieve, then mix them well in the quart of ox-gall; put all together into a three-pint stone bottle well corked; set it to infuse in the sun, or by the fire, six weeks together, stirring it once a day; then strain it from the bottom, and put to every quarter of a pint of this liquor a quart of spring-water, otherwise it will be too thick; set it a little to clarify, and bottle it; put some powder of pearl in the bottle; wash with it.

For a Cold, Dr Radcliffe's Receipt

Make some sack-whey with rosemary boiled in it; mix a little of it in a spoon with twenty grains of Gascoign's powder; then drink half a pint of your sack-whey, with twelve drops of spirits of hartshorn in it; go to bed, and keep warm; do this two or three nights together.

A Method to cure a Cold

Showing: 1 What the catching of cold is, and how dangerous; 2 A present and easy remedy against it; 3 The danger of delaying the cure of it. Taken from the celebrated Dr George Cheyne's book entitled *An Essay of Health and Long Life*, inscribed to the Right Honourable Sir Joseph Jekyll, Master of the Rolls; where, on pp. 129–30 of the eighth edition, he says that Dr James Keill, in his *Statica Britannica*, had made it out, beyond all possibility of doubting, that catching cold is nothing but sucking in, by the passages of perspiration, large quantities of moist air, and nitrous salts, which by thickening the blood (as is evident from bleeding after catching cold) and thereby obstructing, not only the perspiration, but also all the other finer secretions, raises immediately a small fever, and a tumult in the whole animal economy, and, neglected, lays a foundation for consumptions, obstructions of the great viscera, and universal cachexies; the tender, therefore, and valetudinary, ought cautiously to avoid all occasions of catching cold; and if they have been so unfortunate as to get one, to set about its cure immediately, before it has taken too deep root in the habit. From the nature of the disorder thus described, the remedy is obvious: to wit, lying much abed, drinking plentifully of small warm sack-whey, with a few drops of spirits of hartshorn, posset-drink, water-gruel, or any other warm small liquors, a scruple of Gascoign's powder morning and night, living low upon spoon-meats, pudding, and chicken, and drinking everything warm; in a word, treating it at first as a small fever, with gentle diaphoretics; and afterwards, if any cough or spitting should remain (which this method generally prevents), by softening the breast with a little sugar-candy, and oil of sweet almonds, or a solution of gum-armoniac, an ounce to a quart of barley water, to make the expectoration easy, and going cautiously and well clothed into the air afterwards: this is a much more natural, easy, and effectual method than the practice by balsams, linctuses, pectorals, and the like trumpery in common use, which serve only to spoil the stomach, oppress the spirits, and hurt the constitution.

A Receipt for the Gravel

Put two spoonfuls of linseed just bruised into a quart of water, and a little stick of liquorice; boil it a quarter of an hour; then strain it through a sieve; sweeten it to your taste with syrup of marshmallows.

Excellent for Worms in Children

Take fenugreek seed and wormwood seed one pennyworth, beat and searced; mix it well in a halfpennyworth of treacle; let the child take a small spoonful in a morning fasting, and fast two hours after it; do this three or four days.

For a Cold

Take rosemary and sliced liquorice, and boil it in small ale, and sweeten it with treacle, and drink it going to bed four or five nights together.

To Stop Bleeding in the Stomach

Take oil of spike, natural balsam, bole-armoniac, rhubarb, and turpentine; mix these together, and take as much as a large nutmeg three times a day.

The Tar-pills for a Cough

Take tar, and drop it on powder of liquorice, and make it up into pills; take two every night going to bed, and in a morning drink a glass of water that liquorice has been three or four days steeped in; do this for nine or ten days together, as you find good.

To cure an Ague

Take small packthread, as much as will go five times about the neck, wrists, and ankles; dip them in oil of amber twice a day for nine days together; keep them on a fortnight after the ague is gone.

For a Looseness

Take sage, and heat it very hot between two dishes; put it in a linen rag and sit on it.

Another

Take frankincense and pitch, and put it on some coals, and sit over it.

For a violent Bleeding at the Nose

Let the party put their feet in warm water; and if that does not do, let them sit higher in it.

For a Purge

Take half an ounce of senna, boil it in a pint of ale till half be consumed; cover it close till the next day; then boil it again till it comes to two spoonfuls; strain it, and add to it two spoonfuls of treacle, and drink it warm; drink gruel, or posset, or broth after it; keep yourself very warm while it is working; or else two ounces of syrup of roses, and drink warm ale after it in the working.

For the Itch

Take elecampane roots, or dock roots, dried and beaten to powder, and a little beaten ginger, both searced very fine; mix it up with fresh butter, and anoint with it in the joints.

For the Dropsy and Scurvy

Take a quart of white wine, six sprigs of wormwood, as much rosemary, half a quarter of an ounce of aloes, the same quantity of myrrh, rhubarb, cinnamon, and saffron; bruise the drugs, pull the saffron, and put all into a three-pint stone bottle; tie the cork down close, set it in a kettle of water and hay, and let it boil three hours; then let it stand a day or two to settle; let the patient take four spoonfuls every morning fasting, and fast three hours after it, and walk abroad; if it is too long to fast, and the constitution will not bear it, they may drink a draught of water-gruel two hours after it; take this till the quantity is out.

For the Jaundice

Take three bottles of ale, half a pint of the juice of celandine, a quarter of a pint of feverfew, a good handful of the inner rind of barberry tree, and two pennyworth of saffron; divide all into three parts, and put a part into every one of the bottles of ale, and drink a bottle in three mornings; you must stir after it.

To make Lucatellus's Balsam, to take inwardly

Take a quart of the purest oil, half a pound of yellow beeswax, four ounces of Venice turpentine, six ounces of liquid storax, two ounces of oil-hypericon, two ounces of natural balsam, red-rose water half a pint, and as much plantain water, red sanders sixpennyworth, dragon's blood sixpennyworth, mummy sixpennyworth, rosemary and bays of each a handful, and sweet-marjoram half a handful; put the herbs and dragon's blood, the wax and mummy, into a pipkin; then put the oil, the turpentine, the oil-hypericon, the storax, the rose-water, and plantain water, and a quart of spring-water, and if you please some Irish slate, some balm of Gilead, and some spermaceti, into another pipkin; set both the pipkins over a soft fire, and let them boil a quarter of an hour; then take it off the fire, and put in the natural balsam and red sanders; give them a boil, and strain all in both pipkins together into an earthen pan; let it stand till it is cold, then pour the water from it, and melt it again; stir it off the fire till it is almost cold; then put it into gallipots, and cover it with paper and leather.

For the Piles

Take galls, such as the dyers use, beat them to powder, and sift them; mix the powder with treacle into an ointment, and dip the rag into it, and apply it to the place affected.

For the Cramp

Take spirit of castor and oil of worms, of each two drachms; oil of amber one drachm; shake them well together; warm a little in a spoon, and anoint the nape of the neck; chafe it in very well, and cover warm; anoint when in bed.

For a Cough

Take conserve of roses two ounces, diascordium half an ounce, powder of olibanum half a drachm, syrup of jujubes half an ounce; mix these, and take the quantity of a nutmeg three times a day; in the morning, at four, and at night.

For a Dropsy

Take three ounces of the outward bark of elm, boiled in three quarts of water till a third part is wasted; drink nothing else; to make it pleasant, you may put in some sugar, or wine, or elder-wine, or syrup made of dwarf elderberries.

To make Cashew Lozenges

Take half an ounce of balsam of Tolu, put it in a silver tankard, and put to it three quarters of a pint of fair-water; cover it very close, and let it simmer over a gentle fire twenty-four hours; then take ten ounces of loaf sugar, and half an ounce of Japan earth, both finely powdered and sifted; and wet it with two parts of Tolu water, and one part orange-flower water, and boil it together, almost to a candy-height; then drop it on pie-plates, but first rub the plates over with an almond, or wash them over with orange-flower water; it is best to do but five ounces at a time, because it will cool before you can drop it; after you have dropt them, set the plates a little before the fire; they will slip off the easier; if you would have them perfumed, put in ambergris.

For Obstructions

Put two ounces of steel-filings into a quart bottle of white wine; let it stand three weeks, shaking it once a day; then put in a drachm of mace; let it stand a week longer; then put into another bottle three quarters of a pound of loaf sugar in lumps, and clear off your steel-wine to your sugar, and when it is dissolved, it is fit for use; give a spoonful to a young person, with as much cream of tartar as will lie on a threepence; to one that is older two spoonfuls, and cream of tartar accordingly.

For a Rheumatism

Let the party take of the finest glazed gunpowder as much as a large thimble may hold; wet it in a spoon with milk from the cow, and drink a good half pint of warm milk after it; be covered warm in bed, and sweat; give it fasting about seven in the morning, and take this nine or ten mornings together.

For a Dropsy

Bruise a pint of mustard seed, scrape and slice a large horseradish root, scrape a handful of the inner rind of elder, and a root of elecampane sliced; put all these into a large bottle, and put to it a quart of good stale beer; let it steep forty-eight hours; drink half a pint every morning fasting, and fast two hours after it; you may fill it up once or twice.

The Bruis Ointment

Take of rosemary, brown sage, fennel, camomile, hyssop, baum, woodbine leaves, southernwood, parsley, wormwood, self-heal, rue, elder leaves, clowns' all-heal, burdock leaves, of each a handful; put them into a pot with very strong beer, or spirits enough to cover them well, and two pounds of fresh butter from the churn; cover it up with paste, and bake it with bread; and when it is baked, strain it out; when it is cold, skim off the butter, melt it, and put it into a gallipot for use; the liquor is very good to dip flannels into, and bathe any green bruise or ache, as hot as can be borne.

A good Vomit

Take two ounces of the finest white alum, beat it small, put it into better than half a pint of new milk, set it on a slow fire till the milk is turned clear; let it stand a quarter of an hour; strain it off, and drink it just warm; it will give three or four vomits, and is very safe; and an excellent cure for an ague taken half an hour before the fit; drink good store of carduus tea after it, or else take half a drachm of ipecacuanha and carduus tea with it.

Another Vomit

Take rectified butter of antimony, digest it with thrice its own weight of alcohol; a single drop or two whereof being taken in sack, or any convenient vehicle, works well by vomit; it was a secret of Mr Boyle's, and highly valued; and by him communicated to the admiral Du Quesne; it is likewise recommended by Dr Boerhaave.

An Ointment for a Scalded Head

Take a pound of May butter without salt out of the churn, a pint of ale, not too stale, a good handful of green wormwood; let the ale be hot, and put the butter to melt; shred the wormwood, and let them boil together till it turns green; strain it, and when it is cold, take the ointment from the dregs.

Another way to cure the Piles

Take two pennyworth of litharge of gold, an ounce of salad oil, a spoonful of white-wine vinegar; put all into a new gallipot; beat it together with a knife till it is as thick as an ointment, spread it on a cloth, and apply it to the place; if inward, put it up as far as you can.

An admirable Powder for the Teeth

Take tartar of vitriol two drachms, best dragon's blood and myrrh, each half a drachm, gum-lac a drachm, of ambergris four grains, and those who like it may add two grains of musk; mix well, and make a powder, to be kept in a phial close stopt. The method of using it is thus: put a little of the powder upon a China saucer, or a piece of white paper; then take a clean linen cloth upon the end of your finger, just moisten it with water, and dip it in the powder, and rub the teeth well once a day, if they be foul; but if you want to preserve their beauty, only twice a week is sufficient for its use. This powder will preserve the teeth and gums beyond any other, under whatever title dignified or distinguished; and what is commonly called a tainted or stinking breath, mostly proceeds from rotten teeth, or scorbutic gums; which last distemper, so incident and fatal to children's teeth, this powder will effectually remove. Indeed there is no cure for a rotten tooth, therefore I advise to pull it out; and if this cannot be effected, the above powder will sweeten the breath, and prevent such tooth from any ill favour. The too frequent use of the toothbrush makes the teeth become long and deformed, altho' it be a good instrument, and the moderate use of it proper enough. After rubbing the teeth with the powder, the mouth may be washed with a little red wine warm, or the like.

To make the Teeth white

Take three spoonfuls of the juice of celandine, nine spoonfuls of honey, half a spoonful of burnt alum; mix these together, and rub the teeth with it.

A Powder for the Teeth

Take half an ounce of cream of tartar, and a quarter of an ounce of powder of myrrh; rub the teeth with it two or three times a week.

To make the right Angel-Salve

Take black and yellow rosin, of each half a pound, virgin wax and frankincense, of each a quarter of a pound; mastic an ounce, deer suet a quarter of a pound; melt what is to be melted, and powder what is to be powder'd, and sift it fine; then boil them and strain them thro' a canvas bag into a bottle of white wine; then boil the wine with the ingredients an hour with a gentle fire, and let it stand till it is no hotter than blood; then put to it two drachms of camphire, and two ounces of Venice turpentine, and stir it constantly till it is cold; be sure your stuff be no hotter than blood when you put in your camphire and turpentine, otherwise it is spoiled; make it up in rolls, and keep it for use: it is the best salve made.

To cure an Ague

Take tobacco-dust and soot, an equal quantity, and nine cloves of garlic; beat it well together, and mix it with soap into a pretty stiff paste, and make two cakes something broader than a five-shilling piece, and something thicker; lay it on the inside of each wrist, and bind it on with rags; put it on an hour before the fit is expected; if it does not do the first time, in three or four days repeat it with fresh.

To take out the Redness and Scurf after the Smallpox

After the first scabs are well off, anoint the face, going to bed, with the following ointment: beat common alum very fine, and sift it thro' a lawn sieve, and mix it with oil like a thick cream, and lay it all over the face with a feather; in the morning have bran boil'd in water till it is slippery; then wash it off as hot as you can bear it; so do for a month or more, as there is occasion.

To make Brimstone Lozenges for a Short Breath

Take flour of brimstone and double-refined sugar, beaten and sifted, an equal quantity; make it into lozenges with gum-dragant steeped in rose-water; dry them in the sun, and take three or four a day.

For a Burn

Take common alum, beat and sift it, and beat it up with whites of eggs to a curd; then with a feather anoint the place; it will cure without any other thing.

To procure the Menses

Take a quarter of an ounce of pure myrrh made into fine powder; mix it with three-quarters of an ounce of conserve of bugloss flowers; two days before your expectation, take this quantity at four times, last at night, and first in the morning; drink after each time a draught of posset-drink made of ale, white wine and milk, and boil in it some pennyroyal, and a few camomile flowers.

To Stop Flooding

Dissolve a quarter of an ounce of Venice treacle in four spoonfuls of water, and drop in it thirty or forty of Jones's drops; take it when occasion requires, especially in child-bed.

To provoke Urine presently when Stopt

In a quart of beer boil a handful of the berries of eglantine till it comes to a pint; drink it off lukewarm.

To draw up the Uvula

Take ground-ivy, and heat it well between two tiles, and lay it as warm as can be borne on the top of the head. The blood of a hare, dried and drunk in red wine, stops the bloody-flux, tho' ever so severe.

For a Thrush in Children's Mouths

Take a hot sea-coal, and quench it in as much spring-water as will cover the coal; wash it with this five or six times a day.

For the Worms in Children

Take mithridate and honey, of each a pennyworth, oil of mace two pennyworth; melt them together, and spread upon leather cut in the shape of a heart; oil of savin and wormwood, of each six drops; of alum and saffron in powder, of each one drachm; rub the oils, and strew the powders, all over the plaister; apply it, being warm'd, to the child's stomach with the point upwards.

For a Weakness in the Back or Reins

Take an ounce of Venice turpentine, wash it in red-rose water, work it in the water till it is white; pour the water from it, and work it up into pills with powder of turmeric and a grated nutmeg; you may put a little rhubarb as you see occasion; take three in the morning, and three in the evening, in a little syrup of elder.

For the Yellow Jaundice

Take a handful of burdock roots, cut them in slices to the cores, and dry them; half a handful of the inner rind of barberries, three races of turmerick beat very fine, three or four tabes of the whitest goose-dung; put all in a quart of strong beer; cover it close, and let it infuse in the embers all night; in the morning strain it off; add to it a groat's-worth of saffron; take half a pint at a time first and last.

An approved Remedy for a Cancer in the Breast

Take off the hard knobs or warts which grow on the legs of a stone-horse; dry them carefully, and powder them; give from a scruple to half a drachm every morning and evening in a glass of sack; you must continue taking them for a month or six weeks, or longer, if the cancer is far gone.

An approved Medicine for the Stone

Take six pounds of black cherries, stamp them in a mortar till the kernels are bruised; then take of the powder of amber, and of coral prepar'd, of each two ounces; put them with the cherries into a still, and with a gentle fire draw off the water; which if you take for the stone, mix a drachm of the powder of amber with a spoonful of it, drinking three or four spoonfuls after it; if for the palsey or convulsions, take four spoonfuls, without adding anything, in the morning fasting.

To give Ease in Fits of the Stone, and to cure the Suppression of Urine, which usually attends them

Take snail shells and bees, of each an equal quantity; dry them in an oven with a moderate heat; then beat them to a very fine powder, of which give as much as will lie on a sixpence, in a quarter of a pint of bean-flower water, every morning, fasting two hours after it; continue this for three days together; this has been often found to break the stone, and to force a speedy passage for the urine.

Broths, &c., for the Sick

To make Broth of a Calf's Head

Take half a calf's-head, without the brains and tongue, wash it clean, cut it to pieces, put it into a gallon of water, set it over a slow fire. When the scum rises skim it clean, and put in one ounce of ivory shavings, one drachm of mace, one nutmeg sliced. Boil it till half is consumed, and then strain it. Drink three pints a day, either with sugar or a little salt.

To make Broth of a Knuckle or Scrag of Veal

Take any part of a knuckle or scrag of veal, put it into a pot with as much water as will cover it, one ounce of hartshorn shavings, half an ounce of vermicelli, two blades of mace, and three cloves; boil it an hour and a half. If the patient be costive, boil in it a quarter of a pound of currants, and sweeten it with Lisbon sugar.

To make a Strengthening Drink for very weak Persons

Take one pound of silver-bellied eels; cleanse them and cut them into small pieces, put them into a pot with five quarts of water, one ounce of sago, a crust of bread, a top of mint, a small handful of pennyroyal, a drachm of mace, as much nutmeg, and a small stick of cinnamon; boil it till half is consumed. Drink of it as often as thirsty.

To make Chicken Water

Take a cock or large fowl, strip off its skin, and bruise it with a rolling-pin. Then put it into a saucepan with two quarts of water, a crust of bread, and an ounce of French barley. Let it boil till half the water is evaporated, then strain it off, and season it with salt.

To make Barley Water

Take a pound of pearl barley, and two quarts of water; let it boil half an hour, then strain off the barley, and throw away the water; put the barley into three pints of fresh water, and boil it till it comes to a quart; strain it off, and sweeten it to your palate, adding to it two spoonfuls of white wine, or milk.

To make Seed Water

Take of coriander seed, caraway seed, cubebs, sweet fennel seed, and aniseed, of each half an ounce, bruise them and boil them in a quart of water; strain it, brew it up with the yolk of an egg, and add to it a little sack and double-refined sugar.

To make White Caudle

Take four spoonfuls of oatmeal, two blades of mace, a piece of lemon-peel, cloves and ginger of each one quarter of an ounce; put these into two quarts of water, and let it boil about an hour, stirring it often; then strain it out, and add to every quart half a pint of wine, some grated nutmeg and sugar.

To make Brown Caudle

Take six spoonfuls of oatmeal, a bit of lemon-peel, and two or three blades of mace, put them into two quarts of water, let it boil as before, and strain it. Then add to it a quart of stale beer, not bitter, and some sugar; let it boil, and then put to it a pint of white wine.

To make the Pectoral Drink

Take of China root one ounce, sarsaparilla, comfry, and liquorice, of each half an ounce, orrice and elecampane, of each one quarter of an ounce, yellow and red saunders, of each two drachms, aniseed one drachm, Malaga raisins half a pound; boil these in a gallon of spring-water, till half is evaporated, and then strain it off, and sweeten it with syrup of maidenhair.

To make artificial Asses' Milk

Take of pearl barley two ounces, of eringoroot, and China root, of each one ounce, Japan earth one drachm, white maidenhair and honey of each one ounce, ten snails bruised; boil these in three quarts of water till half be wasted. Drink a quarter of a pint of it, mixed with an equal quantity of warm milk from the cow, and sweetened with syrup of balsam of Tolu, morning and night.

To make Chicken Broth

Take a chick just killed, bruise it, put it into a saucepan with five quarts of water, a blade or two of mace, a small piece of lemon-peel, one spoonful of ground rice; boil it till but two quarts remain.

To make Water Gruel

Take a large spoonful of oatmeal, and a pint of water; mix them together, set it on the fire, and let it boil for some time, stirring it often; then strain it through a sieve, and add to it a good piece of butter, and a little salt, stirring it constantly with a spoon, till the butter is melted.

Directions for Decorating, &c.

The Price of Materials for Painting

	£	s.	d.
One hundredweight of red lead		18	0
One hundredweight of white lead	1	2	0
Linseed oil by the gallon		3	0

A small quantity of oil of turpentine is sufficient.

The red lead must be ground with linseed oil, and may be used very thin, it being the priming or first colouring; when it is used, some drying oil must be put to it.

To prepare the Drying Oil

Take two quarts of linseed oil, put it in a skillet or saucepan, and put to it a pound of burnt amber; boil it for two hours gently: prepare this without doors, for fear of endangering the house; let it settle and it will be fit for use; pour the clear off, and use that with the white lead, the lees or dregs being as good to be used with red lead.

For the Second Priming

Take a hundredweight of white lead, with an equal quantity of whiting in bulk, but not in weight; grind them together with linseed oil pretty stiff; when it is used put to it some of the drying oil above-mentioned, with a small quantity of oil of turpentine; this is not to be laid on till the first priming is very dry.

To prepare the Putty or Paste to stop all joints in the Pales or Wood, that no Water may soak in

Take a quantity of whiting, and mix it very stiff with linseed oil and drying oil, of each an equal quantity; when it is so stiff it cannot be wrought by the hand, more whiting must be added, and beat up with a mallet till it is stiffer than dough; when your second priming is dry, stop such places as require with this putty; and when the putty is skinn'd over, that is, the outside dry, then proceed and lay on the last paint, which is thus to be prepared: take of the best white lead, grind it very stiff with linseed oil, and when it is used put to it some of the drying oil, and some oil of turpentine; thus will the work be finished to great satisfaction, for it will be more clean and more durable that it can be perform'd by a house-painter, without you pay considerably more than the common rates. Repeat this preparation once in five years, and it will preserve any outworks that are exposed to the weather time out of mind. But for rooms or places within doors, proceed thus:

The Wainscot Colour for Rooms

When you mix your last paint, add to your white lead a small quantity of yellow ochre, and use it as above directed; it is now the universal fashion to paint all rooms of a plain wainscot colour; and if it should alter, it is but mixing any other colour with the white lead instead of yellow ochre; there must be bought six chamber-pots of earth, and six brushes, and keep them to what they belong to.

To make Yellow Varnish

Take one quart of spirit of wine, seven ounces of seed-lake, half an ounce of sandarach, a quarter of an ounce of gum-anime, and one drachm of mastic; let these infuse for thirty-six or forty hours, then strain it off and keep it for use: it is good for frames of chairs or tables, or anything black or brown; do it on with a brush three or four times, nine times if you polish it afterwards, and a day between every doing; lay it very thin the first and second time, afterwards something thicker.

To make White Varnish

To a quart of spirit of wine, take eight ounces of sandarach well washed in spirit of wine; that spirit of wine will make the yellow varnish; then add to it a quarter of an ounce of gum-anime well pick'd, half an ounce of camphire, and a drachm of mastic; steep this as long as the yellow varnish; then strain it out, and keep it for use.

To boil Plate

Take twelve gallons of water, or a quantity according to your plate in largeness or quantity; there must be water enough to cover it; put the water in a copper, or large kettle; and when it boils put in half a pound of red argol, a pound of common salt, an ounce of roch-alum; first put your plate into a charcoal-fire, and cover it till it is red hot; then throw it into your copper, and let boil half an hour; then take it out, and wash it in cold fair-water, and set it before the charcoal-fire till it is very dry.

A Receipt for destroying Bugs

Take of the highest rectified spirit of wine (viz. lamp-spirits) half a pint; newly distilled oil, or spirit of turpentine, half a pint; mix them together, adding to it half an ounce of camphire, which will dissolve in it in a few minutes; shake them well together, and with a piece of sponge, or a brush, dip in some of it, wet very well the bed or furniture wherein those vermin harbour or breed, and it will infallibly kill and destroy both them and their nits, although they swarm ever so much; but then the bed or furniture must be well and thoroughly wet with it (the dust upon them being first brushed and shook off), by which means it will neither stain, soil, or in the least hurt, the finest silk or damask bed that is. The quantity here ordered of this curious, neat, white mixture (which costs about a shilling) will rid any one bed whatsoever, though it swarms with bugs; do but touch a live bug with a drop of it, and you will find it to die instantly. If any bug or bugs should happen to appear after once using it, it will only be for want of well wetting the lace, &c. of the bed, the foldings of the linings or curtains near the rings, or the joints or holes in and about the bed, headboard, &c. wherein the bugs or nits nestle and breed; and then their being well wet again with more of the same mixture, which dries in as fast as you use it, pouring some of it into the joints and holes where the sponge or brush cannot reach, will never fail absolutely to destroy them all. Some beds that have much woodwork can hardly be thoroughly cleared without being first taken down; but others that can be drawn out, or that you can get well behind, to be done as it should be, may. *Note* The smell this mixture occasions will be all gone in two or three days, which yet is very wholesome, and to many people agreeable; you must remember always to shake the mixture together very well whenever you use it, which must be in the day-time, not by candlelight, lest the subtlety of the mixture should catch the flame as you are using it and occasion damage.

An infallible Receipt to destroy Bugs

To every ounce of quicksilver put the whites of five or six eggs; mix them, and beat them well together in a wooden dish with a brush, till the globules of the quicksilver are but just perceptible; then, after having taken the bedstead to pieces, and brushed it very clean from the dust and dirt (without washing), rub into all the cracks and joints the above mixture, letting it dry on; nor must the bedstead be washed at any time afterwards; by the first application they will in most places be destroy'd; if not, a second will not fail destroying them entirely.

An excellent Way of Washing, to save Soap, and whiten Clothes

Take a butter tub, or one of that size, and, with a gimblet, bore holes in it about halfway; put into your tub some clean straw, and over that about a peck of wood ashes; fill it with cold water, and set it into another vessel to receive the water as it runs out of the holes of the tub; if it is too strong a lye, add to it some warm water; wash your linen in it, slightly soaping the clothes before you wash them; two pounds of soap will go as far as six pounds, and make the clothes whiter and cleaner, when you by experience have got the right way; if it is too strong for the hands, make it weaker with water.

To take Mildew out of Linen

Take soap, and rub it on very well; then scrape chalk very fine, and rub that in well, and lay it on the grass; as it dries, wet it a little; and at once or twice doing, it will come out.

To make Pomatum

Take a drachm of white wax, two drachms of spermaceti, an ounce of oil of bitter almonds; slice your wax very thin, and put it in a gallipot, and put the pot in a skillet of boiling water; when the wax is melted, put in your spermaceti, and just stir it together; then put in the oil of almonds; after that take it off the fire, and out of the skillet, and stir it till cold with a bone-knife; then beat it up in rose-water till it is white; keep it in water, and change the water once a day.

To make a sweet Bag for Linen

Take of orrice roots, sweet calamus, cypress roots, dried lemon-peel and dried orange-peel of each a pound; a peck of dried roses; make all these into a gross powder; coriander seed four ounces, nutmegs an ounce and a half, an ounce of cloves; make all these into fine powder and mix with the other; add musk and ambergris; then take four large handfuls of lavender-flowers dried and rubb'd; of sweet-marjoram, orange-leaves, young walnut-leaves, of each a handful, all dried and rubb'd; mix all together, with some bits of cotton perfumed with essences, put it up into silk bags to lay with your linen.

To make the burning Perfume

Take a quarter of a pound of damask rose leaves, beat them by themselves, an ounce of orrice root sliced very thin and steeped in rose-water, beat them well together, and put to it two grains of musk, as much civet, two ounces of benjamin finely powder'd; mix all together, and add a little powder'd sugar, and make them up in little round cakes, and lay them singly on papers to dry; set them in a window where the sun comes and they will dry in two or three days. Make them in June.

To make Ink

Get one pound of the best galls, half a pound of copperas, a quarter of a pound of gum-arabic, a quarter of a pound of white sugar-candy; bruise the galls, and beat your other ingredients fine, and infuse them all in three quarts of white wine or rainwater, and let them stand hot by the fire three or four days; then put all into a new pipkin; set it on a slow fire, so as not to boil; keep it frequently stirring, and let it stand five or six hours, till one quarter is consumed; and when cold, strain it through a clean coarse piece of linen; bottle it, and keep it for use.

To wash Gloves

Take the yolk of an egg, and beat it, and egg the gloves all over, and lay them on a table, and with a hard brush and water rub them clean; then rinse them clean, and scrape white lead in water pretty thick, and dip the gloves in; let them dry, and as they begin to dry, stretch and rub them till they be limber, dry, and smooth; then gum them with gum-dragant steeped in sweet water, and let them dry on a marble stone. If you colour them, scrape some of the following colours amongst the white lead: the dark colour is umber; for brick colour red lead; for a jessamy yellow ochre; for copper colour red ochre; for lemon colour turmeric.

A
Supplement

A full Discovery of the Medicines given by me, Joanna Stephens, for the Cure of the Stone and Gravel; and a particular Account of my Method of preparing and giving the same.

My medicines are a powder, a decoction, and pills. The powder consists of eggshells and snails both calcin'd. The decoction is made by boiling some herbs (together with a ball which consists of soap, swines-cresses burnt to a blackness, and honey) in water. The pills consist of snails calcin'd, wild-carrot seeds, burdock seeds, ashen-keys, hips and haws, all burnt to a blackness, soap and honey.

The Powder

Take hens' eggshells, well drained from the whites, dry and clean; crush them small with the hands, and fill a crucible of the twelfth size (which contains nearly three pints) with them lightly, place it in the fire, and cover it with a tile; then heap coals over it, that it may be in the midst of a very strong clear fire till the eggshells be calcin'd to a greyish white, and acquire an acrid salt taste; this will take up eight hours at least. After they are thus calcin'd, put them into a dry clean earthen pan, which must not be above three parts full, that there may be room for the swelling of the eggshells in slacking. Let the pan stand uncover'd in a dry room for two months and no longer; in this time the eggshells will become of a milder taste; and that part which is sufficiently calcin'd will fall into a powder of such a fineness as to pass through a common hair sieve, which is to be done accordingly.

In like manner, take garden snails with their shells, clean'd from the dirt, fill a crucible of the same size with them whole, cover it, and place it in a fire, as before, till the snails have done smoking, which will be in about an hour, taking care that they do not continue in the fire after that. They are then to be taken out of the crucible, and immediately rubb'd in a mortar to a fine powder, which ought to be of a very dark grey colour.

Note. If pit-coal be made use of, it will be proper, in order that the fire may the sooner burn clear on the top, that large cinders, and not fresh coals, be placed upon the tiles which cover the crucibles.

These powders being thus prepar'd, take the eggshell powder of six crucibles, and the snail powder of one, mix them together, rub them in a mortar, and pass them thro' a cypress sieve. This mixture is immediately to be put up into bottles, which must be close stopped, and kept in a dry place for use. I have generally added a small quantity of swines-cresses burnt to a blackness, and rubb'd fine; but this was only with a view to disguise it.

The eggshells may be prepared at any time of the year, but it is best to do them in summer. The snails ought only to be prepared in May, June, July, and August; and I esteem those best which are done in the first of these months.

The Decoction

Take four ounces and a half of the best Alicant soap, beat it in a mortar with a large spoonful of swines-cresses burnt to a blackness, and as much honey as will make the whole of the consistence of paste. Let this be form'd into a ball.

Take this ball, and green camomile, or camomile flowers, sweet fennel, parsley and burdock leaves, of each an ounce (when there are not greens, take the same quantity of roots); cut the herbs or roots, slice the ball, and boil them in two quarts of soft water half an hour; then strain it off, and sweeten it with honey.

The Pills

Take equal quantities, by measure, of snails calcin'd as before, of wild-carrot seeds, burdock seeds, ashen-keys, hips and haws, all burnt to a blackness, or, which is the same thing, till they have done smoking; mix them together, rub them in a mortar, and pass them thro' a cypress sieve. Then take a large spoonful of this mixture, and four ounces of the best Alicant soap, and beat them in a mortar with as much honey as will make the whole of a proper consistence for pills; sixty of which are to be made out of every ounce of the composition.

The Method of giving these Medicines

When there is a stone in the bladder or kidneys, the powder is to be taken three times a day, viz. in the morning after breakfast, in the afternoon about five or six, and going to bed. The dose is a drachm avoirdupois, or fifty-six grains, which is to be mixed in a large teacup full of white wine, cyder, or small punch; and half a pint of the decoction is to be drunk, either cold or milk-warm, after every dose.

These medicines frequently cause much pain at first; in which case it is proper to give an opiate, and repeat it as often as there is occasion.

If the person be costive during the use of them, let him take as much lenitive electuary, or other laxative medicine, as may be sufficient to remove that complaint, but not more: for it must be a principal care, at all times, to prevent a looseness, which would carry off the medicines; and if this does happen, it will be proper to increase the quantity of the powder, which is astringent; or lessen that of the decoction, which is laxative; or take some other suitable means, by the advice of physicians.

During the use of these medicines, the person ought to abstain from salt meats, red wines, and milk, drink few liquids, and use little exercise, that so the urine may be the more strongly impregnated with the medicines, and the longer retained in the bladder.

If the stomach will not bear the decoction, a sixth part of the ball made into pills must be taken after every dose of the powder.

Where the person is aged, of a weak constitution, or much reduced by loss of appetite or pain, the powder must have a greater proportion of the calcin'd snails than according to the foregoing direction; and this proportion may be increased suitably to the nature of the case, till there be equal parts of the two ingredients. The quantity also of both powder and decoction may be lessened for the same reasons. But as soon as the person can bear it, he should take them in the above-mentioned proportion and quantities.

Instead of the herbs and roots before mentioned, I have sometimes used others, as mallows, marshmallows, yarrows red and white, dandelion, watercresses, and horseradish root, but do not know of any material difference.

This is my manner of giving the powder and decoction. As to the pills, their chief use is in fits of the gravel, attended with pain in the back and vomiting, and a suppression of urine from a stoppage in the ureters. In these cases, the person is to take five pills every hour, day and night, when awake, till the complaints are removed. They will also prevent the formation of gravel and gravelstones in constitutions subject to breed them, if ten or fifteen be taken every day.

J. Stephens
June 16, 1739

Note Mrs Stephens received five thousand pounds reward on her medicine having been tried and approved (March 17, 1739–40). See *London Gazette*, March 23, 1739–40.

A certain Cure for the Dropsy, if taken at the beginning of the Distemper

Take the stems that grow from the stick or root of the artichoke, pluck off the leaves, and bruise only the stems in a marble mortar; to a quart of juice put a quart of Madeira or mountain wine, straining the juice through a piece of muslin; let the patient take a wine glass of it fasting, and another just before going to bed, continuing till the cure is completed. *Note* This cured a son of Dr Moore, late bishop of Ely (who had the advice of several physicians to no effect) and from whom I had the receipt.

For the Rheumatism

Take one handful of garden scurvy-grass pick'd, two spoonfuls of mustard seed bruised, two small sticks of horseradish sliced, half an ounce of winter bark sliced; steep these ingredients in a quart of mountain wine three hours before you take it, which must be three times a day; at eight, eleven, and five, if your stomach will bear it; if not, then twice only, viz. at eight and five, eating and drinking nothing after it for two hours at least; you are to take a quarter of a pint at a time, which you must fill up out of another quart of the same wine; and so continue drinking till both bottles are emptied.

A restorative Jelly for anyone inclining to a Consumption

Take four ounces of hartshorn shavings, two ounces of eringo root, one ounce of isinglass, two vipers, one pint of snails; the snails being washed and bruised, put all these into three quarts of pump-water, let them simmer till it comes to three pints, then strain it off, and add the juice of two Seville oranges, half a pound of white sugar-candy, and one pint of old rhenish wine; drink a quarter of a pint fasting, and the same quantity an hour before dinner time.

For the Bloody-Flux

Take some garlic, press out a spoonful or two, warm it pretty hot, then dip a double rag in it, lay it upon the navel and let it lie till it is cold; then repeat it two or three times; it cures immediately. By this I cured a gentleman who had tried several other things without success.

S. C.

For the Colic

Let the patient, when they find any symptoms of a fit, take a pint of milk warm, put into it four spoonfuls of brandy, and eat it up; and so let them take it any other time; if they are subject to that distemper, it will prevent the fit. This cured Mr Blundel of Hampstead, after he had the advice of several other physicians, and had been at Bath without success.

For an inveterate Looseness

Take a piece of bread of the bigness of a crown piece, toast it hard on both sides, then put it into a quarter of a pint of French brandy, let it soak till it is soft, then eat the bread and drink the brandy at night going to bed; this must be taken thrice. This cured a near relation of mine who had try'd several other things before to no purpose. S. C.

For Dimness of Sight and Sore Eyes

Take eyebright, sweet-marjoram and betony dry'd, of each a like quantity, the same quantity of tobacco as of all the rest; take it in a pipe as you do tobacco for some time; and take of the right Portugal snuff, put it into the corner of your eyes morning and night, and take it likewise as snuff. This cured Judge Ayres, Sir Edward Seymour, and Sir John Houblon, so that they could read without spectacles, after they had used them many years. S. C.

For the Piles, a present Remedy

Anoint the part with ointment of tobacco. This cured an acquaintance of mine, who told it me himself. S. C.

For a Pleurisy

Let the patient bleed plentifully, then drink off a pint of spring-water, with thirty drops in it of spirit of sal-amoniac; this must be done as soon as the party is seized. Approved by myself. S. C.

For a Tertian Ague, a never-failing Remedy

Take stone brimstone finely powder'd, as much as will lie upon half a crown, in a glass of white wine, about an hour before the fit comes; it cures at twice taking. This I had from one that had cured scores with it, and it never failed once.

For a Quinsey or Swelling in the Throat, so that the Patient cannot swallow

Take a toast of household bread, as big as will cover the top of the head, well bak'd on both sides, and soak it in right French brandy; let the top of the head be shav'd, then bind it on with a cloth; if this be done at night going to bed, it will cure before morning, as I myself have had experience of.

S. C.

For a Rheumatism

Let the patient take spirit of hartshorn morning and evening, beginning with twenty-five drops in a glass of spring-water, increasing five every day till they come to fifty, to be continued for a month, if not well sooner. By this I cured a woman that had this distemper to so great a degree that she was swelled in her head and limbs that she could not lift her hand to her head; but taking this, in three days was much better, and in three weeks' time went abroad perfectly well, and has continued so now for above seven years.

S. C.

To Stop Bleeding at the Nose, or elsewhere

Take an ounce-bottle, fill it half full of water, put into it as much Roman vitriol as will lie upon the point of a knife; let the part bleed into it; it will stop it in an instant.

For Convulsion Fits in Children

Take assa foetida and wood-foot, of each one ounce, infuse them in a pint of French brandy; give a child in the mouth three or four drops in breast milk, or black-cherry water, soon after it is born, and continue it two or three times a day for a week.

To prevent Convulsions in Children

Take ten grains of coral finely powder'd, give it in breast-milk or black-cherry water, it prevents their having any convulsion fits.

For the Gout in the Stomach. Dr Lower's constant Remedy

Take of Venice treacle one drachm, Gascoign's powder half a drachm, syrup of poppies as much as is sufficient to make it into a bolus; let the patient take it going to bed.

For an inveterate Headache

Take juice of ground-ivy, and snuff it up the nose; it not only easeth the most violent headache for the present, but taketh it quite away. This cured one that had been afflicted with it many years, and by the use of it, immediately cured him, and it never returned.

For the Jaundice

Take the juice of the leaves of artichoke plants, put it into a quart of white wine; take three or four spoonfuls in the morning fasting, and at four in the afternoon.

For the Piles

Take the duck-meat that lies upon ponds and ditches, let it lie till it be dry, then lay it to the part; it cures presently.

For an Asthma

Take of virgin honey one spoonful, mix in it as much rosin as will lie upon a half-crown, finely powder'd; let the patient take it in the morning, an hour before breakfast, and again at night, an hour after supper; this must be continued a month.

For an inveterate Cough

Take of spermaceti (called by the common people, Parma city) one scruple; put it into the yolk of a new-laid egg raw and sup it up in the morning fasting; it cures at one taking. Approved by several of my acquaintance, whom I knew it to cure.   S. C.

To cure Blindness, when the Cause proceeds from within the Eye

Take a double handful of the top leaves of salary, and a spoonful of salt; pound them together, and when it is pounded make it into a poultice, and put it on the party's contrary hand-wrist (that is, if the right eye is bad, put it to the left wrist), and repeat it for about three or four times, but put on fresh once in twenty-four hours.

If the eye is very bad, use bay-salt.

To make Sage Wine

Take four handfuls of red sage, beat it in a stone mortar like green sauce, put it into a quart of red wine, and let it stand three or four days close stopt, shaking it twice or thrice; then let it stand and settle, and the next day in the morning take of the sage wine three spoonfuls, and of running water one spoonful, fasting after it one hour or better; use this from Michaelmas to the end of March: it will cure any aches or humours in the joints, dry rheums, keep from all diseases to the fourth degree; it helps the dead palfy, and convulsions in the sinews, sharpens the memory, and from the beginning of taking it will keep the body mild, strengthen nature, till the fullness of your days be finished; nothing will be changed in your strength, except the change of your hair; it will keep your teeth sound that were not corrupted before; it will keep you from the gout, the dropsy, or any swellings of the joints or body.

Receipts, or Various Ways of Eating Pickled Herrings

General Directions to be observed before the Cutting Up a Pickled Herring, which way soever it is to be eat

Lay the fish in a pewter plate, or trencher. Beat it on each side, with the flat of the knife, to loosen the skin. Cut a thin strip off the belly, and slit the back, to divide the skin; which then must be strip'd off on each side (with the knife and fingers) beginning at the neck. Take out the roe; and rub the inside, and the whole herring, with the corner of a towel, dipped in vinegar.

First way

The fish being prepared, as above, cut off the head and tail. Then divide the herring into pieces of about an inch long. Afterwards put the pieces together, as though the fish were entire. Then eat it with or without oil and vinegar, new bread and butter, &c.

Second way

The herring lying skinned, &c., in the plate (as observed in the general directions), shave it very thin; and, when cut to the bone, turn it, and shave it in like manner on the other side. A herring may thus be cut so thin that the pieces of it will quite cover a plate.

Third way

The herring being prepared (pursuant to the general directions), take it by the tail, in the middle of which cut a slit, half an inch long, or more. Pull each tip of the tail opposite ways, by which means the herring will be split into two parts. In one of these parts no bone will be left; and the bone left in the other part may easily be taken out (from a new pickled herring) by loosening the bone at the neck, and drawing it along. The two divided parts of the herring may then be laid together, cut it into slices, and eaten between bread and butter; or minced and mixed with a salad of any kind; or else made into a falmigondi, with chicken, rabbit, or veal. They eat very well with green peas, Windfor beans, kidney beans or potatoes if, after these are drain'd off, when boiled, a pickled herring, or more, be thrown into the same water and then taken out, after the water has bubbled up a minute or two. Herring-pickle may be used for that of an anchovy: and a little of this pickle thrown into the butter made as sauce for eels takes off from their lusciousness. In many countries, pickled herrings are made to serve all the purposes of ham, or bacon.

Note Those who are desirous of being still more conversant with various ways of eating pickled herrings, may consult the ingenious Mr Dodd's (lately printed) *Essay towards a Natural History of the Herring*.

Receipt for making Pickled-Herring Soup

Take a quart of split peas. Put to them five quarts of cold water, a quarter of an ounce of whole Jamaica pepper, two large onions, and three pickled herrings (wash'd in two or three waters, and the roes out), skinn'd, and cut to pieces.

Boil all together till a quart is diminished. Pour in a pint of boiling water, and let the whole boil a quarter of an hour. Take it off, and strain it thro' a colander. Throw into the soup seven or eight handfuls of celery, three heads of endive, all of them cut very small (but if on shipboard, where endive is not to be had, a larger number of onions may be employ'd in its stead), together with a handful of dried mint, pass'd thro' a lawn-sieve. Set all these on a fire, and boil the whole near three quarters of an hour, stirring the soup perpetually to prevent burning, which it will do in a moment, and therefore the pot should stand on a trivet.

Bread, cut into diamonds, and fried crisp in butter, must be thrown into the soup, which then may be served up.

To Stuff a Fillet of Veal, or Calf's Heart, with Pickled Herrings

Take two herrings: skin, bone, and wash them in several waters. Chop them very small, with a quarter of a pound of suet. Add a handful of bread grated fine; and the like quantity of parsley, cut very small. Throw in a little thyme, nutmeg, and pepper, to your taste; and mix all together, with two eggs.

Half the quantity of the above stuffing is exceedingly good for a calf's heart.

Stuffing of Pickled Herrings for a Roast Turkey

Wash, in several waters, two pickled herrings; which afterwards skin, and take the bone out carefully. Take half a pound of suet, and two large handfuls of bread grated. Chop the herrings, suet, and bread (separately), very small. Beat these all together in a marble mortar, with the white of an egg; after throwing in a little nutmeg and white pepper.

Pickled-Herring Pudding for a Hare

Take half a pound of the lean of fine veal, which clear of the skin and strings. Two pickled herrings, which wash in two or three waters; then skin, and clear them of the bones. A quarter of a pound of suet. Two handfuls of bread grated fine. A handful of parsley. Chop all the above (separately then mix them; throwing in half a nutmeg grated, a little thyme, sweet-marjoram, and one egg. Beat the whole together in a marble mortar.

A Receipt to dress a Turtle

Cut his head off; cut it all round, and part the two shells, as you would a crab; leave some meat to the breast-shell called the callapee, season that with some kyon butter, pepper, spice, and force-meat balls between the flesh; and bake it with some meat in it, and baste it with some Madeira wine and butter. Take the deep shell call'd the callapash, take all the meat out of it, the guts, &c. open every gut, and clean it with a penknife, and cut them an inch long, and stew them four hours by themselves; cut the other meat in quarter-of-a-pound pieces; take the fins and clean them as you would good giblets, cut them in pieces like the other; stew the fins and meat together, till they are tender, about one hour, and then strain them off; thickening your soup, put all your meat and guts into the soup as you would stewed giblets, season it with kyon butter, spices, pepper and salt, shallots, sweet herbs, and Madeira wine, as you like it, and put it all into the deep shell, and send it to the oven and bake it. Then serve it up.

The following Receipts were inserted in the *Carolina Gazette*, May 9, 1750; and it is presumed that the Introductory Letter will be a sufficient Authority for adopting them into this Work.

From the Carolina Gazette *to the Printer*

Sir,

I am commanded by the commons house of assembly to send you the enclosed, which you are to print in the Carolina Gazette *as soon as possible: it is the negro Caesar's cure for poison; and likewise his cure for the bite of a rattlesnake; for discovering of which the general assembly hath thought fit to purchase his freedom, and grant him an allowance of £100 per annum during life.*

I am, &c.

JAMES IRVING
May 9, 1749

The Negro Caesar's Cure for Poison

Take the roots of plantain and wild horehound, fresh or dried, three ounces, boil them together in two quarts of water to one quart, and strain it; of this decoction let the patient take one third part three mornings, fasting successively, from which if he finds any relief, it must be continued till he is perfectly recovered; on the contrary, if he finds no alteration after the third dose, it is a sign that the patient has either not been poisoned at all, or that it has been with such poison as Caesar's antidotes will not remedy, so he may leave off the decoction. During the cure, the patient must live on a spare diet, and abstain from eating mutton, pork, butter, or any other fat or oily food. *Note* The plantain or horehound will either of them cure alone, but they are most efficacious together. In summer, you may take one handful of the roots and branches of each, in place of three ounces of the roots of each.

For drink, during the cure, let them take of the roots of golden-rod six ounces, or in summer two large handfuls, the roots and branches together, and boil them in two quarts of water to one quart (to which also may be added a little horehound and sassafras). To this decoction, after it is strained, add a glass of rum or brandy, and sweeten it with sugar, for ordinary drink.

Sometimes an inward fever attends such as are poisoned, for which he orders a pint of wood-ashes and three pints of water: stir and mix them well together, let them stand all night, and strain or decant the lye off in the morning, of which ten ounces may be taken six mornings following, warmed or cold, according to the weather.

These medicines have no sensible operation, tho' sometimes they work in the bowels, and give a gentle stool.

The symptoms attending such as are poisoned are as follows: a pain of the breast, difficulty of breathing, a load at the pit of the stomach, an irregular pulse, burning and violent pains of the viscera above and below the navel, very restless at night, sometimes wandering pains over the whole body, a retching and inclination to vomit, profuse sweats (which prove always serviceable), slimy stools, both when costive and loose, the face of a pale and yellow colour, sometimes a pain and inflammation of the throat; the appetite is generally weak, and some cannot eat anything; those who have been long poisoned, are generally very feeble, and weak in their limbs, sometimes spit a great deal, the whole skin peels, and likewise the hair falls off.

Caesar's Cure for the Bite of a Rattlesnake

Take of the roots of plantain or horehound (in the summer, roots and branches together) a sufficient quantity, bruise them in a mortar, and squeeze out the juice, of which give, as soon as possible, one large spoonful; if he is swelled, you must force it down his throat: this generally will cure; but if the patient finds no relief in an hour after, you may give another spoonful, which never fails.

If the roots are dried, they must be moistened with a little water.

To the wound may be applied a leaf of good tobacco moistened with rum.

The Art of Carving

Terms for Carving

Barbel, to tusk
Bittern, to disjoint
Brawn, to leach
Bream, to splay
Brew, to untach
Bustard, to cut up
Capon, to sauce
Chevin, to sun
Chicken, to frush
Coney, to unlace
Crab, to tame
Crane, to display
Curlew, to untach
Deer, to break
Duck, to unbrace
Eel, to transon
Egg, to tire
Egript, to break
Flounder, to sauce
Goose, to rear
Haddock, to side

Hen, to spoil
Hern, to dismember
Lamprey, to string
Lobster, to barb
Mullard, to unbrace
Partridge, to wing
Pasty, to border
Peacock, to disfigure
Pheasant, to allay
Pigeon, to thigh
Pike, to splat
Plover, to mince
Quail, to wing
Salmon, to chine
Small birds, to thigh
Sturgeon, to tranch
Swan, to lift
Tench, to sauce
Trout, to culpon
Turkey, to cut up
Woodcock, to thigh.

Instructions for Carving, according to these Terms of Art

❀

To unjoint a Bittern　Raise his wings and legs as a hern, and no other sauce but salt.

❀

To cut up a Bustard　See Turkey.

❀

To sauce a Capon　Take a capon, and lift up the right leg, and so array forth, and lay in the platter; serve your chicken in the same manner, and sauce them with green sauce, or verjuice.

❀

To unlace a Coney　Turn back downward and cut the flaps or apron from the belly or kidney; then put in your knife between the kidneys, and loosen the flesh from the bone, on each side; then turn the belly downward, and cut the back cross between the wings, drawing your knife down on each side the backbone, dividing the legs and sides from the back; pull not the leg too hard when you open the side from the bone; but with your hand and knife neatly lay open both sides from the scut to the shoulder; then lay the legs close together,

❀

To display a Crane　Unfold his legs; then cut off his wings, by the joints; after this take up his legs and wings, and sauce them with vinegar, salt, mustard, and powdered ginger.

❀

To unbrace a Duck　Raise up the pinions and legs, but take them not off, and raise the merry-thought from the breast; then lace it down each side of the breast with your knife, wriggling your knife to and fro, that the furrows may lie in and out; after the same manner unbrace the mallard.

❀

To rear a Goose   Take off both legs fair, like shoulders of lamb; then cut off the belly-piece round close to the end of the breast; then lace your goose down on both sides of the breast half an inch from the sharp bone; then take off the pinion on each side, and the flesh you first lac'd with your knife; raise it up clean from the bone, and take it off with the pinion from the body; then cut up the merry-thought; then cut from the breastbone another slice of flesh quite thro'; then turn up your carcase, and cut it asunder, the backbone above the loin-bones; then take the rump end of the backbone and lay it in a dish, with the skinny side upwards; lay at the fore-end of it the merry-thought, with the skinny side upwards, and before that the apron of the goose; then lay the pinions on each side contrary, set the legs on each side contrary behind them, that the bone ends of the legs may stand up cross in the middle of the dish, and the wing pinions may come on the outside of them; put the long slice which you cut from the breastbone under the wing pinions on each side, and let the ends meet under the leg-bones, and let the other ends lie cut in the dish betwixt the leg and the pinion; then pour in your sauce under the meat; throw on salt, and serve it to table again.

❀

To dismember a Heron   Take off both the legs, and lace it down the breast on both sides with your knife, and open the breast-pinion, but take it not off; then raise up the merry-thought between the breastbone and the top of it; then raise up the brawn; then turn it outward upon both sides; but break it not, nor cut it off; then cut off the wing-pinions at the joint next the body, and stick in each side the pinion in the place you turned the brawn out; but cut off the sharp end of the pinion, and take the middle piece, and that will just fit in the place. You may cut up a capon or pheasant the same way.

❀

To unbrace a Mullard   This is done the same way as to unbrace a duck; which see.

❀

To wing a Partridge or a Quail   Raise his legs and wings, and sauce him with wine, powdered ginger, and a little salt.

❀

To allay a Pheasant   Do this as you do a partridge, but use no other sauce but salt.

❀

To lift a Swan   Slit the swan down in the middle of the breast, and so clean through the back, from the neck to the rump; then part it in two halves, but do not break or tear the flesh; then lay the two halves in a charger, with the slit sides downwards; throw salt upon it; set it again on the table; let the sauce be cauldron, and serve it in saucers.

❀

To break a Teal   Do this the same way as you do a pheasant.

❀

To cut up a Turkey   Raise up the leg fairly, and open the joint with the point of your knife, but take not off the leg; then with your knife lace down both sides of the breast, and open the breast-pinion, but do not take it off; then raise the merry-thought betwixt the breastbone and the top of it; then raise up the brawn; then turn it outward upon both sides, but not break it, nor cut it off; then cut off the wing pinions at the joint next the body, and stick each pinion in the place you turned the brawn out, but cut off the sharp end of the pinion, and take the middle piece, and that will just fit in the place. You may cut up a bustard, a capon, or pheasant, the same way.

❀

To thigh a Woodcock   Raise the wings and legs as you do a hern, only lay the head open for the brains; and as you thigh a hern, so you must a curlew, plover, or snipe, excepting that you have no other sauce but salt.

A Bill of Fare for every Season of the Year

For January

FIRST COURSE

Collar of Brawn
Bisque of Fish
Soup with Vermicelli
Orange Pudding with Patties
Chine and Turkey
Lamb Pasty
Roasted Pullets with Eggs
Oyster Pie
Roasted Lamb in Joints
Grand Salad with Pickles

SECOND COURSE

Wild Fowl of all Sorts
Chine of Salmon boiled with
  Smelts
Fruit of all Sorts
Jole of Sturgeon
Collared Pig
Dried Tongues, with salt Salads
Marinated Fish

ANOTHER FIRST COURSE

Soup à-la-royal
Carp Blovon
Tench stewed, with pitch-cocked
Eels
Rump of Beef *à-la-braise*
Turkeys *à-la-daube*
Wild Ducks *comporté*
Fricando of Veal, with Veal
  Olives

ANOTHER SECOND COURSE

Woodcocks
Pheasants
Salmigondin
Partridge Poults
Bisque of Lamb
Oyster Loaves
Cutlets
Turkeys' Livers forced
Pippins stewed

For February

FIRST COURSE

Soup Lorain
Turbot boiled, with Oysters
  and Shrimps
Grand Patty
Hen Turkeys with Eggs
Marrow Puddings
Stewed Carps and broiled Eels
Spring Pie
Chine of Mutton with Pickles
Dish of Scotch Collops
Dish of Salmigondin

SECOND COURSE

Fat Chickens and tame Pigeons
Asparagus and Lupins
Tansy and Fritters
Dish of Fruit of Sorts
Dish of fried Soles
Dish of Tarts, Custards, and
  Cheesecakes

ANOTHER FIRST COURSE

Soup *à-la-Princess*
Fish, the best you can get
Calf's Head halfed
Pullets *à-la-royal*
Kettledrums
Beef Collops
French Patties
Pupton of Veal

ANOTHER SECOND COURSE

Ducklings
Quails
Roasted Lobsters
Potted Lampreys
Blancmange
Orange Loaves
Morels and Truffles ragouted
Green Custard

For March

FIRST COURSE

Dish of Fish of all Sorts
Soup *de santé*
Westphalia Ham and Pigeons
Battalia Pie
Pole of Ling
Dish of roasted Tongues and
    Udders
Peas Soup
Almond Pudding of Sorts
Olives of Veal *à-la-mode*
Dish of Mullets boiled

SECOND COURSE

Broiled Pike
Dish of Notts, Ruffs, and Quails
Skerret Pie
Dish of Jellies of Sorts
Dish of Fruit of Sorts
Dish of cream'd Tarts

ANOTHER FIRST COURSE

Green Puery Soup
Fish of Sorts
Tongue Pie
Chine of Mutton, or Fillet of
    Beef stuffed, larded and
    roasted
Pigeons *comporté*
Beef *à-la-mode*
Roasted Ham and Peppers

ANOTHER SECOND COURSE

Green Geese
Sweetbreads roasted
Chickens *à-la-Crême*
Cockscombs and
Stones   *comporté*
Crocande of Pippins
Custard Pudding
Fried Oysters
Butter'd Crayfish

For April

FIRST COURSE

Westphalia Ham and Chickens
Dish of halfed Carps
Bisque of Pigeons
Lumber Pie
Chine of Veal
Grand Salad
Beef *à-la-mode*
Almond Florentines
Fricassee of Chickens
Dish of Custards

SECOND COURSE

Green Geese and Ducklings
Butter'd Crab, with Smelts
  fried
Dish of sucking Rabbits
Rock of Snow and Syllabubs
Dish of soused Mullets
Buttered Apple Pie
Marchpaine

ANOTHER FIRST COURSE

Soup Lorain
Salmon Blovon
Breast of Veal ragouted
Cutlets *à-la-Maintenon*
Pupton of Pigeons
Bisque of Sheep's Tongues
Saddle of Mutton
Almond Pudding

ANOTHER SECOND COURSE

Turkey Poults
Leverets

Green Peas
Bisque of Mushrooms
Tarts creamed
Ragout of Green Morels
Lobsters serene
Fried Smelts

For May

FIRST COURSE

Jole of Salmon, &c.
Crawfish Soup
Dish of sweet Puddings of
  Colours
Chicken Pie
Calf's Head halved
Chine of Mutton
Grand Salad
Roasted Fowls *à-la-daube*
Roasted Tongues and Udders
Ragout of Veal, &c.

SECOND COURSE

Dish of young Turkeys larded
  and Quails
Dish of Peas
Bisque of Shellfish
Roasted Lobsters
Green Geese
Dish of Sweetmeats
Orangeado Pie
Dish of Lemon and Chocolate
  Creams
Dish of collared Eels with
  Crayfish

ANOTHER FIRST COURSE
Soup *à-la-santé*
Calvert Salmon
Haunch of Venison
Venison Pasty
Roasted Geese
Chine of Veal, with Fillets
    ragouted
Beef *à-la-braise*

ANOTHER SECOND COURSE
Pheasants
Peas *à-la-crème*
Peppers roasted
Stewed Asparagus
Codling Tart
Fruit of all Sorts
Fried Lamb-stones

For June

FIRST COURSE
Roasted Pike and Smelts
Westphalia Ham and young
    Fowls
Marrow Puddings
Haunch of Venison roasted
Ragout of Lamb-stones and
    Sweetbreads
Fricassee of young Rabbits, &c.
Umble Pies
Dish of Mullets
Roasted Fowls
Dish of Custards

SECOND COURSE
Dish of young Pheasants
Dish of fried Soles and Eels
Potato Pie
Jole of Sturgeon
Dish of Tarts and Cheesecakes
Dish of Fruit of Sorts
Syllabubs

ANOTHER FIRST COURSE
Soups
Fish of Sorts
Comporté of Fowls
Puplon of Sheep's Trotters
Collared Venison with Ragout
Chickens boiled, with Lemon
    Sauce
Mackerel
Leg of Lamb forced, with the
    Loin fricasseed in the dish

ANOTHER SECOND COURSE
Roasted Lobsters
Pistachio Pudding
White Fricassee of Rabbits
Gooseberry Tarts
Crayfish
Salmigondin
Fish in Jelly
Fried Artichokes

For July

FIRST COURSE

Cock Salmon with buttered
   Lobsters
Dish of Scotch Collops
Chine of Veal
Venison Pasty
Grand Salad
Roasted Geese and Ducklings
Patty Royal
Roasted Pig larded
Stewed Carps
Dish of Chickens boiled, with
   Bacon, &c.

SECOND COURSE

Dish of Partridges and Quails
Dish of Lobsters and Prawns
Dish of Ducks and tame
   Pigeons
Dish of Jellies
Dish of Fruit
Dish of marinated Fish
Dish of Tarts of Sorts

ANOTHER FIRST COURSE

Rice Soup with Veal
A Dish of Trouts
A brown Fricassee of Fowls
A Calf's Head boned, cleared,
   and stewed, with a Ragout of
   Mushrooms
Mutton Maintenon
Rabbits with Onions
Lumber Pie
Ham Pie

ANOTHER SECOND COURSE

A Hare larded
Neck of Venison
Partridges
Ragout of Artichokes
Cockscombs *à-la-crême*
Fruit of Sorts
Currant Tart
Apple Puffs

For August

FIRST COURSE

Westphalia Ham and Chickens
Bisque of Fish
Haunch of Venison roasted
Venison Pasty
Roasted Fowls *à-la-daube*
Umble Pies
White Fricassee of Chickens
Roasted Turkeys larded
Almond Florentines
Beef *à-la-mode*

SECOND COURSE

Dish of Pheasants and
   Partridges
Roasted Lobsters
Broiled Pike
Creamed Tart
Rock of Snow and Syllabubs
Dish of Sweetmeats
Salmigondin

ANOTHER FIRST COURSE

Stewed Venison in Soup
Haddock and Soles
Leg of Mutton *à-la-daube*
Rabbit Patty
Chine of Lamb
Beans and Ham
Neck of Mutton boned and
    roasted with a Ragout of
    Cucumbers

ANOTHER SECOND COURSE

Bisque of Lamb white
Turkeys roasted and larded
Sweetbreads and Lamb-stones
Fruit of Sorts
Morello-Cherry Tarts
Strawberries or Raspberries
Artichokes

For September

FIRST COURSE

Boiled Pullets with Oysters,
    Bacon, &c.
Bisque of Fish
Battalia Pie
Chine of Mutton
Dish of Pickles
Roasted Geese
Lumber Pie
Olives of Veal with Ragout
Dish of boiled Pigeons with
    Bacon

SECOND COURSE

Dish of Ducks and Teal
Dish of fried Soles
Butter'd Apple Pie
Jole of Sturgeon
Dish of Fruit
Marchpane

ANOTHER FIRST COURSE

Green Peas Soup
Fish of Sorts
Geese *à-la-daube*
Stewed Hare
Bisque of Pigeons
Breast of Veal *à-la-crême*
Bisque of Rabbits
Leg of Veal, with Sorrel Sauce

ANOTHER SECOND COURSE

Pheasant larded, with Celery
    Sauce
Potted Wheat-ears
Scolloped Lobsters
Butter'd Crabs
Stewed Mushrooms
Collared Eels
Crocande of Sweetmeats

For October

FIRST COURSE

Westphalia Ham and Fowls

Cod's Head with Shrimps and
    Oysters

Haunch of Doe with Udder *à-
    la-force*

Minced Pies

Chine and Turkey

Bisque of Pigeons

Roasted Tongues and Udders

Scotch Collops

Lumber Pie

SECOND COURSE

Wild Fowl of Sorts

Chine of Salmon broiled

Artichoke Pie

Broiled Eels and Smelts

Salmigondin

Dish of Fruit

Dish of Tarts and Custards

ANOTHER FIRST COURSE

Soup of Beef Bollin

Crimped Cod and Sentry

Pullets with Oysters

Calf's Head *à-la-crême*

Venison Pasty

Beef *à-la-mode*

Ox-cheek, with Ragout of
    Herbs

Lemon Torte

ANOTHER SECOND COURSE

Teals and Larks

Turkeys roasted

Tansy and Blackcaps

Florentines

Scolloped Oysters

Fried Smelts

Cockscombs *comporté*

Fruit of Sorts

For November

FIRST COURSE

Boiled Fowls with Savoys,
    Bacon, &c.

Dish of stew'd Carps and
    scolloped Oysters

Chine of Veal and Ragout

Salad and Pickles

Venison Pasty

Roasted Geese

Calf's Head halved

Dish of Gurnets

Grand Patty

Roasted Hen Turkey with
    Oysters

SECOND COURSE

Chine of Salmon and Smelts

Wild Fowl of Sorts

Potato Pie

Sliced Tongues with Pickles

Dish of Jellies

Dish of Fruit

Quince Pie

ANOTHER FIRST COURSE

Haricot of Mutton

Fish of Sorts

Haunch of Venison

Fillet of Veal *à-la-braise*

Chine of Mutton, with stewed Celery

A Pupton, with Maintenon Cutlets

ANOTHER SECOND COURSE

Roasted Woodcocks

Roasted Lobsters

Buttered Crabs

Larks with brown Crumbs

Fried Oysters round two Sweet-breads, larded and roasted

A Pear Tart

Crocande of Sweetmeats

For December

FIRST COURSE

Westphalia Ham and Fowls

Soup with Teal

Turbot, with Shrimps and Oysters

Marrow Pudding

Chine of Bacon and Turkey

Battalia Pie

Roasted Tongue and Udder, and Hare

Pullets and Oysters, Sausages, &c.

Minced Pies

Cod's Head with Shrimps

SECOND COURSE

Roasted Pheasants and Partridges

Bisque of Shellfish

Tansy

Dish of roasted Ducks and Teals

Jole of Sturgeon

Pear Tart creamed

Dish of Sweetmeats

Dish of Fruit of Sorts

ANOTHER FIRST COURSE

Vermicelli Soup

Fish of Sorts

Jugged Hare

Beef *à-la-royal*

Scotch Collops

French Patty, with Teal, &c.

Rice Pudding

ANOTHER SECOND COURSE

Snipes, with a Duck in the Middle

Broiled Chickens with Mushrooms

Pickles of Sorts

White Fricassee of Tripe

Pulled Chickens

Stewed Oysters

Stewed Calves' Feet

Curdoons.

The Regular Disposition or Placing of Dishes for the Various Courses

Winter

First Course

Gravy Soop remove Chicken & Bacon

Scotch Collops

Giblet Pie

A Fine Boil'd Pudding

Roast Beef with Horse-radish & Pickles round

Second Course

A Turkey Roasted

3 Wood Cocks with Toasts

A Tansey & Garnish with Orange

A Hare with a Savary Pudding

A Butter'd Apple Pie Hot

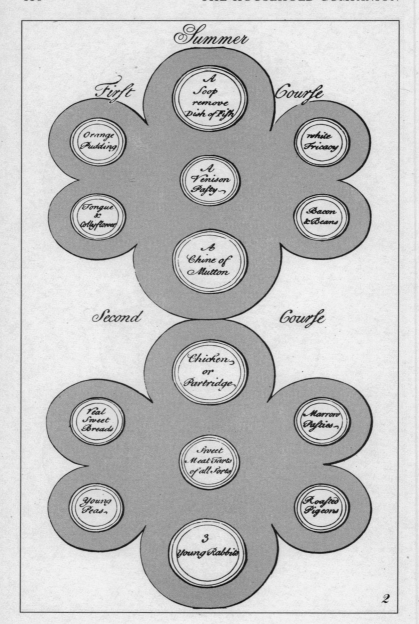

Summer

First Course

A Soop remove Dish of Fish

Orange Pudding

white Fricacy

A Venison Pasty

Tongue & Collyflower

Bacon & Beans

A Chine of Mutton

Second Course

Chicken or Partridge

Veal Sweet Breads

Marrow Pasties

Sweet Meat Tarts of all Sorts

Young Peas

Roasted Pigeons

3 Young Rabbits

2

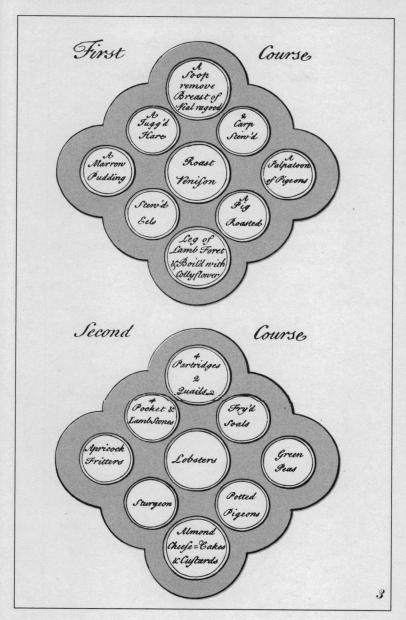

First Course

A Soop remove Breast of Veal ragood

A Jugg'd Hare

2 Carp Stew'd

A Marrow Pudding

Roast Venison

A Palpatoon of Pigeons

Stew'd Eels

A Pig Roasted

Leg of Lamb Foret & Boil'd with Collyflower

Second Course

4 Partridges 2 Quails

4 Pocket & Lamb Stones

Fry'd Soals

Apricock Fritters

Lobsters

Green Peas

Sturgeon

Potted Pigeons

Almond Cheese=Cakes & Custards

3

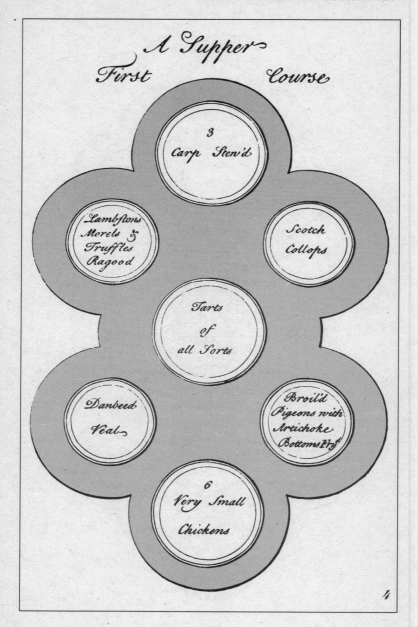

A Supper
First   Course

3
Carp Stew'd

Lambstons
Morels &
Truffles
Ragood

Scotch
Collops

Tarts
of
all Sorts

Danbeed
Veal

Broil'd
Pigeons with
Artichoke
Bottoms Fry

6
Very Small
Chickens